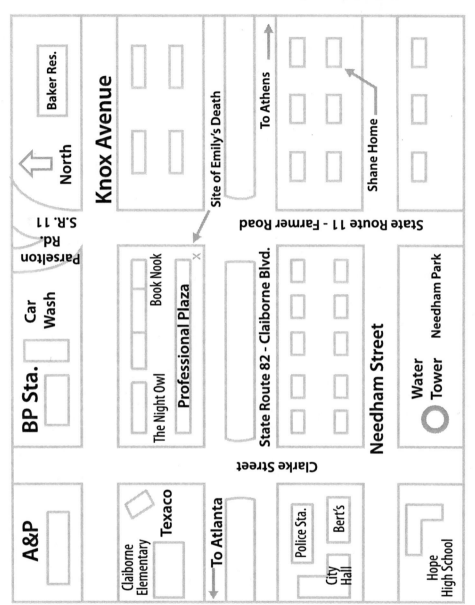

THE TOWN OF HOPE

A REASON TO TREMBLE

BY BOB MUSTIN

ISBN: 1-4699-0897-2
ISBN-13: 978-1-4699-0897-7

PART 1

THE AGONY

CHAPTER 1

THE ACCIDENT

Jason Shane shivered, pulled his parka tighter, and took off toward the accident scene. It was only two blocks from the Shane residence, down Needham Street to Farmer Road and across Claiborne, but the pain in his hip had him hobbling. He was almost there though; an ambulance and a police car sat at the corner, both straddling the curb.

Despite the October evening chill, Jason's blond hair had matted with sweat. He gulped in the damp air and crossed Claiborne, where Emily's bicycle lay crumpled at the base of a power pole. Two paramedics huddled over a stretcher on the sidewalk, Buddy Tarbutton, the responding police officer, a few paces away.

Tarbutton glanced up and nodded hello.

Before Jason could respond, the clatter of a woman's shoes emerged from the night, followed by a large man's flat footfalls.

"Oh, Jason," Wanda Claxton wailed, "I'm so sorry. We were just walking out the door for our bridge night when we heard the collision. We called the paramedics. They had just left a false alarm on the way to Athens, and they came right here."

"Thanks," said Jason.

"Honey, honey," husband Jack said, "she'll be okay, you'll see."

Jason gave the couple a weak smile, stumbled ahead to the paramedics, and identified himself.

"Pulse is dropping," one said, looking up. "Heartbeat irregular."

They had strapped ten-year-old Emily to a long, polished board that had been placed on the stretcher, covered her with a doubled-over wool blanket. Blood had matted her long, blonde hair to a now misshapen face.

"How bad is it?" Jason asked.

"Both legs are broken," said the second paramedic. "Looks like internal bleeding. The car really slammed her, must've hit her head on."

"I think she was coming down Farmer Road and the car T-boned the bike," said Tarbutton. He looked to Jason. "Dance class night, right?"

Jason swallowed. "Yeah. Dance class."

"She's in shock, shows all the signs of a severe concussion," the second paramedic said. "Maybe brain damage."

Jason blinked, unable to digest all this. "Will she live?"

"She's alive," the second paramedic said, "but I can't say for how long."

The first paramedic pressed one of Emily's eyelids open, then the other. "Pupils not responding." He glanced to Jason. "Sir, she isn't responding at all. We need to get her to a hospital ASAP."

Jason took a deep breath. "I'm her uncle. I live with the family, but they're not home yet." He looked away. The ambulance's revolving light spun ethereal red ribbons across the scene. "Take her to Humana Hospital, in Lawrenceville."

"You got it," the second paramedic said. "You know her blood type?"

"A positive," said Jason.

"Good, easy to find." The paramedic stood. "You going to meet us there?"

"Her parents will be home soon, I need to tell them. Just tell the hospital people she's a Shane, from Hope. They know us there. They'll take care of her."

The two paramedics lifted the stretcher and slid Emily into the ambulance. Wanda and Jack Claxton turned, heads bowed, and plodded away. The first paramedic climbed into the ambulance's rear and shut the doors. The second one dashed to the cab.

"I have to file a report," Buddy Tarbutton said. "Hit and run cases like this, we report 'em to the State Patrol. Can you come by later and give us a statement?"

"Yeah," said Jason, "sure." He swayed, took a step, lurched.

Tarbutton caught him, steadied him. "Jason, we'll catch 'em."

"I know."

The policeman patted him on the shoulder, turned and strode toward his car.

Jason bent and retched.

The ambulance flounced from the curb and sped west, Tarbutton's police cruiser following. Within seconds, the ambulance's loopy light and the police car's urgent wail dissolved in the gathering night fog.

CHAPTER 2

ANGUISH

Jason shivered again. Could Emily really be dying? No, he thought, no! But he could tell the damage had been serious; if she lived, she'd probably never be the same again. She wasn't even his child, but she might as well have been. She'd been the centerpiece of his life these past ten years.

Dizziness overwhelmed him, the shock of the accident now fully on him. He staggered to the power pole, caught it with both hands, hugged it as he slid slowly downward. He barely felt the pole's splinters as they jabbed his hands and cheek. His feet tangled in the remains of Emily's bicycle. A handlebar caught his rib cage, and one of the ribs gave. He rolled over to relieve the stabbing pain and, atop the grotesque pile of steel and plastic, he looked skyward.

As he took in the cloud-laden sky, he felt strangely warm. Jungle warm. Off somewhere in the distance, beyond the pain, he heard the sharp, intermittent sound of automatic weapons. He heard screams from the wounded, the yelling and chaos of battle. The acrid smell of smoke and feces and blood was overwhelming. His left hand fumbled along the side of his blue jeans, where the Viet

Cong grenade had shattered his left hip. He felt for the gaping hole in his flesh, the hole that was still there in his dreams, the hole his buddy Leo had pulled together and strapped with a battle dressing as they'd wailed into the din of battle.

Somewhere beyond the streetlights, he saw streams of tracers overhead and heard the dull thump of mortar rounds as they walked slowly toward him. "Medic!" he yelled, "I'm hit!" He began to shake. An odd thought: maybe the shaking would clear the anguish he felt – surely the same agony Emily had felt during the moment of impact.

"No no no no...home...gotta link up. No, go home...don't die... oh, God ohgodohgod...Emily! Where's Emily? Gotta get her outta here. Sarge! Need a medic over here! Oh, it hurts!" He licked sweat from his lips.

His vision seemed to clear a little. He glanced left, then right. Moonlight found its way through the grove of rubber trees where he lay off Highway 13, just south of An Loc. He reached for his rifle, found only concrete. A beer truck rumbled by on the other side of Claiborne, heading toward Athens and the University of Georgia.

He sat up on the mangled bike, head in his hands. He knew what to do. The psychiatrist had told him to breathe deeply. He breathed. Close your eyes, the doctor had said, blank out your mind. Just focus on your breathing. He focused. The terror slowly subsided. Breathe. Breathe. Breathebreathebreathe. Slow down. Gotta take long breaths – long, slow breaths. Long. Slow. Breaths. He breathed, slowly.

His surroundings had quieted, the street a landscape painting. The emotional aspect of his pain had eased, but now his whole body ached. He peered into the dank night. The mortars and tracers and rubber trees were gone. Breathe, Jason. He breathed. As he did so, he relaxed, ever so slowly.

Then pain erupted again. He closed his eyes. Memories of that April day in 1972 rolled through him like a news clip, the highway into An Loc beneath him. Incoming choppers – dustoffs, they called these ungainly aircraft – landed on the road, maybe twenty meters away. Soldiers began loading body bags. The platoon's machine gunner glanced to Jason as he zipped up the bag holding Leo's remains. The film clip reversed – Jason could once again make out his friend running through the trees for a medic. Then the sense of helplessness at the incoming mortar round's mournful howl. He watched the blaze of metal shards lift Leo and fling him into the rubber grove. He remembered the horror of having his own stretcher placed on a pile of body bags in the chopper. "Leo, I'm sorry," he heard himself cry again. There are no sensibilities to the business of war, but to stack the living and the dead in this way was an insanity he still couldn't bear.

Then the road to An Loc transformed. It widened and separated, silhouetted by Georgia pines. Once again, the State Patrol cars and ambulance screeched in, lights flashing, followed by the crackle of static on the nearest cruiser's radio. His brother Pat appeared from out of nowhere, twenty years old again, trying to tell sixteen year-old Jason that their mother and father were dead.

They'd been driving in separate cars to a high school football game in Chamblee and, for some still unexplained reason, their parents' car had sped ahead, veered across two lanes of traffic, and smashed into a bridge column. The policeman said they didn't suffer, Pat had told Jason in the steely manner he always assumed in moments of loss or adversity. Jason could still see the grief in Pat's eyes, the anger in the set of his jaw. He'd clutched Pat that night, clinging to him as if he were a baby. What're we gonna do, Pat? he'd cried. We'll be all right, Pat had said. I'll think of something.

Pat had indeed thought of something. He'd quit college and taken a job in Athens, some twenty miles away. The job had allowed the two brothers to remain solvent and stay in the family home for the months leading up to Jason's graduation from high school. Eventually, Pat had returned to the University of Georgia and finished his degree in business administration. He'd married Yvonne Baker, his high school sweetheart, soon thereafter, and had gone to work for the Stark's Restaurant chain.

Jason had been drafted the summer after his graduation, and three months later, fate had set him down in the dust and noise of Tan Son Nhut airport in the Republic of Vietnam. He'd returned from 'Nam after only five months in-country, had kept an apartment in Decatur for a short while, near the Veteran's Administration hospital. His physical rehabilitation had been brief. But the mental part, the depressions, the nightmares, the delusions, had continued to dog him. Even now, a part of him remained in that place, refusing to come home. Pat and Von had had a spare room in their apartment, so he'd moved in with them. He was still with them twelve years later, when they'd bought back the old Shane home, and for the next twelve years, until Von had announced she was pregnant with Emily. He'd thought Pat would have wanted him to move then, but he hadn't, and Jason was still with them now.

Once again, he took in the street – Claiborne Boulevard, the town of Hope. He breathed deeply. He rose slowly, stood on shaky legs. His body had atrophied over those first years, and his strength had waned for a while, his legs no longer the strong, sturdy legs that had led him to the high school state championship in the mile run. Recently, though, he'd regained some of his strength, and he'd gained back some of his weight. But this trauma, he thought, Emily's death, would surely set his rehabilitation back. The leg below the damaged hip now went numb and folded, and he had to clutch a street sign for support.

He shook the leg, stamped the foot until feeling returned. Good. It would support him now. He took a few unsteady steps and then a deep breath before limping back home.

CHAPTER 3

THE SHANES

Jason glanced up from the antebellum home's front steps. Inside the sitting room bay window, Pat scowled as he paced. He glanced out, saw Jason, and strode out of view, then to the door.

Pat stood a shade taller than Jason's six-foot-two, both brothers with the gangly build of their father. But Pat's body, now taking on the extra weight of mid-life, seemed twice the size of Jason's. His hair, like Jason's, was thinning, but its sandy, wavy texture partially concealed the loss.

Like Jason, he was moody and quiet. But where Jason's self-deprecating sense of humor would surface occasionally between bouts of depression, Pat was uniformly solemn. Where Jason read and imagined, captive to the spirit of ideas, Pat worked. He worked long hours now, always had. He was a reluctant, business-embellishing joiner, associating himself with the Chamber of Commerce, the Civitans, and Edgewood Baptist Church.

And he was a family man. Beyond career, the most defining aspect of Southern males is family, and that mold seemed for Pat an exact fit. He and Yvonne, or Von, as the family called her, had wanted a large family, but Von's several miscarriages prior to Emily's birth had buried that dream.

And although Pat had always found ways to help Jason, he'd never understood his depression. Too, he was vehemently opposed to Jason's sporadic work with movements that Pat considered socialistic. But they were brothers, family. Not much more could be said for their relationship, but so far that had been enough.

Jason limped into the dimly lit foyer.

"Chief Anderson called me here a few minutes ago," said a visibly agitated, pacing Pat. "He told me what happened. Fortunately, someone in this town was considerate enough to tell me I have an injured daughter."

Jason turned abruptly toward the sitting room. "I need to sit down." He made his way across the foyer and collapsed onto an elegantly upholstered easy chair.

Pat followed and turned on a table lamp. He started as he took in the creosote marks and blood specks on his brother's face and hands.

"You're a mess, Jason. What happened?"

Jason slowly passed a hand over his cheek, felt the sting of a splinter embedded there. He pulled it out and flicked away a drop of blood. Then he picked two more from one hand. The broken rib under his jacket was throbbing, but his breathing was returning to normal. "Emily's at the hospital?"

"I just called Von at work. All the agents had gone home and she was about to close up, so she went straight there. I just stopped by to pick you up." He glanced at his watch. "We need to go."

Their route took them five miles out of town to Route 316, and then on a fifteen-minute drive to Lawrenceville and the Humana

Hospital. Jason felt better hearing that Von was already there. If anyone was closer to Emily than he, it was Von. After a while, he steeled himself and prepared to break the usual, stony silence between Pat and him.

"Wanda Claxton phoned about six," he said, as they exited. "She told me about the accident. Then she and Jack called for the paramedic unit. I got over there as fast as I could." He paused. "I think she's in bad shape, Pat. She has a concussion."

Pat's eyes darted toward Jason; his hands clenched the wheel.

"And both legs are broken."

"What? The chief didn't tell me any of that. What else don't I know?"

"One of the paramedics said there might be brain damage."

Pat swore and slammed his fist into the dash, "Why didn't I know this? All the chief told me was that Emily had hit a power pole on Claiborne on her way home, that she'd been taken to Humana."

Jason glanced to his brother. "You don't know how the accident happened?"

Pat swerved into the hospital parking deck. The car nosed down as he jammed on the brakes. "There's more?"

Jason scratched tentatively at another splinter in his cheek. "It was a hit and run."

Pat's chest heaved as he tried to compose himself. "Who did it?"

"Don't know. Wanda Claxton saw the car from a distance, but it was dark."

Someone honked behind them. Pat slammed the accelerator pedal to the floor. The car shot up the parking deck ramp, tires screeching. He wheeled into a parking slot, jumped out, banged his door shut, and strode toward the elevator.

Then he stopped. Jason had propped himself against the car with one hand as he struggled to move his shaky legs. Pat took his arm and helped him toward the elevator. The lift's door closed and they began to descend. "She'd better be all right."

Jason eyed him. "She was hurt bad, Pat. From what I saw, she was in bad shape."

The elevator door opened. Pat burst through and toward the emergency room. Jason hobbled after him.

A short, plump woman with curly red hair looked up from her post at the information desk.

"I have a daughter here," Pat said in a too-loud voice. "A paramedic unit brought her in, from Hope. Name of Shane, Emily Shane."

The receptionist looked over her shoulder to an inner office. "Just a minute." She turned, entered the office, and began whispering excitedly, hands waving. The evening hospital administrator quieted her and summoned an orderly. The orderly raced toward the emergency room. The administrator skirted the reception desk and offered Pat his hand.

Pat didn't take it. "Where's my daughter?"

A shriek. The doors to their right banged open. The orderly guided Von by the arm.

"Pat!" she wailed. "Jason! She's gone, my baby's gone."

"No!" Pat took her in.

A weight seemed to be collapsing Jason's chest. His legs shook. He slumped onto a vinyl-covered couch, closed his eyes, and breathed slowly, evenly. He knew Emily was dead, had known it from the moment the ambulance door had closed. For now, he felt no grief left, only the emptiness that follows such horrific events. He slumped into the couch's back cushion.

A doctor entered from the emergency room, slowly massaging his hands as he neared Pat and Von. He stopped, chin buried in his green scrub tunic. Then he put a hand on Pat's shoulder. "I'm Doctor Yusef Ahmed," he said quietly. "I was on duty when your daughter was admitted."

Pat sniffed and turned. "We know a surgeon here, a Doctor Willis. It's in our records as our preference for emergencies. He should've been called."

"We tried," said the doctor, "but his answering service couldn't locate him."

"Then tell me about my daughter."

"She was dead on arrival," said Doctor Ahmed. "The cause of death was an infarction of brain tissue. The emergency crew did as much as they humanly could, but damage to the head was severe and widespread. There was no way to re-stimulate her upon arrival. I'm so sorry."

"Mister Shane," the supervisor said, "I know this is a very difficult time, but can you and your wife come with me to identify the body?" He reached out to take Von's hand.

Pat pulled her away from the man and led her to Jason.

"All right, where is she?" Pat said to the administrator. "Where's my daughter?"

The administrator led Pat down the emergency room hallway toward a small cubicle where Emily's body lay on a gurney, covered by a sheet.

Jason held Von as she sobbed.

A nurse approached. "Is there anything I can do?" she asked.

"Some tissue, please," said Von.

"And a glass of water," said Jason.

"Oh, Jason," she whispered as the nurse strode away, "why? Why us? Why Emily?"

"I don't know. How could anyone know?"

The nurse returned with a handful of tissues for Von and handed the water to Jason. Then she pulled a small white envelope from her lap pocket. "Doctor Ahmed has prescribed some tranquilizers. There're some here, and a prescription for more. Would you like one now?"

"No," said Von, "just the water."

"Please take them with you," the nurse said, "you may need them later."

Jason took the envelope and put it in Von's purse.

Pat returned from the emergency room and slumped onto the couch beside Von. He sighed. "There'll have to be an autopsy. She won't be released until this weekend."

Jason frowned.

"Crazy, isn't it?" Pat said to his brother. Then he looked to Von. "Are you okay?"

She nodded.

"I'll bring the car around."

With Pat gone, Von turned to Jason. She took in the red, swollen scratches. "You look a wreck, Jason. Did you fall again?"

"I was hassling with Emily's bicycle. I fell, and I think I broke a rib. I guess I'll need to come back here in the morning and let someone see it."

"She loved you so much, Jason."

He sighed. "Yeah."

Von pressed against him, set her head on his shoulder. "You were so good for her. She loved being around you."

"She was good for *me*."

Von nodded. "She tried so hard to help you walk, even when she was barely old enough to walk herself."

Emily had been his only source of happiness in recent years. The depression was terrible; Agent Orange had caused it, some said. Post traumatic stress disorder, the doctors here had claimed. He only knew there was a hole where his soul used to be, and loving Emily had helped to fill it. She was such a happy child; she'd been born to such a sunny disposition. In some ways, she was like the mother Pat and he had lost. Emily would purse her lips, shake her finger, and tell him not to be sad. It'll be better, she'd say, and he'd laugh and hug her, and for a while the depression would recede.

"Pat's here," said Von, "let me help you up."

CHAPTER 4

DAVIS ANDERSON

The following Monday evening, the Shane home opened to visitors. Taking the walkway toward the front porch, each might have glanced up to admire the stained glass windows Von had had installed beside the home's oaken front door. From the steps, and then from the porch, the stained glass mosaic of angelic trumpeters would have seemed to gain life. It would have taken only a scintilla of imagination to see gossamer wings fluttering ever so slightly as those already inside moved through the foyer light.

The door had been left ajar, an invitation to enter unannounced. A book for visitors to sign had been set open on a small table in the foyer. Pat stood at the foyer's far side, in a wide portal to the sitting room, one hand in the two-fisted clasp of J.D. Sims, pastor of the Edgewood Baptist Church. Von clung stiffly to Pat's left arm, a damp handkerchief balled in her hand. Her sky blue, white-trimmed dress would normally have complemented her eyes, which were now twin seas of swollen red. She released for a moment, brushed absently at her blonde shag cut and tucked her dress' collar under her hair's rear hang. Despite tears and an anguished expression, her beauty remained indisputable: a striking, softly angled face, luminescent skin without flaw, and a delicately proportioned figure.

Jason had slumped onto a divan in the sitting room. As friends and neighbors approached and spoke, he would look up and shake hands without reply. Now he glanced to Von and Pat.

Von was upset, more so than Jason had expected. The evening had just begun, and Pat's voice already wore an edge. He'd probably been drinking. It wouldn't show in an obvious way, though. Pat usually drank sparingly, and when he did, it was always gin and grapefruit juice, a concoction that wouldn't easily betray the gin's presence on his breath.

"Brother Sims," Pat was saying, "I'm a forgiving person, you know that. But I won't rest until I find out who killed Emily. And I *will* see her murderer dead."

Reverend Sims sighed. "Please be careful, Pat, not to let vengeance enter –"

"Her killer will get a lethal dose of justice," Pat said, his voice ratcheting higher. "That's a promise."

"Pat," said Von, "this isn't the time."

He spun, clenched her wrists. "Our daughter's dead, Von. When do you suppose the right time will be? How long do we have to wait before we realize the police aren't taking Emily's death seriously?"

Other conversations trailed off as Pat's voice rose to a shout. Noticing, he released Von and turned to the others. "I promise you, I'll find Emily's killer myself if I have to. Justice will be served."

"You have a plan, then, Pat?" drawled a voice from near the front door. The gaggle of visitors parted for a short, stout man in a police uniform. His stubbly brown haircut projected from his head like a phalanx of briars. He had shaved so close his face shone. The pressed uniform stretched to accommodate his broad shoulders. As he crossed the room, his black leather shoes caught the light from the high ceiling's fixture.

Pat sneered. "Well, look who's here. You all know Davis Anderson, the man who's supposed to protect the citizens of Hope." He waved an arm in a mocking sweep. "Come on in, Davis, we were just talking law enforcement. And tell me, is finding the killer of a ten year-old girl exciting enough for you? Or is it more fun chasing teens out on 316?"

Von began to cry.

Pat glared at the chief. "Any idea when someone will begin a serious inquiry into the death of my daughter?"

Hope's unblinking chief of police took in the taller man. "Is there somewhere we can talk, in private?"

Von tugged at Pat's arm. "Go to the kitchen. Please?"

Pat shoved her away. She staggered and almost fell.

Jason struggled up from the divan. A hurried limp carried him to Von. He took her hands, and together they steadied. Then he brushed at a tear that had managed to slip down her cheek to her chin. Embarrassed as the others watched, he let her go. "Pat and Davis should stay," he said. "I don't want you hearing Pat's version of this later, I want it undistorted by hearsay."

Pat thumped his chest with a finger. "This is my business, Jason, not yours."

Jason shook his head. "It's the business of this family, and of everyone who thought enough of Emily and you and Von to come here tonight."

Von had backed away and now stood alone, daubing at her eyes.

Pat took a step, jabbed a finger at his brother. Then he swore and raised a hand, as if to slap Jason.

"Please," the pastor replied, "let's be gentlemen."

Davis Anderson shoved his way between the two brothers. "All right, you two, I didn't come here to referee a fight." He nudged them to arm's length and eyed Pat. "Besides, I don't have much to report. And I don't mind saying it here, in front of everyone." Then he turned a dark look in Jason's direction. "But it's supposed to be a courtesy to share things of this sort with the immediate family first, in private."

"Tell us!" said Jason.

"Please," Von said through her sobs, "please don't fight."

Pat huffed. "Now look what your freedom of information speech has done."

Jason sneered. "Me? I don't suppose your threatening to take the law into your own hands could have had a thing to do with Von's state of mind."

The chief nodded toward the house's rear, gave Pat a push in the direction of the kitchen.

Pat resisted and turned. "Have your say here, Davis, in front of everyone." A narrow-eyed look to his brother. "You and I will talk later, Jason."

The chief cleared his throat. "First, we don't have any hard evidence concerning the identity of the owner of the car that struck Emily." He motioned toward the Claxtons, who stood a step away. "From Missus Claxton's statement, we know the car was weaving after Emily hit the pole. Probably a DUI." He paused. "It was dark. She couldn't tell us the color of the car and she was too far away to make out the license plate. For some reason, she thought it was a Georgia tag, but I wouldn't put her on the witness stand to testify to that. She just had a feeling."

"I'm so sorry, Pat," said Wanda Claxton. "It happened so fast."

The chief took a deep breath and continued. "But there *was* a witness to the accident."

A murmur began to swirl.

"Quiet!" said Pat. He turned to the chief. "Who? Who saw Emily's killer?"

"You all remember Loretta Miller's sister Donna, the one who lives in Memphis. Well, she's been visiting Loretta the past couple of weeks. She was out walking after supper the night the car hit Emily. On Claiborne, down around the elementary school. She heard tires squealing, looked back, and saw Emily on the bicycle, just as it was hit."

Von's crying grew louder.

More murmurs.

"Everyone, quiet!" said Pat.

The chief continued. "She says she stood there by the mailbox and watched the car swerve down the road toward her. It was barely under control when it passed her."

"Who?" Pat said. "Who was it?"

"She apparently got a pretty good look at the car. But getting a decent description from her is another matter. From what we've been able to piece together from her statement, it was a big car, maybe a Chevrolet Caprice."

Animated talk, rising voices.

Pat shouted to silence the chatter. Then to the chief: "I know of several of those in town. What about the color?"

"As you might know, her vision's failing. She said the car was light colored. She called it white at first, then beige, then pale blue. And she didn't get the tag number."

"Philip Agee," Pat said. "I might have guessed."

"Don't go jumping to conclusions," the chief said.

"How many Caprice owners are you going to question," said Pat, "before you pull in Phil Agee?"

The chief drew himself to his full height. His jaw hardened. He looked from face to face. "I don't want to hear this kind of accusation from anyone. Especially you, Pat."

"Got to call the kettle black, Davis."

"Did she get a look at the driver?" someone asked.

"I don't think so," Anderson replied. "She was pretty upset. As the car passed, she thinks she saw the top of a man's head above the headrest. There's absolutely nothing else to go on."

"Why did it take all this time for you to tell us this?" asked Pat.

The chief shrugged. "You know how Loretta is. Her sister is pretty much the same. Two old spinsters who live and breathe for neighborhood tittle-tattle. But the first time one of them's in the thick of something gossipy, they get so scared they can't see straight." The chief's attempt to clear his throat failed. "Could I get something to drink?"

Several liter bottles of Coke sat clustered on a nearby table. One of the visitors scooped a few shards of ice into a plastic cup, poured it full, and handed it to the chief.

He nodded his thanks and drained the glass. "Donna went straight home after the accident and told Loretta what had happened." He chuckled to himself. "They must've thought they were on someone's hit list, because they didn't leave the house for two days. According to Loretta, they talked about it for a couple more days before she decided Donna should report it. By then the details had gotten foggy. We spent all day yesterday taking their statements and trying to make sense of them." He stepped to the table and poured another glass of soda.

"So there *was* a witness," mused Pat. "All this time."

Anderson looked to his mirror-like shoes. "Yes, but as I said, she didn't give us much to go on. I would've wished for a more reputable witness, but we have to take our leads where we can find them."

"When are you going to talk to Agee?" asked Pat.

"He's been out of town. We're looking for him."

"There you go. He's lying low until he thinks this thing has blown over."

The chief jabbed a forefinger. "You need to remember, there's nothing concrete for us to go on at the moment. Anything you might suppose is backed only by the most circumstantial of evidence." He paused to survey the faces about him. "We'll continue to pursue leads, folks. And we'll keep the Shanes informed."

He paused again, as if searching for words. "I know this is an emotional time. But I don't want to hear unwarranted accusations. I don't want to hear talk about taking the law into your own hands. Anger over a tragedy like this can set a town on fire. Just calm down and trust us to do our job."

No one spoke.

"Fine," he said. A nod to the Shanes. "Pat, Missus Shane, I'll be in touch." He brought a hand to his forehead in a casual salute, turned, and strode to the door, past the trumpeting angels, and into the night.

PART 2

THE BROODING

CHAPTER 5

SCUFFLE

With neighbors and family friends gone, the Shanes restored order to the front rooms, washed the dishes, and took the evening's clutter to the trashcan. Thirty minutes later, Von was asleep. Jason sat in semi-darkness in a straight-back chair in the sitting room, facing the front window. The window was a broad one, over eight feet in height, and framed by long, thick, burgundy curtains tied back at their midsection. The windowpanes wore a cloudy coat of moisture from the October night.

Pat stood in the hallway, phone to one ear. The chef of the closest Stark's restaurant, off the highway to Athens, had quit in a fit of pique earlier that night after being insulted by a customer. After a long, placating conversation, Pat sighed and hung up. Then he strode into the kitchen to fix one more gin and grapefruit juice. Lost in thought, he returned to the foyer, and was about to turn off the porch lights when he peered into the sitting room.

"Jason?"

Jason answered as he struggled to stand. He gently rubbed his rib cage, and then probed beneath the protective girdle doctors had had him wear over the broken rib.

"What're you doing up?"

"Thinking."

"Not a sleep problem, then?"

"Not yet." Jason walked past Pat toward the stairs and his bedroom.

"Well, what else could keep my little brother up at this hour?"

"I told you," said Jason. "I was thinking. Just thinking."

"Ah, yes," said Pat, sneering now. "The family philosopher. So deep and yet so fragile. Anything you'd care to share?"

"You're being condescending, Pat. I'm not in the mood." Jason began to climb the staircase, clutching the railing as he went.

"It's only responsible," Pat called out, "to want to know what's going on in my family."

Jason turned, lost his balance. He grabbed at the rail, missed. As he fell, he managed to turn sideways. He wedged his thin frame between the wall and railing supports. He let out a groan as the rebuilt hip hit a stair.

"You're a lot of help," he muttered.

Pat's sneer grew deeper. "But that would have been paternalistic and, oh, yes, condescending, the worst sins possible, according to you." He turned his glass up.

Jason mirrored his brother's sneer. "Been waiting all night for me to fall so you could use that bit of wit?"

"Just an observation." Pat swirled the ice in his emptied glass. "But here's something to think about the next time you ponder the sitting room window: only a few in this world do the real work, take the responsibility. Doesn't keep the rest from complaining, though. Always demanding justice and fair play." He swayed, had to put one foot in front of the other to keep from staggering. "And wanting a say in other people's business." He sipped from the melting ice. "Don't ever embarrass me again the way you did tonight."

Jason laughed. "You weren't embarrassed, you were too drunk. *I* was embarrassed. Your loudmouthed threats embarrassed everyone, including Von."

Pat waved that away. His expression deepened as he looked to the floor between his feet. "I don't know whether you realize it, but Phil Agee had to have an accomplice to stay hidden all this time."

"Surely you have videos of the getaway," Jason said. "Story at eleven on channel five."

"It's your hero. The great liberal state senator, Alan Baxter."

"Shut up, Pat, I won't go for it."

"I'm only making sense and, as usual, you don't want to hear the truth."

Jason looked away. "Baxter wouldn't do that. You're forgetting I know him."

Jason had once considered campaigning for Alan Baxter. He greatly admired his vision of the future, his view of a modern populism, a version of politics for the technological age. But Jason's health had prevented involvement.

"Alan Baxter's a powerful man, and Agee's his friend," said Pat. "He could snap his fingers and make this whole thing go away. But he's too intelligent to do something that blatant. He'd rather make a game of it."

Jason shifted uneasily. Pat knew people, important people. He was probably talking through his hat, but Jason couldn't be sure what his brother really knew about Alan Baxter. "Unlike the ones you favor," he replied, "who are only interested in protecting privilege."

Pat seemed to ignore that, too. After a moment, he said, "Do you ever wonder why some people do powerful things, and others wander through life victimized by everything and everybody?"

Jason grunted. "I suppose there's a personal message for me in this."

"You bet there's a lesson in this for you, little brother."

"Knock off the little brother stuff, Pat."

"Ah, my sensitive little brother."

Jason rubbed his face with one hand. "It has to do with respect. You wouldn't understand."

"Respect? What do you know about respect? You don't even respect yourself. That's what I'm saying to you. If you had any self-respect, you'd pull yourself together. Get some decent rehabilitation. Make your own way in the world. Plenty of others came back from Vietnam and made lives for themselves." He stepped closer, his voice quieter. "You're just wallowing in self pity, Jason, always have been. You could've gone to college, but you let them draft you. Now, after all this time, you still won't let go of the war. Sure, war's a nasty business. Did you think it was going to be like some, what? Some fraternity initiation?"

The furnace in the basement had come on; a cloth on the table in the foyer hung over an air vent, shimmering gracefully.

"You weren't there," said Jason, "you couldn't know. Not in a million years."

"All I know is the same little brother who came to pieces when Mom and Dad died came apart again after Vietnam. You got over Mom and Dad, but Vietnam made you into Humpty Dumpty. You just wouldn't be put back together again."

Jason's face contorted. A tear slipped down one cheek.

Pat cleared his throat, his voice softer, almost tender this time. "You're my brother. I took care of you then." He drained the ice's melted remainder. "I guess I always will."

Jason glared through an onrush of tears. "Do you think I like living here? I know I'm an embarrassment to you. Don't you think I want a life of my own? Do you think I enjoy being a burden to you and Von?" He stopped, choking on a lump in his throat.

"I just want you to be strong." Pat went to his brother, put an arm around his shoulder. For a moment, they held each other. "I'm sorry," he whispered.

The light from the crystal chandelier in the foyer cast shadows on the two as they embraced. The house had grown quiet, except for Jason's asthmatic breathing. Outside, the wind had picked up; the branches of the big oak tree in front of the house swayed, occasionally rubbing against the siding with a fitful scratching noise.

For a while, the two brothers sat on the steps in silence, Pat on a stair below, his back to Jason. His head hung as he ran a finger around the rim of his glass. Jason leaned against the wall, hands cupped over his eyes. Occasionally he took long, slow breaths. The clock in the sitting room ticked the passing seconds.

Pat ahemed and turned. "Ah, look, Jason, I have a lot on my mind. Emily's death." He looked down. "It's affecting things at work."

"It's affecting us all. It's driving us apart."

Pat glanced up. "What do you mean?"

"Well, look at you. You never drink like this, at least you never did before. Von's afraid of you, she cries all the time. You won't talk to her about Emily, and you don't even notice that she's upset. And you and I, we just keep fighting. We're not a family anymore."

Pat didn't speak for a while. "You don't seem to understand. Emily wasn't your daughter. You can't possibly understand the loss. She meant everything to me."

"What about Von and her feelings for Emily, then? And what about me? I loved Emily. If it hadn't been for her these past ten years, well, I don't know what I would've done." A trace of a smile surfaced beneath damp eyes. "She's been like a daughter to me."

Pat shuffled his feet. "You had responsibilities where Emily was concerned. Of course she liked you. You took care of her while Von and I made a living."

"She loved me, Pat. She loved me."

"It was only natural for her to like you; you were her uncle."

"We were closer than that. You and Von weren't here much. I was more of a parent than you."

Pat's voice hardened. "More like an indulgent uncle. You like to talk about respect. I don't think Emily ever treated you with respect. And you spoiled her, you always let her have her way." Pat's eyes narrowed. "Same old story, Jason. You just don't do well with responsibility."

"Do you think she was spoiled?"

"She was a good child, a sweet child."

"Was she spoiled, Pat?"

"She was good. She had a good upbringing, and she had two loving parents."

"Who weren't around very often."

Pat slammed a fist into the wall. "Don't you dare say I haven't been a good parent! It was easy for an idler like you to befriend a ten year old – play with her, give her things, indulge her in ways a good parent would've never tolerated."

"Such as?"

"Such as not making her do her homework."

"She did most of it in school. But then you wouldn't have known that."

"Like not being home in time for supper," said Pat, his voice rising. "Like letting her stay too late at ballet practice."

The house went silent except for the sitting room clock.

Jason's mouth pursed. He slowly doubled his bony fists, relaxed and redoubled them. "So, what's the thrust of this, Pat? It's my fault that Emily was killed?"

"I didn't say that. But the fact remains, she never paid much attention to our rules with you around. It was after dark that night, and rainy. She should've been home, with supper finished, doing her homework." He looked to the front door's guardian angels.

Jason slumped against the wall. "If you had been around much, you would've known how much she enjoyed ballet. She had a real talent for it. The gift of dance is one of personality, and she had it. Angela McCrary told me just two weeks ago that Emily was her best student. And if you knew anything about children, you'd know that when they find something they're good at, you encourage them, you find ways to support them. Angela always stayed late to work with her." He shifted his seat, winced at the pain in his rib cage. "Do you want to go after Angela, too? Threaten her? Have her arrested?"

"Don't give me that!" Pat clumsily swung an arm, struck Jason's shoulder a glancing blow. "You have a remarkable way of turning everything that happens in this family against me. I'm the poor parent. I'm a lousy husband. I'm some kind of crank, crazed by the death of my daughter, who I apparently don't even know, according to you." He stood up. "Go to hell, Jason."

Pat's first step caught Jason in the calf. Jason grabbed the foot with both hands and twisted. Pat fell in a heap on his brother. Hands tugged, first at shirts, then at ears and noses. Jason felt a fist slam against his ear. In reply, he raked Pat's face upward with the palm of his hand. He pounded the side of Pat's face with a fist.

"Stop it, stop it!" Von stood at the top of the stairs in her pajamas. "Stop it, or I'm going to call the police on both of you." She kicked her way between them. "How dare you two fight with each other over Emily. I can't stand this any more. I–I..." She kicked wildly at the two brothers.

Jason rose, quietly climbed the stairway as he held his side, and he stepped past Von. Pat reached out to caress Von's leg.

She slapped him away. "Don't you dare touch me!"

"I was just –"

"Don't say a word, Pat." Von let out a muted wail. "Isn't it enough that we've lost our daughter? That I have to constantly listen to your accusations and threats? Is there any compassion for Emily in you at all? Or are you so full of anger and hate that you don't even miss her?" She bowed her head. "Why can't you cry because your daughter's dead?"

"Von, I'm just trying to do what's right."

"No, you're not. I thought so at first, but now I don't think you care about Emily at all. You don't care about me, and you could care less about this family."

"Von, no, you don't see what I'm trying to do –"

"Yes I do, Pat. I see it more clearly every day. You have an anger in you I've never seen before. It's as if nothing else matters but revenge."

Pat slumped against the wall at the top of the stairway. Outside, the wind's moan grew. "Not you, too," he said, his voice breaking. "I've been through all this with Jason. He doesn't understand the responsibility I have to see justice done." He looked up. "I guess you don't understand, either."

"I understand that we've lost our only daughter. I understand you're obsessed." She fidgeted with the top button to her pajama top. "It was dark that night. A little girl on a bicycle would be hard to see."

"Damn it, Von, it was a drunk driver. I can't prove it yet, but it was Phil Agee. Why are you making excuses for him?"

"I'm going back to bed," said Von.

"Don't you walk out on me," Pat shouted, "I'm talking to you!" He scrambled to his feet.

"No, you're not," said Von. "You're not talking to me at all. You're talking to yourself. In fact, it isn't you talking at all. It's something inside you that's threatened by Emily's death."

"Von, please, help me, help me with this. Don't you see? There has to be justice."

She turned away. "Sleep it off, Pat. Take the day off tomorrow. Go play golf. But just leave it alone. And while you're at it, consider how much you value this marriage."

"Von. Please."

"Sleep in the guest room tonight. I don't want you in my bed." She turned and disappeared into the master bedroom. The door closed and the lock clicked just before the clock downstairs chimed the arrival of the next hour.

CHAPTER 6

THE NIGHT OWL

The previous night's wind had taken the rain clouds away, promising a sky of deep, quiet blue. Along the streets of Hope, the poplars and sycamores and dogwoods were beginning to decorate the season with their colors. Although the wind had left a fresh scattering of leaves and pine needles in its path, this wasn't yet the time of falling leaves.

At the hour of sunrise, the Night Owl diner was a busy place. The greasy smell of bacon and hash browns and omelets hovered outside the diner, its exhaust fans pulling pungent smells from the kitchen and into the open air. At seven a.m. that morning, the door opened to first one man, and then another.

In one corner, a jukebox bubbled and gleamed, its volume turned low, playing a new Carrie Underwood song. All seats at the counter had been filled except the one nearest the cash register, and customers occupied all the booths. One of the men who had just entered, his gray hair tousled, hitched at his khaki pants, straightened his tail-out work shirt, and took the last counter seat. He sipped his coffee and began reading the early morning edition of the *Atlanta Constitution*. He quickly became the recipient of a one-sided conversation with Lucille, one of the waitresses.

Locks of Lucille's curly red hair kept falling across her eyes. She petulantly swept them back over her ears as she worked. "I told my boy friend last night," she said as she sponged the counter top in front of the gray-haired man, "he'd better have a little something serious to say to me, and he'd dang well better say it soon."

"Uh huh," said the man as he glanced over the top of his glasses.

"Well, like I told him, I ain't young as I used to be, and I ain't as patient, neither." She filled the man's coffee cup and returned the pot to the warmer in one smooth move.

"What'd he say?" the man asked, turning the page.

"The usual, a big old nothing. I swear, I'm gonna run him off once and for all. I just don't have time no more for a man who expects the world and takes everything for granted." Someone from the other end of the counter called for more coffee. She grabbed the pot and dashed off.

The next stool emptied and the second man to enter took it. He was a small man with an engaging smile. He unbuttoned his shirt collar and loosened his tie. "Morning," he said in a hoarse voice.

Newspaper man glanced up and nodded.

"Anything new in there?" said the newcomer.

"Nah. Same ol' same ol'."

"Did they put anything in there about little Emily?"

"Who?"

"Little Emily. You know, she was the kid run over by the drunk."

"Emily Shane," corrected Lucille, "Mister Pat's and Missus Von's little girl."

"Yep, that's it," the newcomer said. "Emily Shane. Say, how about some coffee and toast?"

"Regular?" asked Lucille.

"Unleaded," the newcomer replied. Lucille poured a cup of decaf.

"It'll be a minute on the toast," she said. "Cream and sugar's in front of you."

The newcomer nodded his thanks. He added an ample amount of cream and one packet of sugar. "Wonder what's going on with that case."

"What's that?" asked newspaper man.

"You know, little Emily. Little Emily Shane."

Another man had walked up to the cash register to pay his tab. "The police, they dragging their feet. They pretty well know who it is, but they ain't moving on it."

"Why not?" the newcomer asked.

"'Cause they's important people involved, I expect," said paying customer.

"Like who?"

"Well, the Shanes is pretty important here. Long-time family. Well liked. And Mister Pat, he raised a big fuss about it. Says he knows who done it, and I'll bet he knows why." The cash register rang and one of the waitresses took his money.

"How's that?" newcomer asked.

"Well, y'see, it's all around town that Mister Pat is accusing Phil Agee, who is the owner of the biggest real estate company this side of Athens." Paying customer pocketed his change and zipped up his jacket.

The door opened to Pat Shane, and the conversation ceased.

"Morning, Mister Shane," said Lucille. "We ain't seen you in here for a while. Can I get you a cup to go?"

Pat rubbed his hands together. "Thanks," he said, smiling, "but I'll wait until there's a seat. I think I'll have breakfast today."

Newspaper man drained the last of his coffee and folded his paper. "Here you go, Mister Shane," he said, "I need to get on over to work." He stuck the folded paper under his arm and fished in his pocket for change.

Pat smiled again. "Tell my wife hello, will you, Bill?"

"Sure thing, Mister Shane." A big smile spread across the man's face. "You know she don't get to work until eight-thirty or nine, though, but I'll tell her, sure 'nough."

"You still keeping things shipshape over there?"

"Best I can. Missus Von likes me to keep the office looking and running like a million bucks. It lets everybody know we run a good realty office. They's lotsa competition in real estate these days."

"I can imagine," said Pat. Lucille handed him a cup of coffee.

"Say," said newcomer, " I don't mean to be rude, but you're the father of little Emily?"

Pat took a sip of coffee. "That's right." The man seemed familiar, but Pat couldn't place him. Maybe he'd been in his restaurant a few times.

"I was really sorry to hear about the death," said newcomer. "Are the police coming up with anything yet?"

"No," said Pat as he reached, poured in a dollop of cream. "Not much."

"That's awful."

Lucille returned from the counter's opposite end. "Now what can I get you for breakfast, Mister Shane?" She frowned at new-comer. "You going to need a refill before you go?"

"Yeah, one more, if you don't mind."

Lucille sighed and poured his cup so full it sloshed onto the countertop.

"I'm pretty hungry this morning," said Pat. "How about a waffle, two strips of bacon, two eggs, sunny-side up."

Lucille yelled the order to the cook.

"I get grits with that, right?" asked Pat.

She nodded yes, causing a wisp of hair to fall over one eye. She flicked it away.

"At the risk of prying," said newcomer, "do the police have any real leads on the case?"

"Hush, now," said Lucille, "Mister Shane don't need to be bothered with that over breakfast."

"No, it's all right," said Pat.

She said, "Lord knows you and Missus Von have been through a lot. I just don't want any of our customers upsetting you."

Pat shrugged. "It's common knowledge now, I'm afraid."

"So they have something?" newcomer persisted.

"Yes and no," said Pat. "They have some good ideas, but they're a little reluctant to follow up on them."

"Why's that?"

"Here you go," said Lucille, placing a long white plate in front of Pat. "Be a minute on the waffle. Can I warm up your coffee?"

Pat nudged his cup toward her. He turned to newcomer. "There's a witness who saw the whole thing."

A gasp from a nearby booth. The Night Owl's hum of voices quieted.

"It might be best not to say who it is," said Pat, measuring his words. He scooped up a bite of egg.

"Sounds serious," said newcomer.

Pat swallowed a sip of coffee. "Turns out this person saw a big Chevrolet Caprice coming down Claiborne, and the car was weaving. It swung close to the curb, where my daughter was riding her bicycle. It hit her and threw her into the power pole at the corner." He looked around. Every eye was on him. "Poor kid, she didn't stand a chance with that drunk."

"You know it was a drunk driver, then?" said newcomer.

Pat finished his plate and took a last sip of coffee. "Doesn't take a big city detective to figure that out. And who around here drives a big Caprice?"

"Mister Agee drives one," someone said.

"What color was it?" someone else asked.

"It was white, same as his," replied Pat.

"Could it have been someone else's?" asked newcomer.

"Fat chance," said Pat. "This witness saw the man at the wheel."

Another gasp from those gathered around.

"Need I say more?"

"Then why aren't the police moving on it?" newcomer asked.

Pat studied his empty cup. "Agee's been out of town ever since that night. Laying low, I imagine."

"So he'll be arrested as soon as he gets back?"

"Probably not. He has influential friends, you know."

Another murmur.

"Alan Baxter," someone said from the counter's opposite end.

"Yep," said Pat. "They're thick as thieves. Went to college together over in Athens. Agee campaigns for him. Baxter probably owes him a ton of favors."

"It ain't right," someone said.

"You elected him. We all did." Pat looked to Lucille, who had set the waffle before him. "One more cup, Lucille, if you will. There's an election coming up next month. Anyone with friends like Phil Agee doesn't need to be back in the state legislature."

"Now, Mister Shane, Senator Baxter's been good to this county, and to Hope," said Lucille.

"That's right," someone else said. "He got Route 316 finished through here, and look at all the business he's brought into Barrow County."

"I know, I know," said Pat. "All I'm saying is he's made a poor choice of political allies. And friends." Pat turned to face the crowd. "Look, I'm as understanding as the next person, but the fact remains, my daughter's been murdered, by a drunk driver." He tapped his knee for emphasis. "We all know Phil Agee has a drinking problem, and I can tell you personally that he's had his driver's license lifted three times. And three times he's gotten it back within a week of having it pulled." His voice was rising. "Think of that. How many of you would be so lucky? I certainly wouldn't be that fortunate." He lowered his head and scratched his nose. "Whatever his problems are, I wish him well. But I won't stand for the killer of my dear daughter Emily getting off scot free again, just because he has political connections."

"It's not fair," someone said.

"Durn drunk," another answered.

"Big money rules, always has," still another said.

Pat smiled. "As I said, the police claim they're working on it. So the truth will eventually come out. But I've already had a conversation with Chief Anderson, and I can guarantee you they're in no big hurry to pin it on Phil Agee." A pause. Pat's smile grew tense with emotion. "I just hope you folks will stop by and give my wife a few words of comfort as you have the time. She's really taking this hard. Do that for me, will you?"

"Sure thing, Mister Shane," someone replied.

"Maybe we can throw some business her way," said another.

Pat took a long sip from his cup, turned, and asked Lucille for his bill. He looked once more to those gathered around. "Thanks for letting me get this off my chest."

"God be with you and your family, Mister Shane," someone said. A murmur of assent passed through the crowd.

Pat's thoughts found Agee and Anderson again as he walked the three blocks back to the house and his car. High and mighty Davis Anderson may not want to press this case, he thought, and they may never prosecute Phil Agee. But if it does go to trial, I'll guarantee Agee won't find any friends on a jury in this county. The thought of that seemed to make him happy. He started humming. The sun was well up now, and the warmth felt good.

#

The telephone rang at a home in a quiet neighborhood in Athens. The home's owner grabbed the receiver on the first ring. "Yes?" he snapped.

"It's Phil, Alan."

"I'm about to leave for Atlanta."

"I'm sorry. I know you're busy. I'm at the motel."

"I should hope so."

"Can I go home for an hour or so? I need to pick up a few things."

"What things? I'll have someone pick them up for you."

"Well, Alan, I, ah, I just need to get out. It's hard being cooped up like this."

"It could be worse." Alan Baxter struggled to pull on his suit coat as he talked. "I'm going to be late for a staff meeting."

"An hour? Please?"

"No. You'll just get drunk."

"I've got a headache, Alan, a bad one. I didn't sleep much last night."

"Then take some aspirin and go back to bed." Baxter checked the time. "Look, I need to go. I'll send someone by. And I'll call tonight."

"Alan –"

"Goodbye, Phil."

Baxter finished pulling on his coat, straightened his tie, and closed the door quietly, so as not to awaken his sleeping wife. He tiptoed down the stairs, crossed the kitchen and dashed to the garage. He backed his Cadillac out hurriedly, throwing a spray of gravel onto the street. "Idiot's going to cost me, I can feel it," he growled as he drove away.

CHAPTER 7

ANNA BAKER

"Would you like more coffee, Yvonne?" asked Anna Baker.

"Yes, Mama, I would." Von handed her the cup and saucer.

Von sat on one end of a blue brocade couch in her parents' living room, a block away from the scene of Emily's death. Anna sat next to her in a matching chair. For a woman of fifty-nine, Anna was strikingly beautiful. She was short and slim, and Von couldn't remember seeing her looking less than elegant. She had the air of a person always in control of herself and her surroundings. And she was always, no matter the time of day, well dressed. Tonight she wore a gray silk pantsuit and a stark white silk blouse open above the breasts. With her long, steel-gray hair pinned atop her head, she seemed the image of a Greek dowager-goddess.

One long tress slipped across Anna's ear as she took the cup and saucer. She reached for the coffee warmer and poured the cup three-quarters full.

"Just cream, Mama."

In contrast, Von wore a turquoise sweater, no bra, blue jeans, and white sneakers.

"No sugar, dear?"

"No, just the cream."

"Darling, you know I put sugar in your first cup."

"I think it'll be fine without all that sugar."

Anna sighed. "All right. You know, darling, sometimes you're inconsistent."

Von took the coffee and stirred it absently. "I just don't know whether I can stay with Pat any longer, Mama. You know the fuss he stirred up at the Night Owl morning before last."

Word had gotten back to Chief Anderson about Pat's implicating Phil Agee in Emily's death. He'd called Pat that night, and they'd argued. Fortunately, Pat hadn't been drinking and had made no threats, at least as far as Von could tell from her eavesdropping. Jason had heard Pat's end of the conversation, too, and the two brothers had argued after the phone conversation. Pat had stormed out of the house and hadn't returned until the next morning.

"Yes, I heard," said Anna.

"Well, it's just that it's so hard losing Emily, and I-oh..." Von reached in her purse for a handkerchief.

Anna sat back and sipped her coffee.

"I'm sorry, Mama, but I don't know where to turn these days. I'm seeing Pat in a different light. There's a mean side to him I've never seen before."

Anna placed her cup and saucer on the table next to the warmer. She didn't reply.

"I know what you're thinking, Mama. He took in Jason, we have a nice home and a comfortable life. But I'm concerned about other things. In particular, how he's reacting to Emily's death. I don't think he's shown any grief at all."

"Except through his anger."

Von fidgeted. "Anger isn't grief. I swear he doesn't feel the loss as much as I do, if at all. To him it's more an affront to his dignity."

"We all react differently to loss, Yvonne."

"But he seems so compelled to place blame."

"He's a man. He's always looking for a wrong to right. It's a manner of reacting that drives men to wage war. It makes them act first and consider later."

"It goes beyond that with Pat, though," said Von. "It's as if he has to prove he's the one in the right. As long as anyone else has a different opinion, he's never sure he has the high ground."

A car engine's drone filled the room, and then headlight beams swept past. Anna glanced to the clock; it was past time for husband David to be home from his health club.

"But it goes even further," Von continued. She set the cup and saucer next to her mother's. "He's absolutely possessed by the idea that Phil Agee's to blame. He wants to destroy him."

"The evidence is pretty damning."

"Oh, Mama, not you too."

Their attention drifted to the house's rear, and a door opening and closing. David Baker began to rummage through a kitchen cabinet.

"I'm only speaking of the things that have come to light that seem to implicate Philip, Yvonne. Apart from Patrick's reaction to it."

"Mama, you're starting to believe the gossip, too?"

"No, dear. But I do know Philip. I played bridge with his mother for a number of years, during his high school days, and while he was attending the university. She was deeply distressed at times by Philip's, shall we say, his wildness."

In the kitchen, David hummed to himself. Then the sound of the microwave as he reheated the dinner plate Anna had left for him.

"That's what I mean, Mama. Phil Agee has had his problems, and everyone knows he doesn't seem to want to drive a car until he's looped. But that doesn't mean he's to blame."

"It's a pattern, child. His mother, may God embrace her soul, told me many times of his ways."

"Oh?"

Anna shifted in her chair. "He was such an immoral child."

"Good grief, Mama, how can a child be immoral?"

Anna pursed her lips. "Yvonne, you're being rude."

"No, we're disagreeing. You always say that when we disagree."

"May I finish my thought?"

Von crossed her arms and huffed. "Oh, please...all right, I'm sorry."

"Thank you, dear. Now as I was saying. Young Philip was an immoral child. Despite his good Christian upbringing, why, I don't think he ever came to know the difference between right and wrong." Anna placed an elbow on the chair's armrest, her palm alongside her head. For a moment, she lost herself in thought. "I truly think, and this is my supposition based on what his mother shared with me so many times, Philip's version of right or wrong had nothing to do with values or ethics, as you young people might term it. He only knew that some of his behavior brought punishment and some didn't."

A faintly angry expression settled onto Von's face. "Are you saying that Phil may not have minded running Emily down? I mean if he really was the one?"

"Of course not. I'm simply referring to a child's behavior. You have to consider what might develop of such a child as he enters adulthood."

"I don't understand, Mama."

A teakettle whistled in the kitchen.

"There's one defining difference between mature adults and children," said Anna. "The immature among us will justify their motivations by blaming something or someone else. If you watch, ever so carefully, you'll notice that most adults behave as brazenly, as willfully as children. And they learn to shift blame most adeptly. An honest, mature person has a sense of right and wrong and will attempt to atone for unwise behavior by accepting the consequences of what's been done. A child such as young Philip wishes to escape those consequences. In adulthood, Philip has consistently used that darling personality of his to charm away the consequences. The shame of it is that the more successful he is at exercising his charm to get out of scrapes, the less the likelihood that he will ever mature. Sadly, these people deteriorate with time. They are the real victims of their success at avoiding the normal consequences of life.

"So I'm saying that, if Philip really is the one responsible for Emily's death, he's aware of the gravity of his act. But he won't experience guilt over it. His fear is the fear of the disapproval of others, the fear that he won't be able to charm his way out of his dilemma."

"But why is Pat so bent on destroying him?" Von leaned forward. "I mean, why can't he just let the police handle the case? It would do so much to bring peace back to the community. And to us."

Anna inclined her head, as if she were looking for something on the room's ten foot-high ceiling. "I don't know, dear," she said at last. "Patrick and Davis were in high school together. Perhaps there's some old enmity between them. Has Patrick spoken of such?"

"No, I don't think they've spoken a hundred words to each other in the time that I've known Pat. Until now, that is. And I've never noticed any unpleasantness between them. No, I can't think of a thing."

"Then perhaps it's what you might call a power play between them," said Anna.

"That's silly, Mama. Davis is a city employee and Pat's a business-man who doesn't even work in Hope." Von pursed her mouth. "No, that's crazy. I know Pat isn't interested in politics, any more than other civic-minded people. I can't speak for Davis, though. They say he wants to run for the legislature, but he's a very good police chief. Everyone says that."

"Such competitiveness doesn't display itself in the political arena alone, dear."

Von slumped into the couch's back. Her face contorted, and she daubed at her eyes. "That's too complex for me right now, Mama. I miss Emily. I want my family back." She began to cry in earnest.

"Now, Yvonne, you really must get beyond these outbursts. Get a hold on yourself, or they'll never let you go."

Von choked off the crying. "Mama, I'm scared."

"Dearest, you're acting as though you're the one responsible for Emily's death. You really must be strong."

"I can't. Don't you understand? My family's falling apart." More crying.

Anna reached, grabbed Von by the shoulder, and shook her. "Yvonne! Stop it this instant!"

Von's crying stopped. "Mama –"

"I mean it, Yvonne. Someone in your family must be strong through all this."

"I can't do it, Mama, I just can't."

"Yes, you can," said Anna, "and you will."

Von began to cry silently now, her shoulders rising and falling. "It's all I can do to make it from one day to the next. I-I don't have Pat for support anymore, and now I don't have you."

Anna leaned forward and stroked Von's arm. "Be strong, child," she said. "Just be strong."

"How can you say that? You've never been through this kind of loss."

Anna settled back, again looking to the ceiling. She breathed deeply. "Yvonne, there's something I must tell you."

Von wiped at her eyes.

"There was a time..." Anna pulled the top of her blouse together at the throat with one hand and glanced toward the door leading to the hallway and the kitchen. "There was a time when your father and I, well, when we had problems."

Von looked up.

"It was a most unfortunate time. We were young. Your father was working so hard trying to establish the food distributorship that has been so good to us."

Von's mouth fell ajar. "Mama, what're you telling me?"

"Child, you really must stop this interrupting. This is difficult enough with your father here." She cast another glance toward the house's rear.

"You don't mean –"

"What I mean, Yvonne, is that there was a woman at the grocer's where your father maintained an office. They developed a friendship, and the friendship became more."

"Daddy had an affair?"

"Yes." Anna looked to her lap.

"But who – how could it have happened?"

Anna's mouth drew to a thin line. "It's enough to know it happened. I'm only telling you this to make a point. Those were difficult years for the two of us, especially for me."

"I can imagine, Mama."

"I don't think you can, even now." Anna leaned forward and took in her daughter through narrowed eyes. "You have as yet lost nothing, Yvonne."

"How can you say that? Emily –"

"Loved ones will always die, dearest. It's a part of life. None of us will escape it. There's a certain equality in it. The only unknown is when." She paused. "You've lost nothing until you've lost trust in one you hold dear. Until you're with that person day after day, until you sleep beside him, cook his meals, knowing that the intimacy you have shared and which you hold most dear now belongs to another."

For a while, neither spoke. David Baker had gone upstairs, the only sounds those of his movements in the rooms above.

"You and Patrick still have one another, Yvonne. Do not be weak, child. Whatever strength he may possess, which may enable him to endure this loss, is not his to share with you. The only strength you will ever have is your own."

"Mama, you don't realize –"

"Dear, during those years, which were the most difficult I have ever had to endure, the only strength I had, the only solace, was that which lay deep within my own soul."

Upstairs, the shower began to run.

"That strength is within you too, Yvonne. You must refrain from your tendency to rely on the strength of others."

"I...I just don't know what to do," said Von.

"What you must do is gain back your husband's dignity. This town is afire with the death of Emily, and it's Patrick's doing. If you allow it, he'll destroy this town, and himself as well."

"I know, Mama. That's what I've been trying to tell you."

"Your mistake has been to allow Emily's death to become a barrier between the two of you. Because of his anger, he's lost your sympathy, your approval, and he's provoking the passions of Hope in an attempt to regain you."

"You can't honestly mean that all this drama he's stirring up is his way of reconciling with me."

"That is exactly what I mean. Two persons looking outward in the same direction, even in anger, can sometimes heal differences between them. The problem now is that his anger has made him susceptible to an even greater danger."

"I'm still not sure I understand what you're implying," said Von. "Is this what you meant when you said there was a power struggle going on between him and Davis Anderson? That rather than trying to make sense of Emily's death, and accepting his own pain and grief, Pat's chosen to project his sense of loss on Phil, and Davis is in the way?"

"Very good, dear," said Anna. "With the emotional state he's in, he won't mind destroying the whole town in order to get what he wants. Isn't it ironic that one's refusal to deal with one's own feelings might eventually destroy something greater?"

Von's palms went to her face. "I still don't know how to help."

For a while they were silent.

"Tell me," Anna said, "what do the police know about the circumstances of Emily's death thus far?"

"No more than you heard three days ago."

"There's no more?"

"Only a few minor details."

"And they are?"

"Pat's been checking around, calling motels, looking for Phil. He's called some garages and the like, looking for his car. And he found evidence of it, Mama, at a body shop in Gainesville. It's not a very well run business, and they don't keep records." She paused. "Pat talked to one of the shop mechanics, and he said for sure it was there the day after Emily's death."

"Have the Hope police sent anyone up there?"

"No, Pat hasn't told them. I don't think they would, anyway. It's out of their jurisdiction."

"But surely some investigation is ongoing."

"Pat called the state's Bureau of Investigation."

"And what's come of that?"

"Nothing. The governor has ordered a freeze on hiring, and the GBI is shorthanded. It's been in all the papers."

Anna ran a hand through her hair. "All right, is there anything else?"

"No, that's all we know."

"Well," said Anna, "I somehow get the feeling that Patrick is walking where angels fear to tread." She drummed her fingers on the arm of her chair. "Yvonne, you really must try to mend fences with your husband and divert his attention away from this investigation. It has an awful smell about it."

"Do you think Pat's in danger?"

"I can only say, dearest, that it's always best to stay clear of such things. One never knows what danger lurks near such predicaments."

Von sighed. "I'll do what I can."

Anna leaned forward. "No, dearest. That's not good enough. You must keep Patrick away from this."

"Mama –"

"No, dear, do it. Think of the damage to the town. And think of the embarrassment to this family."

"Is that it, Mama? Your interest in this is to keep you and Daddy from being embarrassed?"

"I'm thinking of you, Yvonne, and your husband. In this town, your dignity is your greatest commodity; it's the source of your well being, your security."

Footsteps sounded on the stairway.

CHAPTER 8

DAVID BAKER

A humming David Baker strode into the living room in a terry-cloth bathrobe and slippers. His face still wore a pink tinge from the shower, and he'd combed his thin, gray, still-wet hair over the crown of his head. He was a stocky man, and the robe was spread at the lapels, exposing his broad, bare chest.

Anna crossed her arms over her chest. "David, how many times must I tell you not to dress so informally when we have guests in the house?"

He looked around the room. "Where?"

Von suppressed a smile.

"You never know, Yvonne could have brought friends with her."

David winked at Von and cupped a hand behind one ear. "What's that? You say she has friends with her?" He playfully pinched Anna's shoulder. "Looks to me as though it's only her mother."

Anna huffed and looked away. Then a reluctant smile.

"What's kept you two in here all evening?" David asked. "You could've solved the national debt by now."

Both women twisted uncomfortably in their seats.

David looked first to Von then to Anna. "Uh oh, it's worse than I thought. The gossip channel must be back on."

Von smiled.

"Really, David," said Anna, "must you trivialize everything? You're so childish sometimes."

David chuckled. "I do what I can to support my inner child, but I still can't be assured that my family likes him."

Von laughed outright; Anna shook her head.

The phone rang. David answered it in the hallway. "It's for you, Annie. It's Louise."

Louise, Von's younger sister, was having trouble with her youngest of three children. And she and her husband Jacob were at odds over it.

Anna rose and left the room. "I'll take this upstairs," she called out. "Would you please hang up?"

Von picked up the coffee warmer and the cups and saucers. Returning from the kitchen a moment later, she found her father waiting in the hallway with the telephone receiver in his hand. His eyes darted at the sound of telephone voices.

"Okay, I'm off," he said to Anna and Louise, "Bye, you two."

Von opened the hall closet, and as she put on her coat, she sensed her father watching. Smiling, she turned and kissed his cheek.

"I know you need to go, honey," he said as they hugged, "but I just want to tell you again, if there's anything your mother and I can do, well, don't hesitate to let us know."

She held him tightly. "Oh, Daddy, I love you truly."

He kissed her blonde hair. "I love you too, honey." He gently pushed her to arm's length, hands on her shoulders as he studied her.

"I heard bits and pieces of the chat with your mother." He tousled her hair. "Look, I know it's been hard on you, and I know Pat's been a bitter pill to swallow lately. I just want you to remember you're not alone."

Von turned away and choked back a sob. Then she buried her head in her father's broad chest. "I miss Emily so much."

"Me too, baby, me too. And so does your mother." He draped an arm about her shoulders. "Here, sit back down for a minute. I'll make us both a cup of tea. There's still water in the tea kettle."

"Daddy, I'm floating in coffee as it is."

He shushed her, and then he walked her to the couch and took her coat.

He returned a few minutes later with two steaming mugs of peppermint tea. Von told him most of what she and Anna had talked about. He sipped his tea and said nothing until she was done.

"Honey," he asked, "really, how are you doing with all this?"

"I'm scared, Daddy. I'm afraid Pat will do something rash." She looked down. "I don't want to have anything happen that will hurt you and Mama."

"That sounds more like your mother than you."

"But she did make me realize how much damage Pat can cause with his accusations."

David, unsmiling now, said, "I have to agree with her on that." He punched his tea bag with a finger as it floated in his cup. "I know this town, and there are things that would be awfully messy if they were stirred up. But tell me, what's Pat up to, exactly? I know he's going after Phil Agee, but what's his plan?"

"I honestly don't know, Daddy. All I really know is he keeps saying he wants to see justice done." She held her mug with both hands, taking in its warmth.

David smiled. "Well, he sure set Davis Anderson on his ear with the fuss he stirred up at the Night Owl."

"It may be partially my fault," said Von. "He and Jason had an awful fight the night before." She looked into her mug. "And I said some pretty hateful things to Pat. I made him sleep in the guest room."

"That would have done it," said David, laughing. "But you know you wouldn't have said anything you didn't honestly feel was deserved. I know my little girl."

"Oh, Daddy," she said, "I wish I could be as sure of Pat as you are of me."

David slid across the couch and put his arm around her. "He's doing the best he knows how, Von. Look at his adult life, having to take responsibility for Jason, and running a house, and having no parents, and all that. He's a stiff upper lip kind of guy. It's his strength. It's gotten him through life. This drama of his, it's all part of a coping mechanism."

"Daddy, I'm afraid I've been living an illusion with Pat. I always thought he was a caring person, a person I could depend on to do the right thing when the going got tough." She drew in a long breath and let it go. "I feel as if I don't know my husband at all. It's like I'm living with a stranger."

"Honey, there's a little part of each of us we never show to others, even if we live with them all our lives." He finished his tea and set the cup down.

From Knox Avenue, in front of the house, came the sound of tires screeching, accompanied by the dull thud of an automotive sound system. A moment later, they saw through the front windows the sweep of a red police light, as it followed the teenager across town.

"There's something about growing up and getting married that brings things up in you. Things that otherwise you might never have known about yourself."

"I guess so. At least that's the way it's become for Pat and me."

"But there's so much good about Pat that you might find it easy to overlook at a time like this." He reached, tousled her hair again. "Whatever his faults, you know he worships the ground you walk on. You know that, don't you?"

Von blushed. "Daddy!"

"No, it's true. Why, he may love you even more that I do. It's the thing I like most about him."

Von took his hand as she let her head fall to his shoulder. "You're so sweet to say that."

"I know, honey."

They laughed together.

He kissed her forehead. "You should be getting home. I could talk with you all night, but you have to work in the morning. Unlike an old retired fella like me."

"I just wish I could feel better about what Pat's doing."

"Sometimes you just have to let a thing run its course."

Silence. Then Anna's voice came to them from the upstairs hallway as she made a point to Louise.

"Daddy, I don't know what to do next."

"Neither do I," he said. "But I do know this town."

"You said that." She searched every feature of his face. "Do you know something Mama and I don't?"

"No, sweetheart. But I've lived in Hope all my life, and I know how things happen in a town like this." He looked away. "You need to realize that all police forces work deliberately. Let them investigate at their own speed. And for goodness' sake, keep Pat out of it."

Von held her hands to her face. "I don't know how," she said softly, "I just don't know how."

"It's hard, I know, but please try. You can't afford to aggravate the process."

"Daddy, you're making this sound awfully sinister."

"I guess I am."

"Then is there something going on here, something you don't want me to know about?"

"No, I don't think so. It's the people and the roles they play in this town." He rubbed his chin thoughtfully. "Pat's convinced that Phil Agee has killed Emily, that's common knowledge. But Phil Agee's an integral part of this town. A somewhat minor part, but a part. You can't tinker with the way things are – and with the ones running things – without expecting something to happen."

"I still don't understand," said Von. "Honestly, it sounds like there's something dark going on. Who is this person or group that runs things?"

David exhaled. "It depends, from time to time. It depends on the situation, on what it is that threatens the way things are."

"You mean it's just resistance to change?"

"Sure, that's partly it. But it's more than that." He thought for a moment. "For instance, if I tell you to quit your job and stay home, what would your reaction be?"

Von gave him an annoyed look. "I don't think you'd ever do that."

"Probably not, but if I did, and you were convinced I was serious, what would you say?"

"I would tell you whether I work or not is my decision, and you have no right to tell me otherwise."

"Yep," David grinned, "that's exactly what you'd say. But what if I had good grounds for saying that? What if you had three kids at home who were being neglected, and what if one of them was getting into trouble?"

Von's brow knitted. Then her lips drew to a thin line. "I would think about it very seriously, and then I would say you were meddling. That it's still my decision."

One of David's eyebrows arched upward. "Why?"

"Oh, Daddy. Honestly, you can be so aggravating. I know you're alluding to Louise."

"I'm just tweaking your nose, sweetheart. Why?"

"Oh, I suppose because I'm an adult, and I deserve to make my own decisions."

"Even if those decisions are wrong or foolish?"

"Daddy, you once told me when I was little that I would never learn anything about life if I didn't start making my own decisions."

"Unlike Louise, you were a mama's girl then. You wouldn't do anything without asking her first."

"But I'm willing to take responsibility for my decisions now. If I'm wrong, I know I'll learn something from it."

David slapped his thigh. "Exactly right, sweetheart. You have control of your life if you can make something positive out of anything you decide." He leaned back and folded his hands in his lap.

"A town like Hope it like that, too. It can tax us, it has law enforcement authority over us, all powers we give the town. And a town will be just as resistant to being told it's doing something wrong as you are." He rubbed his nose as he considered. "A town's like a living, breathing thing. And it can sometimes be like an unruly beast. It can be hurt, wounded, if you will. And when it's hurt, it won't tuck its tail and run. It will do absolutely everything it can to protect itself. To show itself to be in the right."

"But I still don't understand what that has to do with Phil and Davis and Pat."

For a moment, David said nothing. "Well, you see, each one of them represents an aspect of the way things are in Hope. Phil has a big real estate agency and is well connected politically."

"You mean Alan Baxter."

"I mean the one and only Alan Baxter. Pat's a prosperous businessman and comes from one of the original families in Hope. Came here before the town received its charter in the late 1880s. And of course, there's Davis, who has law enforcement power."

"Each one's a major piece of Hope," said Von. "Now Pat's upsetting something here, and that threatens to change the way things are. That's what you're getting at, isn't it?"

David nodded.

Anna had appeared from the hallway and now stood in the center of the living room. She had changed to a flannel nightgown; her long, steel gray hair cascading over her shoulders. Even though dressed for bed, she looked most beautiful.

"I had hoped you would be home by now, Yvonne, and in bed for the night." She turned a dour expression to David. "And just what sort of tales were you telling our daughter?"

"We were talking, just for a few minutes, Mama," said Von.

David laughed. "I thought I'd try to explain to your eldest daughter just what sort of rock this town is built on, Annie."

Anna tapped a bare foot. "Yvonne, you really must learn to be more aware. It's eleven-thirty. Had I not been on the telephone with your sister, I would have long since been in bed."

"How is Louise?" asked David.

"She's doing much better. The child has been trying her severely. She's simply in need of rest and reassurance."

David smiled. "Reassurance is a rare commodity these days. Worth many shekels."

Von put a hand over her mouth to conceal her smile.

They rose, and David held her coat as she slipped into it. "I'll walk you to the door, sweetheart."

Von took a few steps toward her mother and then came to an awkward stop.

"Good night, Mama."

"Good night, dear," Anna said. She made no move toward her daughter.

Von walked past her and to the front door. Her father followed and opened the door. They embraced one last time as the cold air rushed past them.

"There was a time," said David, "when I wondered why I ever married your mother –"

"Daddy, I understand."

He placed his fingers to her lips. "The problem was, I didn't understand how to coax her from behind that wall of propriety she hides behind. She's really a good person, you know. Almost fun sometimes. You just have to know how to melt the ice."

"You do have the gift, Daddy."

"You do, too," he said. "Use it on Pat."

She squeezed his hand and then turned and descended the steps, down the walkway and past the envelope of light cast by the front porch lights. She turned the corner onto the driveway.

A moment after she was gone, David walked to the edge of the porch and gazed upward, past the eaves of the house. The stars shone brightly, blinking in their silent, eternal manner. He took them in. "Hey, you guys," he said, "You know what's going to happen, not me. Please don't let my family get hurt."

CHAPTER 9

CONFRONTATION

The following Saturday morning – Pat had slept fitfully. At five a.m., he rose for good. By his third cup of coffee, he'd made a decision. To hell with Davis Anderson and his police force. Phil Agee's left a trail a mile wide, and I'm going after him.

By seven a.m., sunlight began to flood the kitchen. He was always in a good mood after he'd made a hard decision, and now he leaned back, propped his feet on the antique wooden kitchen table, and scanned the *Atlanta Constitution.* This was an election year, and brief articles on local and regional campaigns consumed the front section.

On page five, an article caught his eye. State Senator Alan Baxter, currently campaigning for reelection to his fifteenth term in office, had been asked about his rumored intent to enter the gubernatorial race two years hence. Too early to consider that, Baxter had told the reporter. My only concern is in listening to my constituency and, God willing, carrying their mandate once again to the State Capitol in January. Then there was a brief quote of support from his longtime friend and campaign contributor, Philip Agee.

Pat smiled as he folded the paper. So he's in the area. He thumped the paper as he thought. It'll be that much easier to find him. Neither Von nor Jason was up yet, so Pat quickly showered, dressed, and walked the three blocks to the police station, where he knew Davis Anderson would already be on duty. No one sat behind the desk in the day room. A jocular back-and-forth came from the station's two back rooms.

He was about to announce himself when the door behind him opened to Buddy Tarbutton, who carried a large, greasy paper sack from the Night Owl – breakfast for the early shift.

"Be right with you," said Buddy. He disappeared into a rear office. Minutes later, he returned to the front desk, Pat pacing about the large, gray-painted dayroom.

"You need to see the chief?" Buddy shook salt and pepper over his breakfast. He popped the plastic cover from his coffee, shook in two packets of sugar, and stirred the mixture with a plastic knife.

"I don't think so," said Pat, "I'm sure you can get me the file you're keeping on Emily's death."

"What is it you want to know, Mister Shane?"

"I want to see what you've done so far."

Buddy sniffed, bent over his breakfast, and began eating.

"Well," said Pat, "how about it?"

Buddy shoveled in a forkful of eggs and grits, chewing deliberately. "I'm not sure I can do that."

Another officer emerged from the rear office, toothpick in mouth. He zipped his jacket and announced that he was going on his rounds.

Buddy nodded and returned to his breakfast.

Pat watched the glass door close behind the officer, and then he turned and slammed the desk with both fists. "Are you telling me that I can't see the file?"

Tarbutton drew back. "It's not our policy to allow examination of files –"

"Those files aren't protected by law," Pat said. "Any lawyer can get them. A reporter can get them. So let me see the damned file!"

Buddy pushed his breakfast away, jaw set. "Can't do it. Sorry."

Pat slammed the desk, again, striking an ashtray a glancing blow and dumping its contents over his shoes. "That file is about my daughter! She was killed within the jurisdiction of this police department, and I want to know what you screw-ups are doing to find the man who killed her. Am I going to have to get the file myself?"

"You'd better not try, Mister Shane." Buddy rose and leaned forward, palms on the desk.

Pat grabbed a file from a nearby pile. Buddy reached, clutched one leaf of the manila folder. Pat jerked it away. The folder tore. Letters, reports, business cards and other bits of paper cascaded across Pat's shoes.

"That's it," Buddy yelled. "You're under arrest!"

He scrambled from behind the desk, seized Pat's arm, and caught his neck from behind. Pat kicked wildly, but to no avail.

"I know my rights," Pat croaked through the chokehold, "I'll sue the whole damned lot of you."

Davis Anderson entered from one of the back rooms, a plastic fork in hand. He sauntered to the front of the dayroom and turned to face the two men. A trace of a smile crept onto his face. Pat had stopped his struggling, his face an explosive red.

"Do you think you can behave now?"

Pat nodded.

"Let him go, Buddy."

Tarbutton pushed him away. Pat tried to speak but could only cough.

"Get him some water," said Anderson.

Buddy returned with a paper cone of water. Pat sipped, chest heaving.

The chief chuckled. "You'll be okay," he said. He motioned Buddy away.

Anderson grabbed Pat's shoulders and turned him toward the building's rear. "Get into my office." There, he pushed a chair toward Pat. "Sit." He returned to his breakfast, Pat gasping in air. A few moments later, he leaned back, coffee cup in hand. Pat sat, head down, saying nothing.

"You all right now?"

Pat nodded.

Anderson studied him as he sipped his coffee. "What the hell did you think you were doing out there?"

"I want to see the file on Emily," Pat said. "I have a right –"

"Your rights are going to disappear mighty quick if you don't stop interfering. I ought to put you in jail. Damn it, nobody comes into my police station and causes a commotion like that. I ought to charge you with attacking an officer of the law."

"I didn't attack him," Pat said. "I had a folder, and –"

"Shut up!"

Pat jerked upright, glared – and then he slumped again.

Now," said the chief, "just tell me what the hell's going on with you. You used to be a reasonable person. People looked up to you."

Pat sighed and said nothing.

Anderson's voice softened. "Pat, you and I have lived in this town all our lives. Even so, we don't really know each other. That is, we're not friends." A pause. "But you realize I have responsibilities."

"Yeah," Pat mumbled, "don't we all."

"That's right. Family, profession, community."

"And more," said Pat.

"And sometimes there's not enough of us to go around."

"I just want to see some progress –"

"Look, Pat, I'm trying to keep things on a professional level, but things are going to get personal fast if you don't get a grip." Anderson leaned back in his chair. "Okay, tell me, how do I get this job done and keep you from interfering?"

"I want to know what you know..."

"...about our investigation into Emily's death."

Pat sat up straight. "You're holding out –"

"Like hell I am. You've been all over town raising a ruckus about this investigation, implying that my department is crooked and covering up God knows what about Emily's death. If I hear one more thing about this, I'm going to arrest you for interfering with an investigation."

Pat's eyes narrowed. "Then prove me wrong."

The chief reached into his top drawer and pulled out a thin folder. He tossed it on the desk. "This is the file we have on Emily's death. It contains everything we have and everything we're looking at. I want you to sit down in the lobby and read it. When you get through, bring it back in here and we'll talk." He stood up and nodded toward the door. "Go on, now," he said, "I'm busy."

Pat took the folder and turned to the door. He stopped. "Tell me one thing, Davis. Where's Phil Agee?"

"We're working on that."

"You don't know where he is?"

The chief blinked. "No."

Pat sat on the day room couch and opened the file. He read the police report on the accident. Then Jason's statement, and the statements of Mrs. Claxton, who heard the accident and reported it, and then Loretta Miller's and her sister Donna's. There were several telephone memos, mostly calls attempting to locate Phil Agee, made by a junior officer. Pat noted a number on a scrap of paper, with an underlined business name: Jackson's Body Shop in Gainesville, the one that had reported Agee's car there. Then another telephone memo, written the day Emily was buried: Senator Alan Baxter had returned a call to Chief Anderson. A telephone number scrawled at the bottom of the pink form in a different color ink. Pat didn't recognize the exchange; it wasn't local and wasn't from Athens. He memorized the number, placed the slip back in the file.

Anderson's office was empty; water was running in his private rest room. Pat tossed the file on the dayroom desk and left the station house.

As he reached his front doorsteps, he turned and took in the street. Frost steamed from the roofs of the homes on Needham Street. He shivered and went inside. There, he heard the shower running in the master bath. The television in the upstairs den blared; Jason was gorging himself on CNN's morning news coverage. Pat entered the kitchen and noticed a half-full pot of coffee. He filled his travel mug and eased out to his car.

At Knox Street, he took the left fork toward Braselton, then Route 53. Passing under I-85, he couldn't help remembering the horrendous accident that had claimed his parents. The chief was right, he thought. There's so much responsibility for a family man. And, he considered, no one ever seems to appreciate the sacrifices I've made, the corners I'm always cutting to keep the family solvent. More and more, it seemed, all he heard were complaints. It didn't feel like familial teamwork, it felt like conflict management, and no one seemed to care about the discord slowly simmering within his own over-amped psyche. What was he supposed to do about Emily's death, pat Von on the back and say, Now, now, sweetheart, everything's going to be okay? Well it wasn't okay, so why soft-pedal it? His only consolation lay in finding whoever had killed his only child, and he was sure it was Phil Agee.

Okay, he had to admit the chief was right on another count, too. There's no proof, nothing that would hold up in court. But Pat had the feeling that no one was really looking. Why the resistance? Maybe that answer would come when he found something missing, something that would incriminate Phil Agee.

But that could be as impossible as tracking your tax dollars. Pat was behind on his tax payments for the year. The hell with 'em, he thought. They play a shell game with my tax money, so I will too. What's fair is fair. They do it to make it easier to wheel and deal, to buy the votes necessary to finance some agenda or another. Think about it; legislators, lobbyists, and bureaucrats, all bribing each other with our money. And why? Somehow stirring these nefarious activities into a borderline-legal stew amounted to the creation and accumulation of political power. All those November promises? Nothing but bait. Send me to Congress or the State Capitol, and

I'll do wonderful things: hold down welfare, open a new military base in your neighborhood, fight Communism, or whatever other idealistic thing they could dream up. The joke's always on us. We send them up there to protect the use of our money, and they spend it like drunken sailors. They're like so many marionettes, with unknown hands pulling the strings.

Were these same things going on in Hope? The same misuse of tax money? Probably, Pat mused. He knew the city council members and all the recent mayors. But, he realized, he knew surprisingly little about how the city was run. He knew who the influential residents were, had known them all his life. But were the same deals made here as in Washington and Atlanta? Were pockets being lined in the same way? Was there a corrupt network built into the system to protect well-connected people like Phil Agee when they screw up?

Ahead, the city limits sign for Gainesville, and then a Waffle House. He pulled in to refresh his coffee. Then, a mile or so north, Route 53 appeared to dead-end. He turned north, toward the lake. Soon, a ramshackle metal building emerged, its windows coated with years of grime, the metal sides and roof rusted almost to dust and dappled with tar patches, beneath a thicket of pines. A large, chipped and fading sign in the gable proclaimed Jackson's Body Shop. A high wire fence, sagging deeply in several places, enclosed the building's rear. Pat pulled in and turned off his motor. The garage was closed.

He'd know Phil Agee's car if he saw it: a white 2005 Chevrolet Caprice. But now he wasn't sure what he hoped this trip would accomplish. Maybe he'd see a dented front fender. Maybe there'd be a smudge of Emily's blood there that he could sample and have tested. That is, if the car hadn't already been cleaned up and re-paired. But maybe there'd be something incriminating inside. The garage's sliding front door had been padlocked. He walked to the fence on one side of the building. He found a small, grime-covered window. No one inside the darkened garage. He tried to open the window. Locked.

Back at the building's front, he looked down the road both ways. No one seemed to be about. He walked to the building's opposite side. A small metal door to the shop office was locked. He vaulted the sagging fence. At the rear of the building, he found another door, a wooden one. He tried the doorknob. Open.

The inside smelled of rubber and auto exhaust and dust. There were three cars inside, and a van, all apparently to be re-painted. The white Caprice wasn't among them. He walked qui-etly through the place, thinking. An inside door to the office stood open. He entered and looked about. A large file cabinet had been shoved against one wall, next to a metal desk strewn with papers and invoices. He opened each of the file cabinet drawers. Nothing but account folders in the top two, and none had been marked with Agee's name. The bottom drawer held old magazines.

Pat sifted through the papers on the desk. Then he stopped, something registering. He again sorted through the papers. On one paper, he saw a name: Agee. The bill was for thirteen hundred dollars, and had been marked paid, dated the previous day. He was about to drop the bill when he noticed something else – at the top of the invoice, below the address, a handwritten note. Call when ready, it read, and a number had been scrawled just below. Pat's heart pounded. It was the same number he'd read on the police station's phone message form regarding Alan Baxter. He folded the invoice and pressed it into his wallet.

He returned to his car, so delighted with his find that he failed to notice an elderly woman standing on the porch of a small white frame house across the street. Had he glanced her way, he would have seen her writing down his tag number.

#

Alan Baxter glanced back toward his Cadillac, and down the parking lot. Then he knocked on the motel door. It opened immediately.

"I brought you some food, and a few other things."

Phil Agee took a grocery bag Baxter had been holding.

"Thanks, Alan. I was getting tired of hamburgers. You eaten yet?"

"No. Can you cook?"

"Sure." Agee rummaged through the groceries, removing several bags of frozen vegetables, a canned ham, two loaves of bread, some sandwich meat, and six tins of tuna. "It'll take just a few minutes to whip something up. What else did you bring?" He peered into the second bag and let out a triumphant yip. He held the six-pack of beer overhead, like a trophy.

"That's for me," said Alan. "It's been a tough day."

"You've gotta let me have it," said Phil.

"No."

"Tell you what." Phil pulled a frozen apple pie and a half-gallon of ice cream from the second bag. "Let me have one beer, and I'll serve dessert, too."

"All right," Baxter said. "You can have one with dinner. Just one, now."

"I cook better with a beer in me, Alan. And I know a few tricks to dress this bland stuff up. It'll be good, you'll see."

"Christ almighty, Phil, I've been negotiating with Republicans all day, and now you. You can have one with dinner."

"But Alan –"

Alan jerked the six-pack from Phil, took one for himself, and shoved the rest into the motel refrigerator. He twisted the top from the bottle. "Now, tell me what you said when you called the body shop."

"I just wanted to know when my car would be ready, Alan, that's all." Phil turned his back, ripping open one of the bags of vegetables.

Alan sighed. "Why did you have to tell them it was me calling?"

Phil turned. "I don't know, I guess I thought it'd move things along."

"Well, it did. They worked all night, finished it. I happened by and picked it up."

"That's great, Alan. I can get my car back now. It's awful being stuck in this room all day."

Alan frowned as he thought. "Things seem to be blowing over, so I suppose I can bring it over here tomorrow." He cocked his head to one side. "You sure that's all you said when you called the body shop?"

Phil turned, the bag of vegetables cradled in both hands. He scowled, and then the smile flooded back. "Sure, Alan. Look, it's no big deal. I didn't tell him a thing."

CHAPTER 10

DIFFERENCES OF OPINION

The following Tuesday morning, a new spate of fall weather announced itself with a blustering cold front. Great sheets of rain and lightning poured down on northeast Georgia. They beat dark, blood-like rivulets into the pine-covered, red clay hills. By eight-thirty p.m. the storm had spent itself, the rain refined to a near-invisible mist. Then an advancing wind began to hiss as it flowed through the poplars and pines.

Hope's streetlights projected a ghostly mix of light and shadows. On a night such as this, at a time of such natural power, most residents of Hope were burrowed safely into their homes, watching the nightly news, doing homework, or washing the supper dishes. Those who ventured forth hurried, scurrying into a corner mart for bread, milk, or cigarettes, bent into the wind as if its strength threatened to strip them of life itself.

But there are always safe harbors on such nights. The bright blue neon sign mounted atop the Night Owl beckoned, as might a beacon to seafarers. Light from the diner's interior fluorescent fixtures set the front windows aglow, inviting passers-by to enter and eat. Inside, coffee brewed, the deliciously tart odor of grilled cheese sandwiches and chili tempted, and Lady Antebellum sang of needing someone.

Newspaper man sat at the counter reading a Tony Hillerman novel over a bowl of chili. Gus, the diner's owner, an affable, overweight man of eighty, worked his way into a booth by the front window and combed back his shock of gray-black hair with one hand. He turned his portable radio's antenna until he found Atlanta's WSB radio station, and then he adjusted the tuner. Newcomer sat two booths away, only fragments of his grilled cheese sandwich, dill pickle, and steak fries remaining. He'd propped his feet on the seat, his back to the window. He probed his mouth with a toothpick.

Two women sat talking in the middle booth. One, a schoolteacher, still attractive despite the bodily exaggerations of middle age, wore a red jogging suit. The other woman, the town librarian, was slight, elderly, and known town-wide as Granny. Her nearly eighty years had burdened her with hearing loss, and she alternately smiled and frowned as the other woman talked in her quiet, conspiratorial manner. The gossipy pair was known locally as Radio Hope. On this evening, one recurring thread wove itself through their talk: the person who had killed little Emily Shane.

"I swear to goodness," said Granny, wiping her mouth with a paper napkin, "it's a crime the way that poor family's been treated. I would never have thought such tragedy would've been visited on God-fearing souls. And the way they've been treated by young Chief Anderson, why it's positively sinful."

The schoolteacher snorted in derision. "They keep doing it to themselves, Granny. Especially the husband."

"I know it seems that way, honey, but families are so vulnerable when they're emotionally distraught."

"Of course they are, but that's no reason to walk all over a police investigation. I have to wonder, if they're taking the death so hard, then why the vendetta?"

Granny licked ice cream from her lips. "It's not right though, hon. It's Chief Anderson's responsibility to be a little more under-standing."

"Oh, good grief, Granny," said the schoolteacher, her voice ris-ing, "he's just trying to protect the town. Being the daughter of a policeman, I can tell you, police work is underappreciated. They do so much. They're so highly motivated. And all we do is com-plain when something goes wrong."

Granny finished her pie and patted her mouth with the napkin. She reached into her purse, found a tube of lipstick and a mirror, and retouched her lips. "You're right as rain, of course. I just think the Shanes are getting a bum rap."

The schoolteacher choked on her coffee. "Bum rap?" she said, laugh-ing. "That doesn't sound like you talking. Where'd you pick that up?"

Granny smiled. "Some of those very children who learn Shake-speare from you. They do come to the library once in a while."

The schoolteacher chuckled. "Obviously, our efforts at culture aren't enough to keep them from mongrelizing English."

"I think Shakespeare would be enthralled, hon. Language needs to be nudged out of its old habits every now and then. And, as you know, Master Will Shakespeare took a few liberties with words."

"Well, if liberties with language are good things, then you should come to my next faculty meeting and explain a few things to the principal."

Newcomer had risen. He smiled as he neared. "I couldn't help overhearing you talk about the little Emily Shane tragedy."

The schoolteacher turned in her seat and peered over her glasses. "Is that what we were doing?"

Newcomer held out his hands in a gesture of apology. "I guess I'm being rude, aren't I?"

"That's all right, young man," said Granny, "we did refer to the Shane family's troubles."

Newcomer edged closer. "I was just wondering how it's affecting the town – you know, are people up in arms over this, or what?"

"You look familiar, young man," said Granny, "but I can't place you."

"I'm from Athens. I drive for a long distance courier service as a freelancer, and I'm through here now and then on business. I've been following the story, and I was just wondering if there were any new developments."

"That's not what you asked," replied schoolteacher. "You wanted to know if the town was up in arms."

"That would qualify as a new development, hon," said Granny.

"It could also qualify as a catastrophe."

"When I first heard about it," said newcomer, "it struck me as an awful, awful tragedy. You know how such things stay on your mind. You can't help worrying about the family and wondering why it happened."

"There's no why to it," said schoolteacher, "it's senseless."

Gus turned off his radio. "If you ask me, the townsfolk need to do something about it."

Schoolteacher sighed. "We are. Our police force is investigating it."

"That's not what I mean," said Gus. "We oughta have a show of support for the Shanes. Maybe we could have a rally in the school gym, make some speeches, have punch and cookies. Almost nobody went to the funeral."

"Not everyone knew about it," said Granny.

"That's my point. We should let 'em know we care." Gus glanced to Granny and schoolteacher. "You ladies need anything else? More coffee?"

"Decaf," said schoolteacher.

"I'm fine, hon," said Granny.

"How about you, sir?" he said to newcomer.

"No thanks. I really need to go."

Gus rose and returned with the decaf.

"Aren't you afraid," said schoolteacher as she stirred her sweetened coffee, "that with the feud brewing between Pat Shane and Davis Anderson, a gathering like that would be a slap in the face to the police?"

"Not really," said Gus. "The chief would be mighty thin-skinned to think that. I think the Shanes deserve a little sympathy."

"The point is," interjected Granny, "that they both need to chill."

Schoolteacher laughed. "There you go again, Shakespeare. But you're right. You can bet Davis Anderson would think the rally was Pat Shane's idea. And what if Shane gives a speech and gets all wound up? In the state of mind he's been in lately, no telling what he'd say. He'd probably start a lynch mob and go after Phil Agee."

"Where is that guy, anyway?" asked newcomer. "Last I heard he was on the lam somewhere."

"You need to be careful with that sort of talk," said schoolteacher. "He hasn't been accused of anything, except by Pat Shane."

"He still ain't showed up, though," said Gus. "It's beginning to look awful suspicious."

"Hey Gus!" said newspaper man from the counter. He'd risen and had his wallet out. "How much is the chili?"

"What'd you have with it?"

"Just water."

"That'll be three and a quarter," said Gus.

"Just leave it on the counter?"

"Naw, let me have it. I'll forget it's there." Newspaper man fished three ones from his wallet and produced some change. He eyed the two women. "You folks talking about the election?"

"We're talking about Emily Shane," said Granny.

Newspaper man shook his head. "It's awful. Missus Von don't hardly come to work these days."

"We been talking, and I come up with an idea, Bill," said Gus. "We should do something nice for the Shanes, show 'em we care."

"Like what?"

"Like a big rally in the school gym."

"I still say you're playing with fire," said schoolteacher.

Gus shook his head. "It'd be a 'We love you, Emily' kind of gathering. Maybe we could put up a little plaque in her memory. Something to show 'em we care about 'em."

"Now is not the time," said schoolteacher.

"I kinda like it," said newspaper man. "Missus Von could use some cheering up."

"That may just make it worse for her," replied schoolteacher.

"Well, I don't see how," said newspaper man.

"She has a point," said Granny. "It could be taken the wrong way. And if Chief Anderson and Mister Shane start feuding in public, well, it could make the town awfully uptight."

"Uptight," said schoolteacher. She rolled her eyes and snickered.

"Does Phil Agee have any friends?" asked newcomer.

Newspaper man tsked disapprovingly.

"I thought he was a popular guy around here."

"Was," said Gus.

"Surely he has friends."

"Not many."

"One, really," said newspaper man. "And he's a state senator. Name of Alan Baxter."

"I know the name," said newcomer.

"Some say he's going to run for governor," said Granny.

"He's done a lot for Hope," said Gus.

"So he's pretty well liked here?" asked newcomer.

"He's too ambitious, if you ask me," said schoolteacher. "When you get as powerful as he is, you tend to forget about the people who put you there."

"How wretched is the poor man," said Granny, "that hangs on princes' favors."

Schoolteacher smiled. "The real Shakespeare, eh, Granny?"

She nodded. "Part of Henry the Eighth, I believe."

"What's it mean?" asked Gus.

"It means don't get indebted to powerful people," said schoolteacher.

"There ain't enough influence potential in Hope to pop a cork," said Gus.

"Except for Alan Baxter," said Granny.

"But his is in Atlanta."

"In Atlanta and around here, too," said schoolteacher.

"Well, you can bet he shoots real bullets there," said newspaper man.

They laughed.

"Just don't cross him and his kind," said schoolteacher. "They can ruin a life in a minute that took years to build."

Gus rose and took his place behind the counter. "I got to get rid of the rest of this peach pie," he said. "Who wants a piece? It's on the house." Everyone except Granny accepted, so he cut the remaining pie into three pieces. He warmed them and added a scoop of French vanilla ice cream to each. "I ain't gonna carry 'em over there," Gus said, grinning.

He watched them as they ate, wiping his hands on the front of his white shirt. "I got a little coffee left, too." He poured fresh cups for newspaper man and newcomer and began filling the dishwasher. Then he wiped the counter and cleaned off the griddle.

"That was mighty good," said newspaper man.

The others offered a chorus of agreement.

Gus turned and smiled. "While y'all were finishing the pie off I was thinking. I believe I will put together something to show a little bit of sympathy for the Shanes."

"Well, don't let it get out of hand," said schoolteacher.

Gus nodded. "I was thinking things would go better if we had it here, though. Put up some decorations and serve a few snacks. You know, with cokes and coffee."

"That'd be nice," said Granny.

"I can help you get everything ready," said newspaper man, "and clean things up afterwards."

"What about some night during the week, say mid-month?" Gus asked. "I'll let everybody know. I'll put up some posters and have some flyers made up."

"Who do you think will come?" Granny asked.

"Everybody in town, I hope."

"You reckon Phil Agee'll come?" asked newspaper man.

They laughed.

"You know, it's something to think about," said schoolteacher. "You don't need anyone causing a stink that night. After all, this is a public place."

"I wouldn't worry about that," said Gus, "people'll be in and out. There won't be but a few here at a time."

"Mister Agee prob'ly ain't coming back, anyhow," said newspaper man. "We ain't seen hide nor hair of him so far."

"Trust me," Gus said to schoolteacher. "There won't be a problem. You'll see."

"I hope you're right," she said.

"I need to go," said Granny. "It's past my bedtime." She hugged schoolteacher and waved to the others. "Y'all come visit me, you hear? You can always learn something new at the library."

# # #

With his customers gone, Gus counted the day's proceeds and prepared a bank statement for the next day's deposit. He looked around for a sign of anything he might have forgotten to do. Mornings were such a rush time. Best to get everything done before he left. Seeing nothing amiss, he turned off the lights over the counter.

A Reason to Tremble

Tomorrow he'd begin plans for the Shane gathering. It'll be a nice evening, he thought. We ought to have more events like that. It'll draw the town together, make a positive impact on the whole community. He nodded his satisfaction. It'll be a night the town will long remember.

CHAPTER 11

ANALYSIS

Jason woke early, as was his habit on the days of his psychiatric counseling. He sat at bed's edge as he struggled to overcome the effects of his medications, massaged his legs, probed his ankles and feet for signs of numbness. With this ritual over, he stood slowly, unsteadily. He bent slightly to the left and then to the right to test the rebuilt hip. Today the pain was faint, and he could feel the warmth of blood circulating in his legs. He always enjoyed this flush feeling. When it wasn't there, he felt disconnected, and the simple act of walking would have to be forced and constantly directed. He took a few unsure steps around the small room – just enough to gauge his ability to walk. A smile crept across his face, and he sighed happily.

Then to his bathroom and a shower. After toweling off, he stepped onto the scales. He was almost up to a hundred and sixty pounds.

He blew his hair dry, shaved, and dressed. He stood before the full-length mirror mounted on the back of his bedroom door and surveyed himself. He'd struggled into a pair of loose-fitting khaki pants and a long-sleeved white shirt with bold, colored stripes and a button-down collar – items Von had helped him buy. He pushed a wisp of fine blond hair out of his face. On most days, he refused to face this reflection, but he was feeling good so far, and what he saw made him feel even better. He groped his way down the steps and hobbled to the kitchen.

Today the coffee Pat had brewed smelled especially good. He thought about having one small cup, then thought better of it. Given your medications, you're ingesting too many chemicals, he imagined Dr. Aaron Berg saying. So he set out a box of tea. As the water was heating, he buttered two pieces of toast.

Twenty minutes later, he steered his old two-door Toyota into the parking deck in front of Lawrenceville's Humana Hospital. His habit was to minimize walking, so he parked in the far right corner of the first tier, adjacent to the newly constructed medical office building. He took the elevator down to the open crosswalk and fought his way through a humming wind to the medical building and Doctor Berg's office. Eight-thirty – he was exactly on time.

Doctor Berg, in his early thirties, was already sporting the sagging facial features of late middle age, and to add to it, he wore thick glasses rimmed in wire. A prominent nose produced for him a fluffed but hawkish face.

He nodded Jason to a chair in front of his desk as he scribbled on a pad. Finally, he looked over his glasses and smiled. He pulled a notebook from his lap drawer and slipped into the chair opposite Jason.

"And how have the last two weeks been?"

Jason looked away. "We're still trying to adjust. Emily's death has been really hard on the three of us."

"How are you dealing with the loss yourself?"

Jason shook his head. "I miss her. I miss her a lot."

"She was a very important element of the progress you've made these past few years."

"We were very close." Jason's face contorted and he slumped, head in hands.

"Grief is a healthy response to loss. Is this what you're feeling now?"

"I keep reliving the day she died."

"Let's talk about that."

Jason tried to, but he could only shake his head and mutter.

"Deep breath," the doctor said.

Jason calmed. "I keep seeing her lying there on the ground."

"Tell me about that moment."

Jason talked of the shock he'd felt when Wanda Claxton had called, and of the dread minutes afterward. He'd been so slow getting to the scene of the accident. Finally there, he'd felt so helpless on seeing her disfigured and bloody body.

"I could hardly recognize her," he said. He told of his conversation with the two paramedics, of the decision to bring Emily to Lawrenceville.

"And the decision felt right? That, is you're not questioning your ability to make such decisions?"

Jason nodded, his legs writhing. He exhaled. The doctor tapped his pencil on the arm of his chair and waited. Again, Jason couldn't speak.

"More deep breaths," the doctor said quietly.

Jason breathed in, the air coming in short, nervous spasms. When he could speak, he said, "Something else happened then."

"After the ambulance left?"

Jason nodded.

The doctor scribbled in his notebook. "Can you talk about it?"

Jason took several more deep breaths. "I was there."

The doctor leaned forward. "You were there –"

"In Vietnam. When I was hit. When Leo was killed."

"Can you describe it for me?"

Jason's forehead bled a sheen of sweat. Slowly, he began to describe the scene.

He finished, and the doctor asked, "How are you doing with the lithium?"

"Same as always. It keeps me even. I'm groggy when I get up in the morning, though."

"Were there any physical symptoms during the seizure?"

Jason nodded, feeling along his left hip with his hand. "I felt the whole thing. At An Loc. Me getting hit. Leo getting blown away. The chopper I rode out in, me lying on Leo's body bag." He slid downward as he sat, elbows digging into the chair's armrests.

"You had pain, there in your left hip?"

"Yeah."

"Was it bad?"

"Now that I think about it, it wasn't so bad. I could stand it." Jason's head jerked up, something of a smile on his face. "I remembered to breathe, doc."

"And did it help?"

"Yeah, after a while, I came back."

"You returned to reality at that point?"

"To this one, yeah."

Jason had insisted from the start that his visions were just as real as the world he regularly saw with his eyes open. It had almost earned him a tour in the mental ward at Bethesda before he was discharged. But Doctor Berg had understood. Sort of.

"We'll return to that," said Doctor Berg. "And that was the end of the experience?"

Jason's head hung. "No," he said quietly.

"Tell me, please."

"Mom and Dad – the accident. I saw it happen. I saw the police. Everything. I was so scared."

"Please go on."

"It was brief," Jason replied. "I remember talking to Pat. He said everything would be all right." He looked away and shook his head. "I was really scared."

"Once again, abandonment is the issue." Doctor Berg tapped his notebook. "This is good, Jason. It's still surfacing under extreme emotional stress, but you're becoming detached from the trauma. You've reported it in precise detail, which hasn't been possible before, when your emotional identification with these events was so strong. You remembered to breathe during the hallucinations, and it apparently grounded you quickly and effectively. You're connecting it to the root cause, which is, of course, the loss of your mother and father."

"I didn't talk about this to anyone, though."

"Were you afraid to?"

He sighed. "I don't want anyone to think I'm crazy."

"It's important to understand your beliefs about this, Jason. First of all, do you think you're crazy?"

"No. We've talked about this before. I know I overreact to trauma, and you know what I think about that. I think my body holds the memory so strongly that it allows my psyche to enter a separate reality. An independently created loop of time in which the war is still going on. It goes back to Einstein's theories on relativity and the independence of effects in space-time."

"Yes, I know," the doctor replied. "I've been reading some of the texts you've mentioned." He chuckled. "I have to know at least as much as my patients, if I'm to be their doctor."

"Which books?"

"Ken Wilber's book. Some of Dr. Leary's later work. Pretty radical stuff for a classically trained psychiatrist." He smiled. "I consider myself on the cutting edge of my field in adapting Grof's theories to my practice. The breathwork is so effective in dispersing traumas."

"And are you buying into any of this other stuff?"

"Let's just say it's interesting. If I were to buy into it completely, I would have to believe that wherever your consciousness leads you, however it might decide to express itself, is perfectly appropriate. Our world would be a composite of many separate expressions of reality, and my training won't allow that. I work under the assumption that the collective consciousness desires one completely defined and structured reality for us all."

"But isn't that belief at the basis of all prejudice, and doesn't it further stimulate separation between people?" Jason paused.

The doctor offered no reply.

"It's a paradox," said Jason, "but the insistence on a consensus reality means that one person or group of people get to dictate how it's to be expressed. If anyone else has a slightly different take on reality, they find it undermined by being labeled immoral or worthless. Or crazy."

"But that's why you're here. You want to fit in. To be accepted."

"That's your viewpoint," replied Jason. "Mine is that I want to be rid of the pain. The pain caused by my experiences. The fear of it, the pure horror of it. Not necessarily lack of acceptance or fear of abandonment. I can accept living in two worlds if I can get over the horror I associate with one of them."

"It's undeniably true that you're unusually sensitive to emotional experience. In fact, you're tremendously responsive to emotional stimuli in general. That's why your relationship with Emily has had such a healing effect." The doctor rose and poured a glass of water. He remained standing behind his chair, holding the glass. "You're slowly coming to terms with your emotional pain. And it's because you've discovered something to supplant it. In other words, you had begun replacing the horror of your experience in Vietnam with your love for Emily." He took a long drink of his water. "But now we have a new problem. The experience that has brought you so much healing has been taken away in a most traumatic manner."

Jason's head hung. "You're right, she was the most important person in my life." He looked up. "So where do we go from here?"

The doctor sat. "In work like this, there are no magic answers. Progress comes as the fears and their consequent bodily traumas are faced, one by one, and allowed to dissolve." He paused and, as Jason nodded, he continued. "If we were to proceed too quickly, if too many aspects of your trauma were opened at one time, it could cause extreme chemical imbalances. Imbalances that would be difficult if not impossible to repair."

"I understand all that. But how do I replace Emily?"

"I don't think you need to," said Berg. "What I'm seeing from your experiences of the past two weeks indicates that you're able to withstand the debilitating effects of these traumas as they come up. Even with the reappearance of hallucinations, you didn't lose your ability to function." He smiled. "Your grasp on reality."

"This aspect of the composite reality."

The doctor smiled. "Of course. And at this moment, you seem to be dealing with Emily's death in a more positive manner than Pat. You're doing better, perhaps, than Von."

Jason stuffed his hands into his pants pockets as he thought. "Pat's really a mess. I think Von's okay, though." He looked up, smiling. "In fact, I know she is."

"It's important that you begin to act from this newfound state of emotional independence. While you're still expressing a great deal of fear concerning such issues as abandonment, acceptance, and security, you aren't letting them further traumatize you. Which means you're more resilient emotionally. Both concerning your Vietnam experiences and your family life."

"What are you saying, Doctor Berg? That I'm ready to be on my own? Get a job?" He sneered. "Have a family?"

The effects of Agent Orange on Jason had been devastating. Besides the constant burden of depression, impotence had been an off-and-on issue – for conjecture, at least. For what seemed ages, he'd been in no shape, physically or emotionally, to consider a romantic relationship.

"As the healing progresses," Berg went on, "nothing in that respect is impossible. But we must approach it slowly. You may find your body responding in ways you thought impossible. You may lose certain functions, regain them and lose them again. There are many stages to rehabilitation of any kind. The key is to keep your mind on consistency." He shifted in his chair. "And to anticipate a question, rehabilitative progress doesn't mean you're free of trauma. The true test is how you respond to it. After you leave today, I want you to think about the way you handled yourself in the minutes and hours after Emily's accident. It wasn't necessary to sedate you or hospitalize you, as before, when much less significant traumas arose. You'll see what I mean."

Jason rose to go. As he stood he swayed back and forth, trying to stretch his leg muscles. Unsure of their flexibility after this long sitting spell, he sat down and began to rub his thighs and calf muscles in long, kneading motions. He looked up to see Doctor Berg watching. "I do this every day," he said. "I couldn't get around at all if I didn't do it."

"I was just noticing how well you seem to know the muscle structure of your legs," said Doctor Berg. "Do you know the upper body as well?"

"Not really. I do most of this work on my legs. Sometimes the arms. I read some medical books on anatomy and learned the basic muscle structure. And I asked a lot of questions when I was in the Veteran's hospital, right after 'Nam."

Doctor Berg nodded. "In some future session, let's talk about occupational options. I think you might have some skills in physical therapy."

Jason laughed. He waved both hands before him. "Healing hands, huh, doc? I'll think about that."

"Good." Doctor Berg smiled and then scribbled in his notebook. "We'll put the topic on our list."

Jason rose once more. He bounced slightly as he tested his legs. "See?" he said, "they're better." He strode to the table where the water pitcher sat and poured a glass. He drained it.

"Do you have anything else for today? Anything with the family?"

Jason returned his glass to the table, a pensive expression on his face. "Yeah, there's one more thing." He returned to his chair. "It's Pat."

"All right."

"He's taking Emily's loss extraordinarily hard. His personality has changed."

"In what way?"

"He's become violent."

"Toward others, I assume?"

"Well, yeah. He's convinced that a person named Phil Agee is the one who hit and killed Emily that night. He's trying to provoke the whole town into blaming this man."

"How do you see that as violent?"

"He's had several arguments with Hope's police chief. Almost been thrown in jail. He's beginning to be verbally abusive to Von. And he and I had a fight."

"A fight?"

Jason looked up, a sheepish smile on his face. "Yeah, a real one. We were arguing one night, and before I knew it we were slugging each other. Von had to stop it."

Doctor Berg bent to his notebook. "What were you fighting about?"

"Ah, nothing, really. He said I was wasting my life, and I said he wasn't a good parent."

"The two of you suffer similarly from the death of your parents. However, each of you plays it out differently. You orchestrated a passive dependent role, and Pat assumed the role of decision-maker."

"But I never wanted to be the weak younger brother. I didn't decide that."

"The roles are often arbitrarily taken, in the throes of trauma or emotion. But there are always compensations. Often it has a lot to do with your sense of self-esteem. Your beliefs about yourself. You've compensated for this passive role by developing an active, inquiring mind. Pat compensated for his more active family role by diverting his attention to work responsibilities. However, you and Von, no doubt, have had a damping effect on that. And Pat has clearly allowed it."

"But why this abusive reaction now, after Emily's death?"

Doctor Berg gazed to a large picture window overlooking the north Georgia countryside. "He had developed an equilibrium in his life. His traumatic response was hidden within the family structure he allowed to be created. His passion is, no doubt, to protect and defend each of you."

"Yep," Jason nodded, "you got that right. He's the knight in shining armor, always riding to our rescue. And then reminding us of it."

"But Emily's death threw his creation out of balance. With Emily dead, two things happened." He lay his notebook and pencil down. "First," he said, holding up a finger, "the family was a buffer, a protective padding over his own emotional scarring. Emily's death took part of that away, and now his own feelings of helplessness and abandonment are coming to the surface." The doctor held up a second finger. "Next, it took away his ability to come to the rescue. Emily was dead, and she couldn't be saved. The only reaction left for a person in his emotional state is to find someone to blame and to go after them with all due vengeance."

Jason nodded slowly. "That explains a lot. He's been suffering as much as I have all these years, then."

"Perhaps more. You've been dealing with it more openly. And that's been a strength in that for you. In the days and weeks to come, you'll see."

PART 3

THE HUNT

CHAPTER 12

FAMILY MEETING

Pat sat at the kitchen table, his supper before him. Von and Jason had already eaten, the dishwasher loaded and the kitchen cleaned. On a normal night, Jason would be watching public TV, as the anchors tried to divine the mood of voters in the upcoming national election. Tonight, however, he was restless and had gone for a walk. Von was talking to her mother on the upstairs phone.

To improve Pat's spirits after his weekend in jail, Jason had grilled a dozen chicken breasts and Von had cooked an early batch of collard greens. Together they'd made a sweet potato pie, prepared and cooked green beans and yellow squash. As an afterthought, Von had driven to the grocer's for a packet of meal for cornbread. Thus Pat's favorite dishes lay before him; but he wasn't in the mood.

The previous Saturday, the GBI had informed Anderson of Pat's visit to Jackson's Body Shop. Anderson had told no one; instead, he'd driven to Gainesville to interview the lady who had made the phone call. Then he'd visited the garage, talked at length to the workers and Randall Jackson, the owner. The chief had returned to Hope and placed a series of calls. Then he'd done nothing more until this day, Friday morning.

The chief had waited across the street from the Shane home until Pat climbed into his car, prepared for the drive to his Athens office. Then Anderson pulled into the driveway, blocking Pat's path. Pat, dumbfounded, climbed out without a word of protest. Anderson pushed him into his cruiser and drove away, all in the space of three minutes.

But as Anderson drove, Pat began screaming threats. He bloodied his hands on the metal cage separating the front seat from the rear. At the station, it took three police officers to restrain him long enough to book him and throw him in a cell. An hour later, the booking complete, the chief called Von. She and Jason waited anxiously until mid-afternoon for bond to be set, but they were unable to post the ten thousand dollars until late in the day. Von refused to talk to her husband on the drive home. Jason, though, had spent most of the early evening listening to Pat's rants.

Finally, Pat began to nibble at his dinner. Rising, he poured a cup of coffee and cut a piece of the sweet potato pie.

The front door opened and closed, rattling the kitchen windows. Seconds later, Jason appeared in the kitchen entryway. He cut a piece of the pie and sat.

Pat spoke and turned to his coffee. Von's telephone conversation ended, and she too made her way to the kitchen. As she walked past, she allowed one hand to slide across Jason's shoulder. She picked up Pat's plate and emptied it.

"I knew you'd like the potato pie," she said with forced cheeriness.

Pat didn't respond. He slowly finished his coffee, rose and poured another. Then he turned to Von and Jason. "I really do thank you both for getting me out of there."

Pat returned to his seat, frowning. "I've had an opportunity to do some thinking today." He paused. Neither Von nor Jason spoke. "There was a moment today when I realized how much you both mean to me. Von, I'm so sorry. Jason, I've been hard on you." A sigh. "It's tough to know what to do sometimes."

"Well, what's done is done," said Jason. "Now, if you and the chief will leave each other alone –"

"That's another thing I've been thinking about," Pat said. "I'm convinced he's covering up for Phil Agee. And I keep getting in his way."

Von punched hands into hips. "Pat, for crying out loud."

"No, no," he said, "I know what you're thinking. And I don't blame you. But I'm sure the man's covering up."

"If there really is something going on behind the scenes," said Jason, "well, I think you ought to leave it alone. You're in over your head."

"I can't let it go," said Pat, his voice rising, "until I know the truth. "

"You've already been charged with interfering with an investigation," said Von. "Don't you think that's truth enough for a while?"

"Yeah," said Pat. "That's why I, that is, we, need to take another approach." He bent to his coffee. "I think we need to hire a private investigator."

Jason uncrossed his long legs beneath the table. "Right. That would be all the excuse Davis Anderson would need to lock you up for good. Maybe Von and me, too."

Von now stood beside Jason. "I won't allow this family any more loss or humiliation." She brushed at a tear.

Pat sniffed. "I wish you were as interested in the truth, the *real* truth, as you are in our image."

"Don't you see that Von's right?" said Jason. "What more can we expect to do, other than cause ourselves more embarrassment?"

Pat leaned to one side and pulled his wallet from the back pocket of his trousers. He extracted the invoice he'd taken from Jackson's and tossed it across the table to Jason. "For one thing, we can find out who's at the other end of this."

Jason examined it. "Where did you get this?"

"I found it in the office at Jackson's."

Jason slid the invoice back. "Does Anderson know about this?"

"Nope. He asked where I was that day, what I was doing, what I saw." He waved the invoice. "But this little jewel was never mentioned. I guess I have to give him credit for not going through my wallet."

Jason frowned. "What can the invoice possibly prove?"

"You see that phone number, where it says call when ready?" He thumped the paper. "That number's connected, not only to Phil Agee, but to Alan Baxter." He told Jason and Von of the Alan Baxter telephone memo in the police file, and the coincidental appearance there of that same phone number.

"That doesn't necessarily prove anything," said Jason. "Why drag Baxter into this?"

"Look, you have to get beyond your hero worship," Pat snapped.

"He's no hero, he just happens to be promoting things I believe in."

"Hero worship."

"Will you two stop it?" Von said.

Jason glared at Pat. "Baxter is one of the few good ones. There are always a few bad apples around, maybe even on the senator's side. But I resent your trying to make him a part of this thing."

Pat sneered. "Blinded by hero worship."

"Stop!" Von cried. "I mean it!"

The brothers quieted.

Then Jason said to Pat, "Well, the fact remains, you're deep in this already."

Pat shrugged.

"So what makes you think the chief wasn't acting on his own?"

"I don't think Davis Anderson would've had the nerve to arrest me unless someone convinced him it was in his best interests. Or maybe I was a threat. The good chief's too much of a political animal not to test the winds before he does something like this."

"But what threat could you possibly be, and to whom? We only know what they've told us. Anyone else would've eventually connected Phil Agee with Emily's death, considering the circumstances."

"You're losing your good name in Hope, Pat," Von said. "Our family is a laughingstock."

Pat glared. "Don't quote your mother to me, Von. Tell the old lady the truth will eventually come out. And when it does, she'll owe me an apology."

"I'll have you know, my mother is very concerned –"

"With her family's reputation," said Pat.

"That's not fair!"

"But it's the truth."

Von stamped a foot and looked away.

"I'm going to settle this once and for all," said Pat. "I'm going to hire a private investigator."

"You must have some sort of death wish," said Jason. "A private investigator won't find out anything about this case without the police's cooperation." He pointed a gaunt finger at Pat. "And it won't take them long to figure out who hired him. For Christ's sake, you'll be back in jail in a week."

"I have a right to legal discovery. Not even Davis Anderson can take that away from me."

"I'll remind you of that the next time the jail door slams behind you."

"Look," said Pat, "I have a plan. There's plenty of circumstantial evidence to connect Agee with Emily's death, and I think Davis Anderson will try to keep it circumstantial. He won't open it up enough to expose any real evidence."

Jason rubbed his face. "I can't imagine why a straight shooter like Davis Anderson would want to stage a cover up."

Pat leaned forward. "We don't have to concern ourselves with that. At least not right now. We'll just take the little tidbits he throws our way and let our private eye follow up."

"And maybe step on the chief's heels in the process."

Pat stood, poured the last of his coffee in the sink. "One thing I realized in jail today. You have to be patient."

Jason glanced to Von, distress in her eyes. "You know what, Pat? You've lost it. We could excuse your anger at first, but all this plotting, well, it's crazy."

Pat smiled. "You just have to know how to handle a situation like this. We have to keep a buffer between Davis Anderson and us. That's where a private investigator –"

"No, Pat," said Jason, "not we. You. If you go through with this, you're on your own. I'm not going to be a party to your private war with Davis Anderson." He glanced again to Von.

"I don't want you doing this, Pat," she said. "There's nothing we can do to bring Emily back. Nothing. And there's absolutely nothing to gain from any of this plotting of yours. You'll lose your job, what's left of your dignity, and you'll destroy what's left of this family." She looked down. "I've tried to be understanding and supportive, but I don't know you any more. I wish I knew how to help you, but I don't."

Pat pounded the table. "I'll do this myself, then. To hell with both of you. I've never had any help doing anything, anything that really mattered, and I don't need any help now. So stay out of my way. I'm going to find my little girl's killer."

Von turned to Jason. "Please, do something!"

Jason wanted to run, to leave this far, far behind. He saw himself running down the street, running faster, down the Interstate's grassed median as it wound northward. He ran faster, the cold fall air coursing through his hair, domestic conflict nipping at his heels, a demon he could no longer avoid. Just like Vietnam, he thought. I can't outrun this. I have nowhere to hide.

"All right, then, let's look at this," he heard himself saying, an idea beginning to form, an idea he wanted no part of. "What can you possibly find out that the police haven't?"

Pat gave his brother an odd look. "We can chase this phone number down, for one thing," he said, again waving the invoice. "And I don't think we've heard the whole truth from Jackson's Body Shop. Why was Agee's car being repaired? Where are the damaged parts? And there must be a witness who saw more.

Someone who can identify the car, who got the tag number or saw the driver."

Neither Von nor Jason raised an argument, so he continued. "If we can find out anything – anything – we'll have just cause for going directly to the GBI, without fear of reprisal. And if we can get them involved, maybe we can kill two birds with one stone. We can find out who really killed Emily." He looked to both of them. "Davis Anderson has been dragging his feet on this investigation from day one, and I want to know why. Who is he protecting?

"I really have given this some thought," he said, a pleading tone working its way into his voice. "I'm not as deranged as you think; I plan to stay out of Davis Anderson's jail. And who knows? Even if Davis does find out who this private eye works for, we may find out something valuable, something to keep him off my back."

Von burst into sobs. "I'm sorry, I just can't listen to any more of this."

Jason patted her hand. "It's okay." During Pat's speech he had been thinking; the idea he wanted no part of was crystallizing. "I can't believe I'm saying this, but there's some logic to your thinking, Pat. Maybe there is a way to find out enough to close the book on Emily's death and allow us to get back to normal. I think we *should* hire a private investigator."

"Jason, no!" said Von.

"No, I think that's the way to end this."

"You surprise me, little brother," said Pat. "I thought you'd fight me to the bitter end."

Jason huffed. "Let's get one thing straight before we go any further. I don't like what you've been doing, and I think hiring a detective is dangerous."

Pat sat back. "Then what are you saying?"

"I have a friend. We were in the same unit in 'Nam. His name's Wilton Byrd, and he's a private investigator. He's smart enough to find out a few things discreetly. I think we should hire him, but I'll only agree under my terms. I want him to look at the evidence already available and evaluate it for us. If he says there's nothing of substance to be pursued, then we forget the whole thing. And that means you, Pat."

"We don't have the money," said Von.

"That's another condition. I have some money saved over the years from my disability allowance, and I'll pay for his services myself. When my money runs out, the investigation ends."

"Anything else?" asked Pat.

"Yeah, one more thing. I'm in charge of everything relating to the investigation. I have the final say in all decisions about whom he talks to, what he looks for. I'll report to the two of you, and listen to your suggestions. But I have the last word." He cleared his throat. "Maybe that'll keep you out of jail, Pat."

Pat eyed his brother. "And if I don't agree?"

"Then you'll start meddling again. You'll screw up and, as I just said, you'll end up in jail. And if you do, I won't get you out. I won't come to see you. I'll forget you exist."

Pat stared at his younger brother for a moment, then his wife. "Von?"

"I just want it to end," she replied softly.

"But what do you think of Jason's idea?"

"I hate it!" A moment of silence, and then a long sigh. "If you'll agree to do it his way, I won't fight it."

"And if I don't?"

"Then you and I are through."

"Meaning what?"

"Meaning I'll leave you. I'll divorce you."

Pat looked down and said nothing. He turned to the kitchen sink and gazed out the window above it. "Tell me more about this friend of yours, this Wilton Byrd."

Jason told them he'd met Byrd on the plane during the long ride from California to Vietnam. They'd been assigned to the same unit there. First Infantry Division, 28th Infantry. 2nd Battalion, Bravo Company. The Big Red One. Wilton was black, from a poor Charlotte, North Carolina, neighborhood. Like all of them, he was cautious at first in combat situations, but had fought bravely in the months before Jason was wounded.

A couple of years ago, Jason had received a letter bearing a Decatur, Georgia, postmark. It had been from Wilton, a stock letter announcing his services as a private investigator. Jason had written him, and Wilton had responded. In his reply he was all business, avoiding the more normal reminiscences about the war, something Jason considered logical, considering what they'd been through during the war. Jason remembered that in combat, Byrd had been the mature one among frightened children, the one who knew instinctively when to take chances in the field and when to be careful. He'd been distrustful of whites, though; he didn't talk much to anyone except the other black soldiers. Jason and Leo and Wilton had helped build a firebase near the Cambodian border in Tay Ninh Province before the massive North Vietnamese Army movements began in that area. They'd fought side by side there, saving each other's ass more times than he cared to remember. The experience had galvanized their friendship, and it had helped bridge the rifle company's racial tensions.

"What do you know about him now?" Pat asked.

"The basics. I know what kind of person he is. I trust him. And I know he can take care of himself in tight situations. He's level-headed, both feet on the ground."

"People change."

A corner of Jason's mouth turned up at the irony in that. "I'll tell you what I'll do. I'll make an appointment with him, and we'll talk. I'll make an evaluation, and you, Von, and I will talk again before I make a decision. Fair enough?"

Pat continued to stare out the kitchen window. "You're calling the shots now, little brother."

Jason waited, wondering whether Pat would say more. But his brother now seemed to be lost in the reflections shimmering on the windowpane. The stairs in the hallway creaked quietly, and Jason turned to realize Von was gone.

"It's settled, then," he said. "I'll call him tonight."

CHAPTER 13

GOING TO ATLANTA

In late fall in Georgia, in the southernmost foothills of the Appalachians, the season speaks most beautifully to those who rise early. Before the sun begins its slow climb over an eastern horizon made irregular by tall pines and gently weathered hillsides, a misty cloak hugs the earth. It has spread through the night, thickening as it filled the valleys and spilling over the hills like a carelessly thrown quilt. Within this nebulous blanket, the rhythms and melodies of the natural world lie subdued, reduced to one pure, somnolent tone.

Among the spires of the tallest pines, where this blanket is most like air, the sun's first splendor runs like a field afire. It dances across the pine tops in a spectacle of color. A spread of pure fire so masterfully composed that no human hand could possibly reproduce it, fills the sun's corona with indescribable shades of blue and red and gold. Unable to withstand such magnificence, the trees, the pastures, even the earth itself, fall under its spell and submit to its textures.

Jason watched the dawn from the upstairs family room's large bay window. He'd tossed all night, his sleep intermittent. Finally, he'd risen at five a.m. to his usual ritual of breathing, stretching, and bending. Now he stood with a steaming cup of tea in hand, transfixed by the dawning day. A leaf detached from a nearby oak pressed itself against the window before slipping groundward. The wind caught others and swept them in a pointillist stream to the street's gutters.

His tea had grown cold, so he inched downstairs to the kitchen and warmed the teakettle. The house's central heating system clicked on, and within seconds dry, warm air enveloped him. The teapot began its whistling. His tea made, he struggled up the stairs to his room, bathed, and dressed for his meeting with Wilton.

Pat wasn't up yet, nor was Von. Jason crept downstairs and quietly closed the front door behind him.

After a stop at the Night Owl, he took the southern route to Route 316, and from there southbound on I-85. It was almost eight a.m., and the sun had risen from a swollen red to a smaller yellow sphere. He opened the pint carton of orange juice he'd bought, along with his two bacon and egg biscuits, and he took a long drink

This immediate stretch of Interstate was almost empty, except for a line of trucks ahead in the rightmost lane. He ate one of the bacon and egg biscuits, alternately sipping from his orange juice. He turned on his radio. The signal sputtered and wavered, so he turned it off.

As he came closer to Atlanta's metropolitan sprawl, the traffic thickened and crawled. He edged forward, taking in the swaths of fall colors. This was the time of year the hills and mountains of north Georgia seemed created for. The hot, sticky summer days were gone. Autumn brought with it a sense of being reborn; a time to feel the sun's warmth blended into soft, chilling breezes, to feel the body's sweaty humors being washed away. A certain music filled the air in autumn here, the music of harvest. Most of the farms and dairies had long since given way to suburban development; still, corn stalk teepees and piles of pumpkins proliferated in parking lots. The last tomatoes waited to be plucked from backyard gardens. And, one might imagine, the sound of a fiddler happily sawing out a jig behind an unpainted shed on a lonely hilltop.

Jason unwrapped the remaining biscuit. He licked bacon grease from his lips and thought about his conversation of two nights ago with Pat. He really had no quarrel with Pat's cover-up theory. He, too, now suspected something was amiss, but he couldn't bring himself to point the finger at Phil Agee and the senator. Somehow, it seemed too convenient. But he had to consider Agee's disappearance and the total lack of evidence pointing in any other direction.

But why, really, had Pat found it so easy to obsess over Phil Agee? Could Pat be the one with something to hide? He thought about the family's finances. Emily's burial expenses were going to be a financial burden. Von, who worked as a contract and financing specialist at the town's smaller real estate brokerage, had been at work sporadically these past weeks. He knew her last paycheck was a small one. Pat's responsibility for a chain of restaurants carried the demands of a competitive business. He knew little about Pat's role in that, but his businesses had to be suffering, at least a little, from inattention.

And I'm a financial burden to them, too, he thought. He considered the little ways he impacted the family. Frequently cold in winter, he was always nudging the thermostat upward. He stayed up late at night, watching television long after the others went to bed. And he was there often during daytime hours, with the air down or the heat up, while Pat and Von worked and Emily attended school. He bought foodstuffs and his own clothes, but he ate common meals with the family, and Pat covered Jason's occasional laundry tab along with his own. Could there be financial pressures he was unaware of, pressures Pat could no longer withstand, a basis for his irrational behavior?

The Interstate had long since widened behind him. He drained the orange juice carton and tossed it onto the opposite seat. What if Pat were the culprit here, taking advantage of a freak accident to ruin Phil Agee, who owned the larger real estate agency in Hope? If Agee were ruined, would that benefit Von, consequently the family finances? Had Pat invested in Von's brokerage with that in mind? Was Pat that mercenary? How had Von gotten the position there? He couldn't remember. It was probably there in his subconscious somewhere, swept under a blanket of self-absorption and depression. How well, really, did he know his brother? Ah, this is crazy, he thought. Plots and sinister schemes sure can be conjured up when you're looking for them.

He considered the scant evidence surrounding Emily's death. We know nothing, he thought. Absolutely nothing. Well, we do know, thanks to Loretta Miller's sister, that a large car hit Emily. But for Donna's testimony, we wouldn't know even that. No wonder Pat was frustrated with the police. We were so concerned with the pain of losing Emily that even now we've barely absorbed this remarkable lack of evidence regarding her killer.

There were some new developments, though, but they were small and unrewarding. Yesterday, before Pat's release, Jason and Von had called on Chief Anderson. After angrily chastising them for interfering in the case, the chief had responded to their urgings and sent an officer to Jackson's to report on the garage's connection to Agee. Anderson had called Pat just last night and read the report to him. Randall Jackson, the proprietor of the body shop, had stated that he'd replaced the front bumper and had done some minor touch-up work. Where had the bumper gone? Sold for scrap the same day it was removed, Jackson had claimed.

One of Pat's constant preoccupations was the exact date the car entered the shop, and Jason had posed the question to Anderson. Again, Randall Jackson had kept no records on that. We don't keep good books, Jackson told the officer, but he was sure the car was there on the Monday before Emily was killed.

Had anyone seen blood? Who brought the car in? Had anyone noticed anything else, anything vaguely suspicious? No, the chief had replied to Jason and Von's barrage. Randall Jackson had been virtually void of memory, it seemed, but he was pretty sure the car had been left there before opening time with a note, the morning of October second. No, on second thought, someone had brought it in that morning, but no one knew who it was. Upon deeper questioning of the body shop employees, not even that fact could be agreed on. It was a dance of convenient ignorance, Pat had said later.

As if that weren't frustrating enough, Pat had called Loretta Miller, only to find out that Donna had returned home to Memphis three days earlier. As far as we now know, thought Jason, Donna is the most direct link to the identity of Emily's assailant. What more does Donna have locked in the recesses of her mind about that night? We may never know.

As he continued south, his mind drifted to the towns passed along the way. Buford. Dacula. Sugar Hill. Lawrenceville. Duluth. Now he passed Lilburn. Next would be Norcross. All names of separate communities as little as twenty years ago, they had been caught in the sprawl that engulfed so much of the South.

The suburbs. Then the exurbs. First connected by two lane highways. Then more lanes. Often these roadway embellishments coincided with the first sprinkling of shopping centers, office parks, and high-priced subdivisions. Then came the massive strip developments, the chain eateries, the gas stations, the convenience stores. All gradually taking away both the identity of these small towns and their commercial purpose and strength. And then more lanes jammed between the clutter of commercial development. Gwinnett County, through which he now drove, had once been a place of pristine beauty, where dairy farms dwelled in quiet interdependence with pine and hardwood forests, small lakes, and red clay hills. No longer an anchor for the heady, creative ambience of Atlanta, the county had become a brutally implanted showcase for investors and builders. And it only served to spread the complexities of urban life across a wider palette.

Jason had often considered the nature of this phenomenon. To him it seemed most similar to the swarm of armies that had swept across the nation-states of Europe from the thirteenth century to the time of the Italian Renaissance. Instead of great generals leading armies of knights and serfs, there was a consortium of heavily financed investors, politicians, bankers, developers, and architects. Together, they preceded an army of contractors armed with bulldozers, concrete trucks, brick, and structural steel. Instead of conquering another people in the cause of religious ideologies, or to extend the glory of a king, they attacked the earth itself, preaching commercialism. Pushing trees, grasses, and soil away, their mechanized truncheons beat back nature to construct the commercial citadels of today. It was a sick joke to Jason that so many took the old biblical mandate to subdue the earth so seriously. As if it were an enemy.

Now look at us, he thought. We've finally decided there may be some intrinsic benefit in cooperating with the earth's own processes, so we've spawned a worldwide environmental movement, an ad hoc army to defend the earth. But in establishing this new side to our collective personality, we've pitted it against our industrial and commercial lifelines in true adversarial fashion.

His pensive expression gave way to a wry smile. The human processes that had created a series of unconnected and pristine tribal cultures had eventually produced cities, with their mercantilism, guilds, and mills. Western ways then gave us technology to help support our self-created world. But now, as we struggle to relearn the lessons of the earth's sophisticated, integrative nature, we realize we've very nearly cut ourselves loose from it. And so we have the paradox of a world culture tied together by communication and transportation infrastructures never seen before, at war with itself. Like a cancer. The disease so representative of the twentieth century.

The bottom line here, he mused, must be conflict. No matter how well intentioned, no matter how enlightened we become, we'll never truly progress until we manage to rid ourselves of our attraction to conflict. We'll continue to wage war with each other over religious rights, human rights, gender rights, enfranchisement rights, economic rights, civil rights and all the other inequities we can uncover in an asymmetric world.

A pickup truck, which had been in his blind spot, darted forward. The driver cut sharply ahead of Jason, awakening him from his reverie. He jammed on his brakes, barely avoiding an accident. He'd heard someone say recently that when you come to Atlanta you have to drive like an aggressive paranoiac.

Ahead, from the east and the west, rose a braid of concrete ribbons, the multilevel highway interchange connecting I-85 with the beltway encircling Atlanta. Twenty years earlier, this complex of structures would've seemed futuristic, but now drivers within the streams of automobiles barely noticed this grand architecture.

Jason passed through this concrete gateway and into the inner core of the metro area. We notice so few things, he thought. We just use and move on. We buy things, casually use them, cast them aside, and look for more. It was a materialistic quest for something more. But that something was never where we were looking, never in our hand. It was somewhere else, over some future horizon.

We're all that way, he thought. If not by outright design, then we choose circumstances that shunt us away from the beauty, the mystery of the present, into the unknown of the future or the dreamtime of the past. Look at me. I'm probably going to pay a friend to look for something that may not exist. A something, existing or not, that has torn my family apart, something that may threaten the well being of Hope.

Ahead, the multi-laned roadway twisted through a passageway of bridges and walls. And somewhere within that, the future of the Shane family lay for now, it seemed, in the hands of Wilton Byrd.

CHAPTER 14

WILTON BYRD

Jason had scribbled Wilton's directions onto a piece of notebook paper, which now lay in his lap, directing him to take Clairemont Road. Exiting, he drove past a short strip of businesses and restaurants and then along a tree-lined street through manicured lawns and aging but well kept middle class homes. This gave way to the business district of Decatur. Clairemont dead-ended before him, at the town square, the old granite courthouse at street's end. Two short blocks to the left, he found Wilton's office on Chapel Street, a building with green clapboard siding fronted by a wooden deck.

He clumped up the three wooden steps to the deck. To the right, a small brass plaque had been engraved:

WILTON BYRD
PRIVATE INVESTIGATOR

He was about to knock when the door flew open and he was face to face with a muscular black man, some three or four inches shorter than Jason. The round face and clear, white eyes were as Jason had remembered, as was the square-set jaw and sardonic expression. The nappy black hair was longer, with streamers of gray. Jason grinned as he offered a hand.

The man brushed Jason's hand aside and grabbed him in a bear hug. "Damn, look at you!"

Jason returned the hug. "Wilton Byrd, Private Investigator," he said. "Man, with a vibe like that, you could be the star of a TV show."

Wilton chuckled. "I ain't notorious enough yet. C'mon in, man. It's not the Atlanta high rise scene, but it's home."

Jason stepped into a large, carpeted room. A picture window beside the door admitted a barrage of light. A small, cheap desk had been shoved against the longer wall, with a telephone, for a non-existent receptionist, the phone a risen monument amid a stack of postal clutter and a small, framed picture of an attractive black woman. To the room's opposite side, a couch of wooden framework and thick, cloth cushions covered with brightly colored African designs. A low table before the couch, strewn with magazines, completed the room's décor.

To the rear, a series of portable, cloth-covered partitions formed a room separator. A door stood ajar to the left. Byrd led Jason there. The office had been sparsely and cheaply furnished. A newspaper lay open on a battered oak desk.

"I was catching up on the politicians," said Wilton, nodding toward the newspaper. "Nothing but a bunch of clowns. The white guys want to worship the stars and bars, the black guys are making like slaves about to break out of the plantation, and the women are dissing the outhouse jokes."

There had been a movement to remove the confederate symbol from the Georgia flag in a long-ago session of the legislature. Predictably, it had become an enduring issue before being resolved. The growing body of black legislators had used the older flag as a rallying cause to unite their numbers. And several vocal female legislators continued to be appalled by the men's raunchy humor in the Capitol's halls.

Wilton grabbed up the newspaper, motioning toward a small, ratty couch. "Let me get us a cup of joe." He strode away before Jason could object and returned moments later with two steaming mugs. A playful expression creased his face. "Nothing but quality for customers of Wilton Byrd." Then he disappeared again, this time behind the partition, and returned pushing a swivel chair. He pulled a pint bottle of Jack Daniels from his rear pocket and dribbled some into his cup.

Jason smiled. He remembered Wilton's propensity for doing outrageous things. It gets people off their high horse, he'd once said in 'Nam. Especially officers. High and mighty assholes.

Wilton, noticing Jason's look, said, "Hey, isn't this what private dicks are supposed to do?" He took a sip of his doctored coffee. "The man you see before you is a hard driving private eye, just like in the paperbacks."

"It was three in the morning," said Jason, "and Wilton Byrd couldn't sleep. His fists were sore and he was horny."

They laughed.

Wilton eyed Jason, let out a breath. "III Corps, War Zone C, Republic of Vietnam," he said softly. "Dodged shrapnel and watched each other's back. The Cong. The North Viets. Civilians. Officers trying to establish a wartime record at our expense. And our own brothers." He whistled out a long breath and bent toward Jason. "You give a kid an M-16 or a grenade launcher, like they did over there, without teaching him any discipline, and he's a walking time bomb. How many times we see it, man, after a firefight? Some kid who's already crapped his pants, puts his weapon back on rock and roll, and he runs screaming into the jungle, hosing down everything in sight. We'd find him later on his haunches, out of ammo, and crying like a ten year-old."

Jason nodded. There were precious few people to trust there, yellow, white, brown, or black. You took your friends where you could find them, but knowing you'd better not get too close. They might not be there tomorrow.

Man, he thought, I'd better knock this off, or I'll be back at the shrink's tomorrow. I'm here on family business. He took a sip from his mug and read cautious thoughts in Wilton's expression: We had ties back then. Wore the same clothes, sweated in the same stinking jungle. Look at this guy now, dressed like a goddamn yuppie. Probably living in a big house, money sticking out of his pockets.

Why you in the 'Nam, man? Wilton had asked him once. Mom and Dad died, Jason had told him, and that put me and my brother on hard times. I couldn't afford college, so I enlisted. Huh, Wilton had replied, hard times is temporary to folks like you. The system always pulls you white folks back up. Not like my people. If we get ahead, it's only until we mess up. Then it's back to the 'hood, the mills, the ditch digging.

Wilton cleared his throat, breaking the silence. "How can I help you, man?"

Jason slumped into the couch back. "I don't know where to begin."

"Yeah, you do. Day one. The beginning."

Jason took a deep breath. He told Wilton about Emily's death, about his ensuing sense of loss. About Von and Pat and how they expressed their grief so differently. About Pat's suspicions, about his challenging the local police, his attempts to investigate the case on his own. He told Wilton about Pat provoking the town against Phil Agee and about Agee's ties to Alan Baxter. About Pat's growing feud with Davis Anderson, and the chief's increasingly heavy-handed manner. And, finally, about the way the family seemed to be coming apart at the seams.

Through all this, Wilton said nothing, nodding at certain points, shifting in his chair, and fingering his mug. Jason finished, head bowed.

Wilton drummed his fingers on the mug. After a long silence he said, "What d'you think you're gonna get from me? The police ain't gonna cooperate with me if they won't work with one of their own."

"Pat and I, we've talked about that. There are a few things the police know that have potential. We know what those things are, but we can't follow up on them. And Pat's in a hell of a position since his arrest. One more bad move and he'll go to jail, sure as the world." He sighed. "Anyway, we can't afford the legal bills."

Wilton sniffed. "Then how you planning to pay me?"

"I have some money saved up from my disability pay. When it runs out, well, that's it."

Wilton's expression softened. "You're talking about this like you're on the outside looking in, man. How d'you feel about it? I mean, what d'you think is going on?"

Jason looked down. "Everything's changed since Pat spent the weekend in jail. Before that, I think I was trying to defend my own turf, you know, protect my place in the family. But I think the family's gone now. I didn't really realize it before this moment, but I'm on my own."

"Then why're you here?"

Jason looked up. "You mean why me, instead of Pat?"

"I mean, if the family's shot to hell anyway, why do you bother?"

Jason's gaze drifted as he thought about that. "Pat's been the strong one since mom and dad died. He's taken care of me since I had my ass blown off in 'Nam. Now it's my turn."

"Sounds like you're going through some changes with this."

"It's like it was in 'Nam, I guess. When your back's against the wall, you can't sit back and watch."

"But you're not freaking out, like your brother."

"I guess we've swapped roles. Like I said, it's my turn."

Wilton rubbed his chin. "Okay, so tell me. Why did you guys come to me? Plenty of guys doing this work. What d'you think a black private investigator from Atlanta can do with all these crackers from, what is it, Hope?"

"It was my suggestion. I knew you were doing this work, and I thought –"

"Yeah, but why me?" Wilton persisted. "If I walk into your town and start asking questions, I'll attract more attention than Santa Claus."

Jason answered, his words like cautious footsteps. "I'm getting as paranoid about this as Pat. If there's really a cover up, then who's in on it? Or better, who's not?" He paused. "I know it's been a lot of years since we spent time together, you and I. A lot of things can happen over so much time. People change. I realize we don't really know one another anymore. But I need someone who can't be bought off. There're too many people involved in this who have clout. No doubt about it, you're a risk, because you're not local. But I think I know you well enough to know no one could buy you off."

"Everybody has a price," said Wilton. "How d'you know I won't let one of these crackers slip me some cash? Promise me some big business deal to let this case slide?"

"I don't. That's why I'm here. To make sure. To check you out. To see if I can trust you."

Wilton smiled. "That's the man I remember. No bullshit, just the truth, straight up. Now I'm beginning to trust *you.*"

"You'll take the job?" Jason leaned forward.

Wilton shrugged. "I might get hassled in that town by some of the locals. Someone might shove a gun in my ribs. Then I'd cut a trail."

"Maybe, but I don't think so."

"Why not?"

"Nothing I can put my finger on. It's just a gut feel. Besides, it's the way you were in-country. People don't change that much."

"Now you're thinking like a private eye," said Wilton. "If I help you out, I'm gonna need that in you. There'll be times when there ain't no facts to be had. You have to let your gut lead if you want to flush out the truth. If you can think like that, then we can communicate."

"Good," said Jason.

Wilton gestured expansively. "A black private eye poking around in a town full of whites. I ought to have my head examined."

Jason grinned. "Then let me turn the tables on you. Since you're black —"

Wilton looked at both hands, then laughed and slapped a knee. "Well, how 'bout that? I am black, ain't I?"

"– given that," said Jason, "why would you consider coming to Hope and helping me look for a needle in a haystack?"

"I didn't say I want to." The playful expression had returned.

"C'mon, man," Jason laughed, "give me one straight answer before I start paying your bills. Why? Why take this case?"

Wilton sighed. "Seriously."

"Seriously. It might be awkward in the extreme."

"Everything's awkward when you're a snoop." Wilton finished his coffee and set the cup on the floor. "But do you know why I do this? You know why I make my living as a private investigator?"

The telephone rang before Jason could formulate a reply. Wilton made no moves to answer it. When the answering machine clicked, he said, "Let's go grab some lunch. We got a lot of catching up to do."

CHAPTER 15

REMEMBERING A NIGHTMARE

They took the front steps and followed a narrow driveway to the back of the frame building. The drive sloped downward, revealing a lower second story. Wilton's baby blue Ford Taurus sat on a small paved lot in the rear, just below a large double door positioned between four long, flat windows on the building's back side.

"I live down here," said Wilton. He laughed, loudly. "It's the biggest damn bedroom you ever saw. Used to be a conference room for the lawyer who rented it before me. With Jonelle living here, we can afford the whole house. I can't ever get away from my work, anyway."

Jonelle Parks was Wilton's live-in; they'd been living together for almost five years. When Jason had called Monday night, it was her deep, sexy voice he'd first heard at the other end. She'd seemed pleasant. If that was her picture on the receptionist's desk upstairs, she was a strikingly beautiful woman, with rich, mocha skin and long, wavy hair.

"When do I get to meet her?" he asked.

Wilton glanced at him. "You want to meet my lady?" Smiling, he braked, pulled his cell from a pants pocket, and dialed. His face brightened. "Hey, baby. How about meeting me and Jay for lunch? At Morrison's. We'll be there in fifteen minutes. Mmm, you too."

"Tell me about her," Jason said as Wilton closed out his cell.

"You'll meet her. Then you can tell *me* about her." Laughter.

"C'mon," Jason said. "What sort of lady would give you the time of day?"

"She's a very cool lady, man. Strictly no hassle. Understands the private eye thing. Gives me space."

"You said she works in a bank?"

"A loan officer. Educated. Got a finance degree from Morehouse."

"Keeps your books, I bet."

"Keeps all of me. That includes the books."

They laughed.

Wilton glanced to Jason. "You got a lady, man?"

For a moment he didn't answer. "Don't think I could manage the real thing."

"Yeah?"

"It was the Orange. Remember the day I got sprayed?"

It had been one of the few lulls in the fighting in the five months Jason spent in Vietnam. He'd walked with an ambush team to another firebase one day. Rumor spread later that the area was used by CIA operatives experimenting with chemical warfare, defoliants, even airborne LSD. A small prop-driven plane had flown over them, spreading a thick cloud of dust, like an old fashioned crop duster on a Georgia farm. They'd developed blisters, and they'd kept them for weeks. One of the guys had even lost his sight from the spray.

Wilton nodded. "Yeah, I know. It was all over the place."

"Bad side effects. For me, it was depression. All kinds of chemical imbalances. Off and on impotence."

"Bad, man. Really bad. The war ain't never gonna be over for some of us."

"Hard to make peace with it, all right."

After being wounded, the chopper had carried Jason to a hospital in Saigon, but pain and drugs had clouded his memory of that time. A month later, he'd found himself in the hospital in Bethesda, Maryland. It was several months before he heard anything about Bravo Company. While checking out of the treatment facility at Bethesda, paperwork in hand that would lead to his discharge, he met a guy in a wheelchair. Both the man's legs and one arm were gone, and he was wearing a fatigue jacket bearing the Big Red One insignia. The guy told him of the beating Bravo had taken at the hands of the Cong. The Viet Cong forces, the man said, were still moving in a steady stream through Cambodia and into the heartland of South Vietnam. Bravo Company had taken severe casualties; though as in all forward areas, details were sketchy. What you heard was always unsubstantiated. It never seemed to end, the guy in the wheelchair had groused. You're lucky you got out early.

Morrison's parking lot was surprisingly empty for lunch hour, and Wilton parked near the door. The cafeteria line was short and they quickly found a booth.

"What about you, Will," Jason said between bites, "what happened to you after I left 'Nam?"

Wilton chewed. He clearly didn't relish talking about it. "Funny," he said at last, "but I was watching you and Leo get choppered out when this five-striper caught me and said I was up for R and R. He said I could catch the last dust-off out of there." Rest and recuperation. It was the breather they all lived for, between the long, intense months in the bush.

Wilton sliced into his roast beef. "The chopper was full, and it was the next day before I got to town." He shook his head as he chewed. "The very next day, man, the day after I left, the firebase was overrun. Almost everyone we knew bought it." He paused to chew another forked piece of beef. "I reported to HQ in Saigon when I heard about it, but everyone was busy making excuses for the offensive, and a lot of people like me got lost in the shuffle. I reported in every Monday, even started drawing my paychecks. But they never reassigned me."

He took in a gulp of water. "You believe that? Seven months sitting around Saigon. I just sat and watched the new guys come in from stateside and get dumped into the meat grinder." The meat grinder was their term for that particular sector where Bravo had positioned itself, right in the middle of the enemy's infiltration route. "And I watched 'em come back out, some of 'em in pieces." He shook his head. "I felt bad, really bad, y'know what I'm saying? But there was no way I was gonna get on a chopper and go back in there without orders."

"There you are," a female voice said, accompanied by the clack of high-heeled shoes. Her gray suit pants hinted at slim, well-proportioned legs.

Wilton stood. "This is my old 'Nam buddy, Jay Shane, the one I told you about."

Jason stood up, took her tray, unloaded it, and then he took her extended hand. Tall and lithe, she was even prettier than the picture.

"Wilton's told me a lot about you since you called," she said as they sat.

"Yeah," said Wilton, "I told her I was going to relieve some cracker of his money, and she wanted to know who." His sober expression weakened, and he winked at Jason.

Jonelle's lips tightened. "Jay, I hope you'll excuse this man's mouth."

Wilton's body jerked, and then he laughed, waggled the foot she'd spiked with a heel. "Damn, baby, that hurt."

Without replying, Jonelle bent to take her first bite.

"Women always want to be your mother," Wilton said to Jason. "Like they got to tame you."

"Mothers always leave their work unfinished," Jonelle replied.

"Raising Will," Jason said with a grin, "that'd be a tough job."

"It is," said Jonelle.

"Hope it pays well."

Jonelle rubbed her shoulder against Wilton's and smiled. "It's a labor of love." She looked to Jason. "What were you two talking about when I came in? You both seemed *so* serious."

Jason looked away. "We were catching up."

"I'd love to hear about it. Just take up where you left off. I'll ask questions, fill in the gaps."

Jason looked to Wilton. "You went stateside seven months later."

"Yeah, I was stationed in California for a few months, and the talk was about more advanced infantry training. You know, so we could do a second hitch in 'Nam. So I volunteered for Military Police school. Went through that in Virginia, and when I graduated, they sent me to Fort Polk, in Louisiana, for duty."

Jason finished his meal. An elderly woman in a cafeteria uniform approached, took his tray, and refilled his iced tea glass.

"That's where the private investigator thing started, I guess," said Jason.

"Not yet, not yet." Wilton set his fork on his plate and looked down as he chose his words. "You remember how we always thought the MPs were a big deal, tin gods with arm bands? Always so tough, whacking guys and tossing them out of bars?"

Jason nodded. "They controlled the streets, had to be tough guys."

"They were taking orders. They didn't do anything they weren't told to do."

"They didn't seem all that regimented," said Jason, "at least not over there. I remember in Saigon, all kinds of things happened spontaneously. They were just winging it, defending themselves, don't you think?"

"Wasn't that way, not exactly. There were policies, unofficial ones."

"For example."

"For example. At Fort Polk, a lot of the brothers went through there, some back from the 'Nam for more training. They stuck together, didn't take orders. The post commander told our CO to have us make regular rounds of the barracks, check for fights. We had a couple of NCOs with us, both staff sergeants, one white, one black. I always thought those two stirred up more fights than they prevented, and it was mostly brothers who got whacked.

"I found out later that our CO had a policy and the noncoms were carrying it out. The Old Man figured if you intimidate the brothers, the whites won't start anything. It would look like the

MPs were doing it for them. So we would go to check on fights and, whatever else came down, a couple of brothers would always get whacked. Control by intimidation." His mouth drew into a taut line.

"What it came down to is everybody shied away from the brothers who came back from 'Nam. They were good with weapons, didn't like the military, and didn't take nothing off nobody."

The elderly waitress returned and took Wilton's and Jonelle's trays. She poured Wilton another cup of coffee. Time had moved beyond the lunch hour surge, and the cafeteria had emptied.

"Your story," said Jason, "sounds as paranoid as my brother Pat's thing about the police in Hope."

"Listen to the man," said Wilton. "He probably knows more than you can imagine."

"It's hard to believe law enforcement people could be that cold with the people they're supposed to protect."

"Then you better let me finish my story." Wilton took a sip of his coffee and leaned back. "I eventually saw what was really going on, you understand? My discharge came up, and I got the usual pep talk about careers and the re-up bonus. I didn't care about the bonus, but it was a wad. I didn't have anything else back home except the mills, so what the hell, I'll re-up. Maybe I can be a positive force in all this, you know? So I signed up for a four-year hitch and stayed with the MPs. "It was boring duty for the most part, but I was in a position to see things most GI's never see."

"Different places, different posts?"

"No, man, it was the nature of the duty."

"Secret stuff?"

Wilton smiled grimly. "Yeah, it was secret all right. We looked after drunk officers. Pulled them out of flophouses. One general was smuggling dope back from 'Nam. We stood guard."

"You're kidding."

"No, man. It's the truth."

"I can't see you doing all that. I mean, it just doesn't fit."

Wilton sighed. "You make it fit. You learn to take orders. That way, you ain't really doing it yourself. It ain't real." He'd been holding his coffee cup, fingers dancing on its surface. He set it down with precise movements, as if it were dangerous. He looked up, his hands shaking.

"A few years later, it got very, very real. There was this master sergeant in our unit who was banging some colonel's wife. The colonel found out soon enough, and he paid a visit to our CO. By then, I was almost over my third hitch. I was a staff sergeant, up for another stripe. Well, the Old Man called me in, told me what was going on. Asked what I thought should happen to the master sergeant." Wilton sighed.

"I see where this is headed," said Jason.

Wilton looked to Jonelle. "Yeah, but I want to finish it." He took a last sip from his coffee. "He asked me what I thought should happen, so I said there wasn't much that could be done, seeing as how the colonel's wife had started it. He agreed, but he said someone should teach the master sergeant a lesson. I didn't volunteer, so he assigned me to night duty.

"Well, the very next night, a master sergeant showed up on my shift, and he paired with me for patrol duty. He drove us into town to an apartment complex, and we waited. About midnight, the sergeant who was humping the colonel's wife drove up. My partner ordered me out of the car, and we stopped the guy, cuffed him and brought him over to our car."

"Didn't he put up a fight?" Jason asked.

"He was drunk. He couldn't have fought with his mama and won. Then my partner gave me his stick and told me to work out on him. I wouldn't do it, so he turned the guy around, grabbed the stick and whacked him. Whacked him bad. Kept whacking him."

Wilton leaned forward, and Jonelle began to stroke his neck. "You never told me."

"Never told anybody, baby." Wilton looked to Jason. "That master sergeant, he didn't come to work for a couple of days, and then they court-martialled him for going AWOL. He lost a stripe. Lucky for me he didn't say nothing. It was set up to hang the beating on me if he made a story out of it."

"How would they have implicated you?"

"The other master sergeant would say we were making sure the guy got home safe, then he'd say I got abusive. You know, nigger MP goes wild with stick in hand, beats up on a superior NCO."

"Sounds like they put you in an awkward position," said Jason, "but how could you have possibly known what would happen if that master sergeant tried to cause trouble?"

"I heard part of it from other noncoms, the sergeant corps grapevine. The rest I read between the lines. That was when I decided to get out. Halfway to retirement, and I got out."

"And then you came here?"

"I went home to Charlotte for about six months, stayed with Mama. Thought about things, made the rounds of the mills, looked for work. Applied for a job on the police force. They offered me a slot, but I decided to turn it down. So I moved here, took a construction job while I got licensed as a private investigator." He paused. "I told you I took up this work for a reason."

"You did."

"I'm not a crusader, can't afford to be. But I can help people in this job. I could have helped that master sergeant. I could have helped someone like me."

"That can be dangerous," said Jason.

"You have to pick your fights. I'm no walking suicide case."

"He won't take the easy money," said Jonelle. "Always has to have a cause."

Wilton turned. "I chase plenty of cheating husbands and wives, baby. You know that. I do a case or two a year for local police forces, even did one for the FBI. Military connections got me that one. It pays the bills, you know? But if someone comes in with a discrimination hassle, or a corrupt landlord deal or a businessman who won't pay his help, I give it priority."

"Even if it doesn't pay," said Jonelle.

Wilton shrugged. "I always get paid. Maybe not on time, but I always get paid."

"He's got accounts outstanding that are three years old," Jonelle said. "I get so scared. Sometimes we get really low on money. We wouldn't even be able to afford a doctor if we needed one."

"I don't take chances, so I don't need doctors. But the money's coming, baby." He grinned. "I'll get rich off of Jay."

"If I pay my bills," said Jason.

"You'll pay. I can run faster than you."

Jonelle picked up her shoulder bag. "I need to get back to work."

"Want me to walk you out?" Wilton asked.

Jonelle smiled. "If you have to ask, then no."

Wilton's grin grew broader. "I'll make it up to you, baby. Tonight."

She kissed him and turned to Jason. "Jay, you seem good for my man here. Don't let him get into trouble." She left.

"What else do I need to tell you about my problem?" Jason asked.

"Nothing," Wilton replied. "Let me think. I'll call you tomorrow."

Jason looked down. "We need to discuss fees –"

"Later," said Wilton.

"But I want –"

"Hey, man," said Wilton, "don't worry. I'll take your money. We'll work it out."

"But I don't want to have any misunderstandings."

"Then be cool about it," Wilton said. "Jonelle would call you a cause. This business your family is going through is why I do what I do. I've heard enough already to know your family is getting muscled. Let me think about it. We'll find out what's happening. I'll call you tomorrow."

CHAPTER 16

THE CHANGING FACE OF POLITICS

It was almost nine a.m. when Jason rose. As he sat on the edge of his bed, blinking himself into consciousness, he could hear Von's movements as she prepared for work. He tugged on his bathrobe and made his way to the kitchen. The newspaper lay strewn across the kitchen table from Pat's reading. He put the kettle on, made a cup of tea, and scanned the front section.

A picture of Alan Baxter shaking hands with the Speaker of the Georgia House of Representatives had been set just below the headlines. A power shift was afoot in Georgia's legislature, and Alan Baxter now played a key role in the political maneuverings. An alliance forged more than two years earlier between the governor, the speaker, and the lieutenant governor had held through the last election, but was now dissolving. The Republican Party had been an on-again-off-again factor in Georgia politics over the past couple of decades – until recently. The Dixiecrats of thirty years ago now counted themselves as Republicans. Many conservative businesspersons from the northern states had moved into Atlanta and other Georgia cities; their numbers were largely Republican as well, and this shift in population and political preference had manifested in the Georgia Legislature. The Democrats feuded within their own party, along lines drawn by special interest groups and lobbyists. Meanwhile, the Republican suburbs were moving their candidates into the House and Senate.

The governor, recognizing the changing direction of political sentiment in Georgia, had been slowly distancing himself from traditional Democratic causes, and now sounded remarkably like a Republican. Ordinarily, a political shift of this nature by a governor would have been deadly for his party. But through astute political maneuvering, the Democratic power troika was attempting to preempt Republican issues while trying to hold onto the traditional Democratic voting base.

And Alan Baxter was gaining recognition as an adept navigator of these political waters. A brilliant student of political science at the University of Georgia prior to obtaining his law degree there, he had used his old-family political connections well. With the help of a former patriarch of the state Democratic Party, he'd been elected to the House at age twenty-five. He'd quickly found his footing within the halls of power, and at twenty-nine was elected to the State Senate – with the blessing of the governor.

Baxter had become a political theorist who felt equally comfortable with farmers, urban liberals, ethnics, and the educated elite. He'd written a book of folk stories compiled from conversations with voters around the state. He'd taught political science in a private women's college in Gainesville. And he was widely known as a proponent of computer technology in education. His membership in the National Rifle Association was controversial, as was his occasional crossing of party lines on high profile votes. But the common thread through his career was decidedly Democratic, always nipping at the heels of Republicans and errant Democrats. Now he was stepping forth into party leadership. The editorial Jason had before him described Baxter as a synthesizing force for the state Democratic Party. Alan Baxter, it said, can be the glue holding the faithful together through the election. He can be the one to define the governor's increasingly Republican posture as the Democratic New Wave. If Alan Baxter can stay the course, the Party will owe him a huge debt of gratitude, and he will undoubtedly be the leading gubernatorial candidate two years hence.

Jason lay the paper down and was about to get up when Von brushed past his chair. He filled with the scent of her, the mixture of soap, bath oils, and perfume. Her blonde hair was growing longer, adding an extra inch or two to its hang over the collar of her suit coat, and that added to her winsomeness.

"Don't get up," she said, "I'll make you another cup." She bent and kissed him lightly on the neck. "Thank you, Jason."

His face suddenly warmed. "What for?" he managed.

"For seeing your friend Wilton. For helping us find a way out of this. And you did what I couldn't do. You diverted Pat's attention back to normal things."

They'd had a family meeting the previous night, after work, and Jason had relived his meeting with Wilton Byrd. Pat had demanded to know every word of their conversation, but he'd said nothing as Jason related Wilton's own suspicions about Anderson's handling of the case. Then Pat had begun to squirm and started to leave the room.

"Wilton said he'd call soon," Jason had finished, and they'd all gone to bed, seemingly content.

"I'm off to work," Von said. She filled her travel mug. "Call me at work after you and Wilton have talked again." She turned and smiled.

Jason returned the smile. He watched her leave by the back door.

He lay aside the special pre-election section he'd been reading and scanned the local news section. The items featured there were almost exclusively concerned with the Atlanta metro area. Occasionally there would be an article concerning the outlying areas, like Hope, but that was rare.

It's a shame, he thought, that there weren't more local newspapers. A daily paper had been published several years earlier in Gwinnett County, the largest county between Atlanta and Hope. But the Atlanta paper had run them out of business by lowering their daily price in that area.

There had been two papers in Atlanta before Jason was sent to Vietnam, but they'd merged into virtually identical papers, and that now reminded him of a radio report he'd heard recently. A media study had undertaken to evaluate freedom of the press in each country of the world, and the study had ranked the United States twentieth. The reason, the report had stated, was that common ownership of so many elements of the media, as had happened with Atlanta's newspapers, typically stymied substantive political and social dialogue. In the countries of Western Europe, for instance, the press stimulated a wider variety of viewpoints on critical issues, hence theirs were freer presses.

How ironic, he thought. We send troops at the drop of a hat to defend democratic initiatives in other countries. Maybe we should pay more attention to the way our own version of representative democracy is evolving.

The phone rang: Wilton.

"Well, I thought about it," Wilton said in his deep basso. "So now I need to know all the hard facts you have on hand."

Jason once more told him everything he could think of. The large car that had killed Emily, probably a Caprice, light colored. Donna Miller's sketchy testimony. Jackson's body shop and the supposed date of October second for admission of Phil Agee's Caprice for repairs. And about the phone number Pat had found in Jackson's shop, which matched the one on the Alan Baxter phone memo in the police file. "Not much, is it?"

"It's plenty," said Wilton. "You'd be surprised how little I get to go on sometimes." A pause. "Yeah, this is plenty. I can't blame your brother for getting mad at the police, you know? They could've run a long way on this." Another pause. "Has Agee given a statement yet?"

"They can't find him. He's been in and out of town, but he's not staying at home. Pat thinks he may be helping Baxter with his reelection campaign. He could be anywhere in the state."

Wilton issued a drawn-out expletive. "Man, do you realize how bad this case stinks?"

"I'm beginning to. But Pat's getting edgy again. I suspect he wants to do some more snooping himself."

"Is he gonna keep it together?"

"It's hard to tell with Pat. He's so unpredictable these days."

"Okay, we need to set some priorities. Decide where to dig first."

"Let's look into that phone number," said Jason. "Pat really wants to pursue that, and I need something to calm him down."

"How about this Donna Miller? How do I reach her?"

"She lives in Memphis. I guess the best way is to talk first to her sister, Loretta, here in Hope."

A long silence from Wilton. "If none of this gets us anywhere, I'll have to visit your police force, and maybe Jackson's, but I don't want anyone to know I exist yet. Need to know what I'm dealing with first."

"What are you going to do with the phone number Pat found?"

"Call it. But not before I find out as much as I can about who and what's at the other end." Another pause, and then Wilton laughed. "Hey, man, you haven't even given me that phone number yet."

Jason clambered up the stairs, phone in hand, and found the pocket-sized notebook he'd bought the day before to keep track of data on the case. He read out the seven-digit number.

"What's the area code?" asked Wilton.

"Isn't any. It came off the police phone memo like that."

"And you're long distance from Atlanta."

"And so is Gainesville. My bet is it's between here and there. It would be a local call from both places, so it's probably on the border between the two."

Wilton laughed again. "Hey, man, you're catching on."

"I want to be in on it when you call the number," said Jason.

"Not my usual M.O., but okay. You want to come to my office? I should have my snooping done in an hour or so."

"I can be there in an hour."

"Solid. See you then."

Jason heard the phone click at the other end, and then a soft whir. He frowned and hung up. But he was excited; it felt good to be involved in something on his own again. One of these days, he thought, one of these days... He began humming a song he'd been hearing on the radio, and even managed a few slow, shuffling dance steps.

The drive to Decatur went quickly, and exactly one hour later, he stood at Wilton's door. He rang the bell and, receiving no answer, he turned the knob and walked in. As he pushed the door shut he heard the sound of footsteps at the building's rear.

"I was downstairs." Wilton held up a brown folder bulging with a thick computer printout. "Don't ask me where I got it."

He threw the folder onto the coffee table in front of the couch. "Let's check this thing out." They sat. Wilton turned pages as Jason looked over his shoulder. The computer printout consisted of row upon row of telephone numbers, listed in ascending order, by exchange, and accompanied by alphanumeric codes. Wilton pulled the scrap of paper from his pocket, on which he'd written the telephone number: 555-2246.

Wilton quickly flipped through the pages and found the exchange matching the number. He scanned the ascending numbers, flipping pages until the phone number appeared. Beside the number, an accompanying code in capital letters: RSNN DLTH.

"What does that mean?" Jason asked.

"It's the phone company's customer code for this number. It doesn't mean much, just the phone company's way of cross-indexing the numbers. The first part represents a street or, if the number is commercial, it's a code for the business. The second group of letters is the city location for the number."

"Duluth, then," said Jason.

"Right," said a grinning Wilton. He eyed Jason. "How about the first grouping?"

"It must be a business."

"Right again, Sherlock."

"Do you know?"

"I'm guessing," said Wilton, "let's check it out." He picked up the Yellow Pages book and found the listing he was looking for. Then he tapped it and turned the book to Jason.

Jason followed his finger to a boxed ad on the page. "Residence Inn," he read. The telephone number was 555-2000. "Room number 246?"

"Right you are, my man."

"Do you suppose this is as obvious as it seems?"

"The truth is always plain as day."

"Then we've found out where Phil Agee's been hiding."

"I'd bet on it." Wilton's grin broadened. "See how easy this private eye stuff is?"

Jason edged forward. "All right, let's call."

"I better do it," said Wilton. "Pick up the phone on the desk by the door."

Seconds later, a ringing at the other end. A man answered.

"I'm trying to get in touch with a Philip Agee," said Wilton. "Would that be you?"

"Who is this?" the voice asked.

"Is this Mr. Agee?"

"I don't know you." The line went dead.

"Damn," said Wilton.

"That was Phil Agee," said Jason. The voice was more somber than he'd remembered, but the tone and lilt of his words was easily recognizable.

"We scared him," said Wilton. "He might take off on us. Maybe that call wasn't such a bright idea."

"He won't know who called."

"He'll damn sure know who didn't call." Wilton redialed the number. Busy. "He's on the phone, trying to find out what's going on. We better get over there before we lose him."

They hurried out. Fifteen minutes later, they were speeding north on I-85. They took the Steve Reynolds exit, the motel to their right.

"There it is," Jason said. He pointed toward a white Caprice parked just ahead. They drove slowly past. The tag indicated Barrow County as its home.

"Number 246," said Jason, pointing to a room number listing in front of the Caprice. Wilton drove past and backed into a parking place on the opposite side of the drive, affording them both a good view of the car and the entranceway leading to the room.

"What do we do now?" Jason asked.

"We wait." Wilton replaced his mirror sunshades with a less conspicuous pair from the glove compartment. Picking up a tiny tape recorder, he began recording the time, the motel room number, the tag number. He recorded a detailed description of the building and of the other cars parked nearby.

An hour passed. Jason shifted restlessly. At periodic intervals, Wilton spoke into the recorder, giving the time and movements of tenants and workers and vehicles.

Another hour. The sun had shifted sharply in the late afternoon sky, casting long shadows across the parking area. A middle-aged woman in a white smock pulled a long cart around the corner and into view. She stopped at the entranceway in front of the Caprice. Wilton and Jason watched as she knocked on a door, once, twice, then a third time. Receiving no response, she pulled a key from her belt and opened the door. Moments later she returned, carrying a load of towels and sheets.

"Damn," said Wilton.

"He's not there."

"We didn't get here fast enough." Wilton tapped his fingers on the steering wheel, looked at his watch. "You hungry?"

"Starving."

"Let's go get a burger. We can be back in fifteen minutes." Wilton spoke a few more words into his tape recorder and pulled away.

They returned a half hour later. As Wilton made the turn into the driveway leading to Agee's room, Jason grabbed his arm.

Wilton braked. "What?"

"Pull over, out of sight."

Wilton backed the Taurus smartly into a vacant space.

Jason pointed to the Caprice. Another car, a beige Cadillac, blocked their view of the motel room. A man sat behind the wheel, his face exposed to their view. Another man stood leaning against the car's opposite side. "The guy standing up, that's Phil Agee," Jason whispered. "And the guy in the car is Baxter."

Wilton spoke briefly into his tape recorder. Then Baxter started his engine and Phil Agee entered the building. Wilton and Jason slid out of view as the Caddy drove past. Wilton recorded the car's make, the tag number, and a description of the driver.

Jason let out a long breath.

"You okay?" Wilton asked, chuckling.

"Guess I'm a little disappointed. I didn't want the senator involved in this."

"You get used to people disappointing you after a while," said Wilton. "It comes with the job."

Jason tried to smile but couldn't. He began breathing deeply; finally his anxiety began to ebb. He sighed. "I hope he didn't see us."

He didn't," said Wilton. "And remember this. They're in the open and we're the invisible ones. That's our advantage for now."

# # #

The senator's cell phone rang. "Hello, Phil."

A weak, embarrassed laugh at the other end. "Do I call you that often, Alan?"

"Constantly. What do you want?"

Agee cleared his throat. "I need something to take my mind off all this."

"No booze, Phil, or I'm through with you."

"Can you give me something to do, Alan? You know, keep my mind occupied? You said to keep my mind off that phone call, and I want to get sober, Alan, just like you said."

The senator stopped for a red light, reached to the back seat for his briefcase. "All right, Phil. I have some people I was going to call. They're old supporters, but they need to be stroked." He read off the names.

"I know them, Alan, every one of them."

"That's why I gave them to you, they'll remember you. Call them and chat it up, will you?"

"I'll do it right now, Alan. Thanks."

CHAPTER 17

EXPOSED

They sat in silence. Senator Alan Baxter was gone and Phil Agee had disappeared into his suite. The sun was edging past the terrain before them, the sky at the horizon a slow explosion of color. Somewhere nearby, a dog barked, its yelps disappearing in the hum of traffic from the Interstate. Wilton sat upright and grabbed his recorder. He spoke into it. His words came in short spasmodic strings, and then they slowed and ceased. A moment of silence passed, and he placed the recorder carefully in a recess by the transmission console.

Jason cleared his throat. "Well, partner, what do we have so far?"

"Nothing new," Wilton replied, looking straight ahead.

"But we saw Alan Baxter here with Agee."

"That's not criminal activity. No meat."

"We know Agee's registered here," said Jason. "That's hard evidence. He can't deny that. It'll look like flight from prosecution."

"If he's not registered in his own name, you might make that case. But he can still plead ignorance about Emily and say he was here doing business for Baxter's reelection campaign."

"So," Jason said, an irritable quaver to his voice, "are we wasting our time? You said the truth was as plain as day."

"It is for us, but we still have to prove it."

A sigh. "All right, what do we do next?"

"We wait. We keep looking and listening."

"Specifically."

Wilton rubbed his chin. He slid down in his seat as he thought, his knees to the dash. "We have to give 'em both some rope. Take the pressure off. Let 'em have a reason to forget the call."

"That's nothing. We need something solid."

Wilton's head snapped around. Anger flickered in his eyes. "Look, man, if we knew the answers to this we could go after them. We got a little piece of the picture today, that's all. We just have to keep looking."

"We may never have a case at this rate."

"That's right. We may be chasing shadows as far as the law's concerned. And remember, we're on the trail of a powerful state senator. He has friends. He has ways to worm his way out of things like this. You can damn well believe he knows how to keep from being embarrassed by a two-bit private eye."

"So we're just going to sit here all night?"

"He's not going anywhere," Wilton said. "We can come back tomorrow, or in a couple of days." He turned to Jason. "You wanna go to the house?"

"I don't know," said Jason. "I'm tired."

Wilton nodded. "I know that's right. Let's go get some sleep."

"We'll come back tomorrow?"

"Maybe. Let's sleep on it. Then we'll figure out what comes next."

Wilton cranked the car and crept from the motel complex. He made the turn southbound onto the Interstate and entered the stream of cars moving toward Atlanta. In the opposite direction, the automobile headlights formed a constant, moving wall of light.

This was rush hour, the city's daily evacuation in progress. Perhaps a million automobiles were now leaving the dense, downtown business district of Atlanta. Above, helicopters tracked the traffic, reporting congested areas and suggesting alternatives to radio and TV stations.

Jason looked to the darkened sky as one of the choppers passed. He shuddered. Wilton had turned the radio to a local jazz station, and Jason turned it up.

Jason closed his eyes. Medevac choppers returned, the ones he'd seen in 'Nam, and the ones airlifting soldiers in and out of the combat LZs, the landing zones. Then he heard small arms fire, saw tracers in the night sky, against the backdrop of silhouetted rubber trees. He grunted, loudly. His eyes opened wide and he was once again in Wilton's Taurus, on an Atlanta freeway, breathing heavily and clutching the front edge of his seat.

Wilton glanced. They were passing the perimeter beltway intersection now. He reached over and shook Jason's shoulder. "You okay, man?"

"I'm okay," he said, panting. "Just. An overactive imagination. That's all." He closed his eyes and began to breathe deeply.

Several minutes passed. Ahead loomed the Clairemont Road exit. They negotiated the street in silence. In what seemed only moments, Wilton pulled into his driveway.

As the drive dropped and widened, they saw Jonelle's black Miata parked to one side. Light streamed from the series of windows along the backside of the building. Wilton parked his car alongside hers and killed the engine. Jason reached for the door handle. The lock on the door panel snapped downward.

"You ain't going nowhere until you tell me what's going on with you," said Wilton.

"It's nothing. C'mon, let me out. I need some air."

"There was something serious going on with you back there." Wilton paused to evaluate his friend. "You looked like you seen a ghost, man."

Jason buried his head in his hands. "It was the 'Nam thing. I keep living it, over and over."

Wilton sighed deeply and slowly nodded. "Sometimes I wake up, and I'll be yelling, covered with sweat. If it wasn't for Jonelle –"

"I'm okay, really. It's a chemical imbalance. When I get stressed it happens. I don't know why. It takes me back there, I relive 'Nam things, other things."

"What other things?"

"Other times. When bad things happened. Mom and Dad dying. Stuff like that. It's like my body won't let my mind forget."

Wilton nodded. "It's like a demon snuck in and holed up there."

"Seeing Agee and the senator, it scared me. Then I heard the traffic copter."

Wilton eyed him carefully. "You know, I think you better let me handle this investigation by myself. I don't want you coming apart."

"I can handle it."

Wilton shook his head. "Today was easy. It can get hairy –"

"It's okay," persisted Jason. "I can deal with it." He forced a smile. "C'mon, partner, it's good for me. Lets me get all that bad stuff out of my system."

Wilton studied him for a moment. "Damn," he said, drawing the word out, "you're a real badass, you know that? I mean, look at you. You're skin and bones, part of your body blown away. You've got war chemicals in you, your family's coming apart, and you see stuff when you get stressed. Now you're looking at me like a kid wanting to go to the movies. Most people, if they'd been through what you have, they'd be all doped up in a mental hospital."

Jason smiled. "I've had to toughen up, I guess."

Wilton shook his head and laughed. "Tougher than an old boot. You're tougher than you realize, man."

"So what do we do tomorrow?"

Wilton turned away and began drumming his fingers on the steering wheel. "Give me a call in the morning. I have some other stuff to chase down first thing. Some lady wants me to check on her husband. He's writing bad checks. Gambling, or some such thing. Call about eleven."

# # #

The next morning at nine a.m., Jason was sitting up in bed with bits of paper spread out before him. He'd assigned to each scrap of paper a topic of evidence or a potential obstacle to finding Emily's killer. One piece was devoted to the Caprice. Jackson's garage on another. On that one, in parentheses, he placed the phone number for Phil Agee's room at the Residence Inn. He noted the repairs to the Caprice. "Who brought it in?" he wrote. He noted Donna Miller's name on another scrap of paper. Beside the name he wrote "eyewitness." In brief notes, he described what she'd seen: The accident. A man driving. Vague description of the car. He devoted another scrap of paper to the telephone number itself. "Police file – Chief Anderson" scribbled underneath the number. Another carried Phil Agee's name. "FOUND," a note announced in block letters. One carried Senator Baxter's name. "Connection?" he'd written. Pat was the subject of another. A note asked simply, "Crazy?" He picked up another scrap of paper. His face twisted into a scowl. On that one he wrote Emily's name. "Why?" he added below.

He rested his chin on his hands. The fingers of one hand drummed absently on his cheek. He rearranged the pieces of paper, studied each one, as he tried to make sense of what he knew.

Then he remembered something. He snatched the piece of paper bearing Phil Agee's name and wrote on it: "DUI". Then he wrote, "Athens." He'd remembered a previous Agee DUI episode being mentioned in the newspaper, because Agee had been reported missing. A police search had ensued. The car, which Agee had owned before the Caprice, had been found in a ditch on 316. He was probably returning from Athens and a drinking session. A search party had found him soon thereafter, passed out in the woods, a half-mile away.

The article contained the name of an Athens bar from the police report. That fact had been memorable because the local chapter of MADD, Mothers Against Drunk Driving, had fingered the club as a consistent source of drunk drivers. They'd tracked the police reports and traced at least a dozen DUIs to the club, incidents that had killed or injured children. The event had caused quite a flap in the hard-drinking college town.

What was the name of the place? Jason closed his eyes as he tried to remember. Nothing came. He reached for the local telephone directory on his bedside table, the directory covering several local communities, including Athens. He turned to the Yellow Pages section. On the page listing nightclubs, he scanned names. He was almost at the end of the list when he saw it: The Woof. Yep, that was the place, all right. He wrote the name on the piece of paper assigned to Phil Agee.

Then he showered and dressed for the day and made his way downstairs. Just as he sat before a plate of grits, toast, and leftover dinner ham, the telephone rang.

"You ready for another stakeout?" Wilton asked.

"Born ready," said Jason.

Wilton snickered. "Okay, mister born ready, let's meet at Gwinnett Place Mall, out front. My other job for the day fell through. The lady's husband wrote her a letter, saying he was running off with some young thing. She didn't need me to tell her where the money was going, so I'm available. I can leave right now. How about you?"

"I'm eating breakfast," said Jason. "I can leave in about fifteen minutes."

"Hey, by the way," said Wilton, "let's do the stakeout in your car today. There's a chance we'll be conspicuous if we show up in mine two days in a row."

Jason agreed. "And I have some more backup information on Agee for you."

"Yeah?"

"A couple of years ago, he was written up in a DUI article. He ran his car off the road on 316, and slept it off in the woods. He was married then, and his wife had called in a missing persons report. He'd been drinking at a bar in Athens that night, and they mentioned the name of the place. It's called The Woof, off Broad Street, just before downtown." He paused; Wilton said nothing. "I just thought it might be the place where he was drinking the night he hit Emily. That is, if he was the one. We might confirm it, or maybe we –"

"Yeah, I got it," Wilton said. "Could be a lead. I'll see you at the mall in, what, an hour?"

"An hour."

He was about to hang up when he heard a slight whir, then a fainter, softer sound. He hung up and lifted the receiver again. The dial tone seemed normal. He finished his breakfast.

Jason waited in his car at the mall while Wilton ordered a chow mien take-out lunch. Then they drove the five miles to the Residence Inn exit and into the motel complex.

"Pull in close to the outlet drive," said Wilton. "On the opposite side from yesterday."

Jason backed his Toyota in. The Caprice sat in the same spot. Wilton opened his lunch and began to eat.

"I wonder if I should go up there and knock on the door," said Jason.

"Are you crazy, man? You want to blow the whole case right here?"

Jason sighed. "I just want to do something productive."

"We *are* doing something productive. Patience, my man." Wilton finished his meal, placed the containers back in the paper bag and dropped them on the floorboard behind his seat. He licked his lips. "I should've bought something to drink. You remember seeing a drink machine back there anywhere?"

"There was a laundry, just past the first building as we came in. There might be a machine in there."

Wilton looked around to see if anyone was around. Seeing no one, he climbed out and walked nonchalantly around the corner toward the laundry.

Jason slid his car seat back and straightened his long legs. He slipped down in his seat until he could just see Agee's apartment and the Caprice above the dash. Wilton had placed his tape recorder on the dash, and Jason picked it up, fingering each of its tiny buttons as he inspected it. He put the recorder down and pulled the notebook from his shirt pocket. He'd made a number of notes from his earlier information sorting, and he began to go over them.

A moment later, a car engine started. He looked up. Agee had edged the Caprice out of the parking slot.

Jason glanced in the direction Wilton had taken. He wasn't in sight. Jason threw the door of the Toyota open and, clutching his long legs one at a time, pulled himself out of the car. Agee still wasn't looking in his direction. The Caprice was less than fifty feet away. Jason limped hurriedly toward the car. Agee looked up, Jason nearly in front of the Caprice. He could only see Agee's thick, coarse, salt and pepper hair and his jowly face, beads of sweat on his forehead.

Agee slammed the brakes and the car nosed to a stop. Jason placed his hands on the hood of the car and glared. Agee seemed stunned, but the expression quickly turned to anger. Jason walked his hands across the hood of the Caprice as he limped toward the driver's door. Agee sat agape as Jason jerked the car door open.

Agee grabbed the door handle and tried to pull it shut. "Leave me alone!" he shouted. Jason could smell booze on him. "I didn't kill your daughter! Go away!" He pressed the accelerator, and the car leaped forward, jerking Jason along with it. He stumbled and fell. Agee slammed the door, gunned the engine and, tires screeching, made the corner, almost hitting Wilton.

Wilton tossed his drink and dove for a nearby grass plot. By the time Jason had hobbled to his side, the Caprice was gone.

"What the hell was that all about?" Wilton asked.

"I screwed up," Jason said as he helped Wilton up. "I-I don't know what got into me. I saw him get into his car, and I, well, I felt like I had to do something. So I got out and went for him. Don't ask me why. I just did." He turned from Wilton's glare.

"Get in the car," said Wilton, "and be cool about it." They climbed in. "Tell me about it again, and give me the details."

Jason recounted the scant seconds of the encounter: "– and the last thing he said was, 'I didn't kill your daughter.'"

"You said he'd been drinking?"

"I could smell it, yeah."

Wilton leaned back and closed his eyes. He laughed.

"What?"

"Man, if you ain't lucky. He was probably on a drunk, but he had it together enough to know you were a familiar face. He must not've recognized you. He must've thought you were Pat."

"Great," said Jason. "Now Pat will go to jail, sure as hell."

Wilton laughed again. "No, he won't. Agee can't risk taking it to the police. He won't say a word."

Jason considered that. "So our cover isn't blown after all?"

"Like I said, you're golden, man. But you better tell Pat what's going on, just in case they make some sort of move on him."

"Wouldn't their doing that be too obvious?"

"Well, truth is I really don't know what they'd do," said Wilton. "They might figure Pat's working alone and try to off him. We won't know until they play their hand. But I'll say this much. This thing will blow soon. Very soon."

CHAPTER 18

THE SENATOR

Senator Alan Baxter was concluding an interview with a reporter from the *Washington Post*. He sat in a plush easy chair amid his sitting room's other elegant furnishings within his Marquis Hotel campaign suite. He'd dressed casually, in gray slacks, a white sweater over a red and white striped shirt and, of course, his favorite piece of apparel, his imported leather shoes. There was a large picture window behind him, the Atlanta skyline framing his fair-skinned face and fine blond hair. The reporter sat opposite him, a tape recorder to her right on a small, ornately carved wooden table. In her lap lay a notebook. She picked up a ballpoint pen, made a few quick notations, looked up, and smiled.

"Before we close, do you have anything special you'd like to direct to our readers, Senator?" She turned the recorder slightly.

"Only one thing, Beth. The Democratic party in going to be at the forefront of a radical change in politics here in Georgia." He leaned forward. "The citizens of Georgia will now have a stronger voice and a more responsive government. No longer will they have to choose between the politics of yesterday and the promises of tomorrow. On November the seventh, Georgia's voters will cast ballots that will bring them and their government together in a way only dreamed about since the days of Jefferson."

The reporter made some hasty notes and filled the rest of her page with an elegant squiggle to indicate the interview's conclusion. She thanked him and said, "Your proposals are greatly needed in government, Senator Baxter."

"They're not my proposals, Beth," the senator replied as he sank back into the chair cushions and crossed his legs. "Believe me, this is the work of Governor Raines." He smiled. "I'm just trying to spread the word."

"There've been many attempts at reinventing government," said Beth, "but none has been proposed to this depth at the state level." She folded her notebook and dropped it into her briefcase. "It's going to be challenging, even politically risky."

"Not as risky as continuing to ignore the needs of the people of the State of Georgia."

Beth rose and straightened her suit. Alan Baxter led her toward the closed door.

"I expect to be back to cover your gubernatorial campaign year after next." She smiled and extended a hand.

Baxter took it. "I hope you'll come back anyway," he said stroking her hand. He noted the approving blush on her cheeks. He opened the door, allowing just enough room for her to pass by. He was a short, trimly built man, and he rose to the balls of his feet to catch a last scent of her hair. An aide, seeing her depart the room, hurried to her side to escort her from the hotel.

Another aide appeared at the senator's side. The results of a poll his campaign staff had commissioned were in, and the aide summarized it briefly. There was no significant movement for his

Republican opponent. The voter percentages on both sides of the ledger were considered stable through election day, and his lead was ample. Sixty to sixty-five percent had been predicted for Baxter, and twenty to twenty-five percent for his Republican opponent, an Athens lawyer. The rest were as yet undecided. The senator asked the aide a few brief questions of clarification and dismissed him with a pat on the back.

A middle-aged woman waved from behind a folding table laden with telephones, computer printouts and note pads. "Senator, could I please have a word?" She and several other campaign workers were busily answering a jangle of calls. "Sir, you've had a number of phone calls from a Mister Agee. He's on now. He won't leave a number, and he insists on being left on hold until he can talk to you."

The senator frowned. "What line is he on?"

She looked down at the flashing bank of lights. "Line three."

"I'll take it in the other room." He shut the door to the sitting room and picked up the receiver.

"Alan, this is Phil." The usual lilt in his voice was gone, betraying a sense of urgency. His words were soft and slurred.

The senator sighed. "Yes, Phil. Where are you?"

"A pay phone on Roswell Road. Alan, the kid's father showed up. He –"

"Call me back on my private line. This line's not clear. You know the number." He hung up and began rubbing his temples. His cell phone rang, and he answered.

"It was the kid's dad, Alan. You know, Emily Shane, the one –"

"Whoa, Phil. I don't have the foggiest idea what you're telling me. Start at the beginning."

"This afternoon I went out to, I mean, get a few things."

"You went out to get a bottle."

"Some things," Agee repeated. "I got in my car, backed out, and all of a sudden, there was this guy in front of my car looking at me. It was the kid's dad, Alan."

"Was he alone?"

"I don't know. He grabbed the door handle and opened the door. I drove off and left him standing there. Almost ran over some black guy on the way out."

The senator's jaw tensed. "Were they together?"

"Who?"

"The kid's dad and the black."

"Not that I could tell."

"All right," the senator replied. "Go back to the beginning and tell me every detail of what happened." Agee retold his story, interrupted by the senator's constant press for more.

"You say he was limping?"

"Yeah, maybe, I don't know. He couldn't stand up very well. He fell down when I drove off."

"And the black fellow. From what direction was he coming?"

"From the front entrance to the complex. Just walking along, like they do." A pause. "Oh, yeah. I looked back and the kid's dad was trying to help the black guy up."

"Explain."

"He stuck out his hand and was helping him up."

"How much time had elapsed since the kid's dad fell down?"

"I don't know, Alan. I was just about to turn onto the road, you know, out of the complex. I looked back, and that's what I saw."

"All right."

"I can't go back to the motel, Alan. The police are following me. What am I going to do?"

"How do you know the police are onto you? What have you been doing all afternoon?" He heard laughter in the background. He's in a bar somewhere, the senator thought. Then he heard a male voice asking Agee if he wanted anything else. A hand covered the receiver on Agee's end. Through the clumsily muffled telephone the senator heard Agee order another drink.

"I-I've been driving around," Agee said. "I can't go back there, Alan, the police are after me."

"Where are you now? I know you're not at a pay phone."

A pause. "Okay, you're right, I'm in a pizza place on Roswell Road, you know, off the perimeter on the north side –"

"I know where Roswell Road is, Phil. What I want to know is, what are you going to do now?"

"I don't know Alan. Can I come down to your headquarters? Can you put me up?"

"No, you're drunk. I can't have you coming up here with reporters and God knows who else around."

"I'm not drunk, Alan, honest. Okay, I had a couple of drinks, but I'm eating, Alan. I've been eating pizza. Yeah, pizza, and I've only had a couple of drinks."

"How long have you been there?"

"Since about four or five, I guess. I wanted to hole up until rush hour is over."

"Phil, It's almost nine p.m." The door to the room opened and a young man, another campaign helper, peered inside. The senator pressed the phone's mute button.

"I was told to see if you were in here, Senator. There've been some phone calls –"

"From whom?"

"The *Atlanta Journal*, I think, a reporter –"

"Get a number. I'll call back in a little while."

"Y-yes, sir," the young man stammered. He closed the door.

The senator sighed and dropped the phone in his lap. He was getting a headache. He swore softly and picked up the phone. "Is your car there? Phil...Phil!" No answer, but he heard Agee talking. He was telling someone at the bar how rough his day had been. "Phil! Listen to me when I'm talking to you!"

Agee's conversation stopped, and then some fumbling as he picked up his phone. "I'm sorry, Alan, I –"

"Whom were you talking to? And what were you talking about?"

"Nothing, just talk, Alan –"

"You had better keep your damned mouth shut." The senator took a deep breath. "Look, I want you to get back to the motel. Do you have enough money for a cab?"

"I don't need a cab, I can drive –"

The senator closed his eyes. "Let me remind you," he said, biting off the words, "that you have already committed vehicular homicide. That's the reason you're at the Residence Inn in Duluth and not home in Hope. Do you understand your situation?"

"Alan, I don't want to go back there...the police –"

"You'll be fine as long as you get in that cab and go back to the Residence and sleep it off."

"But the police –"

"Get a damned grip on yourself!" Then the senator's voice softened. "Calm down, Phil, just calm down."

Agee choked back sobs. He slurped a drink, breathing heavily. "Alan, I'm really scared –"

"I know you are, but everything's being taken care of."

"Are you sure?"

"Yes. I've been in contact with Davis Anderson, just today. He's stalling the investigation until this Pat Shane thing dies down. That's why you can't go home. You know that. Davis has covered your tracks as well as is humanly possible. You should be grateful."

"I am, Alan. You're a good friend."

"There's a salesman, Phil, an out of state salesman. Drives a car that looks like yours. Davis Anderson will be looking for him soon."

"Really?"

The senator exhaled impatiently. "This will be your cover story, Phil. New evidence will come to light soon, and you can go home. I have one of my people in Hope two or three times a week to keep tabs on things, make sure Anderson and I know what's going on. I have a person constantly looking for things that might go wrong so we can fix them."

"Thank you, Alan. Thank you."

"So I want you to get back to the motel. Will you do that for me, Phil?"

"Okay," Agee near-whispered. "I'll call a cab."

"Good. Before you go to bed, I want you to pour out all your booze. Will you do that? And I want you to sleep off this bender you're on. I'll have the doctor stop by in the morning and give you a vitamin shot. It'll help with the hangover."

"You're a good friend, Alan."

"When you sober up, fix yourself a good meal. And then I want you to call me."

"At the Marquis?"

"That's right. If you get sufficiently straight, I'll bring you down here for a few days."

"That would be great, Alan."

"But if you start drinking, or I find that you've been talking about your situation to anyone, I'm going to put you back in the motel." The senator paused. "Do you understand what I'm telling you?"

"Yeah, sure, Alan, I understand. You'll be proud of me. I can quit drinking, it's easy, I've done it before. I –"

"If you behave, I've got some things for you to do with my campaign staff."

"I can do it, Alan. You'll see. It'll be just like the old days. You and me, running the campaign. You'll see."

"Good. You keep talking that way. I have some preliminary planning to do in Atlanta for the legislative session in January. If you can keep straight, I'll take you along, after the election."

"You won't be sorry, Alan. You'll see."

"Fine. Now call that cab. I'll see that your car gets back to the motel in the morning."

"I will. I'm going to call as soon as I hang up."

"I'll call in exactly one hour. When I call, I'll expect you to be there and I'll expect you to have poured your booze down the drain."

"I'll do it, Alan. Honest. I will."

"And I don't want you to leave even one drink for your hangover in the morning."

"No, Alan."

"You'll call the cab?"

"You're a good friend, Alan."

"I'll call in one hour. Be there."

"I will. You'll see."

The senator hung up. He closed his eyes and once more rubbed his temples. His headache had grown more intense. He fumbled around in his briefcase and found some aspirin. He poured a glass of water and washed down two tablets. Then in the rest room, he ran cold water onto a washcloth and rubbed his face. The coolness felt good, and he began to relax.

He returned to the sitting room, sat, and closed his eyes. The campaign was almost over. This one had been inexpensive and, so far, according to the playbook. He was popular. So far, politics had been easy for him. But there were always debts to be paid, and his were coming due. The patronage he'd received early in his career had not been free. He and his fellow elected officials were nothing more than a front for power brokers, highly financed masters of commerce and industry who sought to direct the activities of government.

We're on the front lines, he thought. The big money guys pay for everything, but we take the chances. We're the ones with our names in the paper. We have to sort out the morality of things. The morality of things. It had seemed so innocent. Campaign laws, written to allow candidates to keep unused funds until some unspecified, future time. It was legal. But he'd never seen the strings on the money when he was young.

Now he would be running for governor, almost as soon as this election was over. Governor Raines had backers who had financed his first gubernatorial race six years earlier. He'd agreed to run for only one term, but four years later his backers refused to let their investment go that easily. They were men from multinational firms, who were used to buying their way into countries. They were Americans, and they bought, used and sold governments here just like they did in every banana republic down the block.

The senator rose, opened a small refrigerator next to the entry door and took a Coke. He returned to his seat, turning the red and white can in his hand. Condensation was already forming on it. He held it to his face. It made him feel childish, and for a moment, happy. He pulled back the tab on the can and took a sip. The pause that refreshes.

Now the same backers who supported Raines, seeking to extend the value gained from their investment, were dealing to support him, Alan Baxter, in a bid for the governor's office. It had been his ambition since college to someday run for governor. When Raines had invited him to dinner on a recent night, and the plan had been laid out for the succession, Alan had been ecstatic. He'd met the governor's main financial supporters the following day. There were Fortune 500 CEO's, airline executives, real estate barons, presidents of contracting companies, all very pleased to meet him, each offering financial assistance in a number of surprising ways. No laws were to be broken, of course. We got the laws written so we could help, one had said. Government should be a partnership with the main economic drivers. Alan had agreed and, of course, he'd accepted their help.

Bank accounts were set up to funnel campaign funds to him, and to finance his favorite projects. He was elected to the boards of several local corporations. You don't have to get involved, they'd told him, but there will be substantial stipends for sitting. You have a great responsibility, and we don't want you to be distracted by a need for personal funds.

But recently, as he'd observed the governor and his political metamorphosis, he realized how deeply Raines was influenced by his patrons. More and more, he saw him as a mindless instrument of these so-called friends.

He smiled as he took another sip. It was ironic that these men wanted so badly to control government. There was so little to be gained from it in a business sense. All they were buying was easy access and freedom of movement. Subject to a haphazard enforcement of regulatory laws, of course. But that was what lawyers were for. There was so much more to be gained from effective, efficient corporate management in a free market environment. Creativity in the market place was where it was at for the future. It was the key to survival. Not governmental access or control.

It was the *idea* of power, he mused, that attracted them to divert their energies so strongly into the political arena. Competition in a truly free market was a great equalizer. But by owning politicians, they perpetuated their godfather delusions. The pitiful masses bowing and scraping before the benevolent political and economic dictators.

Oh, well. He had another problem, more nettlesome at the moment than the power brokers of Georgia, and his name was Phil Agee. Got to keep him on a short leash, he resolved, and out of Hope until after the election. An old college chum, one of his first political supporters and financial backers. The senator smiled as he imagined himself and Phil sitting in a boardroom with his newfound supporters. Not only had the senator outgrown Phil, but Phil was displaying an amazing potential for embarrassing him.

He thought about the night the little Shane girl had died in Hope. He thought about the events he was now trying so hard to cover up. He knew it wasn't the little girl's father in Agee's parking lot. Davis Anderson had tapped their home phone, and both senator and police chief knew the family had hired a private investigator. A friend of the girl's crippled uncle. A black Vietnam vet with an attitude. It doesn't matter, he'd told Anderson, as long as we don't make any false moves. As long as Phil doesn't get jumpy.

He thought back to his college days with Phil. Their pranks. The bag of dog droppings in their economics professor's desk drawer. Taking the Polaroid pictures though a dorm window of a girl masturbating.

But that was freshman year, before Alan had become truly interested in campus politics. As he thought about it, once he'd started running for office on campus, he'd begun distancing himself from Phil, if only a little. Phil was the prototypical irresponsible child. It had been fun back then, but now, well, Phil was a burden in a complicated and very adult world.

The door opened and the young campaign worker stuck his head in. "Senator –"

"Yes, what is it?"

"Sir, Governor Raines is on the phone. Do you have time –"

"Yes, of course." He looked down at the blinking light. "I'll take it here. Thank you." The young man closed the door.

Alan Baxter sighed. He picked up the almost-empty can of Coke and drained it. As he crushed the can's thin aluminum in one hand, a sudden rush of anger went through him. He threw the mangled can at a trashcan across the room. It missed, clanking off the wall and onto the carpet's luxurious pile. He stood there, somehow transfixed by the crumpled red and white can lying on the floor before him. Then he pressed the button and took the governor's call.

CHAPTER 19

COMING INTO FOCUS

For an off-year election, activity had been brisk. As Jason walked, first along Needham Street, then turning right on Farmer Road and, finally, left on Knox Avenue, he noticed the unusually large proliferation of election posters. It was the Saturday before election day, and almost every yard had at least one sign. The area sported layers of posters, stapled to posts, taped to windows, and staked to any available open ground. In front of the A&P grocery on Knox Avenue, campaign workers were handing out leaflets and talking to prospective voters. The owner of the Texaco station on the corner across from the A&P was running for city council, and his station was festooned with balloons and a brightly painted banner, which flapped gently in the morning breeze.

The mayor was holding a rally in front of the car wash across the street from the Night Owl. Someone had set up a boom-box there, and it blasted out country music while the mayor, a quiet but friendly man of about fifty, shook hands and solicited votes. The mayor's opponent, a long-time city councilman, approached in the back of a pick-up truck, stopping to shake hands and distribute leaflets. As the pick-up passed the car wash, the councilman good-naturedly booed the mayor, who smiled and waved, then returned to greeting residents.

Jason stopped to buy a copy of the morning's *Atlanta Constitution* at a newspaper box. Pat usually monopolized the kitchen and the newspaper on Saturday mornings, and Jason's habit was to walk this distance for a paper of his own, then stop at the Night Owl for breakfast.

He scanned the headlines, folded the paper, and turned to watch the pageantry. He smiled as a gaggle of neighbors passed, and then he turned to the Night Owl. Inside, Gus and his wife Alice were clearing booth tables and the counter, the morning's main surge of patrons almost gone.

"Is it too late for breakfast?"

Gus looked to Alice, who said, "I think we can scrape up something. What're you in the mood for, Jason?"

He took off his parka, slung it over his shoulder and ordered grits, toast, a scrambled egg, and a glass of milk.

Gus unloaded an armful of dishes into the sink behind the counter. "Is that white or wheat toast?"

"Wheat."

Gus dropped three slices of bread into the toaster, ladled an ample portion of grits into a bowl, and poured the glass of milk.

"You going to sit at the counter?"

"No, I think I'll sit by the window, so I can see all the goings on."

Gus smiled. "It's really something, ain't it? Election time, I mean." He carried the foodstuff to Jason. "It makes you proud to be an American, don't it?"

"Yep," said Jason as he slid into the booth, "when we do it right. By the way, I'm expecting an old war buddy of mine to meet me. He'll be here any minute."

"An old war buddy," Gus repeated, an approving look on his face. "Where's he from?"

"He lives in Atlanta now. Originally from North Carolina."

"I'll have to meet him," said Gus. "I always do what I can to make vets feel welcome."

"I'll introduce you."

Gus disappeared into the kitchen to begin preparing for the lunch hour rush.

Jason lifted his first spoonful of grits. There was always something about the taste of freshly cooked grits that reminded him of his childhood, of his mom and dad, of less complicated days. When he was done, he pushed his plate forward and peered to the street. The mayor continued to shake hands and chat with passers-by. Two small children tore the crepe paper from his poster-covered station wagon and ran laughing down the sidewalk, the colored paper trailing like the tail of a kite.

The front page of the *Constitution* once again featured the reelection campaign of Senator Alan Baxter. He must own a piece of the paper, thought Jason. Ah, I'm just being cynical. He laughed to himself, remembering that an old sixties segregationist had nicknamed the *Constitution* the "fishwrapper." Its trustworthiness in reporting had in his opinion gone awry, so he'd pronounced it good for nothing more exalted than wrapping fish.

I guess Senator Baxter is just another good old boy, Jason considered. He served as a progressive in a Georgia still struggling with the mindsets of the thirties and forties. But it was also true that the senator's evolving image was slowly casting him as just another cog in the southern political machine. The term good old boy was used, both endearingly and scornfully, to refer to the rural southern male. In recent decades, it had come to include those who struck the pose of the earthy, true-to-his-roots rugged individualist. A wise, if not educated, man who outwardly spurned the establishment, but who lived by the tenet that he who goes along gets along.

"What you expect to learn with your nose stuck in that paper all morning?"

Jason glanced up and smiled. "Just trying to educate myself in the ways of the world."

Wilton chuckled. "Get out on the street, then."

Gus dropped his preparations for lunch and approached the booth. "Can I help you?" he said to Wilton.

"I could use a coffee. Hot and black."

Jason waved a hand in Wilton's direction. "This is my old buddy from Vietnam. We kept each other alive for the better part of five months in the rubber plantation country."

Gus stuck out his hand. "Name's Gus. This is my place."

Wilton took the hand as Jason added more history to his introduction. He glanced about the diner. "You got a fine place here, Gus. A fine place."

Gus pulled back his hand and absently wiped it on his apron. "Thanks. Been here thirty-five years. Served just about everybody in town over that time. You want anything with that coffee?"

Wilton studied Gus' face for a moment. "Got any Danish?"

"Got doughnuts, made fresh this morning."

"I'll take two."

Gus turned away, clearing another booth on his way to the coffee pot.

"Damn cracker," said Wilton.

"Gus? He's a nice guy."

"Did you see him wipe his hand after we shook? Like shaking hands with a black man is gonna poison him."

Jason shook his head. "Are you really that sensitive?"

"When you get treated like poison, you notice it."

"Maybe you shouldn't work so hard at noticing."

"Meaning what?"

"Meaning this is a small town. Everyone's awkward with differences."

"Especially black differences."

Jason sighed. "You know how people are about that. What if I went to your hometown?"

"You'd do okay. You know how to communicate."

Jason chuckled. "If I got a chance to open my mouth with you around."

Gus returned with the coffee and doughnuts. "You need anything, you just holler."

"Thanks," said Wilton. He sipped his coffee.

Gus stood awkwardly before them. Jason and Wilton looked up.

"This is a patriotic town," said Gus, still shuffling his feet. "We always try to let you vets know we appreciate what you done for us. Especially the ones who served in Vietnam. Most people pretty much forgot about you."

"I didn't do a damn thing but get drafted and stay alive," said Wilton.

"Same here," said Gus. "That's how I managed. Just fought and stayed alive."

"You army vet, man?" asked Wilton.

"First Infantry."

"The Big Red One? No kidding?"

"Yep. World War Two. All the way to the end. Crossed the Rhine. It was a long fight. Seems like yesterday, though." He blushed. "I lied about my age to get in. I wasn't but fifteen."

"Us, too," said Wilton. "Big Red One, I mean."

"Yeah?" said Gus. "I didn't know that."

"Can't say as I have a lot of pleasant memories from it, though," said Jason.

Gus stuck out his hand and warmly shook both men's hands. Then he looked over his shoulder. Alice was still in the kitchen. "Breakfast's on the house," he said. "For both of y'all."

"Well, thanks, Gus," said Jason.

"Yeah, thanks, man," said Wilton.

"You fellows need anything, you just let me know." Gus returned to his lunchtime preparations.

"What'd I tell you?" Jason said.

"Smart ass. You set me up."

Jason grinned. "First time I ever heard that about Gus. But you said you had some more news."

"Yeah. This Donna Miller, I called her. Took your advice and talked to Loretta first. Said I was helping your family out. She gave me the number. Good thing, too. They're both a couple of flakes. It would've scared Donna's pants off if I'd called her cold."

"Did she tell you anything new?"

"Pretty much confirmed what your brother got from the police report. She was too scared for much to register after the car hit Emily. When it got past her, she couldn't tell anything. She couldn't see the driver at all. His head was hidden by the front seat headrest. Some little guy, it sounded like."

"Think it might've been a kid?"

"Hard to say. Hard to guess what she really saw. Now she's saying she thought she saw two people in the car."

"Two people? A man and a woman?"

"Sounded like two men. But don't put any money on it. She'll never be any good to you in court. A good defense attorney would take her apart in a New York minute."

"Two men," said Jason.

"Tomorrow it might be two men, a woman, and a cow," said Wilton.

Gus returned with a pot of coffee. "You boys need anything?"

"A fill-up on coffee," said Wilton.

"Nothing, thanks," said Jason.

Gus poured. "You know, I belong to the VFW chapter over in Athens. You fellows ever want to go, I'll introduce y'all."

They thanked him and he returned to the counter. The regular noon customers had begun to trickle in. Newspaper man entered, taking his regular seat at the counter. Newcomer stuck his head in the door for a moment and then disappeared.

"VFW, my ass," said Wilton. "They don't like Viet vets. I went to a meeting in Charlotte once, right after my discharge. I thought being black made you an outsider, but you mention Vietnam to those guys and they step away fast as they can." He shook his head.

"The world was changing," Jason replied, "and the old World War II vets didn't understand about Vietnam. There were a lot of us who worked against the war when we got back. The morality of war was changing, had been ever since Hiroshima. Vietnam was all about business and politics, and that confused everyone. It just wasn't a popular war."

"When was the last popular war you remember, man?"

"You'd be surprised. World War II was very popular in the U.S. Still is. I'm amazed when I read the historical texts at how noble it all sounds."

"Until the bullets started flying and the blood started flowing."

"Sure. You read about D-Day, all the usual snafus of war, the history books make it seem almost lovable, like a Broadway musical."

"Speaking of Athens," said Wilton, "I visited your bar, The Woof, yesterday."

"Yeah?"

"I think I got a fix on this Agee character. I showed some guy, one of the regulars, I think, a photo from the newspaper story you told me about. He said Agee still goes there once in a while."

"I thought as much," said Jason. "But how did the subject come up? I mean –"

"Relax," said Wilton. "I told him I was a reporter from the Atlanta paper, and I was doing a follow-up on the DUI story. It was a good cover. Went to the city library and researched the story. It was in the *Constitution*. Say, you got a camera?"

"Sure. Why?"

"You're my photographer. I need to go back and question the regular bartender. He was out yesterday. Still gonna play up the DUI angle. But I need to find out if Agee was there that night."

"When do you want to go?"

Wilton gulped down the last of his coffee. "How about right now?"

"My camera's at the house."

"Let's go, then."

They rose. Gus waved goodbye. They thanked him again and departed.

As they opened the door to the diner, newcomer was concluding a conversation on the pay phone just outside. He wheeled around, bumping into Wilton.

"Excuse me, neighbor," said newcomer.

Wilton turned slowly, studied newcomer as he entered the Night Owl. "You know that guy?"

Jason peered into the diner. "We speak. I've seen him around town a couple of times lately. But no, I don't know him." He peered into the diner again and shook his head.

Wilton caught Jason's arm and moved him away from the front windows.

"What?"

"That guy," said Wilton, "I saw him yesterday in Athens."

"When you went to The Woof?"

"Yeah. Afterwards. When I got to the joint, I saw a poster for a Baxter rally on campus, sponsored by some student political group. So I decided to check him out. I see why he's so popular. He really reads people well. Gives 'em what they want. But this guy we just saw: he was there."

"A campaign worker? He's way too old to be a student."

"Maybe," said Wilton.

"Or maybe he's just a resident who stopped by to see the rally."

"I don't think so. When the rally broke up, a couple of the students escorted Baxter to his car, so I followed. That guy," he said, nodding in the direction of the diner, "was in Baxter's car. He was Baxter's driver."

The two of them stood at the curb saying nothing. Across the street the mayor and his wife furled their campaign banners, said goodbye to the last remaining well-wishers and tacked a large poster, prominently displaying the mayor's portrait, to a power pole just behind the street curb.

Jason finally broke the silence. "That could mean anything."

"We're starting to see what's really going on," said Wilton. "The thing is, they know they're being watched. And my gut's telling me Agee and Baxter know who's watching."

Jason fidgeted. "How do you figure?"

"Like I said, just a gut feel. It gets like that sometimes. You see more than you realize."

"What do we do, then?"

"Keep looking. It'll come into focus eventually." For a moment Wilton scanned the streetscape. "But we need to watch our backs from now on. We're close to something. Maybe too close." They climbed into Wilton's Taurus and took the turn at the end of the block. Wilton made a quick sweep into the driveway of the Shane home and waited while Jason picked up his camera. Five minutes later, they were on their way to Athens.

CHAPTER 20

ELECTION DAY

Perhaps it was the level of excitement that had been slowly growing over the past month as the elections neared, but Jason couldn't sleep. He rose early, just before six a.m., dressed, and brought in the morning paper.

The front section consisted mostly of the last wrap-up stories on the various campaigns. Page three contained yet another story on Alan Baxter, once again accompanied by a photo, portraying Baxter talking to his aides as he stood in front of a large table in his Atlanta headquarters. As Jason scanned the photo, he noted a familiar face beside Baxter: Phil Agee in a smartly tailored suit, hands on hips.

He tore the photo from the paper. I'd rather Pat see a hole in the paper, he thought. He finished the front section, rose, and rummaged in the pantry for instant oatmeal. He found a new box Von had bought the day before, tore it open and prepared two packs. He read the sports section as he ate. Then his brother's steps clattered on the hall stairs.

Pat began pouring coffee. "I guess I did hear you up early," he said. "What's the occasion?"

"Couldn't sleep. Thought I'd eat and be ready when the polls open." Jason glanced to the kitchen clock. It was almost six-thirty.

"Who're you going to vote for?"

"Thought I'd vote for the mayor again. Phil Agee's ex-wife for city council. And Alan Baxter."

Pat spun, coffee pot sloshing. He glared at Jason. He set the pot on the stove, snatched a cup from a nearby cabinet, and poured. Another daggered look to Jason. He hit the kitchen table with a leg and dropped his cup. It broke, and a spray of coffee rose to soil his trousers. He swore and kicked the cup's largest shard across the kitchen, slipped in the spilled coffee and almost fell. He swore again, grabbed a dishtowel, and tried to blot the coffee stains from his trouser legs. Finally, he stomped from the kitchen, tossing the towel over his head. It landed on the floor at Jason's feet.

Jason sighed and picked it up. Then he dropped to one knee to pick up the broken pieces.

Pat was getting worse. His mood swings had become so volatile that Jason and Von had considered not telling him anything significant about Wilton's sleuthing. They'd deduced from Pat's grumblings that he was spending his time at work arguing with employees over the most minor of issues. When Jason asked Von about that, she told him they were hardly speaking; thus, she knew nothing more.

Minutes later, Pat stomped down the stairs and into the kitchen wearing a fresh pair of slacks and a blazer. He glared at the coffee pot, then at Jason, and stalked out the back way, slamming the door as he left.

Jason breathed deeply, glad to see his brother gone. More and more, Jason had only Von to talk to. Pat was either too preoccupied for conversation, or he was rampaging because the case wasn't moving fast enough. Last night, against their better judgment, Jason and Von had decided to tell Pat about Wilton's visit to Athens and The Woof.

A regular there had confirmed that Agee had spent all afternoon at the seedy bar on the afternoon in question. Agee had borrowed twenty dollars from the customer they'd talked to and had supposedly left him a signed IOU dated October the fourth, the date of Emily's death. But that testimony wasn't as conclusive as it might seem. Wilton had questioned the bartender that afternoon, a beefy Mediterranean type, and he'd denied knowing or seeing Agee there, on that day or any other.

Near the end of Jason's narrative about Wilton's visit to The Woof, Pat had risen, stomped from the house, and driven off. Without a word. Such reactions always had Jason and Von on edge, but then they'd not been surprised.

Jason began cleaning up the kitchen. He placed Von's travel cup beside the coffee pot, lay two pieces of bread on a saucer, covered it with plastic wrap, and set it beside the toaster oven. She was always in a hurry when she came down, hungry and ready for work, and he enjoyed making her morning ritual easier.

Although her estrangement from Pat was building, she was resilient. Despite her on again, off again presence at the brokerage, she was gaining a modicum of focus while grieving for Emily, and the brokerage was benefitting. Now the firm's principals were talking of expansion. And rumors had it that a financial crisis was growing at Agee Realty; as a result, its agents were taking work elsewhere.

On a recent Saturday, while Pat was catching up on paperwork in Athens, Von cleared Emily's room of all but the most cherished mementos. She'd sold Emily's bedroom furniture that day to a young couple down the street. A few days later, again while Pat was working, and with Jason's help, she repainted the room, brought in new furniture, and converted it into a guest room.

After that, she began smiling more as she puttered around the house. She cooked almost every night. Jason went grocery shopping with her, ran errands with her, and his own spirits began brightening. During those times together, she'd impulsively straighten his shirt, comb back his hair, or squeeze his hand. He looked forward to her return home from work each day, and to the gaiety she seemed to be adding to his life. Every few days, he'd walk to the A&P, buy flowers, and set them in a vase on her nightstand.

He straightened the kitchen, and at just past seven took his parka from the hall closet and departed. He walked the two blocks down Needham Street to Clarke Street, where Best's Restaurant, Hope's finest eating place was located, on the same block as the century-old City Hall.

He crossed Claiborne; ahead the elementary school, where he would vote. The line of voters there stretched a half-block to Clarke Street, and some early comers were already emerging past the heavy oak doors of the elegant old schoolhouse. As he came to the end of the line, he greeted the Claxtons. A high school classmate who now built homes greeted him. Ahead, volunteer workers had set up a table and were passing out free coffee to voters. Before the coffee table, just outside the legal distance from the polling place, the mayor and a candidate for city council shook hands with those in line.

Inside, the line split into several branches, and Jason quickly found himself at a table in the auditorium, where he received his ballot. A booth opened, and he slid the punch card into the voting tablet. His voting complete, he picked up a doughnut from a folding table by the auditorium door and departed.

The sky had brightened. He walked down the long sidewalk connecting Claiborne Elementary to the wide boulevard that was its namesake. The line of voters was much shorter now, its end almost at the doors of the school.

Election day. Full of promises and hope and pageantry. The day the people speak. He smiled. He thought of the local election in Hope, and of other small Georgia towns where telegenic young businesspeople were being swept into political office on promises of more local industry and jobs. Of course, these plans were hatched behind the scenes. When enacted, they would benefit the larger landowners, the real estate brokers, and a few businesses and skilled workers not even present in these towns. All this, though, enhanced the political stock of the mayors and city councils.

He remembered the fight in another north Georgia town over zoning. The town had fallen on hard times, and the structures along its main residential street had become dilapidated. A developer, noticing the amount of traffic through this mountain hamlet, had proposed to the city council that the street of once beautiful old homes be zoned commercial and the homes torn down. He and his business associates would build a strip shopping center and stock its shops with cheap, Asian-manufactured souvenirs. Twenty jobs for locals were to be created, paying minimum wage. But some fifty local citizens, including a number of elderly couples and widows, would be displaced.

Secret talks between the city council, the developer, and a local contractor resulted in a resolution to rezone the area. Only after the residents discovered their homes were being condemned, which would require them to move to a rather seedy apartment complex in another town, did the fireworks start. Someone made claims of payoffs, between the developer and the city council. This redevelopment would break historical preservation laws, too, but the relocation of the elderly, demolition of their homes, and construction of the shopping center moved inexorably forward. Eventually, the press coverage died, as did the charges of bribing public officials.

Lost in thought, Jason almost tripped over a large campaign sign for Alan Baxter, which had been staked in a front yard and which projected onto the pathway. He reached out and jiggled the sign. It came loose. He picked it up, took in the life-sized portrait of the senator.

The photograph had the senator smiling, its strong, angular face offset by a pair of sharply confident eyes and a firmly set jaw. It was the face of early twenty-first century politics. Power. Creativity. Deal making. But Jason began to sense other nuances, associative things. An overwhelming sense of ambition. A certain blindness to ethics. A weakness for using public money for personal gain. Even in this poster photograph, Jason thought he could see the influence of unseen faces and an indifference to citizens' needs.

He dropped the poster to the ground and, suddenly flush with anger, he stomped it. His athletic shoes raised deformations on the face of the candidate he'd decided moments before not to vote for, leaving a permanent imprint. "I respected you," he said, "I believed in you." He looked around, suddenly realizing his voice had come in a shout.

He placed the poster in its upright position and, head hung, he detoured toward the Night Owl.

# # #

Meanwhile, staffers from the governor's office were already at work around the state. Field representatives were questioning voters as they left the polling places, asking questions concerning their choices on bond referendums and the several constitutional amendments on the ballot. They asked about the local candidates selected as well as the voters' choices for state legislators and U.S. representatives. They relayed this information to various command posts. There, the data would be sorted and evaluated.

Beneath the capitol's gold dome, eager young interns manned fax machines and telephones and asked questions. Governor Raines walked among the youthful workers, listening, watching. He asked questions, and the answers he received pleased him; there would be no surprises today.

Alan Baxter entered the room.

The governor took Baxter's hand, and then those of Baxter's senior staffer and his good friend, Phil Agee.

Baxter took in the laboring interns. He sighed through his frown.

Governor Raines glanced at Baxter and laughed. "You were expecting to be upset?"

"I'd hate to think the polls we paid through the nose for had misled us."

"This one's boring, Alan. Actually I'd prefer some surprises once in a while."

"You're a short-timer, Governor. Maybe when I have the next election under my belt, I'll be able to see the sport in it."

The governor clapped him on the back. "Believe me, being governor will do nothing to improve your confidence. You just *think* you have enemies now."

Baxter bristled, then relaxed, forcing himself to smile. "I guess I'll always be cautious."

The governor studied his expression. "Well, you can lighten up today. The newspapers will be calling you Landslide Baxter before the day's over."

"It does seem to be going well."

"And it's only just beginning." The governor stepped forward to take a fax from one of the interns. Baxter nodded toward the door. Phil and the staffer turned, and he followed.

# # #

Jason stopped at the Book Nook, next door to the Night Owl. He bought a news magazine, the cover announcing an article on gene splicing, promising insights into its complex legal and moral implications. He paid and tucked the magazine into his parka, dug his hands into his pocket bottoms, and turned toward home. He passed an election poster emblazoned with a perennial candidate's picture. Someone had stuck a bumper sticker across it, like a band-aid. It read: Abortion Is Murder.

The big political names, he mused as he limped along, don't like changing times. So when the times do change, they feel their best strategy is to probe the most intimate aspects of our lives. They don't like reshaping their attitudes to fit the reality of the world, so they declare political war on our intimacies. Sex, for instance. They find ways to inject sex with fear. Fear of AIDS, fear of pregnancy, fear of murdering fetuses. Fear of nudity, of physical demonstrations of affection. They don't understand that sex can be used to draw its partners together, into deeper levels of intimacy, and in today's world this twist on physical intimacy seems to have more value than procreation. So now we're at war with the most primal aspect of our humanity.

I'm one to talk about sex, he thought. Ages since the last relationship. His thoughts raced, trying to keep Von's image from his thoughts. But the image persisted, her clothes melting, revealing luminescent skin and a beautifully formed body. "No," he said aloud, clenching his fists and pounding at the air as he walked. "No no no no!"

CHAPTER 21

BUDDY TARBUTTON

Friday morning at eight-thirty a.m., Wilton sat at his office computer, scrolling through the information he'd gathered while investigating Emily's death. Three days before, he'd decided to visit Hope's police station in hopes of viewing their file on the case, but first he needed to discuss the case with Jason. You got me on this case, and it's not a secret any more, man, Wilton had insisted the next day. Look, we know what's in the police file. Why not be up front about it? Who knows? They may cooperate. Let's have a conversation with the man there, you know? He may have some little thing we can use. People always say more than they mean to.

Pat, of course, had gone into a rampage over their decision. There was no way he would even remotely cooperate with Davis Anderson. Hey, Wilton had shouted at Pat, this may save your ass! Think about it. We're telling him we're on this thing. What if he finds out the hard way? You know what'll happen? He'll think all sorts of wrong things, and you'll be back in the slammer. So back off!

An inebriated Pat had been so frustrated with Wilton's resolve that he'd threatened Jason and Von. Von had thrown his vodka and grapefruit juice glass at him. It had hit him on the shoulder as she screamed for him to leave the house. Wilton had prevented Pat from hitting her; he'd had to throw Pat bodily from the Shane home. Pat had bellowed at them for a few minutes from the front porch, then he'd climbed into his car and left. He hadn't come home until the following evening. You're starting to enjoy this soap opera, Jason had joked to Wilton the following day. What a bunch of rednecks you got in that town, Wilton had replied. Worse than back home. Got to watch my back every step I take. But they *had* decided to talk to the chief, so Thursday morning had found Wilton in Anderson's office. The chief hadn't seemed surprised at Wilton's appearance, and he'd cooperated. He'd talked at length with Wilton about the information each had gathered. He'd reflected somewhat dispassionately on Pat's behavior. Eventually, he'd turned Wilton over to Buddy Tarbutton, who had had desk duty that day. Wilton had read the police file from cover to cover. He'd questioned Tarbutton about the evening of Emily's death, about Donna Miller's testimony. Nothing significant had been revealed.

He scrolled back to the beginning of his own files. Sketchy stuff, truth be known. He leaned back and scratched his chin. There must be something else, he thought, something still not seeing the light of day.

He rose and, deep in thought, wandered to his kitchenette, where a half-full pot of coffee waited. He poured another cup and pulled a packet of sweet rolls from the refrigerator, heated two in the microwave. While the rolls were warming, he returned to his desk, pulled a pint bottle of whiskey from a desk drawer and sprinkled some into his cup. The timer on the microwave buzzed and he set the sweet rolls on a plate.

The phone rang. He started to answer it, but decided to let it ring. On the fourth ring, his answering machine intercepted the call. He could barely hear the machine as it played his prerecorded message, beeped, and then waited for the person calling to speak.

He had not yet confided this to Jason, but the case was looking like a dead end. Plenty of information about the case lay scattered about, but it led everywhere. And nowhere. Just enough to keep you looking, but never enough to point toward a smoking gun. It was, he thought, like many cases he'd investigated. He called them teases: nothing to hang your hat on, just enough to keep you going in circles. Jason was paying all he could afford, but it wasn't enough to cover Wilton's overhead and travel expenses. I'm going to end this, he thought. I can't keep wasting my man Jay's money. He rubbed the back of his neck and considered what Jason's response would be.

He finished his coffee and sweet rolls and pressed the machine's message button.

"This is Officer Buddy Tarbutton of the Hope Police Force." There was a pause before the message continued. "It's nine-twenty, Friday morning. Please call me at the following number as soon as possible." Another pause. Buddy Tarbutton's deep, resonant voice resumed and he gave the number. It was a 706 area code, somewhere outside the metro Atlanta area. "Please don't call the station house if you're unable to contact me at this number." His voice emphasized don't. The message ended.

Wilton sat back in his chair. Tarbutton hadn't been nearly as communicative as the chief during Wilton's visit to the station house. In fact, he'd seemed moody, almost jumpy about the case. Not the sort of guy you'd think would place a friendly call to see how things were going. And the pauses in the message: what was going on at the other end? It sounded as if he was concerned that someone might be listening in.

Wilton sighed. Maybe he has a grudge against the chief. Or maybe he knows something. Or maybe I'm being set up. If it's a setup, who's behind it? Oh, well, he thought, the best way to hunt rabbits is to flush 'em out, make 'em jump. I'll just have to be careful. He replayed the message. He wrote the number and considered. Listen for a phone tap, he reminded himself as he dialed the number.

The number rang two, three, then four times. He was just about to hang up when the ringing stopped. A deep male voice answered.

Wilton identified himself.

Buddy Tarbutton coughed and cleared his throat before saying, "The file you looked at the other day, did you find enough to help you?"

What kind of game are we playing here? thought Wilton.

"The file on Emily Shane. Did you find what you needed?"

Wilton listened to the background noise and decided the phone wasn't tapped. "You tell me," he said.

A long pause. "There are things that aren't in the police file," said Tarbutton.

"What sort of things?"

Another pause. "I don't have anything else to say over the telephone."

"Then where do we go from here?"

"The phones aren't safe. Can we meet privately?"

Wilton closed his eyes. The phones aren't safe. Who are they tapping? Me? I'd pick that up. He groaned. Jay. They tapped the phones at the Shane home. "Where?"

"I have a cabin on Lake Oconee, just south of I-20. That's where I am now. I'm off today. We can meet here."

Wilton thought about it. He's telling me more than I need to know. Maybe it's okay. All right, he decided, I'll go along. "Tell me when, and I'll need directions."

Buddy Tarbutton gave him directions to his cabin. They would meet as soon as possible, which by Wilton's reckoning wouldn't be before one p.m. They hung up and Wilton sighed. They're using taps. That means Anderson's in on it. But who else? And how do I talk to the Shanes without making the cops suspicious? This would take some thought.

It was almost one-thirty when Wilton pulled up in front of the lakeside cabin. He'd thought about having Jay meet him but remembered he had a late morning appointment with Doctor Berg. Better this way, Wilton decided. Less dangerous for my man Jay. He climbed out of the Taurus and looked around. The dirt road leading from the highway lay behind him, buried deep within the pine forest bordering the northern shore of Lake Oconee. The cabin was small, with plank siding and a large screened porch on the side facing the lake. The lot sloped gently downward, through the pines toward the lake, which Wilton could barely see through the lower branches of the pines.

He began to relax. A squirrel chattered from a nearby tree.

An old pickup sat in the drive, rust spots showing through the brown paint, its bed littered with pine needles, beer cans, and a small stack of old newspapers, which protruded from the paper grocery bags they were stored in. Adjacent to the pickup, a small stoop covered the back door. Wilton opened the screened door and peered through the window panel. No one. He rapped sharply three times. No response. He tested the door handle. Unlocked. He opened the door and stepped into a small, rustic kitchen.

He was about to call out when he heard a thud on the ground behind him. He spun, drew back a cocked fist.

"Hey, take it easy," Tarbutton said as he took a step back.

Wilton dropped the fist. "You alone?"

"Yeah," Tarbutton said. "Sorry to give you a start. I walked down to the lake for a while. Like to get out in the sun when I can, especially when it's cold. I heard your car and came on back up."

"That's cool," said Wilton. "I just been a little jumpy lately."

The officer eyed Wilton. "Me, too. Lots to be jumpy about." He nodded toward the living area. "Grab a seat over there."

Wilton strode through the kitchen to the living room, home to a brown leather couch and a matching easy chair, their coverings cracked and splitting. Across the dim room, beyond a large, wooden industrial wire spool that served as a table, sat a dirty plaid recliner. Against the opposite wall, a small metal stand held a portable television, its rabbit ear antenna wrapped with flags of aluminum foil. The bare wooden floor had been varnished years earlier but was now dull with scars and a long-time accumulation of dust. Wilton took the leather easy chair.

Tarbutton had remained in the kitchen. "Beer?" he called out.

Wilton declined.

Tarbutton sprawled across the couch. "This Emily Shane thing, it's getting messy."

"I know that's right. But you said you had some things that weren't in the file."

Tarbutton turned the beer can slowly. "Some things," he said slowly, "that *used* to be in the file."

"Like what?"

Tarbutton drained the can in two long gulps and tossed it toward the kitchen. "I feel like I'm stuck between a rock and a hard place." A pause. "I don't know if I can trust you with what I know."

Wilton shifted in his seat. "Not enough trust to go around these days. I don't have any reason to believe I can trust anyone from the Hope P.D., either."

The officer nodded. Suddenly he sat upright and leaned forward. "Well, I've had enough of the cloak and dagger stuff. I don't really care what happens now. I just want to get what I know into someone's hands. Someone who can use it." Exhaling, he lowered his head. "Got to trust somebody." He got up and plodded into the kitchen.

"Guess I'll take you up on that beer after all," Wilton called out.

Tarbutton tossed him one. "I was the investigating officer on the case," Tarbutton said as he returned to the couch with his second beer. "But you know that. What you probably don't know is that I did some investigating the night of the Shane girl's death, after I escorted the ambulance to the hospital."

"Didn't know that," said Wilton.

"We're a good police force. We're well trained, and we're prompt to follow up on things, despite the size of the force. Chief Davis is a pro."

"I talked to a couple of Bureau friends of mine in Atlanta. They said he knows his business."

"Bureau?" An alarmed look flamed across Tarbutton's face. "GBI?"

"FBI."

Visible relief. "I didn't figure you to be that connected."

"I been around."

Tarbutton nodded slowly. "Maybe you can do something with this, then."

"Keep talking, man."

Both men sipped from their beers. "The chief," Tarbutton continued, "asked me to nose around a little, so I knocked on doors. That's how I happened to talk with Loretta Miller and her sister." He looked down. "The chief didn't tell it to Pat Shane quite this way, but he was right about one thing: they were scared. It wasn't hard for the chief to make them stay quiet."

"Yeah, well, what did this sister know?"

"She described the car and the driver as well as she could. It wasn't hard to ID the car from her description."

"Philip Agee's."

"Right. The next afternoon, I went to see him."

"What day was that?"

"October fifth."

"Was his car there?"

"I can't say, really," Tarbutton replied after some consideration. "His house had one of those old garages, separate from the house, and it was closed up. I wish now I'd looked more closely. Anyway, he was hung over, and he'd already started drinking again. To cure his hangover, he said. So I sat down with him and started asking questions. Asked him where he was the day before. Said he'd had business in Athens and had ended up at a place there called The Woof. Had a few drinks, he said. I asked him where he was about dusk, when the Shane girl was hit." Tarbutton paused to sip his beer. "Well, he started protesting that he hadn't killed her. I told him he wasn't being accused of anything. When he calmed down, he told me first that he'd taken a cab to a motel in Athens, then he said he was at home in Hope. My evaluation was that he'd been too drunk that night to know how to tie his shoelaces. He just plain didn't remember. So the next day I drove to Athens."

"You mind if I take a few notes?" Wilton asked.

Tarbutton paused for a moment. "Go ahead. Just don't write down anything about where you got this."

"You got it." Wilton began scribbling in a small notebook.

"I went to The Woof in plain clothes," Tarbutton continued. "Didn't want to attract too much attention. I talked to the bartender first. He remembered Agee, said he'd gotten pretty drunk that night. Didn't remember him leaving, though."

"The bartender, describe him."

"Big guy. Dark, wavy hair, kinda moody. Name was Vince, I think."

"He said he remembered Agee?"

"Yep. Said he came in every once in a while. Remembered him because he always got good and loaded. Usually closed down the place. Well, anyway, I stayed a while, had a beer. I was just about to go when some old guy slides into the booth in front of me. Vince was in the back room with a delivery man. This guy asked who I was, why I was asking questions about Agee. He was pretty stewed himself, and he was acting nervous, you know? Always looking around before he said anything."

Tarbutton stood up, placed his beer can on the wooden spool. He began to pace.

"Who was this guy?"

"Jake. That's all he'd tell me. Just Jake."

"Go on," Wilton said.

Tarbutton exhaled and sat. "He told me Vince knew more than he was telling. I pressed him on that, and he got real nervous. I asked him if he was there the night of October fourth. He said yeah. Then all of a sudden, he blurted out that some guy had come in and pulled Agee out of there."

"Did he know who this guy was?"

"Nah. But he gave a damned good description of him. He was short, well built, with blond hair. A good looking man. Well dressed. Looked important. Agee seemed to know him, he said. Said the guy intimidated Agee, pushed him around, real quiet like. Agee could barely walk, and the short guy helped get him out of there. They had a fuss just outside the door over whether Agee could drive. This guy had come in a big car, a Cadillac, with some other guy driving. Those two had a few words, and then the little guy tossed Agee into the rider's side of Agee's car. The guy driving the Cadillac took off, and the little guy got behind the wheel of Agee's car and headed toward Hope."

Wilton drained his can and set it down quietly on the floor beside his chair. "You got any idea who the little guy was?"

Tarbutton fidgeted. "I asked a few questions back in Hope, just to confirm my suspicions. It didn't take a good detective to figure out who it was."

"Who?"

"Alan Baxter, the state senator."

A long silence ensued.

"You didn't tell me," said Wilton, "why you wanted to tell me this."

Tarbutton ran a hand over his hair bristles. "I had been keeping the chief informed on the case. He let me nose around all I wanted for the first couple of days. Then I told him about this guy at The Woof, what he'd said, and about the Cadillac. That day he took me off the case, said he'd take over."

"Was that a problem?"

"No, but I went ahead and wrote it up. Put it in the file. Then Pat Shane came to the station house. The chief had been holding the file. I had it for a few minutes, after Shane got through with it. I noticed my report wasn't in it. In fact, all evidence of my investigation had been removed, and another report substituted, one that reported almost nothing. The next day, I asked the chief about it. He said to forget it, everything was under control. I got kind of pissed, told him I wanted to see my report." Tarbutton picked up his beer can, kept turning it. "The chief closed the door. He asked me how much I liked law enforcement. I told him it was a good life. Then he told me if I wanted to keep working in law enforcement in Georgia, I'd better drop the subject."

"And if you didn't?"

"I asked him that, too. He looked at me and told me I could figure out the rest."

Wilton slumped in his chair's back. "Tell me, man, who knows this besides you, me, and the chief?"

"Nobody as far as I can tell. I worked directly with the chief on it. And you can bet I haven't told anyone else. Until now."

"You know this ain't worth the time it took to tell it," Wilton replied, "unless I can prove what you're telling me."

Tarbutton rose, left the room, and returned a moment later. He held two sheets of paper stapled together. "This'll get you started," he said, and handed Wilton the papers.

Wilton took them, scanned the first page, turned to the next – a draft copy of Tarbutton's missing report on his visit to The Woof. "Okay, you did good," Wilton said. He rose.

"Look," said Tarbutton, "use this any way you like. But I'd prefer not to be known as the source until it's ready to go to court."

"Yeah, I understand."

Wilton climbed into the Taurus, reached in his shirt pocket, and turned off the tiny tape recorder. Hate to tape a police officer, he thought, but this one's a witness to a cover up.

CHAPTER 22

A FAMILY WAY

For the past few years, Wednesday night had been reserved as dinner night at the Shane home. On other weeknights, each drifted into the kitchen on their own schedules, preparing a light meal from leftovers or the staples stored in the pantry. Von had encouraged the Wednesday night dinner in order to draw them together, perhaps dining with friends or Von's parents. Pat was to leave work early on that day, as was Von. Jason's recurring depressions were not allowed to be an excuse for his being absent, and he helped cook or, if in a people mood, he would entertain company while Pat and Von put the finishing touches on dinner.

But now that routine had changed. Recent Wednesdays had found Von and Jason together in late afternoon, first at the A&P grocery, then in the kitchen preparing the evening's meal. Jason had taken over the cookouts from Pat who, more and more frequently, returned home too late to tend to the grilling.

On this evening, Jason put on the red and white-checkered apron Von had bought Pat, and he grilled pork chops. Not the usual thin, bony kind always on sale at A&P. This time, he'd talked the butcher into cutting a pork loin into thick slices of lean meat with just enough fat around the edges to give the chops a good taste.

While he grilled, Von cut strawberries, whipped fresh cream, and baked a dozen sweet cakes – a strawberry shortcake recipe of her mother's. Then together they cooked green beans with small, red potatoes and steamed squash. After the vegetables and the ever-present skillet of sweet cornbread were done, Von made cups of hot tea.

They always served dinner on Wednesday in the high-ceilinged dining room between the kitchen and sitting room. The three windows there were tall and majestic, bordered by thick, richly woven burgundy curtains of the same cloth as those in the sitting room. The middle window was a broad bay into which Von's antique mahogany dining room suite partially projected.

As was their custom, they had intended company for dinner. Jason had invited Wilton and Jonelle for the evening, but Wilton had had too much work. He'd spent the afternoon absorbed in a quickly escalating conflict between the owners of a small apartment complex and a group of tenants, one tenant a close friend. Jonelle had called, saying they might still be able to come after dinner for a visit. An hour later, she'd called with apologies; they wouldn't be coming at all.

Jason and Von had kept dinner warm for another hour, waiting for Pat to come home. He neither came nor called, and at a quarter to seven, Von and Jason sat down for dinner. Almost an hour passed before Pat's car pulled into the driveway. Von had heated another teakettle of water, and she and Jason were lingering over strawberry shortcake and tea, discussing Wilton's conversation of five days before with Buddy Tarbutton.

Jason hadn't told her of Alan Baxter's apparent involvement. He had told her about the phone taps, though. Wilton had checked the phones while Von was at work the day after his visit to Tarbut-ton's cabin. Sure enough, the phone was tapped.

Then Jason had asked her casually about a day she'd mentioned when the phones had gone dead, a couple of weeks earlier. It was her day off, and Jason was away. She called the phone company from a next-door neighbor's and, surprisingly, a repairman had arrived within minutes. She went to the mailbox and then talked for a few minutes with the wife of the family. When she returned home, the phone repairman was upstairs. He was checking all the phones for shorts, he'd told her later. Oddly, the next day another phone crew had shown up. She'd told them the phones were all right, and they'd left.

They'd told none of this to Pat.

Pat slammed the kitchen door and wove his way into the dining room. Neither Von nor Jason acknowledged his presence as he entered. His tie was undone, his suit rumpled. He hadn't had a haircut in a month, and his hair was matted.

"You've already eaten, then," said Pat.

"We waited until a quarter to seven," Jason replied. "You know what time dinner's served on Wednesdays."

Pat's chest puffed, his hands on hips. "My work doesn't always end on your schedule," he said, slurring the words. "And please accept my apology for interrupting this intimate little moment." He turned to face Von. "Warm me a plate."

She glanced up, incredulous. "Warm it yourself." Then she re-turned to her shortcake and tea.

"I told you to warm a plate of food for me." Pat glared, first at Jason, then at Von. Von tensed. She rose. Without a word, she walked past Pat and toward the hallway stairs.

"Don't you walk away when I'm talking to you!" Pat bellowed.

Von stopped for a second, and then continued toward the stairs. Jason struggled to his feet. Pat lumbered after Von.

"Von!" Jason yelled. She turned as Pat grabbed her shoulder.

"You're hurting me!" she cried.

Jason limped toward them. He grabbed Pat and shoved him.

Pat shoved back. "Keep out of this."

"Get away from Von," said Jason.

Pat caught his brother's head in the crook of one arm. The two struggled, Von's hands to her cheeks, a horrified look on her face. Jason's grip on his brother broke. Pat pressed harder on Jason's neck. Finally, he shoved. Jason staggered away, bumped the dining room table, and fell to the hardwood floor.

"Pat!" Von screamed. "How dare you act like this!"

He strode to her, one hand raised. A sickening smack as the hand struck her cheek. She fell in a heap. Pat bent, prepared to hit her again.

"Stop!" Jason yelled. "Stop it, you're hurting her!"

Pat remained over Von, breathing heavily. "You're damned right I am. She's nothing but a whore. I know what's being going on between the two of you."

Von stirred and began to pull herself to her feet. Pat again raised the hand.

Jason scrabbled to his feet and lunged at his older brother. Pat lifted Jason off the floor and heaved him toward the table. This time Jason's head hit, hard. He clutched the tablecloth as he fell, dragging china, silverware, and serving dishes to the floor. A raw, red spot rose on the back of his head. He lay unconscious.

Von ran for the door. Pat lunged after her but missed. Then she was outside, on the porch. She scrambled down the stairs to the sidewalk.

"Come back here!" Pat yelled. He stood in the main doorway, bracing himself, a menacing hulk, flanked by the stained glass angels.

"No!" Von yelled. I'm never coming back."

"Von!"

"I'm on my way to Mama's, Pat. If you so much as call over there, I'm going to notify the police. Do you understand me?"

"Come here!"

"No, Pat, it's over. I won't ever be back."

"I'll call tomorrow," said Pat, his voice weakening.

"No, not ever. You're very sick, Pat, and you're dangerous. And don't you dare hurt Jason anymore. I swear I'll take out charges against you if you do." With that, she turned, shivering, and ran. Her steps echoed softly as she disappeared.

# # #

David Baker answered the insistent ringing at the front door. He opened to Von, and pulled her into the foyer. "Baby, you're hurt," he said, brushing her hair back to reveal the fat bruise on her left cheek. "What happened?"

She buried her head in his chest and began to cry.

Anna descended the staircase. "David, what is it? Who..." She hitched her sweater at the collar as Von came into view.

"She's been hurt," David called out. He kissed Von's forehead. "C'mon, honey, let's get you into the living room."

She clung to him as he steered her. They sat together on the couch. "It's all right now, honey," he said softly, "nothing's going to happen to you."

Anna stood before them. "David, how did this happen?"

He glanced up. "Get her a glass of water, will you, Annie? Let's get her calmed down before we start asking questions." Anna left the room. He rocked Von back and forth as she sobbed. A moment later, Anna returned.

"Drink this, baby," he said to Von. "You're going to run out of tears if you don't." He tipped the glass for her. After the first sip, she took the glass and drained it.

Anna produced a box of tissues. Von took a handful.

"Oh, Daddy," she whispered, "I'm never going back to that house."

"It's okay, you don't have to."

"We were having dinner, Jason and I. Pat was late; I never know when he'll be home these days."

"You don't have to talk about that," said David. "Just assure me you're all right."

She sniffed and sat up. "I want to tell you what happened."

"Tell us what you want, baby."

"Jason and I were eating dinner when Pat came in." She paused. "We're not doing well, Pat and I."

"I know, honey."

Von daubed at her eyes. "Well, he came in and started being abusive –"

"He hit you."

"Not at first. Some things were said and, well, I got up and started to leave the room. He grabbed me. That's when Jason tried to pull him away. He hit Jason."

"Did he hurt him?"

"It all happened so fast. Pat knocked him down, and that's when he hit me. I must've blacked out. I think he hit Jason again, and I ran. Oh, Daddy, I was so scared."

David glanced to Anna. "I knew this was coming. I think I need to pay Pat Shane a visit. Annie, take care of our daughter while I get dressed."

"No, Daddy," Von said. "You'll just make it worse. Leave him alone until tomorrow."

"Nonsense. Your daddy has a way with bad guys. Besides, I want to see what kind of shape he's in. And I want to check on Jason."

Von nodded. "Bring back some of my clothes, too, will you? I won't stay in that house another day."

At just after ten-thirty, he returned from the Shane home. Anna was waiting on the living room couch, dressed for the night.

"I put Yvonne to bed right after you left, David," Anna said. "She wouldn't talk to me. I gave her a short bourbon, and she went right to sleep."

David dropped a suitcase filled with Von's clothing at the foot of the stairs.

"How are things there, David?"

He sighed as he fell onto the couch beside her. "All right, I guess. Jason was the only one there. He has a swelling on his head, where he hit the dining room table. He's going to have a nasty bruise on that fair skin of his tomorrow, but he's in good spirits.

He insists he can take care of himself. The house is a mess, of course, what with the scuffle."

Anna reached in her robe pocket, produced a silk handkerchief, and patted at her eyes.

He pulled her to him. She began to sob.

"There, there, sweet."

Moments later, she pushed away.

"I'm so sorry, David."

"For what?" He lifted her chin. "I know you love your daughter."

"Do you?"

"Annie, of course I do."

She took his hand. "I felt so helpless, seeing her bruised and upset like that."

"I think you saw the little girl in her again, sweet. A little girl who's become a very strong, durable, woman. Just like her mama."

Anna looked up. "Is that how you think of me, David?"

He ran his fingers through the long, steel-gray hair sweeping over her shoulders. "I think of you as strong, and beautiful, and loving. And I wonder why some men risk losing all of that."

She smiled shyly. "You did risk it once."

"Sometimes," he said, "the perceptive men among us see how powerful love is and we run from it. To our work. To another woman, who can't love us, but who can be our friend, and who help us make sense of all those powerful adult emotions."

"I tried to be a good wife to you, David."

"No, it was me. I was a lousy husband back then. Much the way Pat is now."

"You always came home."

"I loved sleeping with you," he said. "Still do."

"Really?"

"Now more than ever." He brushed her cheek with the back of a hand.

Anna clutched at the lapel of her robe. "We haven't talked like this in a long while."

David smiled and took her hand. "Is that a complaint?"

"You were so tender with Yvonne tonight."

"You're surprised?"

"You seem so aloof from our problems sometimes."

"Aloof?"

"You trivialize everything so, with those silly jokes."

"I'm your emotional foil, sweet."

"After all these years, I'm still not sure I know you, David."

"We went a lot of years without much to say to each other."

"There was your business. It took a long time to build it."

"Our business."

"But it was yours, David. The girls needed me."

"They needed us both. Together. And we didn't often give them that." Looking down, he sighed. "So many things kept us apart. So many things that seemed necessary at the time."

Anna looked away for a moment. "They were excuses, I think."

He took her hand. "Are we letting Von's predicament frighten us? Things, awkward things, things that might've cost us our marriage happened between us, too."

"But we didn't let them come between us, did we?"

"Something to be said for forbearance." David chuckled, and then his expression turned sober. "But our children, look at them. Both with marital difficulties." A wistful look filled his eyes. "Did we fail them? Did we create this, Annie?"

"Life is experience, David, but ours has been so different from theirs. Everything has changed. They live in a world so different from the world we came of age in. We can learn from our children, I think."

David smiled. "And tell me, wise one, what can we learn from this, you and I?" He placed his hand over her breast and gently squeezed.

Anna's face reddened. She looked down, lifted his hand for a moment, and then returned it to her breast.

David leaned forward and kissed her. The couch cushions shifted, and they slipped to the floor with a thud. For a moment, they laughed like embarrassed children.

CHAPTER 23

PARTY NIGHT

Friday, November the seventeenth. Crepe paper bunting of green, red, blue, and white hung everywhere inside the Night Owl. The strips had been intertwined and twisted into spirals and hung between the ceiling light fixtures. Some had been draped over the door and over the plate glass window at the front booths. As a finishing touch, Gus hung some from the ceiling over the counter. "I'll leave it up for the holidays," he told wife Alice. "It'll draw customers."

So far he'd been right. The colorful trappings, up since Tuesday along with the posters around town to announce the party, had drawn a booming business to the Night Owl. Salesmen dropped by, salesmen who hadn't been to Hope before. Residents of Hope who hadn't patronized the Night Owl in years brought their children by for one of Alice's homemade doughnuts or éclairs. Everyone talked animatedly about the party and praised Gus for holding it. As the word spread, patrons of Pat's restaurants, family friends, sympathizers and well wishers from Athens, Lawrenceville, Braselton, and Monroe called to inquire.

"It's for little Emily," Gus would explain, "she's their only child, and the accident was terrible. We had to do something to make 'em feel better." In fact, the sympathetic and the well-wishers became so numerous that Gus and Alice decided to raise funds to defray the family's funeral and medical expenses.

Davis Anderson had stopped by. He'd told Gus he'd have officers present on the street outside and planned to have at least one uniformed officer on duty inside during the party. I won't risk even an argument over this, he'd told Gus.

Pat, who didn't often spend time on the streets and in the businesses of Hope, had been conspicuously present of late. The Night Owl's patrons termed this visibility and Pat's solicitations of sympathy for Emily as thinly disguised efforts to incite feeling against Phil Agee. But Pat never referred to the connection between Agee and Emily's death; instead, he groused about Agee's drinking, about his failing real estate brokerage and the impact that was having on the town. He bragged about the way Von's employer, Agee's only local competitor, was stealing business and agents away.

At three p.m. this day, Gus stood on a ladder pushing a thumbtack through a fallen section of the bunting, now sagging over the counter. Three high school-aged girls sat at the booth nearest the door, singing "Country Girl, Shake It For Me" along with the jukebox. As Pat Shane entered, their singing turned to whispers.

"Looks mighty good, Gus," said Pat.

Gus tugged at the bunting. It remained in place, and he climbed down and shook hands.

Pat turned as he surveyed the decorations. "I'm so excited about all this. Emily would've loved it."

Gus beamed as he absentmindedly wiped his hands on his shirt-front. "I think we need to do more things like this in Hope, don't you, Mister Shane? It's the sort of thing that brings the town together."

"Yep," Pat said, "I couldn't agree with you more." He glanced at his watch. "Well. Just thought I'd stop by for a minute and say hello. The posters say the party starts at eight p.m. That when you want us here?"

"Seven-thirty, if you don't mind. We moved it up, 'cause of the big crowd that's coming, and we thought the family ought to be here early for a reception line." He paused. "Alice was supposed to call y'all about it."

Pat smiled, turned, and left.

Alice approached from the back room and ran an arm about Gus' ample waist. "Mister Shane sure is in a good mood."

Gus nodded. "I sure hope he stays that way."

"Everything'll be fine. You'll see."

Gus smiled and kissed his wife on the cheek.

#

Six p.m. – the town's streetlights began to glow. Light from the blue neon sign atop the Night Owl shimmered as if it too were excited. Gus stacked plates of Alice's homemade pastries on one of three card tables. On another, a fifty-cup coffeemaker perked happily, surrounded by stacks of the diner's plain white coffee mugs, stainless steel pitchers of cream, and bowls of sweeteners. Alice placed large plastic bottles of Coke and ginger ale on the last table. She'd set large trays of the diner's glasses alongside, and a huge cooler of crushed ice sat below the table.

Gus adjusted the jukebox settings so it would play a continuous but random selection of songs. He turned the volume down - just in case there was need for a speech or two.

By seven, the townsfolk began to arrive. The Claxtons sat in a booth with the mayor, chatting as they ate their supper. In another, newspaper man sat with Granny. Schoolteacher had claimed a booth in the far corner, holding hands with a history professor from the university.

At seven-fifteen Pat arrived. He stood in the doorway for a moment, pressing the collar of his open-necked white shirt over his sweater. Then he brushed lightly at his black corduroy jacket and khaki pants. He'd had a haircut that afternoon. As he walked about the diner making small talk and shaking hands, approving comments rose. This was the old Pat Shane, they said.

Pat poured himself a cup of coffee and then hugged Alice. "You and Gus are angels. Absolute angels." He held her hand as he spoke.

Alice looked about. "But where's Missus Shane? She and Emily were so dear to us."

"She's late, isn't she?" said Pat. "But don't let that be a problem. We'll have a fine time, anyway."

At five minutes before eight, Jason, Von, and the Bakers arrived together. Seeing Pat, Von flushed. She stalked her way through the crowd. "I suppose you thought you could ruin this evening, too?"

He glared.

"Alice just called me at Mama's. I didn't know we were supposed to be here at seven-thirty. Alice left a message at the house, didn't she?"

Pat's eyes flickered. "Don't bother me with your little grievances tonight, Von, I want to enjoy this."

The diner had filled to capacity, and the noise was rising.

"You want to enjoy it?" Von sputtered. "This isn't being done for your entertainment, Pat Shane, this is supposed to be a show of sympathy for Emily."

A group of people had begun to gather outside the diner, and the street had become a beehive of celebration. Then the crowd parted for Chief Anderson and two uniformed city policemen. Inside, the three split up. One of the officers poured a cup of coffee and joined the crowd outside.

"Don't talk to me in that tone of voice," Pat said to Von, "I'm not in the mood."

David Baker took Von's arm. "Honey, why don't you try one of the éclairs? Alice made them herself this afternoon." He set himself between the two. "We'll see you in a while, Pat."

Outside, the crowd had moved to the street corner.

"I told you it wouldn't do any good to start a fuss with him, sweetheart," David said to Von.

"I'm sorry, Daddy." She hugged him and then fidgeted with the knot in his tie. "I should've known better. He makes me so angry."

David smiled. "And vice versa. Why don't you mingle a little bit? This gathering is for you, too, you know."

Gus greeted father and daughter. "I was beginning to think y'all weren't coming."

"Alice just called us a few minutes ago," replied Von, "we didn't know –"

"Gus, you outdid yourself," said David. "There are more people here than we had at the Fourth of July fireworks show this year."

Gus beamed. "I sure didn't think this many folks would show up." He glanced to the window. "Got quite a few outside, I see."

David turned. He frowned. "I wonder what's the attraction out there?"

The diner opened, and the outside officer entered. He glanced about for the chief. They conferred, and then both men left the diner.

Minutes later, Jason took a place near the door, eating a doughnut.

The chief re-entered, stopped before Jason, and said, "We need to talk."

"About what?"

"Let's use Gus' back room." The chief started for the rear of the building.

"What's going on?" insisted Jason, limping alongside.

"Potential trouble on the street." Anderson turned the room's doorknob and felt for the light switch. Once inside, he urged Jason into the room. Jason refused.

"What kind of trouble?" said Jason. He turned to eye the diner's front.

"Phil Agee's outside."

Jason's jaw dropped.

"He's drunk. He had some kid drive him over here from Atlanta. He heard about the gathering from someone, don't ask me who. He wants to talk to your brother."

"Oh, man."

"I don't intend to have any trouble over this, so I want you to keep your brother inside until I can get rid of Phil."

Jason laughed. "Chief, I don't have any more control over Pat than you do over Agee."

"You need to try." Anderson strode away.

A loud, angry voice rose from the diner. Then several more voices, all talking excitedly. Jason recognized the loudest: Pat. The chief began making his way through the crowd, but it was too late. Pat had shoved his way outside.

"Jason!" said David Baker, his arm around Von. "It's Phil Agee. Pat's threatening to –"

"Gus!" Jason shouted. He motioned toward David and Anna and Von. "Keep them inside."

Gus nodded. He raised a hand high. "Everybody just stay calm and find a place to sit. Let the police handle whatever's going on out there. Please, don't any of you go outside."

At the end of the block, the crowd had grown to some two hundred. Jason tried to work his way through the throng but couldn't. Ahead, Pat was yelling. Then Phil Agee's and Anderson's voices joined in.

Finally, Jason broke through to the inner circle. The chief stood between the two men, trying to shove them apart. Another policeman, arms around Pat's shoulders, strained to hold him.

Agee backed away, leaned against the front of the white Caprice, a frightened young campaign worker for Senator Baxter behind the wheel. A group of local boys congregated around the Caprice, looking at the huge car, grinning. They drank from bottles inside paper bags. The chief eyed them as they hooted.

"You see what you've done, Davis?" Pat yelled. "The town knows you're protecting a killer."

"Get him out of here," the chief shouted.

"I'm trying, Chief," the policeman cried out. "I need help, get me some backup!"

Pat thrashed furiously.

Phil Agee's angry expression began a slow turn to fear. He backed against the Caprice, hands shaking, eyes wide. "Don't let him get me, Davis, he'll kill me!" He turned and placed a foot on the front bumper of the Caprice, as if he planned to climb atop the car. The young driver scrambled out and elbowed his way to the back of the crowd.

Anderson pushed Pat and the officer toward the Night Owl. "Pete!" he yelled to another officer. "We need backup over here."

Emboldened as the chief and the first officer pushed Pat away, Agee began yelling. "Liar! You're gonn' pay f'your lies, Shane!" Then he staggered toward him. "You ruined my life." He raised his fists. "I'm gonn' kill you!"

When crowds gather in the face of such emotional storms, most stand helplessly stunned and simply watch. But as Pat and Agee yelled, the pair's rage pelted the crowd like sheets of rain. The crowd surged forward. They began to take sides. They yelled, taunted one another. Fistfights broke out. Such moments are impossible to describe: the yells, the awful drench of fear and anger made real. And so the people of Hope unleashed a stream of violence on one another.

The chief scrambled about as the crowd erupted. "Back!" he yelled, waving an arm and pushing at those nearest. "Get back!" He looked around. "Where's Pete?" Then he lunged at Agee, who was now intent on attacking Pat.

Pat had been struggling with the policeman and finally broke free. He sprang toward Agee. Voices rose and fell amid the thump and scuffle of pounding fists and kicking feet. The chief drew his gun, Pat almost on top of him.

"Don't let him hurt me, Davis!" Agee screamed. "Kill him, Davis, kill him!" He caught the chief's gun arm with both hands. They struggled for an instant before the gun discharged. Pat toppled forward. He hung onto the chief and Agee for a moment before falling. Yells swirled.

The crowd surged closer. The chief and his officer began shoving viciously at the crowd, some of whom were fighting back.

Pete made his way to the crowd's epicenter. "Move!" he yelled. He pointed his pistol in the air and fired. "I said move, if you don't want to be arrested!"

"Everybody back!" said the officer who had been holding Pat. He gripped his wooden baton and shoved at those nearest.

The youths, now gleefully drunk, began rocking the Caprice. The crowd backed away. The rocking continued. Then the Caprice turned on its side atop the curb. Glass shattered. Metal groaned.

Two police cruisers lurched to a stop at the corner. Four officers leaped out, waving truncheons. They threw four of the youths to the ground. The others scattered and were gone. Pete holstered his gun and continued shoving at the crowd.

Anderson and his other officer leaned over Pat's limp body. His sweater and pants were soaked with blood.

The chief scrambled to his feet. He grabbed Agee, who had fallen with Pat and was now struggling to stand, threw the drunken man onto his stomach, and handcuffed him.

"How's Shane?" the chief yelled.

The officer glanced up. "Dead."

Anderson jerked Agee to his feet and shoved him toward the officer. "Get him out of here. Book him for murder and then throw him in a cell." He wiped his forehead with the back of a hand. "And get an ambulance over here on the double."

Agee's eyes went wide with fright. "Murder? I didn't do anything. Davis, do something!"

The chief stood to his full height. "I said everyone off the street. Now! Move!" He turned to Agee. "You miserable bastard, you won't cause me any more trouble."

With that, Jason moved away, clung to a telephone pole, his eyes closed. He breathed in deeply. Police officers yelled and shoved, urging the crowd homeward. A wrecker arrived and backed toward the Caprice.

Pete approached Jason. "Sir? Mister Shane? Are you okay?"

Jason's eyes opened wide. He began to sway.

The officer steadied him. "You okay, sir?"

"Yeah," he said. "I'll be okay."

Pete nodded. "Then let's move you back, sir. We need to haul the car away."

Jason glanced to the upended Caprice. He took several steps backward and lost his balance. Pete caught him as he fell. He pulled Jason's arm across his shoulder, and walked him to the Night Owl. Inside, the first booth sat empty. Pete pulled an empty chair to the booth's end and helped Jason sit.

Gus hurried to the booth from the far end of the diner, where David Baker and Von were sitting, arms about one another. Anna sat across from father and daughter, unruffled.

"You need a doctor?" Gus asked Jason.

"Just a glass of water." Jason looked to the officer. "Thanks."

Pete patted him on the shoulder. "Got to get back out there, see if we can get this mess cleaned up."

Jason closed his eyes again and breathed slowly and deeply. He took the glass of water from Gus and drained it.

Outside, the town's paramedic unit had arrived. One medic bent, treating cuts and bruises. Two others, in white coats, were lifting a stretcher holding Pat's body.

A wail from the far side of the diner.

Jason made his way down the row of booths to Von. He bent and hugged her to him.

"It's over, Jason," she whispered, "it's finally over."

"No," he replied. "It's not over yet."

CHAPTER 24

SORTING THINGS OUT

In small towns, the end of tempests such as that of the previous evening rarely means calm. By eleven a.m. the next morning, bedlam reigned at Hope's police station. Phil Agee had been booked and was now occupying one of the three small cells at the station's rear. Reporters from nearby media outlets were questioning Chief Anderson about the death of Pat Shane. Outside, on the street in front of the station, dozens of Hope's residents yelled out questions to the police officers standing just outside. Some wanted news of Phil Agee's fate. Jason and Von had demanded that Pat's body be released quickly by the Barrow County coroner's office, and the more judicious in the crowd kept calling out for the coroner's report. A mobile television unit from an Atlanta station had parked, antenna extended, just around the corner on Clarke Street.

Inside Agee's cell, Doc Shannon, once physician to most of Hope's residents, quietly closed the cell door. Pete stood nearby. The doctor, an elderly man thinned by age, stood erect. His steel-blue eyes took in every nuance of the cell and its occupant.

The doctor turned and smiled. "No need for a sedative. He had enough scotch last night to put a rhino to sleep. All I had to do was get him to calm down a bit, and now look at him. A fire alarm wouldn't wake him." He glanced to the adjoining cell. "Let me get a blanket out of that one, Pete. His body temperature's dropping, and it's cold back here."

Pete took in the loudly snoring Agee. "Hard to believe he set off all that." He glanced in the dayroom's direction, where reporters were still shouting questions at the chief. He opened the cell next to Agee, took the blanket, and handed it to the doctor. Doc Shannon shook out the blanket's folds and covered the sleeping man.

"That about it, Doc?"

The doctor chuckled to himself. "Until he wakes up. Then you're going to have your hands full."

"Something funny, Doc?"

"Not really. It's just that last night was the most excitement this town has seen since the fire of forty-seven." He sniffed. "I was here then, too. We had to rebuild a few buildings after that. But this time resurrecting Hope is going to be much harder."

"Yeah, well, it ain't been much fun so far."

The doctor patted the young policeman's shoulder. "You're doing fine." He stepped away, and for a moment he peered at the young policeman through his bifocals. "You're a good police officer, Pete. I heard nothing but good things about the way you handled your part of it last night."

"It was tough. Knowing all those people, and the Shanes and Mister Agee and all the others."

"But that's when a good police force is at its best. When you know the people, you care about what happens."

"It was hard to know if I – if we – did the right thing last night. It all happened so fast. I keep asking myself, could we have done it differently?"

"There'll always be room for doubt with those you live around and care about."

Pete breathed deeply and whistled out an exhale.

Doc Shannon draped an arm over Pete's broad back. "I'll come back about midafternoon and see how your troublemaker's doing."

They left the cellblock, passing through a large metal door that led to the hallway and the dayroom, where reporters had pressed in close to Chief Anderson.

"And then Philip Agee grabbed your arm –" one of the reporters, a short, stout black man with a northern accent, said to the chief. Other reporters stood, heads bent, scribbling.

"He grabbed my arm with one hand," the chief said slowly, precisely, "and with the other, he placed his index finger on the trigger. Then he fired."

"How was that possible?" asked another reporter, a tall, strikingly beautiful woman, her long, wavy brown hair hanging almost to the belt line of her blue jeans.

"My finger was outside the trigger guard," said the chief. "I had simply drawn the gun in an effort to intimidate Shane."

"Do you always draw your weapon when you're mediating an argument?" the first reporter asked.

"I thought the safety was on. It happened quickly. It was an instinctive reaction. There was no time."

"You pulled your weapon as an instinctive reaction," the female reporter said, holding her tape recorder closer.

Anderson blinked. He was screwing up this interview. He could see the morning's headlines: UNARMED HOPE MAN SHOT BY POLICE. GUT REACTION, SAYS CHIEF.

A woman entered the station. "Excuse me, Chief Anderson," she yelled above the others' questions, "I'm from WSB TV in Atlanta. Are you available for a short segment on the Shane death?"

The chief's cell phone rang. He held up a hand for the questions to stop.

"Chief," said Alan Baxter, "do you have a few moments for me?"

"Yes, of course. I have reporters in my office right now, though."

"Can you get rid of them? It's important."

"I'll put you on hold."

He shooed the reporters. "Okay, folks, that's it for now."

"Chief, just a couple more questions," the male reporter called out.

"We'll file a report late today," said Anderson. "It'll contain all relevant information on the incident. If you want to call later, someone will let you know when it's ready."

"Who's on your telephone line? Is it about the Shane death?" the blue-jeaned reporter asked.

"What do you mean by relevant information?" the male reporter pressed. "Does that mean there are some things you won't be releasing?"

The chief's jaw hardened. "That's it for now." He shooed them again, and then he looked to the television reporter. "I'll meet you outside in ten minutes."

Anderson put the phone to his ear as he strode to his office.

"How's our friend doing?" asked Baxter.

"Sleeping it off. He's quiet as a mouse right now."

"I've already rounded up legal representation for him. As soon as I can, I'll arrange bond and get him out of there."

"That's going to be difficult, sir."

"Oh?"

"Some of our good citizens saw fit to contact GBI last night. There were a couple of agents on my doorstep at six-thirty this morning. He's to be moved to Athens tomorrow, and the GBI is to bind him over to the Feds."

A moment of silence. "What's the beef?"

"Police indifference and negligence. That we caused the riot and the death. They don't like it when citizens complain to the State about local law enforcement agencies. It means they have to stick their noses into local matters, and they don't like being drawn in unless it's supporting some agenda of their own."

Another silence. "What do they know?"

"Don't know. They know what I told them about the death. But you can bet they'll be looking under rocks. Covering their own asses, and all that."

"Don't worry, Davis, it doesn't have to be a problem."

The chief slumped into his chair. One more bit of intrigue to manage, he thought. "How the hell did Agee end up here last night, anyway? You said you'd keep him out of town until we could get this thing managed."

"Why couldn't you keep your man Shane under control, Davis? And did you have to charge Agee with murder?"

"The whole thing happened so fast. He wouldn't leave and he wouldn't shut up. Then he grabbed my arm. The whole thing pissed me off. I shouldn't have had to deal with it."

"I'm pissed, too, Davis. At you. You should have wound this thing up by now. Thank goodness the election's over."

"Senator, footprints have popped up all over the place. It's way too messy."

"You're right, of course. But hang in there, Davis. Let's all keep our cool, and it'll be handled. It just takes time for the wheels to turn. Remember that when you're in the House of Representatives two years from now."

The operative word now is *if*, the chief thought. *I wouldn't be having this conversation if I weren't counting on this creep to help me run for the House.* He slowly expelled a breath. "At least Pat Shane's not a problem anymore."

"There's always that. But back to Agee. I want you to arrange bond."

"Can't do it. I don't know that judge. I don't know how she'll see all this."

"What's your guess? About the bond amount, I mean."

"A couple million, at least. Maybe no bail at all unless I reduce the charges."

"All right. Call me when something breaks. You have someone you can trust to look after this?"

"Me. Just me."

"The fewer the better. Especially now."

"I'll call you as soon as I know something."

"Oh, and by the way, Davis, I was just wondering. Who really pulled the trigger last night?"

A sneer crept across the chief's face. *You son of a bitch,* he thought. *I'm not going to give you anything you can use against* me. In fact, now's a good time to make a point. "You don't really expect me to answer that over the phone, do you, Senator?"

The senator's hearty laugh resounded. "Don't get bitter on me, Davis. There had to be precautions, you know that. Come to think of it, I really don't want to know. Call me."

"As soon as I know something."

# # #

Jason and Von were just rising. It had been a difficult night. There had been visitors until after midnight, and neither Jason nor Von had slept well. Von now sat at the kitchen table, slowly stirring her coffee. Jason limped in, sat, and leafed absentmindedly through the morning paper. Then he propped his head on his hands, face buried in his palms. Von slowly pushed her coffee away.

"How are you this morning, Jason?"

"I'm okay."

"I wish I could say I was."

He let his hands fall to his lap, and he began to stare at a spot on the wall beyond Von. "I should feel something. I should feel relieved. Or guilty. Abandoned. Angry. I should feel something, but I don't."

Von's face twisted. "Jason, why did this have to happen? First Emily and now Pat." She began to cry.

Jason rose, shuffled his way around the table, and hugged her. Her soft sobbing grew louder. She turned and buried her head in his chest. "I'm so sorry," she said when the sobbing had subsided.

"I'm sorry you had to be put through this. Pat was my problem, not yours."

"Well. I'm glad one of us can cry over Pat."

Von pulled a matted tissue from the pocket of her robe. "You loved him, Jason. We both did."

He returned to his seat. "It's probably the lithium. Hard to clean out my tear ducts when I'm taking this stuff."

Von blew her nose. "Honestly, you're so hard on yourself."

A long silence.

"What do you want for breakfast?" she asked.

He turned to check the clock. "You mean lunch. I don't know. I'm pretty hungry. We didn't eat last night, if you remember."

"How about waffles? Waffles and bacon and scrambled eggs. It'll cheer us up."

"You don't need to do that, Von. We can go to the Night Owl."

Von reached and squeezed his hand. "I'm not ready for a crowd."

He smiled. "All right, waffles and bacon and scrambled eggs it is. But I'll help."

A half hour later: The telephone had rung several times while they were eating. They'd ignored it.

"It just occurred to me," said Jason. "You didn't stay with your parents last night."

Von reached across the table and took his hand again. "This is my home, Jason. I wanted to be here. With you."

He didn't remove his hand. "The exile is over. The king is dead." He shook his head. "I'm sorry. That was a tasteless thing to say."

"But it's true." She rose and refreshed her coffee. "Are we going to be able to stay here, Jason?"

"In the house?"

She nodded. "I realized this past week just how much it means to me to be here. I don't know what I'll do if I have to leave it forever."

"There are unhappy memories here, Von."

"What happened last night, well, I don't feel responsible for it."

"Of course you're not responsible. Why should you be?"

"There were so many things in my relationship with Pat to feel guilty about. But as I watched him deteriorate these past weeks, I knew they weren't my fault. Pat did it to himself." She looked away. "Someday soon we'll talk. I need to tell you some things." She leaned forward. "But I want you to know you belong here. I need you here."

For a while, silence hung between them.

"Von, you know I can't stay."

"No?"

"Pat left me nothing. He would never have left me anything. I'd be even more of a burden than I have been."

"But where would you go?"

"I don't know. Somewhere. I'll manage."

Von rose, took him in her arms, and kissed him. "You don't have to leave," she whispered. "Please. Stay here, with me."

He pushed away, hands on her waist. "Just like you Shanes," he said with a weak smile, "always insisting."

"You think I'm being pushy? I don't mean to be."

"I think you're Emily incarnate."

She smiled. "That sounds like a compliment."

"It's most definitely a compliment. Emily was my life."

"Then you'll stay?"

"I can imagine what your mother would say."

"We don't have to listen."

He frowned. "You're really serious about this?"

"I want you here, Jason. With me."

He looked away. "You'll fall in love again. There'll be someone else for you. Someone who can give you a good life."

"All I know is I want you here now, in this house, with me." She bent to kiss him again. This time the kiss lingered.

For a while, they held each other, saying nothing.

"This town will never be the same," he said.

"I know. Neither will you and I."

"It was more than Pat's death. Something changed in this town last night."

She cocked her head. "I don't understand."

"Call it a loss of innocence. Remember when Emily was three? She peeked into your bedroom, and you and Pat were making love?"

Von's face reddened. "Jason!"

"Now, you told me about that yourself."

"I know, but –"

"It's like that, sort of. This town saw a side of itself last night it had never seen before. Pat's death will have the same effect on this town that Emily's had on Pat if we don't get some dirty linen aired. And we better do it quick."

She studied him. "Does this have something to do with Davis Anderson?"

"And others, too."

"But who?"

He turned away. "I need to talk to Wilton. I'm not sure myself what game's being played here. Two heads are better than one, you know."

Von went wide-eyed. "Jason, you know something. Tell me."

"Later. Someday soon we'll have to talk, you know."

"Honestly," she said, half-smiling. "You can be so irritating."

He patted her hand, rose, and hobbled up the stairs to his room.

CHAPTER 25

TIGHTENING THE NOOSE

"My man," said Wilton. "What's going on?"

"Tough night," said Jason. "You have some time for me today?"

"Sure. I'm just sitting around, waiting for lady luck to walk in. Anything in particular?"

Jason paused. They had to be careful with phone calls: they couldn't say too much. But if they said too little, the ones listening at the other end of the phone tap would suspect their cover was blown. "Pat was shot last night. He's dead."

Wilton said nothing.

"I just need to talk," Jason continued. "It's really hard on Von and me right now."

Another, longer silence before Wilton spoke. "Yeah, man, come on down. I'll be here."

A surge of grief; Jason tried to stifle it, but couldn't. His voice cracked as he said, "I can be there in an hour."

"You all right, Jay?"

"Yeah. But let's make it an hour and a half."

"You take care, man."

Jason held the receiver, listening for the usual soft click he'd come to recognize as the phone tap. It was there, in the prolonged electronic deadness. He hung up and slumped against his bed pillows.

His eyes were burning. A lump swelled in his throat, and he gave to grief. An adolescent's loss of parents. Innocence trampled amid the smoke and dust of war. Years of helplessness and depression. And, now, Pat's death. It was as if Pat's final moment had turned from tragedy to gift, as if his death were now serving as the final push, a trigger of sorts, to release the dross of decades. The release was pure; it was primal and cleansing. Tears streamed down his cheeks, dripped from his chin onto his clasped hands. He moaned, and then he screamed. Then something within surged, sweeping him away. But to where? He didn't know.

When the purge was complete, he opened his eyes. As Berg had coached him to do when overcome with his depressive state, he inventoried all aspects of himself: his physical sensations, his breathing. He probed his legs for the tightness Berg believed a symptom of the emotional baggage Jason was still holding onto. Now he noticed none of the usual symptoms. Somehow his senses seemed clearer, sharper. Everything in the room seemed vibrant, alive.

He rose, sat on the edge of his bed and put on his shoes. As he negotiated the stairs, his legs felt stronger. By the time he found his parka in the hall closet and stepped onto the front porch, his breathing had become deeper. A crisp breeze was blowing, and sunshine warmed him. A lone dove cooed in a nearby oak.

# # #

An hour later, he slid onto the couch in the large front room of Wilton's office. Wilton sat backwards in a straight-backed chair, arms folded over the top slat. He listened without interruption as Jason related the story of Pat's death.

"The chief arrested Agee, huh?"

Jason nodded. "He was really pissed at him, that much was apparent. Way more so than I'd ever seen from him before. He's always been such a cool customer, you know?"

"Agee's probably been making life tough for the chief," said Wilton. "I wonder if he arrested him to control the situation, or whether he really means to press charges."

Jason thought for a moment. "I remember Davis saying something to him as he hauled him off: Agee would never cause him any more trouble."

Wilton rose from his chair and began to pace. "Just when I think I'm starting to get a handle on this thing, there's more."

The door from the hallway opened and Jonelle entered, resplendent in a red and black jogging suit. "Are you two as hungry as I am?"

Wilton swept her up in his muscular arms. "Always hungry for you, baby."

She glanced to Jason, rolling her eyes. "He has a one track mind."

Jason smiled.

Wilton turned, eyed Jason. "I've been meaning to comment, man. You look like you're putting on weight."

Jonelle agreed. "You have a good color to you now."

It was true. His appetite had been slowly growing for some time, as had his weight. Doctor Berg had commented on it. This is a healthy sign, the doctor had said. And, yes, he felt better. Better than he had in a long time.

"Not the right flesh tone, though," said Wilton. "We'll have to work on that. Needs to eat more soul food."

"I'll cook for you sometime," said Jonelle. "I'll make some cornbread and turnip greens. And I'll bake a ham."

"We eat that all the time," said Jason. He stood and stretched.

"That's right, I'd forgotten," Wilton said. "He may be a well-to-do white, but he don't eat like most of 'em here in Atlanta, with their mung beans and tofu. He eats like good country folk, black or white."

Jonelle tugged at Wilton's arm. "Come on, you two, let's eat."

"Morrison's again?" asked Jason.

"Cafeteria food's always good," said Jonelle.

"With the old folks," said Wilton. "You always want to eat with the old folks, man."

"You don't have to wash the dishes."

#

After eating, Jonelle dropped them off at the office on her way to the mall. They settled into their seats and the conversation returned to Pat's death.

"The funeral's going to be tomorrow at three p.m. at Pat and Von's church," Jason said. "Von and I would really like for you and Jonelle to come."

Wilton paused, nodded slowly. "Yeah, sure, I'll come. Jonelle said this morning that she wanted to come. We'll be there. Say, what's your gut feel about the circumstances of Pat's death?"

Jason frowned. "What do you mean?"

"I mean, we know a little bit now about what's going on behind the scenes with the chief and the senator, right? And we know what a pain in the ass Pat's been for them, right? Well, it occurred to me that maybe the whole thing was staged to get rid of Pat."

Jason slumped into the couch's back cushions. "No, I don't think so. It was just too crazy." He considered it again and shook his head. "No, no way. It was more like in 'Nam, remember? How the captain always had a battle plan, but it went to hell in the first minute? No, there's no way it could have been worked out the way it happened."

"It was that crazy?"

"In a way, it was like a firefight. Happened all of a sudden, and none of it made sense. The cops were very good at crowd control, though. They had it managed a lot quicker than I would've expected."

"Anderson's good at his job. He knows how to work crowds. All good cops learn that. I found that out in the MPs." Wilton rose from his chair, found the bottle in his desk, and poured a coffee mug half full. He began to pace.

"I think it was an accident," said Jason.

"A convenient accident, I'd say."

"Yeah, well, maybe."

An understanding smile crept across Wilton's face. "If you're right, then maybe the chief was smart enough in the heat of the moment to see a way to dump the whole thing on Agee. Take the heat off the police force and the senator. All their problems go away in one evening of hell raising."

"Maybe," Jason said.

"Maybe, hell. It makes sense. But we've gotta find a way to keep the heat on Agee and Baxter and the chief without getting our butts in a crack, and we gotta do it fast."

"Right. Once Agee's before a jury, we'll never be able to press a case against Baxter. He and Davis will be in the driver's seat forever and ever."

Wilton sipped from his mug. "So what do we have so far?"

Jason shrugged. "Well, you know that better than I do."

"We got the telephone number for Agee's room at the Residence Inn in Duluth. We got Pat's testimony that he saw the same number on a written telephone message from Alan Baxter to the Hope police department." He stopped pacing and turned to Jason. "You gotta get to the police station, pronto, Jay. We need a copy of that memo."

"But I thought it was too circumstantial to be useful. That could be explained away any number of ways."

Wilton took his seat, leaned forward. "We're building a case, man. Its main value is it's the only real piece of evidence that ties Agee and Baxter and Emily's death together. And it's in the police file. It shows that someone there knows something we don't, and they're not doing anything with it. It'll help us make a dent in their credibility." He sipped. "We have the invoice Pat ripped off from the body shop. It has the same telephone number on it, and Agee's name. That only involves Agee and his car, but with the police memo we begin to make a circumstantial case, you see?"

"All right. I guess so."

"And maybe we can use the memo and the receipt to do some arm twisting at the body shop. We might find us a smoking gun yet."

"We've also got Buddy Tarbutton's testimony," Jason said. "That's all we need, don't you think?"

Wilton set his mug on the coffee table. "It could be challenged in court. Maybe Tarbutton has some axe to grind that we don't know about."

Jason shifted, leaned forward. "But you have a draft copy of Buddy's report. And you've got the tape you made at his place, with the story at The Woof the night of Emily's death. Any lawyer for the other side would be hard-pressed to have a jury ignore that."

"A halfway competent lawyer would notice that the draft didn't have a date stamp. Like I said, Tarbutton's story could be made to look like some kind of grudge against the chief because he took the case away."

Jason shook his head. "You sure are good at invalidating your own evidence."

"It's mileage, man. I've had slick lawyers do it to me in court." He walked to the large window at the front of the room and gazed out. Daylight was beginning to dim. "A thought on the tape. A lawyer might ask whether the tape was made with Tarbutton's permission. Tarbutton could say no, and it wouldn't be admissible. But maybe we could approach him with it now. He didn't seem to mind us using the draft report and his name if we could get the case into court." Wilton shook his head. "But what if Baxter's a step ahead of us? The chief and Baxter know what Tarbutton knows. They'd probably try to bump him off if they figured they couldn't keep him quiet."

"You really think they'd try that? I'm still having a hard time believing they're capable of all this."

"And that's what they'd have going for them in court. A competent chief of police and a well-respected state senator, unjustly accused. But back to Tarbutton. If they're a step ahead of us, they've already leaned on Buddy, told him if he cooperates with us in any way, he'll be dog food."

Jason sighed. "You're right. Without his corroboration, the court would have no reason to believe Buddy's visit to The Woof ever occurred. Voice identification technology isn't considered reliable, I know that much. The defense could say we had someone make the tape for us."

Wilton nodded. "You're catching on, Jay. The law ain't necessarily just."

Jason rose. "I need to use the john." He smiled. "But don't forget Wanda Claxton and Donna Miller. They saw things, remember."

"All viable parts of the case, man," Wilton called after him. "We won't throw their testimony out, at least not yet."

Jason returned and sat. "So you're saying at this point all we really have going for us is the telephone memo."

"No. I just remembered something. We've got one other loose end we need to chase down."

Jason frowned, not following.

"You remember on the Tarbutton tape? There was this guy he talked to at The Woof."

"Yeah. What was his name?"

"Jake. We need to talk to this Jake guy." An exuberant look spread across Wilton's face. "You think it's a lost cause, but we're close to making a case. I can feel it."

Jason leaned back. "Will, I only have another five hundred dollars in my savings. And with Pat gone, neither Von nor I have enough money to hire a lawyer. The house is hers, at least for now, but I can't ask her to mortgage it."

"Look, man," said Wilton, "you've paid me all you could. I know that. And I knew going in that I wasn't going to get into a higher tax bracket off you. If we chase down this Jake guy, and it's a blind alley, then that's it. That's all I can realistically do for you, regardless of how much bread you got." He set thumb and forefinger a fraction of an inch apart. "But we're that close to something. So be cool."

"I hate putting you in this position. I don't want you working for free."

"It's okay, man. I want to do it."

Jason sighed. "Part of what I'm trying to say is that even if we find Jake and talk him into testifying to something or other and make Tarbutton's testimony ironclad, Von and I won't be able to afford a lawyer."

Wilton closed his eyes, rubbed his forehead. "How much of this does Von know?"

"She knows about the taps. She figures Anderson did it, but I didn't tell her that. And she doesn't know about Baxter's involvement. I didn't want her put in any unnecessary danger."

"That's cool, man, let's keep it that way. I know a lawyer who might take the case for next to nothing, maybe for free. He's a brother, name of Anthony Brewer. I've seen him in court before, and he's good. A young guy, trying to establish a reputation." He nodded. "Yeah, I think he may be the ticket. But first we gotta find Jake."

"All right, let's find this guy. If you get something really good from him, I'll agree to talk to this lawyer of yours." Jason grinned. "Okay, now I'm feeling it. We're going to solve this thing."

"Solid." Wilton clapped his friend's shoulder.

# # #

Sunday dawned bright and cold. Leaves drifting from their perches were the only blemishes on the day's clarity. The Edgewood Baptist Church sanctuary had been unusually somber at Sunday morning services, and then later at Pat's funeral, as if under a cloud. The townsfolk seemed afraid to speak, lest something erupt again. Reverend Sims' eulogy had been brief and subdued. They'd buried Pat in the family plot among the rolling hills in back of the church. Afterward, as is the custom, the congregation retired to the Shane home for a buffet dinner and reception. Even then, when food usually brightens spirits, few smiled, and even fewer made conversation. They simply ate and went home.

On Monday, Von returned to work. Jason sat alone at home, reading and waiting for word from Wilton. Wilton didn't call until Monday night. He'd returned to The Woof, making sure not to be there on bartender Vince's shift, and he'd asked around about Jake. Jake hadn't been in that day, but Wilton had unearthed the location of a dilapidated boarding house, just down the street where Jake was supposed to be living. He'd found Jake's room, but no Jake. So on Tuesday, Wilton would stake out the place.

He'd also found out that a hearing had been set in District court for Agee, the hearing to be held on Friday, the day after Thanksgiving.

# # #

The next morning at ten a.m., Wilton sat in his Taurus across the street from Jake's boarding house. He had a good description of Jake, and he was sure he could recognize him. It was almost two-thirty that afternoon when a city bus stopped at the corner, and a man fitting Jake's description climbed off.

Sure enough, the man made his way up the boarding house steps. Wilton spoke into his recorder, clambered out of the Taurus, and crossed the street. He found Jake on the second floor, fumbling with his door key. He approached, Jake unaware until they were side by side.

"Hey, brother," Wilton said, "are you Jake?"

Jake wheeled, his forehead home to a large bump. A number of scabbed-over abrasions covered his chin and cheeks, his eyes swollen with fear. His adam's apple bobbed up and down. He was trying to speak, but couldn't. "Who...who...?" was all he could manage.

Wilton grabbed the gaunt man by the shoulders and steadied him. He reeked of body odor and cheap wine. His gray hair had been cropped short and his face was as wrinkled and leathered as that of an Arizona cowboy. Wilton had seen many of his kind before: dissipation had rounded his shoulders, giving the effect of lost height. He looked to be in his mid-sixties, but Wilton guessed him to be in his early forties.

"Hey, be cool, man," Wilton said, "I'm not here to hurt you." He smiled. "I need some information, that's all." He reached down and turned the key, already inserted in the lock, and opened the door. The foul smelling room sat cluttered with dirty clothes, take-out food packages, and empty wine bottles. Wilton pushed him into the room and shut the door.

Jake cowered against the wall. "I...I...don't know nothin'. Tell Vince I don't know nothin'!"

Wilton frowned. "Vince? The bartender?"

Jake nodded.

He gently touched the bump on Jake's head. "Vince do this?"

Jake nodded again.

"All right, sit down, on the bed."

Jake did as he was told, still shaking.

"I'm a friend of the cop, the big guy from Hope." No response. "He told me that you'd IDd a man for him."

Jake shook his head. "No...I don't know nothin'. I didn't see nothin'!"

Wilton knelt, his face inches from Jake's, trying to avoid his fetid breath. The man's teeth showed gaps, the gums raw, evidence of recently missing teeth. "Look, man, what you saw is very important. An innocent man may go to jail unless you tell me what you know."

"I can't –"

"You don't have to worry about anybody but me. I can get protection for you. The GBI can protect you."

Jake's eyes opened wide. "They were there. They watched Vince beat me up. I don't know nothin'!"

"The GBI watched this guy Vince beat you up?"

Jake nodded. "They was in plain clothes, but they was GBI."

"How do you know?"

"I know 'em. I seen 'em with the senator around town, in uniform. They was his guards, or somethin'."

Wilton sighed. "All right, Jake." He pulled out his wallet and extracted a pair of twenty-dollar bills. "You'll be okay, you understand?" He held out the bills. "You take this, get cleaned up, do your wash, and get yourself some food."

Jake reached cautiously. Then he snatched the bills.

"I got eyes on you, so if I hear about you buying any booze with this money, I'm coming back. This time it'll be me that works out on you, you understand?"

Jake nodded.

"You forget you ever saw me, and you get yourself fed and cleaned up. If you do that, you'll never hear from me again. You got it?"

Jake nodded again.

Wilton rose and set a hand on Jake's shoulder. "You take it easy, man."

He turned and left. He climbed in his car, slammed the door, and drove the three blocks to The Woof.

He shut off his engine. No other cars there. Inside, he took a moment to look about, saw only the worn bar, the barstools and the empty, barely lit booths. An array of bubbling neon lights hung on the wall behind the bar, giving the place an eerie feel. A man emerged from the back room carrying a case of beer. Even in the poor light, Wilton knew the broad shoulders, curly black hair and swarthy complexion.

Vince eyed Wilton, set the case of beer on the bar. He reached beneath the bar as Wilton vaulted it. Wilton shoved him against the plank wall with one arm and grabbed his pistol hand with the other. He smashed Vince's hand against the planks. The gun fell to the floor with a clatter.

"You always pull guns on customers?" he growled, hands on Vince's throat. He kicked the gun away.

Vince swung a ham-like fist. Wilton moved with the punch. He caught the arm, threw him to the floor. A grunt, as Vince bounced on the concrete.

It took a moment for the bartender to regain his breath. Wilton had a foot in Vince's crotch, a hand on his throat.

"Let me know when I have your attention, man," said Wilton. "And while you're at it, realize that I can crush your balls and your windpipe at a second's notice."

Vince tensed to struggle. Then his eyes widened as Wilton's foot began to apply pressure. The struggling ceased.

"What you want with me, nigger?"

Wilton laughed. "You call me that? Then what should I call someone who beats up old men, huh?" He pressed Vince's windpipe. The barkeep's face swelled, the veins in his neck bulging. "You like having the power of life and death over someone, huh? What's it feel like to be on the other end?" Wilton jerked his hand away.

Vince swooned, almost losing consciousness before he could gasp in air.

"Now, listen, man. Jake isn't going to say a word. Your whipping made sure of that. So I'm afraid you're going to have to do all the talking." He reached in his shirt pocket and pulled out the tiny tape recorder. He set it on the floor and pressed the record button. "This is November the twenty-first, at The Woof, and I'm talking to Vince, the bartender." He looked down. "Vince, I want you to tell me one thing. There was a man named Phil Agee here on the night of October the fourth. You know the night I mean. A man came in here and took Agee away. I want you to tell my machine who that man was, and I want you to tell me how the two of them left here. In exact detail." He leaned forward slightly, pressing Vince's crotch.

"Yeah, sure," Vince croaked.

"Nice and easy, Vince. Just the facts." Wilton rocked forward on Vince's crotch.

"Okay, okay, I know the night. It was the senator. He was here. –"

"Senator who?"

"Baxter. He came in about five or so. He talked to this guy, Agee, and they argued. Agee was drunk. The senator helped him to his car. He'd come in another car. He told the driver to leave, and he put Agee in his own car and drove off."

"That it?"

"That's all I know."

Wilton pressed down again with his foot.

"Honest! That's all I know."

Wilton picked up the recorder and turned it off. "Okay, now we need to talk, off the record. I still got your attention?"

Vince nodded.

"I did some checking on you. You've done a hitch in reform school at Alto. And you did seven years, courtesy of the State of Georgia, at Reidsville. Assault with intent to kill. Despite all that, I think you're a smart guy, Vince. I think you know this tape, whether or not it can stand up in court, can put you back in the joint, especially if I turn it over to the Feds. And I bet the good senator won't even care. You agree?"

"Yeah."

"This is off the record, remember, so tell me why you're protecting the senator and why you beat up old Jake."

"Asshole!" Vince growled. "You're gonna send me up anyway, ain't you?"

"No, man. If there's a game being played here, it's all yours. I just want the information."

Vince closed his eyes and exhaled. "All right, I'll tell you."

Wilton put the tape recorder back in his pocket, pushed the record button as he let it drop.

"The senator came back that same night," said Vince. "He paid me to keep quiet."

"How much?"

"A lot. Two thousand bucks."

"Just to keep quiet?"

"Yeah. I didn't know he killed that little girl! It was two weeks before I figured out what happened."

"Will you testify to that in court?"

Vince turned away. "No! I can't. He'll have me killed."

"Senator Baxter will have you killed?"

"Yeah. Those two goons of his, the two GBI guys. They'll kill me if any of this gets out. You gotta believe me!"

"Do you really believe the senator would have you killed?"

"I know he would. They made me beat up old Jake. They told me if he said anything about seeing the senator here that night, they'd kill him, and then they'd kill me."

Wilton lifted his foot from Vince's crotch. "Like I said, man, it's your game to play. If you say nothing about this visit, no one else will know, unless I can get this into court. Then I'll use the tape, but by then Baxter will be arrested. I'm only holding you account-able for knowing the senator was here that night, and that he paid you to keep quiet. If the law comes after you, I'll do what I can to make the court believe you didn't know you were covering up a crime. Is that cool?"

"Yeah," said Vince.

"Then you take it easy. And remember this, before you run to Baxter. You don't owe him a thing. He's the one who threatened to kill you, not me."

Wilton rose, picked up the gun, and left Vince sitting on the floor behind the bar. Seconds later, he was on his way home.

CHAPTER 26

JAIL TIME

Wednesday, the twenty-second of November. Stale air filled the visiting room of the old city jail in Atlanta, the only window a two-foot square hole, filled with a pane of grimy glass. On the window's outside, five vertical steel bars had been fixed in place – a reminder of the building's function. The fifty year-old building was more than unkempt; it was deteriorating. The plaster in the visiting room had yellowed and cracked, the linoleum tiles on the floor worn and dirty. Dents of various sizes and a grungy coating of handprints, cigarette grime, and dirt covered the room's steel door and wire-reinforced window. Phil Agee and Alan Baxter sat at a squat, gray-painted steel table. It had been caved slightly in its middle from years of pounding. Its paint was flaking off, exposing rusty metal, onto which years of telephone numbers, names, and various doodles had been scratched.

On Tuesday, the chief of the Athens police force had requested that Agee be transferred to Atlanta. His jail was overcrowded, and he had no interest in managing as controversial an inmate as Phil Agee. So that afternoon, the City of Atlanta Police Department had taken him. The normal place of incarceration, the newer

Pretrial Detention Center, had filled to capacity, which was why Agee was being held, within sight of the golden dome of the State Capitol, in this stale, ramshackle old building.

The hearing had been moved up and had been held this morning. The judge had bound Agee over for trial, principally on the testimony of Police Chief Davis Anderson. The lawyer Alan Baxter had provided was a good one, but the judge, given Agee's DUI record, was in no mood to put him on the streets again. At his lawyer's urging, Agee would submit to psychiatric and medical examination to determine the degree of his alcohol dependence.

The lawyer had been careful to remind the court that nothing revealed in the examinations, beyond Agee's state of substance dependence, could be held against him in court. And he'd further demanded the right to review any transcripts or doctor evaluations. The judge had agreed; her final determination on bond would be postponed for two weeks, pending the psychiatrist's findings.

Agee and Baxter sat facing one another on mangled metal chairs. They were alone. A policeman stood guard on the opposite side of the room's steel door.

Despite the room's dearth of heat, Agee was sweating. He continually pulled at the collar opening of his buttoned blue work shirt. His feet swept back and forth.

The senator crossed one leg over the other, leaned back, and draped an arm over the back of his chair.

A small plastic pitcher of tap water sat on the table, and a stack of paper cups. Agee periodically poured a cup full and drank it in a single gulp. As the two men talked, he wiped his forehead with a shirtsleeve.

"Alan," he said, his voice low and rasped, "you've got to get me out of here. I don't think I can make it another day. That judge, she just doesn't know me as well as you. I won't get in trouble, you know that. Jesus, I need a breath of air!"

The senator smirked. "What you mean is you need a drink."

"Yeah, I really could use one, Alan. Just one. Can you arrange it? Just to calm my nerves?"

The senator re-crossed his legs, "You know I can't do that, Phil. This is a jail, for crying out loud."

"I know, I know, Alan. It's just that it's awful in here. It's cramped and dirty, and I can't sleep. I'm climbing the walls. Please, you gotta do something."

"All I've been doing for six weeks is getting you out of scrapes," the senator said. "You've put my career in jeopardy, and now I'm going to have to spend big money to keep the damage to me under control. Who do you think is paying for your legal representation?" He turned away in disgust. "The least you can do is shut up and be patient."

"I've got a business to run, Alan. My business is suffering. I've got to get home, see if I can get things back on an even keel."

Baxter leaned forward, gripped the table with both hands. "What you need to do is to stay here, to shut up, and let my people do their job. Anyway, you hardly have a business to go back to."

Agee held his face in his hands. "I know. I know I could have spent more time with it. But as soon as I get out, I'll get it back running again." He groaned through his fingers. "Alan, do you really think I have a drinking problem?"

The senator pounded the table. "You've been drinking almost nonstop for two years. You've been like this since Brenda left you. Why did she leave you, Phil? Do you remember why she left you?"

"She said I drank too much."

"That's right. And you weren't this pathetic back then." The senator leaned back in his chair once more. "You had better face the reality of it. You're a drunk."

"You're right, Alan, I need help. Please, help me."

"You're a grown man, Phil. I can't watch you every minute of the day." Baxter paused to take in the distraught man. "Look at what you've done in the last six weeks. You've run over a little girl in Hope. The whole town's on the verge of warfare over it."

"I don't remember doing that, Alan. Why does everyone keep saying that?" Agee slowly shook his head, tears streaming down his face. "I wish I could remember."

"That's exactly my point. When you drink, you don't remember things. And now look what's happened. You've shot the little girl's father, and you're under arrest for murder. For the life of me, I can't figure out how you managed to screw up so bad."

The door opened and the guard, a bulky man, entered and set hands on his hips. "I can only give you five more minutes, Senator. We have others who need the room."

The senator looked up and nodded. The guard left.

Agee muttered, wiped at the sweat and tears with both sleeves. "It wasn't like that, the Shane guy being shot, it was an accident. You've got to believe me."

The senator's mouth tightened to a thin smile. "Then what do you think happened?"

"I know I was drinking. Don't you see? That's why I took the kid from your staff with me to the Night Owl. He had to drive for me. But I didn't kill the little girl."

"All right, give me your version of what happened in Hope."

Agee gulped down another cup of water. "I went there to mend fences, to extend my sympathies, you know? I wanted Shane to know I didn't kill his daughter."

"All evidence to the contrary."

"And then, all of a sudden, Shane was out there in the street, threatening me. Davis pulled his gun, and I thought he was going to protect me, Alan. But he didn't do a damned thing. Shane just kept on coming."

The senator leaned forward. "Tell me then, how did you manage to shoot Pat Shane?"

Agee looked wildly about the room before he settled again on the senator. "That's what I've been trying to tell you, Alan. I didn't shoot him."

His voice had risen. The senator held a single finger to his lips and nodded toward the door.

"I yelled at Davis to help me, to keep Shane away –"

"You wanted Anderson to kill him," the senator said, "You said you wanted to kill him yourself, and then you kept screaming, 'kill him!'"

"I was scared, that's true, but I didn't really want him to shoot the guy. I grabbed Davis' arm, down by the wrist, so he wouldn't, but I never touched the gun. Honest."

"How can you be sure?"

"I remember, don't you see? I remember that much. I was pulling at his arm with both hands, and then the gun went off. That's the way it happened."

The door opened, and the guard reentered. He stood silently, the door open.

"I need to go," Baxter whispered. "You get yourself dried out and calm down. Ask the doctor for a sedative. Just relax. But I need to tell you something."

Agee looked away.

"Look at me, Phil."

Agee turned, eyes downcast.

"You've been drinking too much, you're not thinking right. Your memory is only there in bits and pieces." He placed a palm against Agee's fleshy face and pressed until Agee looked at him. "You're in trouble, Phil, big trouble. There are at least five people ready to testify to Anderson's version of what happened when the gun discharged. No one, I repeat, no one, saw it the way you just described it." He sighed. "Chief Anderson and I will help you, but you've got to trust us. So relax and let us do what we can."

Agee's head hung. "All right, Alan."

The senator smiled. "Today was only a minor setback. Everything will be all right, you'll see."

Agee didn't look up.

The senator rose and walked past the guard. Once outside the building, he stood for a moment, breathing deeply. The tense, stale smell of the jail was still with him, and he wanted to remove even the memory of it. It was mid-afternoon; the bustle and clatter of rush hour had not yet begun. He walked the windy block down Piedmont Avenue to the parking deck where he'd left his car. Minutes later, he circled the State Capitol and merged into the northbound interstate traffic. He kept an apartment in Duluth, near the Residence Inn at which Phil had stayed. He had work to do, preparing for the legislative session, but dealing with Agee had left him drained. He'd go to Duluth, catch a quick nap, eat, and call his wife. Then he'd come back to his campaign headquarters suite at the Marquis, which was in the process of being closed down. It would be quiet there now. All the staffers had been sent home for the holidays. He'd make a few phone calls, read through drafts of proposed legislation for the January session, and he'd relax. Just enjoy the quiet, the solitude, and relax.

# # #

Eleven o'clock that evening had passed. The senator took off his glasses and pushed back his chair. He'd made his phone calls. His mind had gone blank somewhere in the midst of the draft legislation's tedious wording. He rose, stretched, and poured a scotch from the bar in the anteroom. He took a sip, felt its warmth. He'd foregone dinner after his nap, and the scotch was making him woozy. He rose and rubbed his neck as he walked about the suite. When the scotch worked, as it was working tonight, it usually spared him the intense headaches that usually accompanied his most stressful days.

And this day had indeed been stressful. Despite the albatross Phil had become, the senator was reconsidering his decision to throw his friend to the wolves. He walked to the broad window and surveyed the skyline below him. So much had changed in the past thirty-odd years, since he'd graduated from law school at the University of Georgia. Atlanta wasn't just the central city of the Southeast any more; now it was a mature, world-wise metropolis, long past its adolescence, with all the sophistication of New York, Los Angeles, Chicago, and Houston.

Just look at the architecture, he thought. The trends are being set here in Atlanta. Business comes to Atlanta now, not the other way around. And, despite the grumblings of old money and those preferring a return to the bygone era of a friendlier, smaller Atlanta, these changes were good for all of Georgia. Change was good: that was his mantra as he worked the good old boy network each spring in the Legislature.

And, damn it, he thought, I've been a part of it. I've been a major player in putting Atlanta and Georgia on the map. As much as the death of the little girl bothers me, as much as I hate hanging the whole thing on Phil, I'm not going to let a freak accident ruin the chance to continue my work. He took a long drink. For all its imperfections, The System, as he called the ever-present but informal network of power, influence and money, had created all of this. A brave and beautiful city. I think it was Henry Grady, a post Civil War newspaperman, who first spoke that phrase. And now The System's rewarding me, Alan Baxter, with the governorship of the State of Georgia.

Far off, to the northwest, beyond the place where the Interstates split apart, in a quiet neighborhood of elegant and expensive old homes, stood the Governor's mansion. He couldn't see it from his vantage point, but it was there. Waiting. The scotch was working its magic; he felt its giddiness. For a moment, he closed his eyes.

Suddenly the image of that night in Hope returned. He heard the thump and the little blonde girl's cry as Phil's Caprice hit her bicycle, throwing her into the power pole. As much as he tried, he couldn't make the image go away.

What had happened? For all Baxter's characteristic attention to detail, even he wasn't completely sure. He'd arranged to pick up Phil from that fleabag bar he always seemed to gravitate toward on the west side of Athens. Phil had called him at home from there, talking loudly. Why had he even responded to Phil's call? Now, he didn't know. Perhaps it was simply the habits born of their difficult friendship. Or maybe he was afraid Phil would, once again, be picked up for drunk driving in Baxter's own hometown. Another embarrassment for me and for the city of Athens, he thought. And several months in jail for Phil, unless I stuck my neck out once more to get him off. How ironic. Phil's in jail anyway, and he's still a political embarrassment.

Baxter drained his glass. One other possibility occurred, one he'd always evaded – until now. Perhaps he'd come to Phil's rescue that night because he enjoyed controlling him. Maybe he liked getting away with things. Maybe he wasn't concerned with Phil at all. Maybe he enjoyed pulling strings so much that he was addicted to it. In the State Senate, he had to do it; it was part of the political tug of war as the Legislature struggled to represent the will of the people. Maybe control is my addiction, he thought.

He set the glass on a small mahogany table and rubbed his temples. He was getting a damned headache anyway.

He'd intended to simply take Phil home that night, make sure he was safe. That was it. No big deal. Once again he saw Phil sitting beside him in the Caprice, slumped against the door on the rider's side, almost asleep. But the effects of alcohol were always unpredictable, and Phil had suddenly come to life as they'd entered Hope. In his stupor, Phil had seen fit to continue their argument over his ability to drive. He'd grabbed the wheel. The car had swerved, near the intersection of Farmer Road and Claiborne.

I had to hit the drunk son of a bitch, the senator thought. He wouldn't let go of the steering wheel. He was up on his knees in the seat, trying to get between the wheel and me. He smiled now as he thought about it. I punched Phil pretty hard; my hand was swollen for almost a week. And it was amusing now that Phil didn't recall any of that, even the knockout punch.

The senator frowned as the ensuing details returned from memory. He'd grabbed the wheel, the Caprice very nearly out of control. And then he'd heard the thump. He saw the bicycle and the little girl hurtling toward the power pole. It had been one of those moments when time seems to stand still, allowing the full impact to fully imprint on the mind. As he righted the car, he saw her blonde head hit, and then her legs seemed to wrap around the pole. He knew in that moment that the little girl, whoever she was, would die.

"I didn't see her," he said aloud. He looked around to see if anyone had heard, and then he shook his head. He'd called Phil's cousin Willis and had him drive the Cadillac back to the senator's home. Baxter had then driven Phil to the Agee family homestead, just west of Athens, where Phil had been living alone since the divorce. He'd managed to drag Phil into the house and heave him onto the couch. He'd planned to take the Caprice back to Athens in order to keep Phil from driving any more. Instead, as he'd realized the full impact of what he'd done, he'd called Willis again.

Willis had met Baxter at Phil's an hour later in his own car and drove the senator home. Early the next morning, Baxter and Willis had returned to Phil's home. After inspecting the Caprice, Willis had asked how the damage happened. The senator had told him Phil began to fight, just as he'd neared Phil's home, and Baxter had run into a fence post. Willis, who wanted to keep Phil's drinking problems quiet, suggested the body shop in Gainesville. He knew the owner, Randall Jackson, an occasional fence for stolen cars. The business is otherwise legit, Willis had told the senator. I know we can keep him quiet.

Baxter took off his shoes and lay back on the couch. The headache was still there. Maybe this would help.

When he and Willis had returned from Gainesville and the body shop, Phil was awake and drinking. Realizing quickly that Phil had no memory of the night's earlier hours – much less the accident – Baxter had sent Willis out so he could talk to Phil alone. He'd reconstructed events of the accident for his hapless friend. Phil had insisted on driving home. Baxter had agreed only if he followed Phil, so he'd hung back at a distance in the Cadillac. He'd seen Phil hit the little girl. Phil had driven on. As far as Baxter could tell, there had been no witnesses. I'll do what I can to make this go away, he'd told Phil; the car's in Gainesville being repaired. Just keep quiet, and it'll be handled. And unless you want to go to jail, don't breathe a word of this to anyone, especially Willis. After that, Phil had cried at the thought of killing the little girl, and Baxter had known his friend had bought the lie.

There had been witnesses, of course, and an increasingly difficult trail to brush away. Rumors of Agee's involvement had quickly reached Athens, and Baxter had had to assure Willis that his cousin hadn't hit the Shane girl, that it had been someone driving through Hope. Once Willis had bought the alibi, Baxter had started using him to keep tabs on events surrounding the police investigation. Don't bother the police directly, he'd warned Willis. Baxter didn't trust Davis Anderson, but Davis was ambitious, and ambition could always be manipulated. Just poke around quietly. Ask some questions. Help me keep my thumb on the pulse of this thing. From there, it had escalated, culminating in the death of Pat Shane.

The senator thought again of the accident. Why do things like this happen? No matter, he thought. The important thing's to stay the course. I can't let a freak accident spoil everything I stand for. Everything I can yet do for the State of Georgia. But now his mind was clouding; he looked at his watch – well past midnight.

The whole damned thing was Phil's fault. I was only trying to help a friend. Yes, it's best that Phil take the rap. Maybe time in the federal pen will be the catalyst to make him straighten out what's left of his life. No real harm's been done, so far at least. I'm good at damage control. Baxter smiled dreamily as he closed his eyes for the last time that night. Damage control. It was a tool of survival for politicians.

CHAPTER 27

DECISIONS

Wilton's office and residence sat darkened that night, except for the single light shining over his desk. Jonelle was spending the night with her parents in a nearby suburb, so he was taking advantage of the time to page through his computer notes, searching for a clue, some perspective, some stone not yet upturned that would break the Emily Shane case open.

Earlier that evening, he'd bought a small portable radio-tape player, which he'd placed on the file cabinet beside his desk. A local jazz station played quietly. The holiday season was here, and he'd figured he should get a jump on laying in holiday spirits, so he'd also been to the package store. He'd stuck a fresh bottle of Jack Daniels in his desk drawer. Then he'd set a half gallon bottle of vodka and a bottle of brandy beside the radio. He and Jonelle usually threw parties at this time of year, and someone was always showing up at odd times for a drink. He'd also bought a case of beer, now cooling in the refrigerator, and several bottles of wine, stored out of sight in a kitchen cabinet.

He rose and placed a copy of the Buddy Tarbutton tape in the portable player, switched off the radio, and pressed the play button. As the deep, slow voice began, he turned it up so he could hear while grabbing a beer. With his beverage in hand, he fell once more into his chair, the tape droning on.

It finished, and he rewound it halfway, replaying Buddy's telling of his visit to the bar. Then he cued up his own tape synopsizing his visit with Jake. Finally, he played the tape he'd recorded at The Woof, and relived his visit with Vince.

Jake and Vince were variations on a theme he'd come across many times in his work: hoods putting muscle on bystanders to their crimes, even those with less direct knowledge of the crimes. I should be used to it by now, he thought. I shouldn't be this pissed off about old Jake getting busted up. Most like Jake were meek, easily intimidated individuals who had simply happened by and been seen around the wrong someone at an inopportune time or place. All Wilton had to do was remind these hapless people that they weren't alone. That they could be protected, their testimony used to bring justice. But he also realized Jake could never be convinced to testify, and neither could Vince, for that matter. True, they were different strains of streetwise losers, but they knew the threats against them were all too real.

Wilton sipped from his beer and leaned back. The unfolding events disgusted him, though he'd never expected much of politicians such as Baxter; they were servants of the rich, the elite. Everyone knew that. Even the growing number of inner city blacks being elected to city councils and state legislatures knew who buttered their bread.

Wilton had never been that intimately connected with the processes of politics, but he'd seen the changes wrought in those who were. He thought of the woman from his neighborhood in Charlotte who, back in the sixties, had marched with Doctor King in Alabama. After the deaths of King and Bobby Kennedy, she'd run for political office and had won. In that office, she'd been a woman of no little virtue. For many years, she'd represented her people well in the state legislature.

Then, abruptly, she'd run for her district's house seat in Washington, had won, and almost overnight her political postures had changed. She was less radical; she'd moved her family out of their old neighborhood and into an upscale suburb. Why the change of heart? Where had the money come from? How did she explain the sudden loss of effectiveness as she quickly ascended Washington's political ladder? These questions had been on everyone's mind, including Wilton's. And the press had reflected them in their questions to the woman. There was a bigger picture from the vantage point of Washington, she now replied. The wheels turned slower. Please be patient with me. With us.

But the answers to those questions on the streets had been different. She'd paid her dues in the rough-and-tumble world of local politics. She'd done what could be done there. Now it was time for a little payback. Most had nodded, understanding. Some, like Wilton, were not persuaded. If she wants the good life, then she should quit politics. No one said you had to spend your life there. The founding fathers certainly hadn't intended to spawn a culture of professional politicians. Let the lady go to work for one of the big information system companies moving to Georgia. Or there was always the lecture circuit. Or she could start her own political consulting business, or maybe a charity of some sort. Just don't confuse public service with easy street.

Some of Wilton's friends had argued that those opportunities weren't open to blacks very often. We opened up the political system, he'd responded. Didn't we? We can do the same thing with the business world. And we can support those of us in commerce just as strongly as we do those of us in politics. But we don't have the luxury of our own people adding to the corruption of the political system. Let the lady get out of politics. Wilton had never voted for her again.

The tape ended. He pressed the rewind button and finished his beer. No matter which way he turned in this case, the senator was there. Just a step away, quietly covering his tracks. Yes, Wilton was pissed. Unusually pissed for a man who tried to be cautious, who knew the pitfalls of temperament. We always expect so much of politicians and the political system, he thought. That was why it hurt so badly when they display human frailties and, in the case of Baxter, the loss of what remained of their honesty.

He tossed his beer can toward the kitchen and considered how to deal with the good senator. How do we flush him out? He turned to the earlier evidence. How had the senator become involved that night, anyway? Why had he taken it upon himself to see Agee home? And if the senator really was driving Agee home from his drinking bout that night, how had it happened that he'd hit Emily? Is there something I've missed? he wondered for the thousandth time.

He scrolled once more through his notes, stopped at the page on which he'd recorded the substance of his telephone conversation with Donna Miller, and he read her rambling comments. She'd seen one person. Maybe two. Both were men? Or maybe one was a woman. She'd seen one's head above the headrest. Why had she mentioned the headrest? Had her vision and her memory really been that detailed? The senator was a little guy. His head couldn't have been seen above the headrest.

Wilton drummed the desktop with his fingers. He scrolled back to the top of the page, where he'd copied Donna's phone number. He dialed. On the third ring, Donna Miller's syrupy voice came alive.

He introduced himself, reminded her that he'd called about Emily Shane days earlier.

No reply for a moment. "Why, yes, Mister Byrd, I do remember you. You'll have to forgive me, but you caught me napping."

Wilton smiled. "Sorry about that, ma'am, but I was going over my notes from our conversation, and I noticed that on two separate occasions you mentioned seeing a head above the car's headrest –"

"Oh, dear, do we have to talk about that again?"

"Just one question, and then we can talk about anything you like."

"I don't really think I can help, Mr. Byrd. I've just about forgotten everything."

"Can you tell me more about what you saw above the headrest? Was it the top of a head, or what? Just give it a minute, ma'am, no pressure. Tell me what you remember from that night."

A sigh. "Let me see...oh, yes! Now I remember. The man in the car had turned his head, I think, if my recollection is correct –"

"It was a man, for sure?" Wilton said.

"Yes, his head was turned, and he seemed to be close to the windshield. I saw his shoulders up high and he was pulling on something. That's it. Or maybe he was pushing, I don't know."

Wilton shook his head. "That doesn't make a lot of sense, ma'am."

"Now, young man, I may be up in years, but I certainly have good sense. I know a person tugging on something when I see it. Yes, I certainly saw that, and then the car hit the poor little girl."

"You saw that before the collision, then?"

"It was so awful. People should be more responsible."

"Miss Miller, was that person in view after the car had passed?"

A long pause. "No, I don't think so."

A picture slowly began to emerge, but it was still vague. "Thanks, ma'am, I think you helped."

"Have you talked to Loretta this week, Mister Byrd? She really needs to call me more often. She's there alone in that big old house."

"I'll call and tell her to give you a ring. You have a nice evening, Miss Miller."

Damn, he thought after hanging up, what did that old lady see? He typed some more notes into his computer, saved the file, and he stood and began to pace. Then the picture Donna Miller had found so hard to describe jelled. Agee had been in the car with Baxter. Baxter was probably driving. Agee and the senator had struggled for some reason. It was an accident. A simple, stupid accident. And all Baxter could think about was covering his ass. Wilton reopened his computer files and made more notes.

I need to talk to Jay about this, he thought. At best, a well-intentioned state senator carrying a drunk friend home, something we can't prove. Coincidentally, a little girl in the town's been run over. And I'm betting the wrong man's in jail for it, soon to be on trial, for another crime he didn't commit. To try to involve the senator now would really take some fancy footwork. We need a breakthrough, like another witness who saw the whole thing. Baxter's not gonna roll over now and admit he was involved, even if it was an accident.

He rose, opened another beer. He considered taking what he had to the FBI. His connections there would assure him of being heard. Definitely not the GBI, though; the senator was too connected there. Or do we take it to young Anthony Brewer, let him run with it? And to make it all the more complex, there was this rush to convict Phil Agee of Pat Shane's death. We have to get some serious goods on the senator soon, before Agee stands trial. The testimony linking Agee to Pat Shane's death was gonna be too compelling. But everyone connected with Agee's trial is gonna hear the rumors about Agee causing Emily Shane's death, if they haven't already. Agee's only chance, and ours, is gonna be if his lawyer begs for a change of venue.

No, it ain't gonna be possible to take down the senator through Agee's trial; it'd be seen as a cheap shot based on guilt by association, and given the senator's influence, it'd be dangerous politically for the prosecution. No, thought Wilton, we need to take Baxter down now, separate from the Agee case.

A moment later, he dialed. Jason answered on the third ring.

"We just heard on TV," Jason told him, "that Agee's trial has been shifted to Atlanta, so Von and I are going away for a few days, up to Asheville, do some sightseeing, see the Biltmore Estate. We're planning to leave in a few minutes."

Wilton was speechless. Nothing much surprised him these days, but this – some judge giving us more time to dig into this case. And Jay going off to the mountains with his sister in law. That ought to start the tongues wagging in Hope.

"I guess you know what this sounds like," he said. "It sounds like my man Jay still has a little bit of fire left in the furnace."

Jason gave up a hollow, embarrassed laugh. "It's not quite that way. What's up?"

The phone tap was still in place. Wilton considered his words. Ah, what the hell, he thought, let the man go to the mountains, have his fun. "It'll keep for a few days. When're you two gonna be back?"

"Sunday. We want to be back before the Thanksgiving going-home traffic gets heavy."

"Look," said Wilton, "you call me when you get back, and let's get together. I want to talk to you about your future." He and Jason had devised a code to talk around the tap. Wilton was supposed to be selling insurance on the side. Talking about the future was code for the next step in their unfolding efforts to bring Emily's killer to trial.

Jason grunted. He knew as well as Wilton that, despite the continuance, time was getting short. "I can be at your office early Monday," he said, "and we'll see what you can do with an old dried up vet's future."

Wilton laughed. "Okay, you go on to the mountains with that beautiful lady."

Jason laughed too, but nervously. Even he didn't know what to expect of his and Von's time in the mountains. Strange things were happening inside him. All he knew for sure was that something was about to crystallize, something that might change his life. "It's the mountain air," he said. "Just going away to clear our heads."

"Oh, man," Wilton laughed, "I've heard it called everything now. Be cool and have a nice trip."

He rose and wandered back into the waiting room, where he'd left his beer. He tested the contents. Already a little flat, but he drank from it anyway. Then his thoughts returned to the case. "I can't lay it down," he said to himself.

It was true. He'd backed out of plenty of unproductive cases before, and he knew he was beating his head against a brick wall on this one, even though the confrontations with Jake and Vince had re-energized his interest in nailing the senator. But in reality, there was just no way in hell he was going to pin a thing on Baxter. The guy was too smart. He controlled that little sawed off chief of police in Hope, and he had the inside track with the GBI. But there was something here, something Wilton had to unearth – for himself, if not for the Shane family.

He considered the senator. He'd never met the man one on one, but he was betting Baxter had heard of him by now. They were, he thought, a stealth version of good guys and bad guys. On opposite sides of that ever-ambiguously drawn line defined by law, and almost invisible to everyone else concerned.

The floor beneath his feet trembled slightly as a train rumbled through the town of Decatur. Like the train, the senator could certainly be felt, even when he couldn't be seen. There was power in that. Wilton wondered at his own, similar effect on the senator. Looking through the front window, he searched until he found the train, silhouetted by moonlight.

Nah, he thought. I'm just a flea to Baxter. A minor irritation. He deals with the likes of me every day, and he never gives it a second thought. What gives him that ability? Wilton took a long drink, made a face at the flat beer. What does he have that I don't have? The answer: access to information. And the power to withhold it.

Information was power. It was a liquid asset. Information control kept the senator distant, always around the next corner.

But I'm a private investigator, he thought. Information's my game. The senator's beating me at my own game. Not because he's better at it; he's beating me because he has better control of the access.

"All right," Wilton muttered, "one of the rules of this game is to know when to fold a hand and play another. But I ain't ready to fold. There's gotta be a way to get to this guy." He drained the can.

Baxter's not bigger than life, he considered. He makes mistakes. I'll find one. Human nature's a great equalizer. I'll find some weakness, some vulnerability. Let the man pull his strings. All I need is an opening, and I've got him. And I want to see him. I want to see his eyes, up close. No more of this lurking in the shadows. I want him up front, man to man.

He thought of Jonelle, and he smiled. Wilton, she would say, you're like a cat all tangled up in a ball of yarn. Let it go. And she was probably right. But one thing his years as a private eye had taught him: you have to stay with your gut instinct, and for some reason, his gut told him this guy could be had. Jonelle knows how I am with that. She knows I won't take chances. I just have to find a chink in the senator's armor. It comes down to a test of wills, like it did in 'Nam with the Cong and the NVA.

He considered what would come of confronting the senator. In the long run, I may not win it, but the high and mighty Senator Alan Baxter won't get out of it without a few bruises. Ducking justice has its price. He clenched his fists, opened, and re-clenched them. I can handle a few bumps and bruises. I wonder if the senator can?

He breathed out, his decision made. This ain't merely an investigation, it's about the death of a child. Right and wrong. Justice. The senator may not know he's done it, but he's thrown down the gauntlet when he had old Jake roughed up. Wilton thought again of Jake, saw the fear in the drunkard's eyes. No one, not even a drunk, should have to live with that kind of fear. I'm gonna push this thing. To the bitter end, baby.

PART 4

THE FINAL STORM

CHAPTER 28

THE GAME OF LAW

Wilton went to the bank early on Friday morning and all but emptied his safety deposit box. He spent most of the morning at his desk going over the information he'd accumulated on the Shane case: the audio tapes, Buddy Tarbutton's draft report, the invoice from Jackson's Body Shop and the case notes from his computer files. As suspected, the Alan Baxter telephone memo had been unobtainable. Jason had visited the chief and asked to view the Shane file and e-mailed Wilton about it. The memo wasn't there. He didn't bother to ask questions; it was simply one more footprint erased.

Wilton made a phone call. He would take what he had to the young lawyer, Anthony Brewer, and get a fix on their chances in court.

Wilton slid copies of the papers and tapes into a large manila envelope. In another, similar envelope he slipped the originals of each of the tapes, the invoice, and the draft report, along with a disk copy of his computer files. If Anthony was interested in the case, Wilton would ask him for help in securing this evidence. Not good to be holding everything myself, he thought. If rumors get out that the senator might be implicated, there could be a serious scramble to suppress. Let the senator work for it.

He glanced at his watch – eleven a.m. He was to meet with Anthony in thirty minutes. He locked up, dashed out the front door, jumped the steps, and ran down the driveway to his Taurus.

Anthony's office was in the Equitable Building, one of the taller of the older high rise office buildings at Five Points, once the commercial hub of Atlanta. There are many options for traveling by automobile in Atlanta, but none of them are dependably quick. Wilton chose to forego the downtown Interstate, taking the city's surface streets instead. It was a good choice: he heard on the radio as he drove that a tractor-trailer rig had turned over in the southbound lane of the downtown connector, spreading frozen foods across the multi-laned expressway.

The elevator stopped on the Equitable's tenth floor. Wilton looked to his right. Sure enough, a small sign and an arrow indicated the way to Auburn Legal Services, the law firm Anthony Brewer had founded five years earlier. At the end of the hall, he found a double wooden door with the firm's eagle logo on the wall to the left. Below the logo were the names of the firm's members: Anthony Brewer, then Leon Spight and Ja'net Hughes. Wilton entered.

He'd expected to see a prim receptionist behind an antiseptically kept desk and a quiet, somber waiting room filled with business magazines and, perhaps, to hear the anesthetic sounds of Muzak. Instead, the office had no receptionist; the anteroom owned the cluttered ambience of a college dormitory dayroom. Posters of Stevie Wonder, Chick Corea and Babatunde Olatunji, the African percussionist, had been hung on the wall, and a large poster advertising the Atlanta Black Arts Festival. Music flowed from a modular CD player set on a bookcase against the far wall. Wilton recognized the tune as one of his favorites: a popular jazz song from the eighties by George Benson.

The contents of three bags of fast food from a downtown Burger King had been spread across a low table in front of a black leather couch, the room filled with the greasy smell of hamburgers and French fries. A short, squat black man of perhaps thirty, wearing thick glasses and a younger, taller, light skinned black woman, also wearing glasses sat behind the table, eating their burgers. The short man, in a black, pinstriped business suit with a bright floral tie, was Leon, Wilton assumed. The woman, dressed in blue jeans and a tie dyed tee shirt, was no doubt Ja'net. Beside the table, in a leather chair, sat Anthony Brewer. Anthony was in his mid-thirties, but he seemed younger. He sat sideways in the chair, his legs dangling over its arms, reading a paperback.

Ja'net smiled and put down her burger. "Can we help you?"

Wilton returned her smile. "Don't get up," he replied. "I have an appointment with Anthony."

Anthony laid down his book and sprang to his feet. "I know you now," he said as he approached, hand extended. "I remembered the name when you called, but I couldn't place the face. I see so many people in court." He smiled, his eyes and teeth islands of white in the long, black face. Anthony, perhaps three or four inches short of seven feet in height, towered over Wilton. He'd buttoned his gray silk shirt at the collar and he wore no tie. His black wool trousers stopped an inch above his ankles, and Wilton noticed he wore no socks with his lumpy brown loafers.

"It's been a while," Wilton said.

"Right, right. What can I do for you?"

"I have a client who could use some legal help." Wilton looked around. "You got a place where we can talk?"

"We don't have a conference room," Anthony said. "Let's go to my office."

Wilton opened the door to Brewer's office, Anthony following. Inside, a large desk and the three padded chairs before it barely made room for a pair of ceiling-high bookcases. A large, worn, high-backed leather chair sat at a cock-eyed angle behind the desk. On one wall hung a diploma from the Emory University School of Law and a certificate of membership in the Georgia bar, both bearing Anthony Brewer's name. Posters had been thumbtacked to the other wall, the posters mostly for music festivals and concerts.

"Our next expense is a permanent legal secretary," Anthony said as he motioned Wilton toward a chair. The young lawyer sat on the front edge of his desk, his feet on the floor. He shrugged and fashioned a grin. "Someone who can organize this place."

"Looks like a fire hazard to me, man."

"Yeah, it's bad, isn't it? So what's going on?"

"This client," Wilton began. "He's a friend of mine from 'Nam –"

"What's he charged with?"

"He's not. It's a long story –"

"Tell me."

Wilton spoke briefly of the family's conflict with Davis Anderson over the investigation, or the lack of one, into Emily's death, which had led to his own involvement. Then he talked of his decision to seek Anthony's help.

"You say these are white people, and they have no money?" Anthony moved his feet back and forth on the carpet.

"Yeah," Wilton replied. He slumped slightly in his chair. "My buddy can't work, and his brother's only real asset was the house. The wife owns the house now. She works at a real estate firm, doesn't make much. The family put all they made into the house and furnishings."

"Doesn't sound like my thing, man," Anthony replied. "I work the Atlanta scene, and I usually don't take white people."

"I've seen you work," Wilton insisted. "This is your kind of case."

"You said you have evidence. Let's see it."

For over an hour, Wilton laid out for the young lawyer the information he had amassed, explaining how each piece was connected to the death and the apparent cover-up. He showed Anthony the invoice from Jackson's with the Residence Inn telephone number. Buddy Tarbutton's draft report, which placed Agee and the senator together the night of Emily's death.

He played the tapes. Buddy Tarbutton's accounting to Wilton – his conversations with Jake and with the bartender, Vince, which implicated the GBI. Wilton related his confusing telephone conversations with Donna Miller and his own newly formulated theory that Emily's death had been an accident caused by a scuffle between Agee and Baxter as the car entered Hope.

At last, Anthony leaned back and closed his eyes.

"What do you think, man?" Wilton asked the young lawyer. "Do we have a case?"

Anthony exhaled heavily. "It's a very interesting story. I don't think I've heard one quite like it. And believe me, I hear stories, all kinds of stories."

Wilton nodded. "And I've been there personally for most of this one."

"What do you make of the way your friend's brother died?" asked the young lawyer.

"Only the chief knows for sure, but I think he pulled the trigger himself."

Anthony frowned. "If you can connect the senator to any of this, even indirectly, it'll embarrass him politically. Big time."

"A trial would be quick," said Wilton. "To minimize political damage to the senator."

"Yeah."

Wilton shifted in his chair. "So what do you think, brother, do you want to take on the senator?"

Anthony had moved to his chair during Wilton's exposition, his long legs draped across a corner of the desk. "You know what my thing is," he replied. "I like causes."

"Yeah," said Wilton. "Same as me. We both want to see justice done. We both want to do the right thing."

Anthony smiled. "Don't put words in my mouth, man." He looked down, the smile changing subtly into an expression of amusement. "Causes attract me. I like the conflict, you know? I love the ambiguity of controversy."

Wilton said nothing.

The young lawyer swung his long legs to the floor. He leaned forward. "As a lawyer, my job is to interpret facts, to stake out a position. Something happens, you see? There are facts about that. But there're never enough of them to conclusively show how the thing happens. Someone has to fill in the gaps." He gestured toward Wilton. "That's what we use people like you for. To fill in gaps. Just enough to justify our position, our interpretation of what happened." He cocked his head to one side. "You follow?"

Wilton cleared his throat. "Yeah, I follow."

"Good. I'm not sure how much you know about the practice of law –"

"I been on both ends of it," Wilton replied. "And in the middle."

"How's that?"

"Look, man, I know how the law works. I've seen all kinds of things twisted in court, just to make some big shot look good."

"That's right," Anthony replied, the amused expression frozen on his face. "The judges, they do that, too. They hire attorneys to do research for them. They decide which way they want to rule on a case, and they ask their staff to do research. They go out and find precedents for the decisions. And the judges rule their way. To protect someone. To protect the law. With supporting evidence. That's the way we work. We have an agenda, and we support it with whatever facts are around."

This was beginning to sound like a cop-out to Wilton. "That's bullshit, man," he said. "Doing business that way makes a joke out of justice."

"It depends on what you call justice. If it gets down to a judgment over which lawyer was better prepared, then, yeah, you're right, it becomes a joke. Sometimes the way the judges rule, they're only evaluating legal talent."

"A joke," Wilton repeated. One of his fists had clenched. He massaged it absentmindedly with his other hand.

"That's right, my man, it's abused all the time. But don't you see? If we couldn't do that, then the law would always be a simple case of right and wrong. No gray areas. No room for new thinking.

Law uses opinions to explore the gray areas. It seems crazy, but it does that by choosing up sides, by challenging, by exploring those opinions. It puts a lot of faith in our ability to solve problems that way. Develop your opinions passionately, but solve the problem with a reasoned argument."

Wilton's eyes narrowed as he eyed Anthony. "I got a client, man. He and his family would like some legal help."

Anthony's expression remained unchanged. "That's what I was leading up to. Given the nature of the law, your case is fatally flawed. You have no dependable, direct witnesses. What you do have is subject to interpretation." He emphasized the words. "Subject to interpretation." Then he rose and sat again on the front of his desk. "I can see several ways of interpreting the information you have. One of them makes the senator the bad guy. But there are others. You see what I mean?"

"You have to make it airtight. Inside info."

Anthony nodded. "Exactly right." He paused. "I take cases like your friend's all the time, cases in which little people are being pushed around. But I'll tell you, man, I consider this one unwinnable."

"Because of who you'd be up against?"

"And the lack of hard evidence," Anthony replied. "You'd be trying to take down the man, Senator Alan Baxter, and you'd also be taking a big bite out of a local law enforcement agency and the GBI. No judge would want to take this kind of case on your kind of circumstantial evidence. It would be professional suicide."

"Let me see if I understand where you're coming from," said Wilton. "You're saying I've got enough circumstantial evidence to base a case on, but the courts will never look at it on its merits unless I make the case concrete myself and stuff it in their face on a silver platter."

"That's about it," said Anthony. "You have to make it so compelling they can't ignore it. It would be easier if there were an interesting legal precedent involved. Something to get the judicial juices flowing."

"Something besides justice, you mean."

"You still don't get it." Anthony's voice now carried an edge. "What you'd be asking a prosecutor and judge to do is to take on a case that could bring down a major politician. A lawmaker. Maybe his financial backers. And scandalize the law enforcement system itself. In the judge's or the prosecutor's mind, the whole damned power structure of the state could potentially be on trial. No telling what the civil liberties radicals would do with it once we'd opened that sore. You'd be forcing the law and the system it's built around to protect themselves."

Anthony's voice had risen in volume as he spoke. His eyes sparkled. "But I'm not afraid of that, man. I love it! When you get a case like that in court, it's like a basketball game in a one on one situation. Just you, the other guy, and your game."

"So now you're saying you'll take the case?"

"I said it's unwinnable."

"Because of who's involved, and the evidence."

Anthony nodded. "Exactly right. I take cases like this, but not *pro bono*. I only take one like this if I have a good chance to win. I think this one might make it into court, but I'll have to charge your friend a fee if you want me to do the pushing." He shook his head. "I'll take a beating from the district attorney, but I'll do it. For the money."

Wilton shook his head. "You'll have to forgive me, brother, but I thought you were out there to clean up the system for the little people."

"I am." Anthony's smile slackened. "But I have to maintain a reputation. I have to maintain my respect."

"With the system. At the expense of the people's respect."

"There's a bigger picture, man. It's okay to lose cases if you get paid the big bread. Everybody knows the difference between a job lawyer and a cause lawyer. As I told you, I'm into causes. But taking the money lets everyone know you mean business. Otherwise you're just a loose cannon. You pick your fights when a cause is at stake, but you have to win the freebies to stay in the game." He swept his arm before him, encompassing the room. "Does this look like the office of an upwardly mobile black professional? I'll do the pushing for you and, yes, I'll take the money. That way, even if I lose, I stay in the game. So that someday I'll be able to take the one big case, the case of a lifetime, the one that can make a difference."

Wilton looked to the floor. He lost himself in the carpet's texture before he responded. "How much would you charge my man," he said at last, "if you were to take this case?"

"Twenty thousand for getting it to trial should be about right. And a hundred and twenty an hour for prep work. I'd hire you for any additional investigative work. Or you could work that out with your friend. There are money people out there. I can give you names. But I need money for this one. You understand, it's the way I play the game." Anthony folded his long arms over his chest. A long silence. "The best you can hope for," he said in a quieter voice, "is to lay some political damage on the senator. And I will guarantee you that when I'm through with him, in court or out, he'll have to answer some embarrassing questions when he runs for governor. We might even get lucky and scare off his backers."

"But we would still lose."

"Might not even make it to a jury. As I keep saying, it's just not winnable. I wouldn't play it to win." Anthony paused. "I would milk the case for all the political damage I could lay on him, but, no, you don't try to win an unwinnable case."

Wilton rose and collected his tapes and documents, placed them back in their envelope. "Thanks for your time," he said.

"Hey, you're right, it's my kind of case, man," Anthony called out. "You come up with the bread, and the senator and I will get it on. You think about it."

Wilton stopped and turned. He saw the smile on the young lawyer's face. He read the confidence in his posture. He'd leaned back, hands propped on the desk, legs crossed at the ankles. "You know, I've seen you in court a lot of times," Wilton said, "and, man, you're good. You know the law. And you got the presence. I've seen juries come over to your side just on the strength of your presence." He took a step toward Anthony. "But you got one big flaw. And I didn't see it before today."

The young lawyer didn't move, but the self-confident smile had slipped. "Yeah? Talk to me, Wilton, tell me this trash."

"In this whole conversation, I never heard a word of sympathy for the little girl or her family. Where's the outrage, man? Where's the hurt I feel over this thing? A little girl, ten years old, killed in the most senseless way. Sure, it was an accident. But then it was covered up. By a state senator. All sorts of law enforcement people involved. And now the little girl's father's dead." Wilton stepped forward. "Don't you see how sick this is? You're the law, man. And you don't have any compassion for the victim."

Anthony now owned the stony expression of a person chastised. "Happens every day," he said quietly. "Right here in Atlanta. Kids and old people killed in drive by shootings. Family violence. And it isn't little white girls here in this town, man. It's little black kids. Yeah, sure, I've got feelings." He rose from the desk and walked to the window. Clasping hands behind his back, he surveyed the city below. "The law is where the action is. Used to, we could take it to the streets, but we can't anymore. Violence has never really changed anything. The law is limited, but it's our only alternative if we want to change the way things are. If we really want to be on the side of right."

Wilton turned and walked to the office door. "That's true enough," he said, his hand on the knob, "and I think I know it better than you. I've seen enough killing and injustice for twenty lifetimes. But you can't be so detached, Anthony. You can't make a game of it. A little outrage, it's good for the soul."

The young lawyer said nothing. Wilton opened the door.

"Oh, one more thing," said Wilton. He turned again to the street-facing young lawyer. "I hope you get that shot at the big case some day. The one that'll make so much difference. I really do. But don't count on it, man."

Anthony Brewer turned a questioning expression to Wilton.

"All that respect you're trying so hard to earn from those Harvard lawyers and the judges, who owe their souls to big money and influence? They'll give you all the respect you want. But when that big case finally comes down, you're gonna be on the wrong side of it. Think about that, man. Think about it. A whole career, and in the end you get sucker punched.

"Can you live with that, man? Can you live with the death of Emily Shane? With not being able to help all those kids here in Atlanta who die on the streets every day? With street people freezing to death underneath yesterday's newspaper 'cause their existence can't be justified legally or financially? For the sake of staying in the game? Well, at some point, you're gonna have to think about *this*: the man has talked you into looking at the law like it's some kind of sport. He's got you rationalizing all those people away. You've already sold out, and the sad part is you don't know it." Wilton paused. "The law." He spat the words out. "It's not a game. It's about freedom and justice and happiness and peace of mind. It's about life."

Then he stalked out, passed through the reception room, which now reverberated to the music of Stevie Wonder. Wilton knew that song, too: one of Stevie's older ones, "Higher Ground." The song ended as the elevator bell rang. Minutes later, he hit the street.

CHAPTER 28

HEAVEN

A quiet pervades everything else in the North Carolina mountains. Even in late November with the leaves down, this quiet swallows any bustle that intrudes, allowing only whispers, quieting even the sounds of cars and trucks to a soft hum. It's a place for being. A place for quiet contemplation, for simple release from one's cares. It's as if somewhere within us, with our press toward a yearned-for promised land, there's a need to quit the chase for a time, to stop and to enjoy the harvest. And these mountains, knowing the language of this quieter satisfaction, respond in their own way, with a quietude and grace that allows for such restful repose.

As those days in the mountains passed, Jason and Von found themselves driving the mountain ridges and the streets of Asheville, saying little, absorbed in the sleepy mountain ambience. Or maybe the silence of this place was part of a communication to be felt, a conversation wishing to remain unspoken until its magic had healed them both.

On Saturday, they rose early and drove across town for a tour of the Biltmore Estate, a stupefyingly lavish symbol of the opulence that had fed America's early, freewheeling industrialists.

They wandered like delighted children through the expanse of the mansion and, from a promontory at the building's rear, they overlooked a placid lake and the estate's eight thousand remaining acres. The tour ended at noon, and they wound along the three miles of approach road carrying them through a ravine on the estate's north side and toward downtown.

They had a late lunch at a nearby mall and departed southwestward, toward the town of Highlands. They rode in silence. Both had much on their minds, but the words still weren't coming; maybe the mountains' meditative quiet wouldn't allow it. But then they weren't there for idle conversation, they kept convincing one another; they were there to clear their minds.

Toward evening this day, they stopped in Brevard. A tiny restaurant sits on the town's main street. The cool, clear mountain air had whetted their appetites, so they ducked into the tiny eatery for a snack. The waitress, fortyish and heavyset with coarse, graying black hair hanging to her waist, recommended the restaurant's apple cobbler. Von and Jason ordered. The cobbler was indeed delicious.

"Are you going to order another one?" Von teased, eying Jason's empty bowl.

Jason had inhaled his cobbler and pushed his bowl aside to make room for his tea. He licked his lips and rolled his eyes in mock response. Then he laughed.

"It's good to see you laugh, Jason." Von smiled and reached across the table. Jason took the offered hand, stroking the tips of her fingers. She had removed her wedding bands the day after the funeral. Without them, her hand seemed even more delicate. She squeezed his hand, pulled hers back, and resumed eating.

"A Thanksgiving vacation in the Smoky Mountains," Jason said to himself.

"What?" Von said as she looked up.

"Oh, I was just thinking out loud. Life is so strange. Would you have believed, six months ago, that we would be here? That we'd be having a Thanksgiving holiday together in the Smokies?"

"So now I'm strange?" she said, wrinkling her nose.

"No, really." He sighed. "Could you have imagined it six months ago? Could you have even dreamed up the circumstances that brought us both here?" He lifted his mug, cradling it in both hands as he sipped.

Von pushed her bowl away. She looked up with a soft smile and bright, sparkling eyes. "Maybe."

Jason couldn't help but return the smile. "Tell the truth, now."

"I wouldn't have admitted it before, even to myself, but yes, I could've imagined it. I could've imagined us together in the mountains, and I could have imagined even more."

"Funny," Jason replied, eyes flitting to the booth's table, "but I bet your mom and dad couldn't have."

Von's smile slipped. "But I've never thought of Mama as a source of anything funny before."

Jason eyed her. "You know what I mean. I'll bet she's beside herself, what with her little girl out of town with yet another Shane man."

Von stared into her coffee mug. "Everyone grows up," she said. "I am, and so can Mama."

Jason smiled. "Remember their faces when you told them? They looked like they'd just been told their teenaged daughter was pregnant."

Von rubbed Jason's leg with her foot. "I'd hate to disappoint them."

The waitress reappeared. "Anything else?" she drawled, looking first to Von, then Jason.

Jason glanced to his empty bowl.

"I think he wants another dish of cobbler," said Von. She reached and handed it to the waitress.

"Please, no." Jason grabbed the waitress' wrist. "She's a temptress. She knows what this cobbler does to me. It's a pagan broth, I tell you! It dements the mind even as it delights the senses. I may become disoriented and unable to find my way home again."

"It is pretty good, ain't it?" the waitress managed.

"Better than good." Jason rubbed his stomach. His belt, which was worn from years of fastening at the innermost notch, was now pegged two notches toward the tip. "It's divine nectar. Fit for the gods."

The waitress gave Jason an odd look and stepped back. "I'll make out your ticket, then. Be back in just a minute." She hurried away.

"I overdid the compliment," he said.

"You did," Von replied. "Mountain people are reserved. Simple understated politeness would have been enough."

"Fit for the gods..." Jason shook his head again. "That's probably heresy in these here parts."

"Don't make fun. She's sweet."

"But not as sweet as the cobbler."

The waitress returned with the ticket and a small, covered Styrofoam dish. "Just pay up front," she said. "And this is to remember us by." She handed the dish to Jason. He opened it to the aroma of hot, buttered apple cobbler.

"You *are* sweet," Jason said. "As sweet as the cobbler."

"Y'all come back and see us, now." A customer at a nearby table motioned, and the waitress scurried away.

"Jason, we have to send her a thank you card."

He turned the ticket over to see her signature. "Get the address, and we'll send Wilma a card."

"I saw business cards by the cash register. I'll get one."

They rose, paid their bill, and departed. Dusk had come and the town had darkened.

Jason found Highway 64 and pointed his Toyota into the darkness. The road curved sharply, hugging the side of the mountain. For a while, they peered to the sinuous road in silence.

"I hope we're not alienating your mom and dad," Jason said, "with this rash, adolescent behavior of ours."

"We needed this time away." She rubbed his shoulder. "Everyone's confused. I know I am. And a little bit scared."

"Yeah. I just don't want you to lose any more family."

Soft laughter. "Parents are resilient. That's what kids do. Make their parents stretch. Our roles in life are to toughen them up." She placed a hand on his arm. "But we're not up here for them. We're here for us."

Once more, silence took them. They leaned into the curves, the Toyota humming furiously as the road rose before them.

"I talked to Doctor Berg about this trip," Jason said, after negotiating a pair of tortuous curves.

"Did he approve?"

"Yeah." He patted her hand and moved it to her lap. "He said I was handling things very well now. Better than most normal people." He emphasized the word normal.

He and the doctor had also discussed his growing physical attraction to Von, the nearly forgotten sensations he'd begun to feel in her presence, how she was becoming a constant presence in his thoughts. Now is not the time, the doctor had said, to let convention intimidate you. Your brother's gone, and you and Von are making adjustments. The feelings the two of you have for one another may not be permanent, but you need each other now. Be friends. If you're capable, and if there's agreement between the two of you, I see nothing wrong with your being lovers.

Jason had not yet allowed himself to accept that as a possibility. He didn't know why. Maybe it was the years of self-absorption, spent in the hell of parental loss and war trauma. Maybe I can't face having something good happen in my life, he thought. Maybe I'm not capable, emotionally or physically. Or maybe I'm just used to being alone.

Jason cleared his throat. "Doctor Berg said spending this time with you would be good for me. Good for both of us."

"The doctor's a very wise man."

He couldn't see her face in the dark, but he knew the expression that came when she was teasing.

"Did he say anything else? About us, I mean?"

He laughed. "Of course he did. He said that living in the same house with a beautiful woman would spoil me. My expectations of other women would become unreasonable."

A finger dug into his ribs.

"I think I should talk to this Doctor Berg. I need to find out who these other women are."

"But they're all less beautiful."

"Well, there's some consolation in that, I suppose."

The mountain woodlands disappeared in darkness as they entered a tree canopy. Soon, residential lights appeared, glowing like fireflies. The Toyota passed through Cashiers. A sign indicated ten more miles to Highlands and the lodge where they were to spend the night. Those miles were especially difficult, the road narrowing on its winding pathway as it clung to the mountainside.

Suddenly, a sharp turn, and Jason slammed on the brakes as he set the car's wheels into it. A dark form emerged, two yellowed eyes reflected in the headlight beams. The little car skidded to the outside of the curve and nudged a masonry wall between the roadway and the abyss beyond. The car lurched to a stop, the engine dead.

The deer in the road before them raised its white tail, turned to look back and bounded up the mountainside into the wooded shadows. Jason's heart pounded. He let out a long breath and twisted the ignition key. The engine restarted, and he nudged them toward Highlands.

He glanced to Von. "Are you all right?"

Her face's tension shone with the dashboard's dim light. She moved across the seat until she was against him. Her head went to his shoulder.

"I'm okay, I think," she said. "It happened so quickly. Oh...my heart is still racing. Here, feel." She pulled his hand through her open jacket and against her breast.

Minutes later, the sign for the lodge appeared. He turned down a steep incline, parked, and they entered. No one at the reception desk. He rang the bell. Von nestled against him in the cold space. Then footsteps sounded on the stairway behind them.

They turned to see a short, rotund man in thick glasses, wearing blue jeans and a red plaid flannel shirt. He scuttled behind the desk. "May I help you?"

"I'm Jason Shane and this is Von Shane. We have reservations for the night." The man pushed his glasses higher on his nose and flipped through a stack of file cards.

"Here we go. I have a cabin with one queen-sized bed for you right around the corner." He pulled a card from the stack and began scribbling on it.

Jason looked to Von. "We were to have separate rooms. You should have a larger cabin for us."

The man peered at Jason over his glasses and thumbed through the stack of cards once more. "No," he said slowly, "just the one." He looked to Von, then Jason. "You called so late, and this is our last cabin." He smiled. "We have a lot of people in town tonight."

"That's fine," replied Von. "A cabin with one bedroom will do fine."

Jason flushed.

The man beamed. "Good, good." He handed Jason a card to fill out. "We're always full in October during leaf season, but it's unusual this late in November."

Jason filled out the card and pushed it toward the man, who peered at the information. Then he reached into a desk drawer and extracted a key. "You'll be in number twenty-three." He smiled, absently pushing his glasses up his nose again. "It's three cabins down to your left."

They drove the short distance to their cabin and unloaded the car. The rustic cabin consisted of a single, large room with an adjoining bath. It had no heat, but there was a fireplace, stacked with logs and kindling, ready to be lit. Jason opened the vent and held a match to the kindling. A heavy wooden bench had been set in front of the fireplace, and together they pulled it to the hearth-stones. They sat together for a long while, warming. She snuggled against his lean frame.

"We didn't really have a choice, did we?" She stroked his face with a finger.

"We could've slept in the car. Me in the front, you in the back."

"Wouldn't have worked. You're too tall. You would've kept me awake all night."

Jason bent and kissed her. He tried to quiet his pounding heart-beat, but couldn't. He kissed her neck, her ears.

Then he pushed away, cradled her head in his hands. "I don't know if this is right, Von, but I want you. I want you more than..." His sentence unfinished, he kissed her eyelids, her nose, her mouth.

This time it was she who pushed away. "Really, Jason, it's okay."

He released her, rose and began to tug the mattress from the room's four-poster bed. Then he stopped and they moved the bench, dragged the mattress closer to the fire.

The last time he'd felt the ecstasy of lovemaking had been while in a beery haze in Thailand, during one of his breaks from the war. But that hadn't felt like this, nor had his awkward encounters with the only girl friend he'd had in high school. Oh, God! He whispered her name like a mantra. Von. He felt himself begin to shiver.

"Jason, more!" she whispered. "More!"

"I can't. My hip...too weak..." He tumbled from her.

She mounted him, her skin hot against his.

She cried out, loudly, and Jason did, too. An eternity later, she collapsed atop him.

"God, I love you!" he cried.

She answered by placing her lips against his. One last time they kissed. Then he pulled up the sheet and blankets. The fire crackled, a shower of sparks erupting. There was no noise except the hollow cough of the chimney as it drew the heat upward. They lay wrapped in each other's arms and as the fire dimmed, they slept.

CHAPTER 30

DEAD END

Wilton braced himself against the cold, opened the door to his office, and dashed across the deck and down the steps for the morning newspaper. Inside again, he tossed his paper onto the couch and strode to the tiny kitchen at the rear of the large entry room.

While waiting on coffee to perk and his bread to toast, he gazed past the kitchen window to the sky beyond the bare tree branches. A few remaining clouds scurried across the sky's deep blue. A sparrow lit on the tree branch closest to the window, fluffed its feathers into a gray, mottled ball, and hopped to the feeder Jonelle had attached to the window ledge. It pecked at the seeds there, shook itself and flew off.

He was almost through eating when he felt Jonelle's arms slide across his shoulders and around his neck. He bent to kiss her hand. Nine-thirty, and she was already dressed.

"What're you doing up and about so early, baby?"

"I thought I'd go to the mall. Look for a few Christmas presents for my parents. Maybe even something for you, if you promise to behave from now until then."

He reached up and pulled her to him, kissed her. "You sure you want me to behave?"

She affected exasperation as she pushed him away. "I have to watch every step I take around this house. Never know when I'm going to get jumped."

"Keeps you alert."

"Makes me want to go to the mall, so I can have a moment's peace."

"You hurry back, baby, in time for us to play a little before the football game."

"Mother says I've spoiled you, and she's right." Jonelle said. "Now I have to work our love life in around your football schedule."

"You better get on to the mall then."

She turned toward the kitchen door, and then stopped. "Oh, I almost forgot. I was just listening to the radio news, and they said the trial for that Agee guy has been moved up."

"What?"

"It's supposed to start this Wednesday."

"Damn," said Wilton. "Damn, damn!"

"Is something wrong?" She set hands on hips. "You're not still playing around with that case, are you?"

"Nah."

She eyed him. "Wilton, please stay away from that trial. I don't want you involved with anything else concerning Senator Baxter. It's trouble."

He smiled. "No problem. I'll catch the story in the morning paper. That's it." He rose and swept her into his arms. "So when're you going to be back?"

"In time."

She left. The kitchen window rattled as she pulled the door shut.

He poured another cup of coffee, finished his breakfast, and then opened the newspaper. The story about Phil Agee's trial had been buried in the middle of the local news section: "HOPE MAN TRIAL SET." One brief sentence referred to his association with Alan Baxter.

As Wilton read further, he discovered that the case had been transferred to a new judge, who had re-set the trial date. We're anxious, the article quoted the prosecutor's office, to get the case adjudicated before the new year. And the next legislative session, Wilton thought.

He turned through the rest of the paper, his mind still on the article. Poor dumb, drunk Agee. He's being set up, and he doesn't have a clue. What kind of man is this senator, to hide behind an old friend's coattails like that? To let him take the heat for killing Emily? To let him stand trial for killing Pat Shane? At the very least, Agee was provoked into killing Pat. At worst, he didn't do it at all. Wilton sipped the last of his coffee. Jason's gonna have a surprise waiting for him when he gets back. This trial is gonna be slam dunked. Talk about a rush to judgment.

He leaped from his chair, grabbed the telephone on his desk, and dialed information.

"Do you still have a number for the reelection offices of Senator Alan Baxter?" he asked the operator. "I think it's in the Marquis Hotel."

He found a pencil, scribbled the number on the back of an envelope. He hung up and tapped the eraser end of his pencil on the desktop as he thought.

He would confront the senator. But then what? *I'll just get put in the slammer for harassing a prominent, highly visible public servant. Maybe I can follow him. Maybe he'll do something stupid. Or maybe he'll go somewhere or see someone who'll make all these loose ends come together.*

Wilton knew he was grasping at straws, but he wasn't going to let this case go down knowing there was something else he could've done to straighten out this mess. He picked up the phone and dialed the telephone number he'd been given. It rang four, five, six times. He was about to hang up when a youthful male voice answered.

"This is Will Bradfield, of the Associated Press," Wilton replied. "I'm trying to reach Senator Alan Baxter."

"Can you hold on?"

Seconds later, another voice answered, a woman's. She sounded older.

"Will Bradfield, of Associated Press," he repeated. "I'm trying to contact the senator. I'm doing a follow up story on the election."

"I don't believe I know you, Mister Bradfield."

She can't know all the political reporters, he thought. *I'll keep bluffing.* He affected a chuckle. "I haven't been assigned to this region long. I've been stuck behind a desk in New York, editing copy. And then, out of nowhere, I get assigned this story. The senator's considered a national comer, you know."

"It's one step at a time, Mr. Bradfield." The woman's tone had changed from caution to one of prideful pleasantness.

"Would it be possible to contact the senator today?"

"I have two numbers." She repeated them to Wilton.

"If this goes well," he said, "I'll have the senator as a regular assignment. You know, track the next two years leading to the governor's race."

They exchanged a few more words, and Wilton hung up.

He scrambled down the stairs to the living quarters and returned with his telephone number printouts. He looked them up. One appeared to be an address in Duluth; from the looks of the code, it was an apartment complex. The other was for an address in Athens. He found a city map and confirmed the street name. The one in Duluth must be for business. This one, he thought as he tapped the city map, is probably the family home.

He exhaled, rubbing his face with the palms of both hands. All I can possibly do is find the senator and tail him for a while. See if he leads me to anything. It's not much. He sighed, rubbing his forehead. This could be dangerous.

Then he thought of Buddy Tarbutton. It's probably another dead end, but maybe Buddy can tell me something new. He sifted through his files until he found Tarbutton's home phone number. He dialed. A beep, followed by a message replying that the number had been disconnected.

He called the police station in Hope. "Officer Tarbutton isn't a member of the force here any more," the duty officer told him. "He quit last Monday. Went back to North Carolina, I think."

Wilton grunted. Best he could tell, Buddy had enjoyed his job on the Hope police force, for the most part. He was either getting a lot of heat because of what he knew, or his conscience was bothering him. Anyway, that door was now closed.

He glanced at his watch as he hung up. Jonelle would be at the mall all morning, would probably eat lunch there. She wouldn't be home until one or one-thirty. He locked up the office and minutes later entered I-85, bound for Athens. He took the bypass to the east and followed it. The exit he took placed him in a residential neighborhood near the University of Georgia campus. It was an old neighborhood, the homes probably built in the nineteen thirties or forties.

He wound his way into an old subdivision and found the senator's street. One house there, not unlike the others, except that its yard contained a forest of signs proclaiming Senator Alan Baxter's reelection campaign. He drove past. Not too slowly; that could attract as much attention as pulling into the driveway and blowing the horn.

Sure enough, the senator's Cadillac sat in the driveway beside the house. A Chevrolet sedan sat at the curb. He looked in his rear view mirror, noticed movement near the house. A man and woman had emerged from the house and were standing next to the Cadillac. Wilton slowed, almost stopping. The man held the door open for the woman and then circled to the driver's side. No doubt about it, he thought. It was the senator.

Wilton sped up and drove to the next block, where he wheeled into a driveway and reversed direction. He wanted to see the senator up close, to look at his face as the Cadillac passed by. Instead, the senator's car turned in the other direction. Better yet, he thought. I'm in position to follow him. Just for the hell of it.

A car passed Wilton in the opposite direction, the Chevrolet sedan. Intent on the Cadillac, he let the Chevy pass with hardly a notice.

Two men sat in the Chevy's front seats. They were large men, both with the athletic builds of weightlifters. Both men's hair had been cropped short. The older one, sporting a red mustache, wore a blue jean jacket and had slouched against the door on the rider's side, a hand partially obscuring his face. The driver leaned across the steering wheel, the sleeves of his corduroy jacket riding up and exposing thick forearms. He pulled into a drive, turned around, and began to follow. Wilton and the Cadillac were out of sight, winding their way out of the subdivision.

The men in the Chevy knew where the senator was going; it was their job. Ever since the incident in Hope in early October, the senator had made sure his two GBI bodyguards were never far away. They reentered the Athens bypass and turned toward Atlanta, where the senator and his wife were to attend an Atlanta Falcons football game the following day, guests of Governor Raines. The Chevy fell back to a distance of almost a quarter mile and matched the speed of the other two cars.

The senator led the furtive procession onto the perimeter beltway north of Atlanta. A few miles more, and he turned onto West Paces Ferry Road, toward the governor's mansion.

Wilton lost the senator on West Paces Ferry, but realizing his destination, wound his way down the narrow, tree-lined street of upper class homes. He crept past the wrought iron fence of the state-owned mansion. Inside, at the top of the hill in front of the mansion, he glimpsed the Cadillac. Then he tapped the accelerator and continued toward Buckhead, speaking into his tape recorder as he drove.

The Chevy stopped momentarily at the gate to the mansion. The State Patrol sergeant flagged them in, and they parked. The driver made a call. The ensuing conversation was animated but brief. He motioned to the guard that he would circle through the gate and exit.

Wilton glanced at his watch. "Damn, damn, damn!" he growled as he pounded the steering wheel. He'd found the senator's home, had followed him to the Governor's mansion. Big deal. This had informed him nothing. Absolutely nothing. Jonelle was right; I gotta get this off my mind. She'll be home soon. In fact, she may be home already, wondering what's up. He turned toward Decatur and home

He forced his attention to the cityscape and the sky beyond. At least it was a beautiful day. He just might be willing to forego his precious football game. Maybe he and Jonelle could climb Stone Mountain, the gargantuan mass of granite to the east of Atlanta. He thought of the view from there on such a clear day, the brisk wind mingling with the heat of the distant sun. Yeah, that would take anyone's mind off a lost cause. After the climb, they would both be hungry, and a dinner out with a drink or two would be perfect.

Behind him, the Chevy barely managed to keep up. But that wasn't a problem; they knew where Wilton lived, had tailed him there several times. The two burly men were now in a sour mood. The senator hadn't been pleased that this black detective had been following him. He'd told the Chevy's rider that his patience with this tenacious black man was at an end. We'll have to do something about him, he said. The rider murmured acquiescence. Good, Baxter growled. You know what to do.

CHAPTER 31

REVELATION

Jason huffed as he lugged the largest suitcase up the back stairs of the house on Needham Street. He took a deep breath before unlocking the back door. He flicked a switch just inside the kitchen, illuminating the deck and the back stairs, where Von stood with the other suitcase.

She smiled as he turned for her suitcase and shook her head.

"Take advantage of this chivalry while you can." Grinning, he took her bag, and led the way into the kitchen. "I may be a helpless wimp again tomorrow."

"You wouldn't know how to be a wimp, Jason."

"I guess it worked, then."

"What?"

"My twenty years of faking it."

"I wasn't fooled."

He kissed her. "Do you want to christen the master bedroom?"

She feigned a sigh. "We need to unpack. I have work tomorrow, you know."

He lifted her face to his and kissed her again. "I'm not sure, but is this a version of that old I've got a headache thing?"

"I can tell there's only one way to shut you up." She took his hand and led him upstairs.

An hour later they lay in bed, covers drawn about them, wrapped in each other's arms. This time, it had been difficult. Doctor Berg had prepared Jason well for the reemergence of his sexual abilities, more so than for their occasional receding. Their first attempt of the evening had gone nowhere, but finally they'd managed.

"Are you okay?" she whispered.

He sighed. "You mean with being a lousy lover?" He'd told her in Highlands that his abilities might come and go. It was a joke then, as they'd gorged on one another.

She put a finger to his lips and issued a faint sigh. "I haven't been this satisfied in years. Maybe ever."

He kissed her hand and then closed his eyes. He felt incredibly tired, and not a little depressed. For some time he lay, unmoving. Then the bed shook as Von sat up. When he opened his eyes, she was facing him, legs tucked under her. Streams of streetlight cascaded over her, burnishing her naked skin to a phosphorescent white.

She bent, gently stroking his chest. "Jason, I told you there were some things I would have to share with you when the time was right."

He said nothing in reply.

"It has to do with Pat and me." Pausing again, she looked down.

"You don't owe me any explanations."

Her chin quivered, and then a sad sigh. "Please, Jason, this is hard enough as it is." She turned away. "I'm sorry. I'm starting to sound like Mama."

"Bad comparison." He reached for her.

She gently pushed away. "I need to tell you this. Please."

"You have my undivided attention."

"About nine years ago, Pat and I were having troubles. We had a fight one night, and it involved you."

Jason thought back. He'd been depressed during that time, severely depressed. He wasn't eating, and he bathed infrequently. His hair had grown long and stringy. He didn't shave. And for months, he rarely left the house. He'd told no one, but it wouldn't have surprised anyone who knew him that he was contemplating suicide.

"Pat wanted to commit you," she said. "Your depression affected him so. He was going to put you in a hospital...for the rest of your life. He couldn't face you any longer, Jason. I've always thought that you reminded him of so much that had gone wrong in his own life."

"I guess you're talking about Mom and Dad's death."

"And your going to Vietnam and coming back so damaged. He tried to be a parent to you, and when you allowed yourself to be drafted, it made him feel like a failure, especially when you came back wounded and depressed. He thought you had been running away from him, and he felt so guilty about it."

"He was always taking on too much responsibility for his own good."

"And then me. The miscarriages. They strained our marriage." She placed her hands over her eyes.

Jason sat up and embraced her. "Are you okay?"

She nodded, but the soft light betrayed tears. "Then he ran away from me, Jason. He started drinking and had a series of affairs. I thought Emily's birth would bring us together again, but it didn't, not really."

He lay back, turned to the window, and for a moment watched the bare branches sway on the oak outside. The wind emitted a slow, hissing sound as it swept past the house.

"I never imagined."

"Oh, he never flaunted it, but I knew him. I knew what he was doing. After a while, I confronted him. I suppose I thought that if he could send you to a mental hospital, well, then he wouldn't find it hard to leave Emily and me."

"He wouldn't have done that, Von. He was too proper. I mean, he had a pretty rigid idea of what a family should be like. He tried his best to create that, and to include me in it. At one point he might've been discouraged enough to commit me, but that was my fault. Even so, he'd have never abandoned you and Emily." A sigh. "But then, what do I know? He was only my brother."

"So after he admitted to the affairs, we had this big fight, about a lot of things, including you. I told him that if he had you committed, I would leave, too. And I'd take Emily."

"I'm glad I was oblivious."

"Then he did something I'd never have expected. He broke down and cried. He didn't say another word, he just cried. Then he left the house and didn't come back for three days. When he did come back, we talked again. I was sure he'd leave for good. So I asked him where he'd been. He told me he'd been with a woman, his latest affair. The one that's been ongoing these past years."

Jason swallowed. "Who was it?"

"She manages the Stark's restaurant in Athens."

Jason knew her, had met her – Judy something. She was a long-time manager there, had been a Stark's employee almost as long as Pat. She was an attractive woman, very businesslike, in Jason's estimation. She was short and shapely, like Von. And she had a lot of Von's mannerisms. He'd heard, from Pat's secretary and others, that Judy had been married three times, but the talk now was that she devoted too much of her life to her career to make room for a man. Except for a man as devoted to Stark's as she was.

"I guess I should have suspected something of that sort," he said.

"That's where he went every time he left here. To her place, in Athens."

"But why did you put up with it? That is, if you knew so much about it?"

"I was afraid of life on my own, especially with Emily. Even more so after she died."

"Then I was just someone to escape to, a way to avoid loneliness?"

"No." She held his head in her hands and kissed him.

"Then why? Why do you want to be with me?"

"I watched you struggle so hard to regain your life, Jason. To be the person you wanted to be. I saw it working. I watched you with Emily. I saw your strength when she died, then again when Pat died. I realized how much you meant to me. Had always meant to me."

"It was inspiration, then. That's all I was. Inspiration."

"More than that. My marriage to Pat has never been a fulfilling one."

"Because of me."

"Because I chose a man who was afraid to face his own fears and insecurities. And I couldn't see that because I was afraid to face some things in my own life. Mama. My belief that I needed someone to take care of me."

He began to feel an ache somewhere deep inside. He swept her up; he wanted to lose himself in her.

Again she pushed away. "I have to finish this, Jason. After Emily died, and especially after Pat's death, I realized I had nothing, I had no one. Except myself. And I suddenly realized that if I were to be a part of someone's life again, I would want it to be with someone like you. Someone who loved life enough to fight for it. Someone who needed nothing except his own sense of self worth. I realized how much we have in common. Even in our weaknesses."

He took her in, and this time she didn't resist. So delicate. So vulnerable. The way I've always felt. So helpless. But we're not helpless, really, he thought. Neither of us.

"I love you, Jason. Very much."

Despite the embrace, she shivered.

"You need to put something on."

"And we need to unpack and fix something to eat."

Minutes later, they clattered down the stairs in bathrobes. They lugged the two suitcases upstairs, unpacked, and took their dirty clothes to the washing machine, just off the kitchen. While the washer chugged, they made sandwiches and warmed some home-made soup.

After they'd eaten, the doorbell rang.

"It's Mama and Daddy," Von yelled over her shoulder as she opened the front door. She hugged her father, and then looked past him to her mother. "What are you two doing out on such a cold night?"

"Your mother and I are on a new togetherness kick," said a smiling David. "Every night since Thanksgiving we've taken a walk. If we're going to grow old together, we might as well get tired to-gether." He pulled Anna to him and kissed her cheek.

"We saw your lights on, dear," said Anna, "and we thought we would stop by for a minute. How was your trip?"

Jason entered the foyer and placed an arm around Von's shoulders. "It was nice, very nice."

Von glanced to Jason, and then her arm circled his waist. "Have you been to the Biltmore House before? It's absolutely beautiful. You must see it sometime."

"Actually," David said, "we have seen it." He glanced to Anna. "You remember, sweetheart? Back in the sixties, I think it was. We drove up there with your cousin Vera and her fiancée."

"Yes, David, I remember." She took his hand. "But come along. We must finish our walk. Yvonne, you and I will talk tomorrow."

"We have some hot water in the kitchen," said Jason, "wouldn't you like a cup of tea before you go back out?"

Von stiffened and pinched him.

Anna looked from Von to Jason, and then to David. "Aren't those the matching bathrobes we gave to Yvonne and Patrick two Christmases ago?"

Von hugged Jason to her. "Yes, they are, Mama." Her voice had gone shrill.

"And how do you happen to be wearing your brother's robe, Jason?"

David pulled on Anna's arm. "C'mon, Annie, let's go. You and Von can talk bathrobes some other time."

Anna remained motionless, eyes leveled on Jason. "I've asked Jason a question, and I'm waiting for an answer."

"It was handy." Jason glanced to Von. "I –"

"Mama," Von said, "you may as well know now, since you've made it your business. Jason and I are in love. We took this trip to sort out our feelings." She let her hand slide into his. "And to get to know each other better."

Anna's eyes narrowed. She shook away David's hand and took a step forward. "This is the most unseemly thing I could possibly imagine you doing. I can't tell you how disgusted I am."

"Let's finish our walk, Annie." David placed his arm around Anna's shoulder. "The air will cool you down."

She brushed the arm away and glared at Von. "Yvonne, there are things more important than the pleasures of the flesh, and I thought I had reared you in that knowing."

"Mama —"

"Don't interrupt me when I'm talking to you!"

"You're in my house, Mama. I will interrupt you any time I please. How dare you come over here and pick a fight like this."

David let out a long breath and stepped away.

"Why don't we go into the sitting room," said Jason, "and talk this out?"

"No!" Anna's eyes flashed. "I will not sit down with the two of you half naked. You are both so shameless!"

"You came over here uninvited, Mama." Von cinched the belt on her robe. "Don't expect us to be dressed for Sunday school whenever you decide to drop by on a whim."

"You're sassing me, Yvonne, and you're being a tramp."

"I can't be as cold and heartless as you, Mama. I have to act on my feelings. That's what you don't like. You don't have any feelings. Do what Daddy says, go home."

"Very, well, Yvonne, I'll go. But I will tell you that you have shamed this family. You would not restrain Patrick and his behavior, and I now understand why. You are as shamelessly vulgar in your private habits as your husband was impetuous in public." Her knuckles paled as she clenched the collar of her jacket. "With Patrick gone, you'll have to face the reality of supporting yourself. You're on your own now, Yvonne, and I will also tell you that you'll have no help from us."

Anna turned to Jason. Her lips curled downward as she surveyed him. "And I'm certain that your man of the moment will not be able to help you in that respect."

Von bit into her bottom lip. Her eyes reddened as tears snaked down her cheeks. "Get out of my house, Mama!" She stamped a foot, fists clenched. "I don't need your help. I don't want your help."

"Good-bye, Yvonne." Anna turned abruptly. Then she stopped, chin raised. "Are you coming, David?"

"I'll be along in a minute."

Anna strode across the porch, down the steps, and into the dark. Jason held Von as she cried.

"Honey," David said, "you know how your mother is when –"

"Oh, Daddy, how could you let her say all those terrible things? Do you feel that way too? Do you hate me, too? Just when I'm the happiest I've been in years? Please tell me I haven't lost you, too."

He cleared his throat. "Sweet, your mother and I are getting along better than we have in years. Don't ask me to provoke her now. I just can't do it." He reached out and took her from Jason. "I love you, sweetheart."

Then he turned and strode after Anna.

CHAPTER 32

FRIGHTENED TOWN

Jason rose early on Monday morning. Von was still in the shower as he pulled his parka from the downstairs closet and set out for the Night Owl. The sun rose behind him as he walked. He was still sleepy, barely noticing the gentle rush as the air warmed, stirring the smallest of the bare branches overhead. A piece of paper rattled across the sidewalk and clung for a moment to a thin, wrought iron post supporting a neighbor's mailbox before it tumbled into the street.

Neither he nor Von had slept well. The visit from Anna and David had ruined their first night home. Anna has the ability to do that, whenever she wishes, he thought. It's almost as if she instinctively knows how to sabotage things she doesn't like. Around one in the morning Von had shaken him to tell him she was having trouble sleeping. That wasn't news; he'd been tossing, too. He volunteered to sleep in his old room, in more familiar surroundings, and Von didn't protest. But Jason didn't sleep well there, either, and he suspected Von had continued her tossing long into the night.

He glanced through the Night Owl's front window and waved to Gus, who was busing a front booth. He bought a copy of the morning's *Constitution* and tucked it under his arm. A longhaired youth burst through the door of the Night Owl, almost bowling Jason over.

"'Scuse me," the boy mumbled without looking up. He turned toward the parking lot around the corner.

Jason smiled and said nothing. He entered. The diner had already filled, so he took a chair to one side of the door, shook out his paper, and scanned the front page.

"You want a cup while you wait?" a voice sounded above the usual chatter.

"No, thanks, Lucille," Jason called out. "I'll wait until I can order."

Lucille nodded and began sponging the counter in front of newspaper man. She bumped his mug, sloshing the contents. With hardly a glance, she picked up the mug and wiped, repositioning it in front of the unperturbed man.

Jason turned to the sports page and began glancing through the scores. The door to the back room opened. Gus emerged, shaking hands and exchanging hellos. One of the Hope police officers vacated his stool at the counter, so Jason folded his paper and slid onto it.

"Morning," he said to the breakfasters on either side. Both men gave him strained smiles and returned to their eats. Jason frowned and shrugged. Lucille took his order, and he resumed reading his paper. The man on his right stood and paid. A young woman sitting in a chair by the door rose and started for the stool. Jason greeted her. The woman grimaced, shuffled her feet, and returned to the chair by the door.

"You want that cup of tea now?" asked Lucille as she placed an oblong plate with an omelet, toast and grits in front of Jason.

He nodded. "It may be my imagination, Lucille," he replied as she returned with a cup of water and a saucer stacked with tea bags, "but I could swear I'm making your customers uncomfortable."

"Yeah, well, people are funny sometimes." She hurried to the other end of the counter to refill a mug.

Jason ate in silence. Then he turned in his seat to survey the dwindling crowd. A booth emptied. Moments later, schoolteacher and a regular customer of Gus', a beefy, handsome man in his early forties, a house renovator, entered and took seats there. Jason lifted his cup and smiled. They nodded in his direction, then bowed to their menus.

Lucille set a check by Jason's mug and turned to pour coffee for the man next to him. He paid and, mug in hand, he slid into the booth beside schoolteacher.

"I know I'm interrupting, but do you all mind if I ask you both a question?"

"Free country," replied regular customer as he gazed into his coffee mug. Schoolteacher turned in her seat to face Jason, slouched against the wall, and said nothing.

"It's not that I'm feeling particularly insecure, but it sure seems everyone is going out of their way to keep from speaking to me this morning."

"It ain't your imagination," said regular customer.

"Well, what's going on, then?"

Schoolteacher made a wry face. "The town's still upset over Pat."

Jason didn't reply.

"We hear you took up where your brother left off, chasing after Emily's killer," said regular customer.

"In a manner of speaking, I guess that's true."

"Well, we're against it," regular customer said. He looked down. "I don't speak for anybody but myself, though."

Jason turned to schoolteacher. "You, too?"

She sat upright at that, holding her mug out, a barrier between them. "I think so. The town needs a rest. Your brother's death has everyone a little unhinged. Please don't provoke anything else."

Jason said nothing. Gus approached the table and quietly refilled regular customer's mug.

"Gus," said Jason, "maybe you can shed a little light on this for me. Would you sit for a minute?"

Gus nodded. "Let me put this pot up." He turned, filling mugs as he went. He took a seat beside regular customer.

"My two friends here," said Jason, "are telling me the town's developing an allergy to the Shane family."

Gus said nothing.

"You see it that way, too?"

After a moment, Gus said, "We're all mighty sorry 'bout your brother. He looked to his hands.

"And Von and I can't thank you enough for the good will your party generated for us."

Schoolteacher snorted. "Yeah, that was some outpouring of good will, all right. Half the people in town were fist fighting and calling each other names. The out of towners, too."

"That part of the evening was insane," said Jason "There's no explaining what happened."

"The town's scared," Gus blurted. "That feud between your brother and Phil Agee stirred up something. Something bad."

"We don't want you stirring up something else," said regular customer. "We don't want any more killing."

Jason was becoming exasperated. He understood, but Emily's death, it seemed, had been lost in the shuffle. "Don't you care that someone killed a ten year old girl, that this person is still free?" He'd tried not to make his question sound like an accusation, but he knew it had had a pitiful, begging inflection.

"You should have left it to the chief," said regular customer, his jaw firmly set.

Gus nodded. "We can't let people take the law into their own hands. Look what happens."

"But the chief wouldn't pursue the case. He avoided involving Phil Agee."

"Who's to say that Phil did it?" said schoolteacher. "That was something your brother started, and the whole town bought it."

"Not everybody," said regular customer. "I never did."

Jason, remembering differently, gave him a faint smile. "Who do you think did it, then?"

"The chief says it was somebody from out of town," said Gus. "Somebody passing through."

"Then why didn't he say that from the beginning? Why didn't he make an arrest, or at least exonerate Agee? That would've quieted the town." Jason looked away. "It might've saved Pat's life."

"Maybe he didn't have it all put together soon enough," said Gus.

"Or maybe he was protecting someone."

"You're starting to sound like your brother," schoolteacher said. "That's what's set the town on edge. We don't want to go through that again."

"We pay the chief and his force to protect us," said Gus. "We oughta trust 'em to do their job."

"Back to my question, though," said Jason. "Who's this suspect? Is the chief onto anything? Or is this just another smokescreen?"

"Mister Shane," said regular customer, "I think Phil Agee would've never been under consideration if it hadn't been for your brother."

"I understand what you're saying," said Jason, "and I understand why you feel that way. But I have to keep asking: Is anyone concerned about Emily? Don't you realize you're just wishing her death away?"

"What's done is done," mumbled regular customer.

Schoolteacher set a hand on Jason's arm. "Emily's death was a terrible thing, and Pat's even more so in a way, but we have to move on. We can't let this thing grow and grow. You saw how the fight erupted that night, everyone taking sides. If that happens again, it could destroy the town."

Jason blinked, trying to parse his thoughts. The diner was almost empty now, as was the street. The sun had swollen on the horizon. A stray cat, something of a mascot to the diner, was pawing the front door. Unable to entreat anyone to let her inside, she wandered out of view.

"Well, I think Phil Agee's innocent, too," said Jason. The words came involuntarily, though slowly; it felt as though they'd been stuck in his throat.

"Sure 'nough?" Gus responded.

"When did you come to this?" asked schoolteacher. "After Pat died?"

"I never did buy into it, at least not completely." Jason said. "It always seemed too easy an answer. I've known Phil all my life. I know how he is when he's been drinking. But even in his most irresponsible moments I couldn't picture him hitting Emily and driving away."

"Well, who do you think did it, then?" schoolteacher asked.

"Yeah," said regular customer. "If it wasn't Agee, then who was it?"

"I don't want to say." Jason leaned back and let a sigh escape. "Maybe you're right. Maybe we should just drop it."

"I want to know who you think did it," said schoolteacher.

The other two leaned forward and nodded.

"Look," said Jason, "it's easier to spit out a name and make accusations than it is to prove things. If I've learned anything since Emily's death, it's that."

"But, still, you have your ideas," schoolteacher persisted.

"Who, Jason?" Gus asked. "Who do think did it?"

"It was Alan Baxter."

Schoolteacher slapped the table. "Oh, for the love of Pete, you're as full of it as your brother."

"What in the world," Gus said.

"He was seen driving Phil around that night. It all fits, believe me."

"I don't buy it," said regular customer.

"I don't, neither," said Gus.

"That's all right. We can't prove a thing. We don't have credible witnesses, and the evidence is sketchy at best. But he did it. I'm sure of it."

"I'm not listening to any more of this," said regular customer. He picked up his ticket and handed Gus a five-dollar bill.

Gus rose to let him out.

"Jason, you can't even think such a thing," said schoolteacher.

"Don't worry, I'm going to drop the whole thing. And you're right, I can't put Hope through this. I sure don't want to put Von and me through it."

Alice emerged from the back room door behind the counter and edged up to Gus.

He turned, took his wife's hand. "Something wrong, sugar?"

"I just got a call. There was a news bulletin on the television." A tear curled down one fleshy cheek. "Phil Agee's committed suicide."

Gus hugged her to him.

Schoolteacher groaned and covered her face with her hands.

"There, you see?" shouted an eavesdropping customer. "You see what you and your brother did to this town? An innocent man has done died." For a moment, the man leaned toward Jason, fists clenched. "Damn you to hell, Jason Shane!"

CHAPTER 33

A DIRTY JOB

Wilton spent Monday morning going through police accident files as part of a research project he'd contracted with an insurance company. He went home for lunch and lay sprawled across the couch in his office, eating a bologna sandwich. His radio turned up and an airy jazz tune playing, he half-listened until the ensuing five-minute news broadcast began.

The announcer: "Philip Agee, prominent Georgia businessman and political supporter of State Senator Alan Baxter of Athens, died in his jail cell in Atlanta today. An apparent suicide, Agee was to go on trial Wednesday in the shooting death of a neighbor in his hometown of Hope. Agee is reported to have been despondent over the shooting. He's survived by two sons. Divorced two years ago from the former..."

Wilton bolted upright. He tore the plastic wrapper from his unread morning paper and scanned its pages. He didn't find a mention of Agee's death until the obituary page, in an article separate from the normal death notices. He scanned it, then read it again, slowly and carefully. Nothing more than he already knew.

The rest of the day went by in a blur for Wilton, his thoughts tumbling between Emily's death, the senator's ensuing intrigue, Pat's death, and Agee's suicide. By evening, he'd resolved to take what he had to the FBI. He had friends there. He would call Jason later about it, but for now he'd assemble what he had, wash his hands of the whole mess. Tapes, reports, computer files, the whole shebang. There was a chance the Feds could make something out of it, he figured, outside the political structure of Georgia law enforcement. At nine that night, he called his FBI contact and told him the whole story.

Tuesday morning, he was still collating his files and tapes as Jonelle came upstairs for coffee. She bent, idly reading the text spewing from the chattering printer.

She straightened. "This is Jason's case. It's about that Agee guy, and Senator Baxter. Why?"

The printing stopped. He smiled and took the stack of paper from his printer. He smiled. "Don't worry, baby, I'm getting rid of everything tomorrow. Giving it to the FBI."

She looked away. "You promised me. You promised me you'd give this up."

"That's what I'm telling you." He reached for her hand. "I'm getting rid of it. Giving it up to big-time law enforcement." He clutched her shoulders and pulled her to him.

She drew away. "I know you Wilton. I know that look in your eyes. You aren't giving it up, you're just calling for help."

"Don't be that way, baby."

A moan. "It's hard enough for me that you do the work you do. But now you're lying to me. You promise me you'll drop this thing, and you just keep doing it, behind my back." She clacked a heel against the floor, stalked to the coat closet, and pulled out a jacket.

"Jonelle, I'm just trying to shut it down. You know I can't leave things hanging."

She strode toward the front door, Wilton following. She turned. "I'm going away for a while. I need to think." She wiped away a tear. "I'll be at mother's."

"You're gonna come back, right?" His voice had gone hoarse.

"I'll call."

"I love you, baby."

She kissed him lightly. "I'll be back during my lunch hour to pack a bag." She left.

# # #

Alan Baxter's two GBI bodyguards noted Jonelle's departure. One of them reached for his cell phone and pressed a speed dial number. He began to speak, but a loud, angry voice at the other end interrupted. He tried several times to break into the constant stream of words, but couldn't. He pulled nervously at one down-turned terminus of his red mustache. Then he nodded. "I understand," he said. He swore as he closed the phone.

"What was that about?" his partner asked.

The redheaded man slammed his fist into the dash. "He said to get out of here."

"What?"

The red-haired man repeated it, voice rising.

The driver shrugged and cranked the engine. "Where to?"

"Drop me off at my apartment. You go home and play with your kids."

The driver turned, directing the car toward Clairemont Road. "You going to tell me what's going on?"

The redheaded man looked straight ahead. "No. But do yourself a favor and see if you can get reassigned. Maybe get the hell out of this line of work."

The driver frowned. "What about you?"

"I got a job to do. A dirty goddamn job."

"Again?"

"Yeah."

"Why us? We're GBI agents, for chrissake."

"I'm taking you out of it. Like I said, you go home. It's just me this time."

"You sure, partner?"

The redheaded agent reached into his jean jacket pocket and pulled out a pack of cigarettes, lit one. "You know the score. I don't have a family. No parents. No wife. No kids. And I owe the bastard a favor that won't ever be paid off." He rolled the side window down an inch and exhaled toward the breach. "Not until one of us is dead."

That evening, the red-haired man stepped out of his apartment, locked the door, and ran down the steps through a lightly falling rain to his car, a rusty Pontiac compact. Instead of his blue jean jacket, he now wore a three-quarter length gray topcoat. He poked through the glove compartment and pulled out a heavy blue steel cylinder. He tossed it in his hand, feeling its heft, and then let it drop into his coat pocket. Before he cranked the engine, he patted the bulge under his coat.

He was a cautious man. He'd learned to trust no one, and to check twice on himself. Satisfied that the thirty-eight-caliber pistol and silencer were in their proper places, he backed out of his parking place. From there it would be at least a thirty-minute drive to Decatur and Chapel Street. He lit a smoke.

The radio played faintly, and the slap and whine of the windshield wipers all but drowned it out. He wanted to take his mind off the task at hand, so he turned up the volume. A talk show host changed the topic from the high salaries of professional athletes to a political drama involving a small island republic in the Caribbean. The island's government, struggling economically, was threatening to expel all American business interests, mostly banking and trading companies. The country's leadership had been negotiating with business magnates in France, who had promised economic aid to the beleaguered republic if it would grant most favored nation status to France, thus providing a source of increasingly hard-to-get fresh foods and a freewheeling banking atmosphere. The French would help clean up slum neighborhoods on the island and provide teachers and jobs. And the island's government, to further its stature with the people, had seized the opportunity to abandon its protective treaty with the U.S.

The show host tried to provoke an ineloquent but liberal-minded caller into saying that he thought the U.S. deserved this political slap in the face. It was just a business decision, the next caller resolutely repeated. The U.S. shouldn't allow its ideological leanings to interfere with deals that were in the best interests of the people.

Talk radio irritated the driver of the Pontiac, although he constantly found himself listening to it. It was mindplay verbalized by lazy people with nothing better to do. People who could never back up their opinions with facts. The world was full of them. He'd met many in his life.

His life. Alan Baxter had long ago emerged as a permanent fixture of his life. *How did I ever let him get a toehold?* He drew smoke in and exhaled. *It didn't matter now.* The situation in Hope had taken an ominous turn. This black guy, Byrd, had talked to an FBI agent. Some friend of his at the Bureau. An old army buddy, the senator had informed the driver. And the FBI agent's supervisor, being the good bureaucrat, had called the GBI to discuss jurisdiction. This ended up in Baxter's ear, and he'd ordered the GBI to retain jurisdiction. The FBI had been relieved to be out of it.

So here I am. The man smiled as he reflected on his forty-seven years. He'd grown up poor; in rural Georgia the only work available to his kind was on the huge peanut farms. He and his three younger brothers had spent their summers working those fields for less than minimum wage, turning over most of the money to the family and keeping only enough for an occasional new pair of blue jeans, a new shirt, and a rare pair of new boots. The four of them eventually saved enough to buy a junked pick-up. They managed to get it running during the following winter, and it became their only mode of transportation to school, jobs, and football practice.

Football. His salvation. He was big for his age, and he was quick. As a freshman, he'd started at fullback on offense and linebacker on defense. He excelled at football. When his father became ill and died during the summer between his junior and senior years, he determined to quit school, for the good of the family. In this small community, his coach was the first to know of his decision, and he paid a visit to the fatherless family. He would see the local plantation owner and make sure the hapless family members weren't left lacking. But in return, the oldest brother had to go back to school and play football.

He now entered Atlanta's perimeter highway and neared I-85. The rain was falling in sheets. He turned the radio up. A caller lamented the lack of football rivalry between Georgia Tech and the University of Georgia. They were in different conferences now, and their interest in each other had been dwindling for a while. The traffic on the perimeter slowed to a halt. Ahead, nothing but a hazy ribbon of red taillights.

Football had been the source of his first realization that he could survive without his hands in the sandy soil of south Georgia's farm country. He made All-State in his high school conference, and a scholarship to the University of Georgia followed. During his first month on campus, he joined a fraternity, courtesy of an alumnus. He maintained better than average grades in the off-season in a business administration curriculum.

As fate would have it, Alan Baxter was a fraternity brother. During the football player's sophomore year, in a bar in Athens after a football game, the player was provoked into a fight. He inflicted mostly superficial damage on the other youth, but it was enough to outrage the pummeled youth's father, a prominent lawyer. The footballer was arrested, then released, and it died there. Baxter was a senior that year, already a potent political force on campus and around town. He pulled a few strings.

Traffic began to move. The agent took the Clairemont road exit and turned toward Decatur. The rain was now a patter on his windshield. The young football player had visited Baxter in his room at the frat house and had thanked him. I'll never forget your help, he told Baxter, truly meaning it. A year and a half later, nearing graduation, his mother died and Baxter called him. Baxter offered his condolences, and the conversation drifted to other things. You want to stay out of Vietnam? Baxter asked. Yeah, you bet, the younger man replied. Petition for an exemption, Baxter said. Your brother's already over there. Federal policy allows for exemptions so that families like yours aren't required to take on an inordinate portion of the war burden. He wondered why Baxter had kept up with him so closely, and later wrote him, asking what was behind the constant attention. I know how to help people, Baxter wrote back, and I like doing it. Besides, that's what fraternity brothers are for.

But his soldier brother was later killed, just weeks before he was to have returned stateside and, in a fit of anguish over the death, their youngest brother committed suicide. The agent's remaining brother left Georgia and the agent never heard from him again.

But after the agent's college football career ended, he was drafted anyway. He spent a little over a year in Germany before a hardship discharge initiated by Alan Baxter brought him home. Out of the Army and footloose, he refused to go back to the farm. After months of bumming around the country, he rented a small room in Americus and went to work for the fire department. The idle hours bored him, and he managed a shift to the police force.

He stopped at a red light, just minutes from Wilton's place. He touched the bulge beneath his coat. The light turned green.

During one of the man's years in Americus, the governor had barnstormed the town with an entourage of state legislators, which included Alan Baxter. The two fraternity brothers talked briefly, and a month later, the young policeman received a notice asking him to apply for a position with the Georgia Bureau of Investigation. The pay was good, and he took to investigative work like a duck to water.

But he'd developed a taste for women, expensive women. Suddenly, his paycheck was far from adequate. For a while, he became a passive participant in the burgeoning drug trade along the state's coast. Internal affairs quickly noted his lack of attention to the trade. His supervisor relieved him of his duties and began paperwork to dismiss him from the force. Once again, Alan Baxter intervened. Truly penitent, the young agent was ecstatic to be included in Alan Baxter's personal service as a state-salaried bodyguard.

Looking back, though, he could see now that the senator had for years manipulated his loyalties, and his life. He had willingly involved himself in questionable activities for the senator, and under the senator's powerful wing, he'd always been insulated from repercussions. Until the recent intrigue in Hope, he'd rationalized the senator's demands away as simply taking care of messy political business. But no longer. The incident involving the senator's friend, Phil Agee, the little girl in Hope, and the ensuing whitewashing of a local investigation there had brought it all home to him in plain language. He was breaking the law for the senator.

As he neared the house, he braked to glance through the building's front window. A light shone in the rear of the front room. His prey was home.

CHAPTER 34

NO FEAR

Earlier that day, a long, a slow rain had washed Hope's streets clean, leaving the asphalt with a glistening sheen. Jason parked his Toyota in front of the house, the rain still beating the old car's top like a tin drum. He was tired. As he stepped out, he lost his balance, fell back against the car. He swore. Drenched and barely able to move, fatigue and irritation gave way to wild laughter. Finally, he took a deep breath and made his way up the sidewalk to the front porch steps.

As he grasped the rail, he saw Von's shadow behind one of the front door's stained glass angels. The porch lights came on. She came to the door, still in her business suit, shoulders folded forward, a hand to her face. She was crying.

He embraced her, asked what was wrong.

"It's been an awful day," she cried, wriggling deeper into his arms. The two of them lurched precariously.

"Let's move inside before I fall and take you with me," he said.

She took his arm, helped him through the door, and then stopped and eyed him. "You're soaked. Please change clothes before you get sick."

"Yes, ma'am," he said, giving a weak grin. "Think I'll sit down first, though." He draped an arm over her shoulder, hers around his waist, and they made their way down the hallway to the kitchen.

Von said, "I'll make a pot of tea." She motioned him to one of the straight-backed chairs tucked under the old antique table.

He slumped onto it. Now that he was inside, he realized that hunger loomed. "I have a better idea," he said. "Let's order something to eat."

"We have Cokes in the fridge," said Von. "Would you like pizza?"

"I was thinking more along the lines of Chinese. Hwang's is delivering now."

"Should I order tea, too?"

"Just the food. Maybe it'll cheer us both up." He tried to laugh, but only managed an awkward gurgle.

She placed their order. He struggled to his feet and hobbled to the refrigerator. He pulled out a large bottle of Coke, found two plastic tumblers in the adjacent cabinet, and poured them full.

She eyed him again. "Jason, please change clothes. The last thing you need is a winter cold."

He left without a word and returned ten minutes later. She turned to him, crying.

"Tell me," he said softly.

They sat.

"Jack called me in as I was locking up tonight," Von began.

Jack Wilkins was the lead broker and a one-half owner of the real estate agency Von worked for. He'd been good to Von. He'd allowed her to work irregular hours, let her have time off when Emily died. And he was a source of comfort following Pat's death. She'd told him about her need for a trip to the mountains over

Thanksgiving to sort things out, and he'd let her have the time off. A nice guy. A good friend

"What did he want?"

"He and his two partners have had phone calls. People want to be comfortable with a company that helps them get a loan and buy a house, and they don't feel comfortable with a Shane helping them anymore."

"Maybe we should change our name, then."

"I'm serious, Jason. This is about my livelihood. It's about our life." She pressed his hand. "They've let me go."

"Just like that?"

She reached for her purse, rummaged, and slid a check on the table. "This is my severance pay."

Good old Jack, thought Jason. The check had been written for a full two weeks' pay, as if she were a salaried employee. Von hadn't worked a full week in months. Jack hadn't needed to do this.

"What are we going to do?" she said. "I feel so alone."

He walked his chair closer and hugged her. They'd discovered that Pat had left an annuity for enough to pay off the house. But there were taxes, and insurance bills. Their credit charges were minimal, but without a decent source of income, their credit card debts would soon mount. His small stipend from the military would barely pay for his basics. What, indeed, would they do?

He'd spent the morning looking through the jobs section of the *Constitution's* classifieds and the afternoon chasing promising leads, in places as far away as north Atlanta. A slow economy burdened the region, and permanent jobs were scarce. He needed work sitting down, and that ruled out many possibilities. Too, his history of depression and lack of a work record would hurt him.

Local and state governments hired disabled vets, but you had to take tests. Interviews would be months away. And in Hope, the business people had listened politely but had offered nothing, even the ones with help wanted signs in the windows.

"We'll think of something, you'll see," he said as he stroked the back of her neck.

The phone rang and she picked up.

"Mama?"

Jason's eyebrows lifted. Had the ice lady melted? he wondered. Von tried to speak a couple of times, but wasn't able to. Slowly her face contorted, and a tear slipped down one cheek. She spoke again only at the end, to tell her mother goodbye.

"I can guess," said Jason.

"I don't know who she thinks she is," said Von. She swiped at a tear with the back of one hand and sat.

"She won't have anything further to do with you until you get rid of me."

Von nodded, sniffing. "She thinks she can run my life."

"She's used to thinking that way. You've deferred to her in almost everything your whole life."

She shook her head. "Sometimes it seems all she and I do is argue."

He made his way to the refrigerator, fumbled ice into his tumbler, and again flopped onto his chair.

"The two of you argue," he continued, "but then you let her have her way. Or you sneak around her, patronize her. You get away with it because your dad's taught you all he knows about avoiding confrontations." He took a long drink. "He's raised avoidance to an art form."

Von's eyes narrowed. "Well, how do you expect us to act? You know how strong-willed she is. Maybe we should have had constant fights, like you and Pat."

"Maybe. But the bruises from avoidance can hurt a lot longer than those from a fist fight."

Von lowered her head. Her shoulders shook as she cried. "I can't stand it any more. I want to leave this town."

He bent to her. "It'll be better tomorrow."

"This is our hometown, Jason, and we're being treated like lepers. Something awful has happened to Hope." She reached into her purse for a tissue.

"It would've happened anyway, Von. Pat was so intent on avenging Emily's death that he didn't realize he was opening up something else here. Sort of like lifting a pretty rock and discovering there are spiders and scorpions underneath. He opened things up publicly, and the people here, well, they couldn't ignore it. Hope's a private town, and it wasn't prepared to have its dark side see the light of day. You and I are still here, and visible, and that helps remind everyone that they've swept something ugly under the rug."

The doorbell rang. Jason turned, pulled his wallet from a hip pocket, and limped toward the front door. Moments later he returned with the Chinese. The fragrance of soy sauce filled the kitchen, and they ate ravenously.

Von pushed her bowl away and said, "I have an idea."

"Good," he replied. "I'm fresh out."

"Why don't we sell the house? We can move to Atlanta. We can both find jobs there. Make new friends. We can start over, together." She glanced down for a moment, and when she looked up, a broad smile had taken her.

He'd thought of leaving Hope, too, but now there seemed to be too many reasons not to. "If we were to leave like this," he said, "we'd be avoiding things we need to deal with. Your mother would be a ghost, haunting our lives. She'd find a way to drive a wedge between us no matter where we were. No, we need to face her every day, show her we're sure about us, sure about who we are. We need to be here to confront Pat's reputation, too. And maybe we can help Hope face its hypocrisy, the urge to shove awkward things out of sight. I'm convinced that the only way to do either is to be as unlike Pat as possible. To show a different kind of strength. To smile, to live in this house, with all its memories, to have a good, loving life together, to step out into this town every morning and make it a good day."

She took his hand and looked away.

Despite his Pollyannaish talk, he felt fear knotting in his solar plexus. For the first time in his life, he had something he wanted. He loved Von and he was afraid of losing her over such an important thing: how they would face their future in a town that sought to shun them.

Odd, but two weeks before, it had been he who had wanted to leave Hope. But a sense of destiny was rising in his life, and now in their life together – an opportunity in their middle years, to finally make their lives work. To heal a lifetime of emotional scarring, and as Von had said, that would mean starting over. No, leaving Hope now meant those wounds wouldn't heal. They had to stay, to fight for their dignity, for their mutual identity, on the only battleground that mattered. It was time to risk. He knew if he gave in to fear now, he'd eventually lose Von. He'd lose everything.

"We've done nothing wrong, Von," he continued. "We have nothing to be ashamed of. We've done everything we could to find Emily's killer and keep Pat from destroying himself. We haven't succeeded, but in the process we've both grown stronger. This is home. It's ours. No one can take it from us. And look at the two of us. Look what we've done. We've found what everyone wants. We've found hope in another person, the kind of hope that can only come from facing the depths of our own selves."

She looked up, searched his expression.

He smiled, despite the thumping in his chest. "I want to stay here. With you."

His words had had their effect. Determination swelled in her, too; he could see it in her eyes. She reached, and they clung to one another for a long while.

Finally, her elbow slipped on the table's surface, pushing her food container and upsetting her Coke. She lunged away, too late to prevent the drink from spilling in her lap. She began to laugh, head bowed into cupped hands. When she looked up, her eyes were wide open, alive.

Jason laughed with her. He rose and found a dishtowel to blot the drink from her clothes.

"Leave it," she said. "We don't have to be so proper all the time. It'll be a symbol, something to remind us that life is crazy."

"As if we need a reminder."

Still laughing but softly now, she took the dishtowel and began daubing at her soaked pantsuit.

"A symbol," Jason said. "Something we can remember always. A memory, indelibly etched on our lives. And our clothes."

She gaily tossed the cloth toward the sink. "And what, precisely, is this going to be a symbol of?"

"No fear," he said.

She repeated it: "No fear. Yes! Who's afraid of Hope?" There was a heaping portion of irony in that, and they laughed together.

CHAPTER 35

FACE TO FACE

The redheaded man drove past Wilton's building and turned around. He drove once more past the house and parked against the curb across the street, two houses down. The rain had slowed to a cold mist, and overhead he caught glimpses of the moon as clouds fled silently to the south. He saw no one else on the street. He climbed from the Pontiac. Still no one. He stood, looking and listening. No faces at windows along the street. No cars moving.

He strode across the street to the building's wooden deck and stopped once more to look, to listen. Nothing. He loped down the sloping driveway to the house's rear. One car there, Wilton's Taurus. Good. He tested a side window – closed but unlocked. This was going to be easy. His plan dictated the use of the front door, but now he had an alternate entry to the house.

He froze. A window on the second floor of the house next door rattled. He stepped into the shadows. The window glowed with light now. An elderly woman struggled to close the window. She shook its bottom panel once, twice. The window slammed shut. She pulled a pair of curtains across the window and doused the light. The man looked around once more. Nothing moving.

He strode back up the driveway, stopped in the shadows at the edge of the deck to un-holster the thirty-eight and attach the silencer. He unbuttoned his coat, pulled one arm inside, leaving the sleeve flaccid. Then he stepped lightly onto the steps leading to the deck. No noise. Three more steps across the deck to the door.

He leaned to the door and listened. Faint music inside. He tried the doorknob, slowly, slowly. A smile crept across his darkened face. Unlocked. He pushed the door open and stepped inside. The clack of a computer keyboard. He pushed the door shut. Its locking mechanism clicked, loudly. The keyboard clatter stopped. The man took two, then three more steps across the room, as silently as a cat.

"Jonelle?" The rollers on Wilton's chair bumped across the floor. "Baby, is that you?"

The redheaded man strode in, blocking the partition opening, his gun pointed at Wilton's chest.

Wilton rose to a crouch, jaw set. "Who the hell…" Then his expression shifted as he realized who the man was.

"Shut up and sit," the redheaded man said, the gun now pointed at Wilton's head.

Wilton hardly gave the gun a glance. "You work for Baxter."

The man pushed Wilton back to his desk chair. "Sit. Hands on the armrests. Do it!"

Wilton complied.

The man turned the chair, pushed it roughly against the opposite wall, the gun barrel between Wilton's shoulder blades. Desk drawers opened. Papers shuffled and then whispered onto the floor. Wilton's hand darted to his shirt pocket, jabbed at his recorder's button.

"Where's your piece?" the man asked as he turned to Wilton.

"Downstairs, in the bedroom. In my chest of drawers."

"Where's your girl?"

"She won't be back tonight, she's visiting family."

The chair spun, Wilton once more face to face with the agent.

"Then why were you calling out for her?"

Wilton let out a slow breath. "We had a fight. I thought she might be over it, and maybe she'd come –"

"Call her," the man said. "Ask whether she's coming back tonight."

Wilton picked up the phone and punched in the number. It sounded three times before she answered. "Hi, baby."

"Wilton, it's you?"

"I wanted to hear your pretty voice before I go to bed."

"I'm sorry I left like that," she said. "I'll be back tomorrow. You know I can't leave you for very long."

"Sure, baby, I love you, too."

They said their goodbyes. Wilton held the phone for a moment, and then he hung up.

"I can tell by your face," the man said. "She won't be back tonight."

"Yeah."

While Wilton was on the phone, the agent had completed his provisional search of the cubicle. His only direction from the senator was to make this look accidental. He'd planned to have Wilton commit suicide. Shoot himself with his own gun. But another idea had begun to form, and this one was better, much better.

The man eyed the half-gallon of vodka on the file cabinet. "We need to have a drink."

"Hey, c'mon, man, don't play games with me. What d'you want? Why did Baxter send you here?"

"We're going to have a drink. Then we'll talk. Open that vodka."

Wilton complied.

The man nodded toward the kitchen. "Get up slowly. Get some ice and two glasses."

Wilton rose, eyes fixed on the man, and then he walked slowly, deliberately toward the kitchen. He opened a cabinet and brought out two glasses. He retrieved a small container of ice from the refrigerator. The man motioned him back to his chair, and then he backed into the kitchen and dragged a chair into the cubicle. He sat backwards, his arms over the back support.

"Pour," the man said.

Wilton dropped three ice cubes in each glass, then a portion of vodka. He handed one glass to the man. "What you want to talk about?"

"Drink," the man commanded.

Wilton drank.

The man sipped his own.

"You're too late to snuff me," said Wilton. "I've already given everything I have to the FBI."

The man sneered. "I hate liars. You didn't see the Bureau guy at all. They've waived jurisdiction."

Wilton looked away. He'd received the call from his friend less than three hours earlier, saying the Bureau would waive jurisdiction. It would be the GBI's ball game. "You guys get around."

"When we have to. Drink. All of it."

Wilton drained the glass, made a face as he swallowed. He hated vodka; this was to have been for Jonelle and her array of mixers.

"Pour," the man said.

Wilton poured the glass halfway full. "I must really have Baxter worried."

"Pour it full."

Wilton poured the glass to the brim.

"Drink."

Wilton drank that glass, then another. And another. He blinked as he drank the last one. "You goin' to snuff me?" he said. He knew he was slurring, and his vision was doing crazy blips, like an old television with no horizontal hold.

"You're a nosy son of a bitch, even for a private snoop," the man said. "But, yeah, you're already a dead man. Courtesy of Senator Alan Baxter. Now shut up and drink."

"Hey, I know I can't get t'the senator. He's too good. Too far out ahead o'me. Controls too many people. 'Sides, it was an acc'dent. He ran over the girl by acc'dent. I figured'out. Drivin' Agee home that night. He tol' you that, I bet."

The man said nothing, but one eyebrow arched. He made a motion to turn the glass up.

Wilton complied. "Hey...I'm...I'm gonna throw up," he mumbled.

"Then throw up."

Wilton tried to rise, but couldn't. He looked at the man and blinked. "Help me up, man."

"If you can't get up, then throw up right here."

Wilton's brain felt like mush. He sank back. The motion disrupted what was left of his equilibrium. Something jerked him forward, and he felt a well of hot, acidic fluid in his mouth, felt it explode outward. He closed his eyes, his head full of the foul taste, and he fell from his chair to the floor. He looked up, trying to locate the man. Everything swam. He rolled over, breathing heavily. "Help me," he whispered.

He heard the man rise and walk from the room. Wilton fumbled in his pocket for the tape recorder. He managed to slide it across the floor, under the closet door.

The man returned. He lifted Wilton's head. "Drink this," he said, pressing another glass to Wilton's lips.

Water filled Wilton's mouth, and he swallowed. His breathing grew less labored.

"More?"

"Yeah," Wilton whispered.

Once more the cool water.

"Better?" the man asked.

Wilton nodded.

"Drink this."

Wilton's mouth burned with new vodka. He held it in his mouth, refusing to swallow. The man's gloved hand clamped Wilton's nose shut. Wilton coughed and swallowed. He was becoming less conscious of the man, of the room, of his own body. The burning fluid entered his mouth again and again.

He rolled over, groaned. He struggled to his knees, only to spew bile onto the wall before him. He managed a sitting position. A warm wetness spread through his crotch and then down a leg of his jeans. Odd. He couldn't see anything distinctly, but his hearing was unusually acute. The man gave him more water. Then Wilton retched again.

The man swallowed hard. The smell in the room was overwhelming. He rose from his crouch, turned his face into the crook of an arm to keep from throwing up. He sipped lightly from his own glass of vodka. The sight of this black man, on his knees and throwing up, disturbed him. He thought of his father, dying of tuberculosis at the age of forty. He remembered the landowner for whom his family had toiled coming to their weather-beaten rental house the morning his father died. The redheaded youth had come to the door, and the man had handed him a hundred dollar bill. He would send someone over to bury his father, the man had told him.

The agent thought for the first time in years of the letter he'd read, informing him of his brother's death in Vietnam. He'd stepped on a personnel mine, shredding both legs. The blast had set off a firefight, and before a medic could reach him, he'd bled to death on a narrow dirt road separating two rice fields. He remembered the brother's scared, confused letters during earlier months. Neither he nor his buddies could make sense of the war. He would just keep his head down. Pray for me, the letters said time after time, pray I'll make it home.

Death, the agent thought. He was old enough to have seen a lot of death, and he'd grown afraid of its eventuality. Strange, but as he watched this Byrd fellow struggle to breathe, to stay alive, he determined to save himself from the same struggle. Life, despite its thrills and joys, just wasn't worth the fight it would eventually take to keep it.

He took a deep breath, seized the bottle of vodka, and poured it straight into Wilton's mouth. Wilton coughed and spewed fluid onto the man. Then he groaned and went limp, a thick, yellow fluid dripping from one corner of his mouth. Minutes passed.

The man checked his pulse. Still alive. He picked up the bottle of brandy.

Then he stopped to search Wilton's desk. On top, next to his computer, he found a stack of audio tapes, neatly labeled. Good. He searched his computer disks. Taking the most likely ones, he scrolled the computer's hard drive files, deleted a few that seemed to be related to the Hope case. Just to be sure, he pulled the plug on the computer. Re-plugging it, he watched the screen. He un-plugged and re-plugged the computer once, twice more, in rapid succession. Good. The computer's hard drive had frozen.

He unscrewed the top from the brandy bottle and poured the amber liquid over Wilton, soaking his clothes. He lit a cigarette, and held the burning end to Wilton's shirt. Nothing. Too wet. He stuck the cigarette between Wilton's fingers and struck a match, holding the match to Wilton's shirt. Nothing. He lit another, hold-ing the fabric up to the heat of the match. The sweet fragrance of brandy grew richer, and the material ignited.

He watched as the fire spread. Wilton's dark skin distorted smoothly, then wrinkled. Then came the acrid odor of burning flesh. He unscrewed the silencer from his pistol and dropped it in his coat pocket, returned the pistol to his shoulder holster, pulled his arm back through the sleeve of his coat, buttoned up and, look-ing back once more, he strode to the door and was gone. A minute later, the Pontiac engine's initial roar dropped to a hum.

Mission accomplished. The fire had not yet spread. He'd not been seen. He drove the car to the end of the street, passed the transit station and headed north toward the Interstate. He would drop the tapes and computer disks in a dumpster a block ahead, and when he reached home he'd call Baxter at his Duluth apartment.

He would make a brief remark to the senator, something he'd just rehearsed. He would say it forcefully, but calmly. The senator wouldn't enjoy its implications; he would be outraged, in fact. He would sweat for a couple of days, the agent thought, and then he'd learn that it had all been a bluff, that the FBI wasn't coming for him. Well, to hell with him. The slimy little creep deserved to sweat for a while. Then he'd hang up. He'd attach the silencer to his thirty-eight. He imagined pulling the trigger would be easy. There would be a shock, but no pain.

No pain. He found that concept hard to imagine. He still lived with the agony of the life he'd been born to. He didn't know why, but over the forty-seven year span of his life, through decent times, worse and better ones, he'd never shaken it. He hadn't been able to drink it away, spend it away, or fuck it away. Sometimes he thought it was just fear, programmed into him in his youth by his family, by their numbing poverty. Some sort of emotional slavery, that was all he could call it. At other times, he hated himself for being too damned sensitive about things like that. So. What to make of what he was feeling now? He just didn't know. But after tonight he'd feel it no more.

CHAPTER 36

POWER AND JUSTICE

A few minutes past midnight – Jason fumbled for the bedside phone. Von stirred, but the soft, regular rhythm of her breathing continued. He gently rubbed her shoulder with his empty hand as she nuzzled closer for warmth.

"Hello?" Someone was jostling the receiver at the other end.

A woman's voice stammered and then choked.

"Who is this?"

"It's…it's Jonelle."

This wasn't the relaxed, sultry tone Jason associated with Jonelle. She began to cry.

"What is it? What's the matter, Jonelle?"

"Wilton," she said. "He's dead."

"Dead? What do you mean? How?"

"He burned to death…" Crying interrupted. "…old couple across the street…saw fire. Something moving. They went outside. Wilton…ambulance came…he's dead."

"Where are you?"

"At the house…Mama and Papa came…police just left." More crying.

Von worked her way to a sitting position beside Jason. She yawned, eyes still closed. "Who is it?"

"Jonelle. Something's happened to Wilton." He returned to the phone, Jonelle still crying.

"It was terrible," Jonelle cried a moment later. "He was so burned...they took him to the morgue...I couldn't recognize...he ran outside."

A deep male voice began consoling her.

The receiver at the other end changed hands, and Jonelle's father announced himself. His voice faded as Jonelle took back the phone. She tried to speak but couldn't. Then her father again.

"Jonelle wants to know if you can come," he said to Jason. "Her mother isn't doing well with this. I need to take her home."

"Of course," Jason replied. "I can leave in five minutes."

"Her mother and I will stay until you arrive."

Jason sighed heavily and hung up. He lifted his legs to the edge of the bed, and while he was rubbing them, Von switched on her bedside light.

"I need to go," he said. "I think Wilton's been murdered."

Von gasped. "But how? Who..."

"He was burned. I promised Jonelle's dad I'd come."

She slid to his side. "I'm going too."

They dressed quickly. Jason's legs were shaking, so Von insisted on driving. Forty-five minutes later, they parked on Chapel Street. Von helped him out of the car, and as they stepped onto the wooden deck, the door opened. A heavyset black man filled the doorway, bald head aglow with moonlight. He smiled weakly and extended a hand.

"I'm John Parks," he said. "You must be Jason."

Jason nodded and introduced Von.

"Come in, please."

The door closed behind them. Jonelle was sitting on the couch with her mother, both crying. The resemblance was striking; but for the streaks of silver in her hair and the subtle facial changes that come with age, the older woman could have been Jonelle's twin.

Jonelle ran to Jason. "Who did this?" she whispered between sobs. "Why?"

He kissed her hair. "Tell me what you know."

"Will you be all right, honey?" Jonelle's father asked. "We're leaving."

"I'll be all right, Papa."

The older couple buttoned their coats and departed.

After composing herself, Jonelle told Jason of Wilton's odd call that night. Something was wrong; it had been entirely out of character for him. So she'd decided to check on him. When she arrived, two elderly neighbors were standing just off the deck at the front of the house, talking to a pair of policemen. Wilton's blackened body lay on the walk there. An ambulance had just arrived, and an investigation team. One of the paramedics pronounced Wilton dead.

From that point, Jonelle's account was foggy, but she'd run inside, through the awful smells, to the mess in the cubicle. A policeman had heard her wails, had come in and calmed her. Then she'd called her father and, after the investigation team had left, Jonelle and her parents had cleaned up the vomit and bits of refuse from the fire.

Jason crossed the room and peered over the police barrier tape to the partitioned area. The sweet, burnt aroma of the brandy hung in the air, and the sour smell of vomit mingled with disinfectant. A few tiny fragments of burned cloth and paper still lay scattered about. An oblong area of the floor had been scorched. He turned and asked, "Had he been drinking?"

"No," Jonelle said curtly. "Wilton never drank much. He liked a little buzz, but too much drink got in the way of his thinking." She pointed. "There was a bottle of brandy beside the CD player, and a bottle of vodka. They were empty and lying on the floor when I got here, but the investigators took them. Anyway, he wouldn't have drunk the vodka; he hated it." She sniffed. "I told the police that, too."

Hers would have been Jason's description of Wilton's drinking habits, too. "The police have anything to offer?"

"They simply said it looked like he'd been on a bender. Passed out, spilled the brandy on himself. A cigarette ignited him."

"A cigarette?"

"They found a couple of burned cigarettes. One was a butt, the other almost whole, between Wilton's fingers." She looked away, her face twisted with anger. "He didn't smoke, Jason."

Jason sighed. "He'd been working on our case again."

She nodded. "He said he was going to take it to the FBI. There must've been something new. He promised me he'd drop it, but he didn't. He couldn't let go."

Jason glanced to Von. Her expression brimmed with questions.

"We had a fight about it this morning," said Jonelle, "and I left, to think. I was so scared for him. When I came home at noon to pack, he gave me the originals of the tapes, and a paper copy of his computer files. They were all up to date, he said. But I know Wilton. He wouldn't have done that if he weren't scared."

"What did you do with his files?"

"I have them in a safety deposit box at the bank."

"Did you tell the cops about the files?"

She shook her head.

"Did you listen to the tapes? Did you read anything?"

She said no.

Jason began to shuffle through the mess on Wilton's desk. After a moment of pacing about the cubicle, he threw open the closet door, peered in, and closed it.

"Jason, what do you know?" asked Von. "Tell me."

Jason stopped. He'd seen something. He opened the closet door again. He picked up the tiny recorder, held it out on one palm.

"That's Wilton's," said Jonelle. "It was in the closet?"

Jason popped it open. A small tape, partially wound. He rewound it and pressed the PLAY button. Wilton's voice, tinny and artificial. Then a new voice. He rewound a few feet of tape, pressed PLAY again.

As the tape relived Wilton's last minutes, Jonelle began to wail. Von held her, led her to the couch in the waiting room. Jason followed with the tape. They continued to listen.

Jason stopped the tape and slumped into the nearby chair. "There's no doubt that Alan Baxter killed Emily. And he might've been behind Pat's death, too." He paused. "We had decided to take it to a lawyer Wilton knew. Baxter has two bodyguards, GBI agents. They beat up a guy Wilton had unearthed, a guy who had a key piece of the story." He shook his head. "I guess somehow Wilton got too close to Baxter. But without a doubt, this tape proves Wilton was murdered, and it implicates Baxter." He held the tiny instrument out on one palm. "This is Baxter's mistake, the one we were waiting for. Now we can get him into court."

"Don't," said Jonelle. "Please! I've lost Wilton over this, and you've lost Emily and Pat. It's too much."

"Jason, I'm scared," said Von.

"And so is Alan Baxter."

"We're in danger, aren't we?"

"Yeah, I suppose we are."

"What are we going to do?"

A long pause. "I don't know. But I'll think of something. Right now I need some air." He zipped his parka and left the house.

The wind hissed. The cloud cover had moved to the south, and the sky sparkled with the cleanliness new weather always brings. Across the street, a Christmas tree had been set in a front window. Cold air had clouded the window, and the tree lights' myriad colors seemed to pulse. Jason clumped down the deck steps. Then his calmness left him. He cried. He kicked at the cold space before him.

Minutes later, he found himself across the street from the transit station. He sat on a bench there. A newspaper box stood close by, the early edition already deposited. This was the twenty-ninth of November. A photo of Alan Baxter had been set on the front page, under the masthead. Jason absently took in the image.

How could Baxter have done this? He closed his eyes and took in breath after breath of night air. Suddenly he tensed. An old, familiar sound filled his ears: the rapid, steady beating of a helicopter's props. A police helicopter looped past the station and then disappeared into the night. He relaxed. A car rumbled by, three teenaged boys out much too late, all sitting in the front seat, stereo thumping. They waved. Jason waved back.

He pounded a cold, tingling fist against the bench's icy slats. Wilton's image came. Such a strong, honest face. Then Baxter's image emerged. This thing, this notion of power, granted by the people, yet so easy to abuse. He tried to imagine Wilton's body – burned to a misshapen hulk. Power like Baxter's, it can do so much good, but it can threaten a good person's right to exist, and that's reason enough for us all to tremble. As he thought about the sort of power Baxter had at his disposal, another image formed – that of some ethereal beast, constantly looking for a weak human vessel to inhabit. All it takes is fear and pride, and it enters.

But I'll finish this, he resolved, for Wilton. I'll find this FBI friend of his. I'll take it to Washington if I have to. Sure, Baxter will fight back. But I'll do it anyway. He turned again to the newspaper photo. Anger rose in him like a storm. Vengeance. I won't succumb to that. His head fell to his chest. I'll do it the right way. I'll find the justice in all of this.

Justice. It's all about justice, isn't it? That's the key. To establish the rightful limits of power. The law, with all its ambiguities and mind games, is meant to be the servant of justice, true justice. Justice is a grand, ephemeral thing; it's life protecting life, an idea you can chase but never quite capture. As with Emily's death, some form of power gone awry can disrupt the law, and when that happens, justice vanishes.

He remembered the tape recorder he'd slipped into his shirt pocket. He took it out, held it to the light. Justice was such a high-minded concept to be subject to pure chance – an accidental tape recording. Pursuing Emily's killer had changed him, his family, the town of Hope. But even so, something told him everything would work out now.

He'd be all right. No more running from his demons. He'd seek them out, accept them for what they are – simply life's tougher acts. Together, Von and he would face Baxter and the town of Hope, and they'd fight their way to a good life, a happy life. And when the going gets tough, they would think of Wilton, and Pat and Emily, and they'd grow even stronger.

He rose. A familiar tune filled his head, a Christmas carol. He hummed it. A smile inched across his face. As he returned to Wilton and Jonelle's place, his steps became stronger, his stride longer. For once, he couldn't feel the pain in his hip, the pain that had for so long been his only companion.

END